DIRTY BEASTS:

LASH

NEW YORK TIMES AND USA TODAY BESTSELLING AUTHOR

JASINDA WILDER

DIRTY BEASTS:

LASH

PROLOGUE

A DEADLY GAME

TATIANA

"**D**RIVE AROUND THE BLOCK, PLEASE, GEORG."

"Yes, Ms. Juric."

I am not my father's daughter; I am my mother's daughter. That said, I was still half-raised by the man, despite my mother's best efforts, which means I'm always alert and aware, constantly scanning my surroundings, which is how I pick up the blacked-out Mercedes SUV that's been following us for the last several miles.

As Georg, my driver, makes a right-hand turn on Vukovara, I remain twisted in my seat, watching the G-Wagen as it slides out into traffic behind us, three cars back. It's a pimped-out ride, as the Americans would say, with oversized spinning chrome rims, thin tires, blacked-out windows, and after-market LED light bars.

I sigh. "Idiots."

"Problem, Ms. Juric?" Georg asks, glancing at me in the rear-view mirror.

"Yes," I snap, annoyed at this ridiculous delay to my tight schedule. "We have a tail. G-Wagen three cars back."

Georg's eyes flick away from mine, scanning our backtrail; his brow furrows as he spots them. He cuts aggressively across traffic and makes a sharp, tire-squealing left turn against the light, eliciting a chorus of honks. He guns the engine at the last second, and the powerful motor sends my BMW 8 series rocketing forward. Another left, weaving around slower-moving cars, and then a sharp, fishtailing right, and then a sudden tap of the brakes and stomach-churning slide puts us underground in a parking garage. Georg slows, then, winding down to the bottom of the garage, backing into a space in the farthest corner.

We sit in silence for ten minutes or so, waiting.

"I believe we are clear, Ms. Juric," Georg says.

"Very well. I have a meeting with Draga and Tomas…" I check my Bulova watch. "Ten minutes ago. Dammit."

I slide my phone out of my crocodile Birkin and ring Draga. She answers on the third ring. "Draga, yes, it's me. I've been delayed—my apologies."

"Not at all, Ms. Juric. Tomas and I have been review-ing the numbers. If you wish, we could have the meeting now. Your physical presence is not strictly necessary."

"Excellent—I have another meeting across town in an hour. Put Tomas on speaker, please."

"Yes, Ms. Juric…here we are." A pause and the rustle of papers as Draga gets situated. "Now. Our numbers this quarter have been excellent…"

I put the tail out of my mind and focus on Draga's and Tomas's reports, digging into the details of my company's latest quarterly reports.

I'm immensely proud of what I've built—I took a quarter-million Euro loan from my father when I was twenty, and over the last eight years, I've grown my busi-ness into ten million Euros per year, with year-on-year growth of twenty-seven percent. Not bad for a girl without a university degree. I did poach my father's second-favorite business advisor—Martin has been indispensable to the process, teaching me much of the fine details of running and growing a profitable business.

When Tata first heard my pitch, he called it silly—the grasping of a bored little girl with too much time and not enough business sense.

My company buys top-shelf couture from around the world a season or two post-trend and resells it in pop-up boutiques, utilizing flash-sales strategies and aggressive pricing to move products, prioritizing stock movement over price tag; we utilize social media as the driver of our primary sales—most of my inner circle executives are social media, marketing gurus. We push heavily on IG, TikTok, and YouTube, resulting in a young clientele with lots of money and huge followings—our growth is as much due to social media word of mouth from our loyal followers as any traditional advertisements. Our pop-up boutiques last for seventy-two hours, with the specific location only revealed via our official socials posts at the last second—the lead-up to the reveal is a bread-crumb trail of hints and clues that eagle-eyed followers can decipher, share, and discuss.

We host clusters of pop-ups in a specific area of a specific city over the course of a month and then move to different cities and start all over again. This has developed a devoted cadre of fans who follow our zigzagging across Europe, following clues and competing to be among the first thousand clients who receive a bonus gift bag filled with collectible pop-up specific swag.

My mind is racing as we shift from numbers to the

details of our next pop-up campaign, back here in our hometown of Zagreb, where we began.

Georg glances at me. "Shall we head to your next meeting, Ms. Juric?"

I nod, covering the mouthpiece. "Yes, Georg, thank you. Just keep an eye out. Probably someone connected to Tata thinking they can use me to get to him."

Georg snorts. "You think they'd know better by now. Your father's methods of dealing with such antics are well known at this point, I should think."

"You would think, yet every year, there's at least one attempt. After Tata took care of the last one so publicly, I had imagined I'd get at least a few months off before the next one."

"Shall I call him, ma'am?"

I shake my head. "Not yet. Perhaps it was simply an opportunistic attempt."

"Perhaps, ma'am."

Georg exits the garage and sets us on a course back across town to my next meeting—a location-scouting endeavor with my advance team.

There's no sign of the tail, so I let myself put it out of my mind, trusting Georg to keep watch as I go over the specs and details of the location we're touring today.

It's an old church in Low Town that's been remodeled into different businesses multiple times over the years; the latest endeavor fell apart when Covid hit, and now it's been sitting empty. It's at the heart of an up-and-coming neighborhood, so a pop-up there now is ideal. We just have to hope it's in good enough shape that we can flip it without excessive overhead—that's part of my business model: we rent in the more expensive areas, but when we do a cluster in an area with lower real estate values, we buy a property, flip it, host the pop-up, and then lease it out, so we make money on the actual pop-up and then again on the property lease; it was tough to get that aspect off the ground, requiring me to put a ton of my capital back into purchasing real estate, which was a huge gamble. Tata advised against it, but it's paid off, as I now own several million euros worth of real estate throughout Europe.

Georg pulls the BMW to a stop in front of the prospective location. It's quiet, a mostly residential area with narrow, winding streets. The church is from the nineteenth century, red brick with twin spires at the front and lovely stained-glass windows that have somehow survived the last hundred-and-some years. There's a decent amount of parking in the area, and a vacant lot next to the church has been fenced off with a chain link, a weather-faded sign advertising that it's been for sale for a very long time.

Ana and Katya, my location-scouting team, are already here, walking around the exterior of the church with their tablets and headsets, styluses scribbling notes, and taking photos.

Georg, who is also my bodyguard, follows me at a precise distance, his gaze restlessly roving the area.

Ana and Katya spot my approach and bustle toward me. "So, ladies. What do we think?" I ask, reaching for Ana's tablet. I scan her notes and photos, and then head for the entrance—the agent gave me the code for the lockbox, which I open and let us inside.

"It's prime, Tati," Ana says, taking her table back. "Our research indicates this neighborhood will see a boom over the next few years—the median age of the residents has gone down significantly over the last five years, and early investors are already seeing growth. I think we should snap it up while we can—the agent has offers in, but they're all low-ball. We can come in high and still turn a profit."

"Do you have any initial thoughts on what we'll do with the space?" I ask.

It's open, with exposed brick walls and newly re-done floors. The roof was redone in the latest remodel in 2019, along with the plumbing and electrical. It has a ton of natural light, and several back rooms as well as a size-able basement.

Katya answers my questions. "We were thinking a restaurant. There aren't many in this immediate area. We've been in preliminary talks with a potential restaurateur who might be interested in the space after we're done.

"It seems like it's in pretty good shape," I say, scan-ning the ceiling for water spots, checking the walls and flooring, testing light switches, and peeking into the back rooms and basement.

"We'll have Jakov do a thorough inspection before we put in an offer, but it looks great to us," Ana says.

"Excellent," I say. "Let's move on it. Pending a green light from Jakov, put in an offer ten percent over the high-est current bid, and see if you can nail down the restaura-teur. I'd like to have a lease in place the moment the pop-up is over."

We all exit together and I lock the key back in the lockbox. Georg is in the corner of my eye by the BMW, so I address him without looking.

"Well, we're ahead of schedule, Georg, so perhaps we'll have time to grab some lunch before my next meet-ing. Fancy anything in particular?"

I finish locking the box and give it a tug, and then spin the tumblers. Georg doesn't answer.

Ana and Katya are conspicuously silent—usually, they chatter my ear off in unison every moment I'm within ten feet of them.

"Georg? Did you hear—"

Ana's face is pale and shocked, her lips trembling. Katya looks as if she's about to puke.

"Girls? What's—?"

Georg is slumped over the hood of my car, blood sprayed across the white hood and streaming down, dripping onto the concrete.

There's no one in sight, however—no cars. No threatening male figures waiting to snatch me.

I step in front of Katya and Ana, pushing them together behind me. I reach into my purse and withdraw the little Sig Sauer Tata gave me for my last birthday and forced me to practice with at the range until he felt I was proficient.

I edge the three of us into the corner of the covered entry of the church and instruct the AI voice assistant of my cell phone to call my father. He answers on the first ring.

"Tati, darling. How are you?"

"Georg is dead, Tata."

"What? *How*?"

"I'm in Low Town scouting a location. I went in to look and when I came out he was dead. Someone shot him. I didn't hear anything. There was a car following us earlier, but Georg lost them."

"Stay where you are. I have someone in Low Town

right now. Send me a pin." He waits until he receives the pin I send him. "Stay on the line, darling. I'll be right back."

I keep the phone to my ear with my left hand and clutch the pistol with my right, finger outside the trigger guard as I was taught.

A few moments later, he comes back on the line. "Someone is on the way," he says. "He'll be there in a minute or two. Do you see anyone?"

"No. No one. Nothing. I didn't hear anything, Tata."

A low growl. "The bastards won't give up, will they?" He sighs. "Stay right where you are. My man is driving a black Range Rover. You know him—it's Filip."

My heart is pounding—I'm too scared to be upset, yet, but later I'll mourn. Georg has been my driver and bodyguard since I was in primary school.

A squeal of tires announces Filip's arrival—a black Range Rover screeches to a halt in the road; the driver's door flies open and Filip jogs toward us.

Filip is one of my favorites of Tata's men. He's young, handsome, and nice, plus he's well-groomed and doesn't smoke. He rounds the hood of the Rover and trots up the steps, reaching for my arm.

"I've got you, Ms. Juric. Come with me, please."

I tug my arm away. "Ana and Katya first, Filip."

"My orders are—"

"I don't give a damn!" I snap. "They're my employees and I will not leave without them."

Filip sighs. "Very well." He gestures toward the car. "Ladies—please."

Huddling together, my girls shuffle down the steps, trying to hide their eyes from the gruesome sight of Georg's body and the gallons of blood.

Filip glances back at me, an odd, sad look in his eyes. "I'm sorry, Ms. Juric."

"Sorry?"

I don't get anything else out—before I can utter another word, Filip draws his pistol from the shoulder holster and fires two shots—*BANG-BANG!* Ana and Katya topple forward, red holes blasted through the front of their skulls.

Shocked, I forget my own pistol for a second too long. Filip snatches it from my hand and then puts the hot round barrel of his against my temple. "Let's go, Tatiana. Now."

Tears streaming down my face, I look at him, unmoving. "Filip? What…? I—I don't understand."

"Your father isn't the highest bidder anymore." Filip grabs my arm and shoves me down the steps. My three-inch heel catches on the top step and I go tumbling down, scraping my elbows and palms bloody. I lose both shoes in the process, as well as my purse. Filip grabs my phone, flings it into the vacant lot, and then hauls me to my feet, shoving me toward his car.

He yanks open the rear door. "Get in."

I climb in, looking back at Ana and Katya, face down on the sidewalk, their blood mingling with Georg's.

Filip's dark eyes find mine in the rearview mirror. "No funny shit, Tatiana. The money is for you alive, but it doesn't say anything about hurt. Get me, Princess?"

I nod, fighting to stuff my emotions down so I can find a way out of this. I'm barefoot, without my phone and gun, and now I have no clue who to trust. I thought Filip was loyal. Clearly, so did my father.

We take a long, circuitous route out of the city to the airport; a guard opens a gate and lets us through to a restricted section, where the private jets are hangared. We pull into one of the smaller hangars, passing beneath the hulking, shadowy shapes of small jets and private prop planes. The Rover's headlights flic on automatically in the gloom, illuminating a small folding table at which is a man wearing glasses tapping at a laptop. Beside the table, a man is handcuffed to a chair; his head is hanging, so I can't make out his face, but his hair is long and black, and I see a hint of a long beard.

"What's going on, Filip?" I ask. "Who are they?"

Filip twists in the seat. "Shut up. No questions, no talking."

"This isn't worth it, Filip. You know what Tata does to people who mess with me."

His face contorts into a rage-filled rictus. "Oh yes, I know. His precious princess. Well, *Tati*," he sneers my father's nickname for me, "what my new benefactor is paying me *does* make it worth it."

"Filip, please. This won't end well."

He grins, an ugly sneer. How did I miss the evil in him all this time? "Shut *up*, Tatiana. Remember what I said. The money is for you, alive. Which means I can do whatever I want to you as long as you're still breathing when I turn you over."

I clench my jaw shut—I believe him. When he sees that I'm shutting up, he nods and exits the SUV. Rounding the hood, he opens my door and yanks me out, shoving me toward the table.

"Wait here. Don't fucking move, you snobby bitch."

Filip wiggles his gun at me. "I'll shoot you in the knee if you so much as twitch wrong. Get me?"

I nod once.

He vanishes between the airplanes and returns with another folding chair, which he jerks open and sets down next to the bound man.

"Sit."

I sit, and Filip handcuffs my hands and feet to the legs of the chair; with a horrible grin, he rips open my blouse, baring my braless chest.

His grin widens into a greedy leer. "Better than I imagined, princess."

I lift my chin and glare at him. "Get a good look, Filip. Better enjoy it while you can."

"Thinking your father is coming to rescue you, eh?" He smirks. "Well, we have plans for that."

He tosses the gun onto the folding table; the man at the laptop stops typing, withdraws a pair of rubber gloves from his pocket and a disinfectant wipe from a package on the table, and thoroughly wipes down the weapon. When it's clean, he stands up and crouches in front of the man handcuffed to the chair beside me, who seems to be either unconscious or drugged, as he doesn't resist when Filip's companion presses the pistol into his hand, carefully ensuring his prints are all over the handle. He even ejects the magazine and makes sure his prints are on the slide and hammer as well.

That done, he goes back to his laptop and resumes typing.

A few minutes later, he looks up at Filip. "The package is ready to upload."

"Show me."

The be-spectacled man turns the laptop so Filip can see it and taps the spacebar to play the video. It shows a person, who I assume is the man beside me, shooting Georg, Ana, and Katya, and then shoving me into the Range Rover. If I hadn't experienced the incident myself, I would believe it's real—it's that good of a deepfake.

The man in the video is Roma, unless I'm mistaken. He's broad-shouldered, heavily muscled, and devastatingly beautiful.

Filip nods. "It's perfect, Ivan. Good work. Send it to Stjepan."

A moment later. "Done."

Filip grins at me. "No going back now, princess. Your father dearest thinks *he*," here Filip points at the man beside me, "has kidnapped you." Just then, his phone rings, and he answers it, pretending to be out of breath and upset. "I...I lost her, sir. He came out of nowhere, just bam-bam-bam. I don't know where he got a gun, sir. One second, he was under control, the next, he was gone. You sent me to get Tatiana, and..." he fakes a choked-up pause. "I'm sorry, sir. I let you down—" he listens. "Yes, sir, I understand. I'll find her. No, you don't need to worry, sir. Everyone—yes, sir. We're on it, sir."

He listens a bit longer and then hangs up, grinning at me. "There. That's bought us some time. Now we wait."

He crouches in front of me. "I'm really not supposed to—the new boss wants you for himself. But I figure I can have a little fun with you first. He won't know the difference, will he, whore?"

He fondles my breast with a rough hand and then viciously pinches my nipple, causing me to cry out; my cry of pain only makes him grin more.

"Filip!" Ivan barks. "Enough. Mercado was very clear—he wants her alive. No bullshit. You heard him."

"He won't know, Ivan. She's a loose little slut. Fucks anything that moves, as long he has enough money." He sneers at me, rage-filled. "Not so much as a glance my way, though. I'm just her precious Tata's henchman. She would never dare sully herself with the likes of me."

Oh, the irony. I would have. I liked him. I thought he was cute and kind. It was my father who categorically refused to let me date his men. That was the one no-no he never wavered on.

I don't bother saying anything though—I know well enough that it won't make a difference, now.

Fighting to remain calm, I breathe in slowly and evenly through my nose and exhale the same way through my mouth, ignoring my fear, panic, and humiliation.

Ivan leaves the table to confront Filip. "It's not worth it. We get millions when this is over, Filip. *Millions*. You can have anyone you want, then. Just not her. I know how you feel about her, brother, but she's not worth it. If you soil his prize, Mercado will cut you into tiny little pieces and feed you to his pet fish. So, keep your dick in your pants and your hands off of her, finish the op, get paid, and we can go hunt down some prime pussy. Okay? I know a guy, Filip." Ivan's voice drops to a murmur. "He works for the Syndicate—he can get us into a Syndicate brothel. That shit is *exclusive*, Filip. Like, only the highest rollers get in there. I'm talking the hottest bitches on the planet will be gagging on your cock in..." he looks at his watch. "Forty-eight hours. *If* you play your cards right."

Filip looks at me over his shoulder. "She needs to be taught a lesson."

"She will. Just not by you. You know what they say about Mercado, right? The shit he likes? I promise you, she'll get what's coming to her."

My blood runs cold at the implications.

Filip growls in frustration. "Fuck. No one will know, Ivan."

Ivan shoves Filip toward the exit. "*He* will. You *know* he will. And I know how you like to play, Filip. I've seen what's left of them when you're done."

Filip laughs—a dry, horrible little chuckle. "I wouldn't do that to her. I just want a little taste."

Ivan pulls a baggie of white powder from his back pocket. "I've got something else you can taste. Pure Colombian coke. We each get a whole fucking key of this shit if we pull this off, Filip."

They go outside, huddling together just outside the hangar. Ivan dips into the bag and snorts a hit, tips his head back, and then whoops loudly, handing the bag to Filip.

"Psst." A soft hiss gets my attention, and my head whips around; the man must've been playing possum. "Get ready."

I ever so gently rattle one handcuff. "For what? Unless you have a key?"

His eyes glint in the gloom, and his teeth flash white. "I do not need a key."

I hear rattling, a soft breath as he does something that makes him strain, and then I hear a crack of a joint dislocating. Seconds later, he's crouching behind me.

His voice is hot against my ear. "Do you have any bobby pins in your hair?"

"Yes, quite a few," I whisper.

My hair, black and quite long, is done up in an elaborate updo, courtesy of my glam squad.

I realize belatedly that the man spoke to me in English, whereas I'd been speaking Croatian with Filip.

"Do you know what they were saying?" I hiss as the man runs his fingers over my hair, finding a bobby pin and withdrawing it.

"Yes," he answers.

"Who is this Mercado?"

"A very, very, *very* bad man. I'll explain later. For now, we must go." his English is excellent if accented—Croatian is not his first language, nor is English.

My English is good but not as good as his, so I revert to Croatian—I'm too freaked out and confused to have the brain space to translate my thoughts on the fly right now.

"Can you understand me?"

He snorts. "I speak a dozen languages fluently, Tatiana Juric," he says in flawless if accented Croatian.

"How do we get out of here?" I ask. "There's only one exit."

"Think carefully. Did he leave the keys in the car or did he remove them?"

I close my eyes and focus. "I don't know. I didn't see him take them, but they could be in his pocket. It's a key fob. I don't know."

"Can't risk it, then."

This whole time, he's been quickly and quietly using the bobby pin to unlock my handcuffs. When the last one is unlocked, he grabs my wrist and tugs me off the chair and into the shadows deeper in the hangar. Since he seems to know what he's doing, and since he's a victim of this whole convoluted scheme as much as I am, I opt to go with him.

It's my best shot at the moment. He shoves me ahead of him, and we duck underneath a jet; he puts me behind the front wheel assembly.

"Wait here. If you are squeamish, do not watch."

"I'm not."

"Suit yourself."

I grab his wrist. "Wait—-who *are* you?"

He drops to a knee in front of me, and I can just barely make out his dark eyes and white teeth in the dim light of the hangar—it's past sunset now, the light of day fading.

"My name is Lash, Tatiana Juric."

"You know me?"

"I knew you when you were a gangly, beautiful, coltish teenage girl. I worked for your father."

"I don't recognize you."

He shrugs. "You wouldn't. You never knew I existed."

"But you know me."

"Yes, I do. Only from afar, but I know you."

"What's happening, Lash?"

"A very complicated bit of business, Lovely One." Somehow, he makes the endearment sound like a nickname. "A double cross, among other things."

"My father is going to think you kidnapped me." I keep hold of his wrist—which is thick and dense with muscle.

"I know. I will keep you safe and return you to him. You have my solemn vow." He twists his hand so now he has my hand in his and kisses the back of my palm. "You will be safe as long as you are with me."

"My father will be very angry. And so will this Mercado person." My heart pounds—not from fear, now, but something else. Something to do with this man, his touch, his kiss on my hand. "They'll kill you."

He kisses my hand again, making my skin tingle and tighten; his grin is a flash of white in the darkness. "They will try, and they will fail." He lets go of my hand, creeping backward into the shadows, melting out of sight. "Remain here, and remain silent."

"Okay."

"Tatiana?"

I frown. "Yes?"

Something soft and warm lands on my face and shoulder, smelling of male sweat and cologne. "To cover yourself. Filip will die first for his sins against you, and he will die screaming."

I shrug out of my blazer and then the ruined blouse, and shrug into the shirt. It's huge on me, hanging past my hips, the sleeves around my forearms, even though I get the impression that this Lash isn't much taller than me.

"Thank you," I whisper.

There's no answer.

I peer into the gloom; Filip and Ivan are now smoking cigarettes and passing a flask back and forth.

A patch of shadows shifts.

I can't make out what happens, but Filip's body contorts backward, and he screams as he's hauled into the shadows, kicking. Ivan pulls his gun and fires, the noise deafening and the muzzle flash blinding, but he curses floridly in Croatian.

A second later, there is another long, gurgling scream from Filip, one that trails off slowly.

"Filip?" Ivan calls, his voice shaky.

Silence.

I can just make out Ivan, turning in circles, gun extended, shifting this way and that.

A shadow passes between Ivan and the light from beyond the hangar.

I hear the crack of a bone snapping, and Ivan screams.

"Delete the video," Lash growls.

"I—I can't. I mean, I can delete it, but it won't stop Stjepan from seeing it. He already has. It's too late."

"Then it's too late for you." *BANG!*

Thud.

"You can come out," Lash says in a normal pitch.

I emerge from beneath the airplane and join Lash. Ivan is at his feet, staring sightlessly at the ceiling, a pool of blood spreading beneath his skull. "Now what?"

A phone chimes and Lash bends to retrieve the device from Ivan's pocket; he holds the phone over Ivan's face, and it unlocks.

"Dammit," Lash hisses. "Damn them to hell."

"What?"

"Your father has my friends. This is even more complicated than I thought. Mercado is a very crafty and duplicitous man." Lash pockets the phone. "Come. We must leave this place before their co-conspirators discover their deaths. We will make plans on the way."

He stops to rifle through Filip's pockets, coming up with the key fob for the Range Rover. I climb into the front passenger seat as Lash takes the wheel. The dome lights illuminate him.

He's even more absurdly, devilishly gorgeous in person than in the AI deepfake. His beard is long and shiny and braided to a point at his chest, with elegant, curving mustaches. His hair is bound back in a low ponytail, and his eyes are deep and dark and wise and kind. At least, they're kind as he regards me.

And my god, his body.

Massive, bulging, rounded shoulders, arms nearly the size of my thighs, a heavy, hard chest, and flat, rippling abs. He's scarred all over, as well, speaking of a life of violence.

For a moment, we merely stare at each other.

"You have truly blossomed into a beautiful woman, Tatiana. Given a thousand years, I could not a find the words in any of the languages I know to adequately capture your beauty," he says in English and then switches to Croatian. "You can trust me, Lovely One. I will not rest until you are safe once more."

He makes my pulse race. "I...I..." And, apparently, leaves me tongue-tied. "I trust you, Lash. Perhaps I shouldn't, but I do."

He takes my hand and kisses the back of it, his glittering black eyes never leaving mine. "Your faith in me is a priceless gift, Lovely One." Croatian again. Then back to English. " We must go. Time is short, especially for my friends."

He whips the SUV in a tight circle and nails the accelerator to the floor, and we're off into the purple light of a dusky Zagreb sunset.

And for some reason, I am not afraid, despite the dangerous, deadly game we're caught up in.

Lash will protect me.

CHAPTER 1

THE PRINCESS OF ZAGREB

LASH

MY MEMORY OF ZAGREB IS RUSTY FROM DISUSE, and time is not on my side. In the passenger seat beside me, Tatiana Juric looks frightened but determined, shaken but resolute.

"How well do you know the roads, Lovely One?" I ask in Croatian.

She frowns and sighs. "Not well, I'm afraid. Georg…" she trails off, sniffling. "I trusted him to drive and navigate."

"Filip killed Georg?" I ask.

She nods. "Yes, along with two of my employees."

"I am sorry for your losses," I say.

She shakes her head. "I just…I don't understand what is happening."

"We are pawns in a very complicated game," I tell her. "I do not know all of the details, or even very many of them, but I know the general outlines."

"Could you enlighten me, then?" she says, as we reach the main road leading away from the airport.

I consider. "Some of it. I am a security contractor of sorts for an individual based in Las Vegas, Nevada, in the US." I pause to mentally translate—a complicated process since neither English nor Croatian are my first, second, or even third languages. "There is a man known as Mercado, from South America. He is a very, very bad man. Evil, devious, cunning, and cruel. I do not know how, but somehow he is connected to you and your father, and also those two men back there. There is a plot of some kind against me, my Broken Arrow brothers, and my employer, which somehow involves you, your father, your father's men, and me. Some of my friends are here in Zagreb, held by your father. I cannot guess as to how you are connected to Mercado or why he wants you."

She frowns thoughtfully. "My father is a powerful man in Zagreb, and not just Zagreb but Croatia and beyond. I had assumed this was all something to do with him."

I shake my head. "No, Lovely One. Your father and you are pawns, as am I. I do not know how any of this connects to me and my friends, but I assume all will be made clear in time. For now, keeping you safe is our number one priority. Contacting your father and attempting to get him to see the truth of the situation is second, and freeing my friends is third."

She looks at me. "Your friends' lives are lowest on the priority list?"

I can only shrug. "In my heart, no. But I must be pragmatic. I know your father, and he is not unreasonable. If I can keep you alive and unharmed and get in touch with him, I do not believe my friends' lives are in danger."

Tatiana nods slowly. "Yes. You are right about Tata. But you killed Filip and Ivan. How will you prove anything? Tata won't just take your word for it."

I can only shrug and shake my head. "I know. And I think it will only complicate this situation that Filip and

Ivan were certainly not working alone. Mercado has nearly infinite resources and will turn the full weight of them toward regaining control of the situation."

She sighs. "Tata's resources are not infinite, but he does wield a lot of power in Zagreb. We will have his men to deal with as well."

I glance at her. "Do you know most of his men on sight?"

"Yes," she answers. "Not all of them, but many of them. Why?"

"I respect your father. I have no quarrel with him, and I won't kill his men if I don't have to." I checked my mirrors but saw no sign of pursuit yet.

It's only a matter of time, I know. Mercado's men, Stjepan's.

I drive in silence for a while, and we reach the city after a few minutes; I opt for High Town and the bustle of the newer and more monied streets. We stop at a traffic light and I glance at Tatiana Juric—the last time I saw her she was a gangly, long-legged teenager with big ideas and an even bigger attitude. She had a predilection for glitter, sequins, crop tops, short skirts, big hair, and tall boots back then. Rebellious, defiant, and troublesome. Back then, Stjepan had to employ several men just to keep tabs on his wayward, troublesome daughter and keep her out of trouble. Those men were very busy.

Now, however, she has blossomed into a stunning woman. The long, coltish, gangly legs are now the long, sleek, curvy legs of a beautiful woman in the prime of her youth. The rebellious, hotheaded girl with big ideas is now a brilliant, successful woman with the world at her feet.

She is tall, a few inches taller than me—albeit I am not

a tall man. Her hair is long and jet-black and pin-straight, worn loose around her shoulders. Her eyes are a very dark brown, wide, deep, and mesmerizing. She is slender, but no longer a skinny, knobby-kneed, awkward teenage girl, but rather a curvaceous, slender grown woman.

She is beautiful.

I did not desire her back then, of course—she was a child, a mere slip of a girl, and my employer's daughter. And I knew also that such as she, Zagreb's unofficial princess, was not meant for the likes of me.

The only things that have changed in the intervening years is that she is an adult now, and I do not work for her father. She is still Zagreb's princess, and still not meant for the likes of me.

"What will we do, Lash?" she asks, breaking the spell of my thoughts.

The light turns, and I accelerate through the intersection, checking cross traffic and our backtrail for signs of pursuit—so far, so good.

"First, we get rid of this vehicle," I tell her. "Then we must develop a plan." I glance at her. "Do you have your phone?"

She shakes her head. "No. Filip took it from me and threw it when he kidnapped me. My car is still there, along with my purse and my—my girls. Ana and Katya."

I look her over—my T-shirt is enormous on her. We are nothing if not entirely too conspicuous, like this, me without a shirt, her swimming in mine, and us in this flashy car.

"We need to find clothes and a different car," I say. "And a cell phone. Do you have access to any money without your phone or purse? We cannot risk backtracking across the city to wherever those items are."

"Low Town," she says, absently answering as she thinks. "If you think it is safe, we could go to my flat. My doorman will let me in. I have cash there, and clothes. With cash, we could get a pre-paid cell."

"Is it far?" I ask, pulling over to the curb.

She looks around, assessing our location. "No, in fact, only a few blocks from here."

"Very good. We will have to be quick. I must assume your flat is being watched, but we cannot make our way out of this as we are. We need cash and a phone, and you need proper attire."

Tatiana nods. "I understand. Go to the next intersection and make a right."

I follow her instructions—a few blocks ends up being more like a full mile away, which in city terms is a lot. But we arrive at her flat without issue. It's an old building on a narrow side street, away from the bustle. Formerly a single dwelling, it was renovated at some point in the near past into a handful of upscale flats. It has dedicated parking in the rear, in a small courtyard accessible only via a low, narrow gate with a keypad. Instead of entering the parking lot, however, I circle the block several times, watching. I see no evidence of either Mercado's or Stjepan's men, yet, so I park the borrowed Range Rover a couple of blocks away.

Tatiana moves to exit the car, but I stop her with a hand on her wrist.

"Wait," I say. "We must be cautious."

"What are we waiting for?" she asks. "I've seen no one."

"That does not mean they aren't there," I tell her, watching the mirrors. "Ah, yes, see?"

I point—an older red Skoda passes us and makes the turn that takes them to her building. "I saw them a few blocks back. They are attempting to follow us, but they are not very good. I wasn't sure if they were following us or not until now."

"How do you know they are?" she asks.

"Because they followed us around the block more than once. Which is clumsy work, indeed." I eyed her. "I have an idea, but it would require some trust on your part."

She lifted her chin and regarded me cooly. "What would you have me do?"

I jut my chin at her. "You will walk to your flat from here and I will follow at a distance. It will look as if you are doing the..." I paused, thinking. "I do not remember the words in this language." I switch to English. "The walk of shame. Do you know this?"

Her amused grin is dazzling. "Much to Tata's eternal shame, yes, I do. Perhaps too well." She stares at me, defying me to judge her.

I only smile. "If you are seeking judgment, Princess, you will not receive it from me. You are a woman grown and owe me no explanations for the choices you make in your own life."

She frowns at me. "Princess?"

I shrug. "I always thought of you as the Princess of Zagreb."

She grins. "I like that. Tatiana, Princess of Zagreb." The grin fades. "So, I am bait, then, yes?"

We stick to English, now, and hers is fluent but accented, with occasional pauses to recall the correct word.

I nod. "Yes. But I will not let anything happen to you."

Her lovely dark eyes search me. "I know." She says it simply, quietly, with an assurance that puts a burn in my chest.

"You trust me?" I ask.

She nods. "I do. It is a...a feeling, I suppose. Perhaps you will betray me, but I do not think so." She rests a hand on my forearm. "I have known many of my father's men, and many of his enemies. I know how it feels when a man is good and when he is evil, and you are not evil."

"Most of us are not all of one or the other," I say, "but a little of both, princess. You would do well to trust me only so far as I have earned it."

She shrugs. "What choice have I got, Lash? With this Mercado seeking me, how long will I make it alone?"

"Hours at best."

"And with you?"

"I will die before I let Mercado have you," I say, the words a low, forceful hiss.

She smiles, shrugging—the gesture has an air of resignation. "So then, I ask again—what choice have I but to place my trust in you?"

"None."

She lets out a breath. "I'm going, now."

I pull the pistol from the space between the driver's seat and the center console where I'd stashed it while driving; I checked the load—two rounds missing.

"Go," I tell Tatiana. "You may not see me, but I will be with you all the way, I promise."

She exits the expensive SUV with a single short, sharp nod, and she. A flurry of wind blows, catching the over-sized T-shirt like a sail and lifting it, baring her torso from waist to chest. For a split second, my gaze is fixed on her lovely curves—a trim, slender waist, delicate ribcage, and small, firm, high, round breasts.

In that split-second, a flash flood of desire rampages through me.

But then I remember—as I always do, as I am bound to do by the ghosts which haunt me, and I drop my eyes.

Tatiana presses her arm across her middle to keep the shirt down as the wind gusts, and her deep dark eyes are on me. She knows what I saw, and that I looked away.

For another fraught moment, our gazes meet. She looks away first, and I cannot read her thoughts. She picks her way carefully across the street on bare feet, and I wait until she's a good distance away before exiting the car myself. I leave the key fob in the cupholder and jog after Tatiana.

She rounds the corner and is out of sight—I pick up my pace and reach the corner just in time to see her at the keypad for the gate leading into her building's parking lot.

Two men cross the street after her, closer to her than I am by a few dozen meters.

Shit.

They haven't seen me yet, fixated on their quarry; I collapse against the wall and lean heavily against it, letting my hair drape in front of my face, and adopt a shuffling stumble as if intoxicated or drugged.

They notice me and dismiss me in a single glance.

They hurry after Tatiana, entering the portico that covers the gate and keypad. Tatiana made sure the gate was securely latched behind herself, which pleases me.

One of the men shakes the gate as if he could unlock it or loosen it with a few hard shakes. The other man gives him a disgusted, annoyed look, muttering something to him which I am too far away to make out.

The gate is designed to keep cars out, not people, and they make quick work of scaling the fence between the gate and the wall, a narrow section only a hint wider than a man.

I continue my vagrant shuffle, leaning heavily on the wall and watching through the curtain of my hair.

Once both men are over the fence and out of sight, I scrape my hair out of the way and sprint for the portico. I scramble over and land just in time to see them enter the building.

Time to move faster. I sprint for the doorway and then stop, easing it open and peeking in.

Within, the foyer is bright with sunlight and warm, the light reflecting off of white marble floors. A semi-circular desk with a computer monitor faces the entrance, un-manned at the moment. I hear the elevator whining, and soles squeaking on the stairs.

I jog up the stairs, pistol held close to my body as I crane my head to see up the stairs; I catch glimpses of bob-bing heads and shoulders, and a quiet murmur of voices speaking in Croatian: "...Alive, so no guns."

"I will only scare her."

"Boss says we don't get paid if she is hurt."

"I won't hurt her."

A snicker of laughter. "You always say that, Josip. Your idea of hurting someone is suspect, though."

"Oh shut up, Dario. If enjoy the spoils of work a lit-tle, who will know? Will they believe her? Or me? I won't leave any marks."

"You will get us both killed, Josip. Boss says the client is a big deal and was very clear. The girl is his. I will not help you. I will not be a part of it, and I will tell the truth if I am asked."

"I asked nothing of you, Dario, you useless piece of shit. I will take the risk, and I will have the reward."

Seems to be a running theme, so far. Mercado wants Tatiana for himself, and he wants her "unspoiled."

What does the daughter of a Central European crime lord have to do with a South American drug kingpin? I can see no connection.

Other than me.

I worked for Stjepan when I was younger, and now I work for the Boss, and somehow Mercado has Tatiana Juric in his sights.

I let my mind work on the problem as I ascend the stairs as silently as possible. The two men continue to bicker in Croatian as they make their way to the third floor.

I hear a door creak open, silence, and then the soft thud of the door closing. I sprint up the stairs and crouch near the door, pause, and then ease it open, hoping to avoid the creak by opening it slowly.

It mostly works, and I slip through—ahead of me, the two men amble unhurriedly side by side down the wide but low-ceilinged hallway. The floor here is plush scarlet carpet with gold flecks or designs of some sort, and the walls papered in dated pinstripe wallpaper. The plush carpet silences my footsteps as I creep up behind the two men, wishing I had my knife or a suppressor.

At the far end of the hallway, beyond the men, I see Tatiana. She's playing her part beautifully, walking slowly with an awkward limp, as if she stepped on something in her barefoot journey here. She's mumbling to herself in Croatian—complaining about men, it sounds like.

She reaches the door that I assume must be hers, rattles the handle, and fumbles at her hip as if reaching for a purse that's not there.

The men increase their pace, and one of them produces a handgun from the back of his track pants. The other has a taser, and they exchange a silent but aggressive argument about gun versus taser.

The argument is their undoing.

I move as swiftly as possible on the carpet, creep up behind the taser-wielding thug, and wrap my arm around his throat. He gurgles as I haul him backward, putting his body in front of mine. I grab his wrist and twist the taser out of his grip. His companion has noticed, and his gun lifts. I jab the Taser into the side of my victim's throat and trigger it. He convulses violently, choking noisily. I drop him and let him fall to the ground; his head thunks on the carpet, the plush surface likely saving him from brain damage, not that I care.

His companion, in the split second it took for me to tase the first man, has gotten his gun up and brought to bear on me, for all the good it will do him. I sweep my front foot upward in a sharp kick, knocking the barrel up and away. Landing on that same front foot, I lurch forward and leap, driving my trailing knee as hard as I can into his diaphragm.

He staggers backward, doubling over and vomiting from the force of the impact. I step past him, locking my arm around his head, and twist. *CRACK.* He flops to the floor, dead instantly.

The other thug is still alive, gurgling and gagging, writhing in agony. I crouch beside him. Stare down at him—His eyes are wide, and he's trying to speak, begging for his life.

I grip his trachea and squeeze, watching panic flare in his eyes; his struggles slow and then cease.

Tatiana watches from the end of the hallway, eyes wide. "He was not a threat anymore," she whispers.

"He would have been. He could call for backup. Send a message to his boss or his friends." I rifle through the pockets of both thugs, coming up with spare 9mm magazines for my pistol and an excellent Kershaw folding blade, as well as a few hundred euros.

"Can we not use their phones?" Tatiana asks.

I shake my head. "No. We must assume their employer is tracking them, for one. And for another, their phones are locked."

"Can't you just put it in front of his face and then change the Face ID to yours?" she asks.

I smile. "Face ID these days requires attention. It is almost impossible to spoof or fake. It is an excellent idea, but unfortunately impossible. A burner is best."

"Oh." She unlocks the door with a key. "Shall we?"

"Where'd you get the key?" I ask. "The doorman was gone."

She gives me a saucy wink and a smirk. "I saw the men coming after me and assumed they were there for me. Old Gregor is a lovely man and I didn't want to see him get hurt, so once he gave me my spare key, I told him to go have a smoke."

I followed her inside and closed the door behind me, locking it. "Excellent."

"What do we do about the bodies?" she asks.

I shrug. "Leave them. We have other things to worry

about. By the time the police are called, we shall be well away from here."

"But I thought most murders got solved. Won't they come looking for you?"

I can only laugh. "They can look."

This gets me an odd look from her. "You mean to say they will not be able to find you."

I shrug. "I am not an easy man to find."

Tatiana frowns. "Filip managed it."

I laugh. "Filip managed nothing. Mercado had the jet I was on hijacked. Filip was a blunt instrument at best. A sledgehammer."

"And what does that make you, Lash?"

I consider the question. "Obsidian."

She blinks at this, confused. "The volcanic rock? Black stuff like glass?"

I nod. "When properly worked, there is nothing on earth, man-made or otherwise, that is sharper than obsidian. Obsidian blades are so sharp and capable of creating such precise and delicate cuts that they are used in eye surgery to this day because no steel instrument can be sharpened so finely as obsidian."

She stares at me, absorbing this information, and processing how it applies to the metaphor. "I see."

I shake my head. "We do not have time for metaphors, Tatiana. Change into practical clothing, and swiftly. Jeans or leggings, a shirt, a hooded sweatshirt or some such, and practical shoes." I fix her with a look. "This is not the time for fashion, Tatiana."

She shoots me a look that is equal parts amused, droll, and annoyed. "It is *always* the time for fashion, Lash." She gestures at the kitchen. "There's food if you're hungry."

"Very good."

She heads down the hallway to where I assume her bedroom is, pausing at the door. "Lash?"

I look her way. "Yes?"

She peels off my shirt and extends it to me, managing to keep herself covered in the process. "Here."

Heart pounding, tongue stuck to the roof of my mouth, I move down the hallway and halt within arm's reach.

I take the shirt, keeping my eyes fixed on hers. An expression I cannot read crosses her face, and then she releases the garment and drops her arms to her sides, exposing her bare chest.

My eyes involuntarily flick down, linger, and then I whirl away. "Get changed," I say, my voice a low murmur.

Those who know me—very few people, indeed—know that the quieter my voice gets, the more dangerous I am.

Tatiana is in danger indeed—but not of violence.

My hands shake, and I clench them into fists as I shrug into my shirt.

"Lash?" She sounds puzzled.

I do not turn. "Change, Lovely One."

"What's wrong?"

"Nothing."

I hear her steps. I flinch as if stabbed when her soft small warm hand touches the center of my back. "I dropped the shirt, Lash. You did nothing wrong."

"I know."

"Do you not find me attractive?" So close behind me that I can almost feel her body heat.

My brain scrambled by her proximity. "Yes, Tatiana. I do. Very much so."

"Then I do not understand."

"No. You cannot."

"Lash…"

I pivot on my heel, and she's right there, so close, long black hair draped over one shoulder to cover a breast, pink nipple playing peekaboo through the strands; she's all elegant curves and graceful lines, a dancer's body, lithe and sensuous. Staring up at me, bold and curious.

"So tell me," she whispers.

"It is long in the telling, time is short, and it does not have a happy ending." I brush the pad of my thumb over her lips. "Do not toy with me, Tatiana. I will keep you safe and see you free of this mess. But…" I hold her arms and walk her backward. "I am not the kind of man you should set your sights on, now or ever. I cannot be what you want."

I walk her into her room, release her, turn on my heel, and exit. "Get changed. We need to be gone in the next two minutes."

CHAPTER 2

NICOLAE DRAGOS

TATIANA

I WATCH LASH CLOSE THE DOOR BEHIND HIMSELF, the sting of rejection burning like acid in my gut.

I strip out of my skirt and underwear, leaving them on the floor for once in my life. I dress quickly in my most comfortable jeans, with a soft and supportive sports bra, a fitted white T-shirt, and my vintage leather biker jacket. Heavy black shit-kicker boots complete the look; as well as being cool, the boots are incredibly comfortable, and feature steel toes as an added bonus. I make quick work of braiding my hair and then coiling the long braid into a bun.

Knowing time is short, I grab a small leather backpack-style purse from my closet and stuff a change of clothes into it, along with some feminine products just in case, deodorant, a new toothbrush and travel tube of toothpaste, and...for reasons I don't care to examine too closely at this moment, a string of condoms.

A knock at the door announces the end of Lash's patience. "Are you ready?"

"Nearly," I answer, opening the door and pushing past him.

I go into the second bedroom, which I use as an office; crouching beside my desk, I enter the combination to my safe. Within is the emergency kit Tata has insisted I keep on hand: a fire- and waterproof bag containing cash—ten thousand euros, ten thousand US Dollars, and five thousand in an assortment of currencies; a compact handgun and two spare, loaded magazines; my passport; and a cheap, disposable, pre-paid burner phone with a full battery and a charger with a converter for wall and car use.

I stuff everything but the handgun into my bag; the handgun goes into the pocket of my jacket.

Lash grins at me. "You are your father's daughter, I see."

"For better or worse, yes. When I first moved out to live on my own, Tata gave me this safe with all of this in it. He insisted I keep this emergency kit with me wherever I live, and that I keep the passport current. I've never needed anything but the passport until now."

"Such is the nature of emergencies," Lash says. "Your father has many faults, but he is no one's fool." He glances at my jacket pocket and the weapon therein. "Do you have training with that gun?"

I nod. "Tata makes me go to the range with him every Sunday morning." I shake my head. "I had a gun in my hand when Filip shot Ana and Katya. I...I froze. It was so sudden. So unexpected, and I...I did nothing." My eyes burn.

Lash takes me by the arms, and his deep, wild, dark, and unknowable eyes pierce mine. "You are not a killer, Tatiana. That is a good thing. To carry death on your conscience is a hard thing. Be glad you do not."

"They were sweet, innocent girls," I say, feeling rage boil in my blood. "They had nothing to do with anything.

There was no reason to kill them. Why, then? Why not kidnap me from my bed, or while shopping? Why kill Georg? He was innocent as well."

Lash shakes his head. "Who can know the reasoning of bloody-minded insects like Filip?" He frowns. "Tatiana, about what I said…"

I move past him. "Later, Lash. As you keep saying, we have to go."

He nods, and we leave my flat together, Lash preceding me, gun held in both hands close against his chest with the barrel angled down—a grip unique to those trained in close-quarters combat and room-clearing tactics. My father employs men from all walks of life across his various business interests, both legitimate and otherwise; his bodyguards and enforcers are all exclusively former military and police, and I have enough experience with those types of men to know when a man is an operator, as they call themselves, and when he is merely a thug with a gun.

Lash is an operator, through and through: it is written in the scars on his body, in the brusque efficiency in everything he does, in the lethal, predatory way he moves, in the cold hardness of his eyes.

His hallway takedown of the two men impressed me; it was utterly silent, brutally quick, and accomplished without firing a shot.

I wonder what it says about me that it turned me on. Am I a sadist, to be aroused by the murder of two men?

It wasn't the death that affected me that way, though, I recognize. It was the skill he demonstrated. The feeling of safety and security engendered by his protection.

We're out on the street and Lash has stowed his gun at the small of his back, hidden by his shirt. We walk in silence for a long time, covering block after block, turning at random, circling, doubling back, and crisscrossing our own path until I am disoriented myself.

"Where are we going, Lash?" I ask, after almost an hour of walking.

"Nowhere," he says, eyes roving restlessly. "I am assessing the skill of our pursuers."

"Pursuers?" I check behind us and see nothing, no one.

He indicates a camera atop a pole supporting a traffic light. "They watch us."

"So we wander Zagreb aimlessly hoping to confuse them?"

A shrug. "That is part of it. What I am really assessing—well, testing, perhaps, is the more accurate word— is their response time. They know we escaped their men at your flat. That was an hour ago. If they are watching us as I assume, I need to know how fast they can send more men our way.

"Are we talking about Tata's men or Mercado's?"

Another shrug. "Either—both. They may be the same, also. Remember, Filip was your father's man until Mercado turned him. When loyalty is purchased rather than earned, it becomes a commodity possessed by the highest bidder, and your father is not in the same universe as Mercado on that front."

"He is so powerful, then? This Mercado."

Lash nods. "Oh yes. More so than you can imagine." A newer Lada Niva creeps up behind us. "Your father controls one small city in one small country in Europe. Mercado controls much of Latin America, from the Rio Grande to Tierra del Fuego."

"Oh," I say, processing this. "But we are not in South America. We are in the city controlled by my father."

"For a man worth billions, a man who owns politicians, who controls police forces and can command the generals of armies, it is a simple enough matter to exert in his influence wherever he wishes." Lash nudges me so I am forced to walk with my shoulder brushing the wall, putting his body between me and the Lada still trailing us by a few meters. "If Mercado wanted to, he could have your father assassinated and put whoever he wishes in his place, and then Mercado would own Zagreb."

"What is stopping him?" I ask.

"Value. What does Mercado want with Zagreb, Croatia? It does not factor very heavily in the world of illegal trade. Drugs do not flow through here and neither do guns or women."

"Tata deals heavily in drugs," I say. "Guns and women not so much."

A shrug. "Think of it this way, Tatiana: your father is a distributor. He purchases his drugs from elsewhere—in bulk, yes, by the kilo and hundreds of kilos, but he still purchases and then distributes. Mercado is the *source*. He controls the flow. He produces the drugs, and he decides where they go. *That* is genuine power. I do not mean to denigrate him, Tatiana, but your father is the ant scurrying this way and that with crumbs. Mercado is the hand wielding the entire cookie."

I frown all the harder. "If Mercado is so powerful, then what chance do we have?"

Lash grins. "My employer is the difference."

"Who is your employer?" I ask.

"An excellent question," Lash says. "A powerful

individual. A very mysterious one who deals in information, among other things."

"What is his name?"

Lash shakes his head. "That's the mysterious part. I don't know."

I laugh. "You work for someone, and you don't know his name?"

"I have never met him, only his second in command, Inez. But I see the effects of his power." Lash shrugs. "Where Mercado is the stormtroopers of the cartels spreading murder and destruction in broad daylight, my employer is the whisper in the shadows, a knife in the dark."

"The knife in the dark being you," I say. "The obsidian blade."

He nods. "Yes." He glances back at the Lada. "Are those your father's men? I think they must be, or they would have attacked us by now."

I look and then nod. "Yes. That is Jakov and Tomas."

"Tell me about them."

I shrug. "The bluntest of instruments. They guard shipments, usually. If Tata needs someone intimidated or leveraged, he sends them."

Lash nods. "Wonderful."

All I catch is a blur of movement, and Lash has his gun out—*BANGBANG*! The hood of the Lada sprouts a pair of holes and smoke plumes from the engine bay. It's so sudden that I jump in shock, shrieking. Before I can so much as stammer a question, Lash is at the driver's window, smashing it with the butt of his gun, reaching in and yanking open the door, and dragging the driver out.

"Call Stjepan," Lash growls in Croatian. "Now."

Tomas, the driver, blinks blood out of his eye where a shard of glass cut his face above his eyebrow. He digs his phone out of his pocket and hits a favorite contact. The handset rings, and Lash takes it, puts it on speaker.

"Tomas," Tata's voice barks. "You have her?"

"No, Stjepan, *I* do." Lash's voice is a low growl. "I did not kidnap her. The video you saw was a deepfake. Your man Filip was a traitor."

"Nicolae Dragos," Tata says. "It has been a very long time. Tell me, old friend, why should I believe you?"

"Believe *me*, Tata," I say, taking the phone from Lash. "It was Filip and Ivan. Filip killed Ana and Katya right in front of me. He molested me and he would have raped me. He was working for Mercado. Lash saved me."

A long, tense silence. "Tati, is it you? You say so?"

"I say so, Tata."

"Then you can come home. Lash can deliver you."

Lash takes the phone back. "I am not certain that is a good plan, Stjepan. If Mercado turned Filip, who else in your circle has he turned? Who can you trust?"

Another silence. "Filip was my trusted right hand."

"And Mercado bought him. You cannot trust anyone."

"But I can trust you, eh, Nicolae?"

"I never betrayed you, Stjepan. You know what I went through. You know what happened. Would you have stayed?" He shakes his head. "Nicolae Dragos is dead. He has been dead for many years. Now there is only Lash."

"You always had a flair for drama, Nicolae." Tata sighs. "What do you suggest, then?"

"For one, I am not Nicolae, I am Lash. For another, you release my friends. For a third, you do some quiet investigation into the finances of those you think you can trust. Until you know for sure who Mercado owns and who he does not, Tatiana is safer with me."

"If I release your friends, what leverage do I have over you?"

Lash sighs in annoyance. "You are thinking about this all wrong, Stjepan. You do not need leverage over me. And holding a man like Solomon Cabot is not the leverage you think it is. I do not know the other two, but if they are with Solomon, then you have not one tiger by the tail, but three. Release them, and soon, before you discover what I mean the hard way."

"You have my daughter, Lash."

A sigh. "I do not *have* her, Stjepan. I am *with* her. She is not my prisoner or my hostage."

"Tata—Father," I say, switching to Croatian. "Listen to him. Please. I do not know what is in the past between you two, and I do not care. It has nothing to do with me."

Tata sighs, thinking. "I cannot trust you, *Lash*. When my daughter is returned to me, I will release your friends. I will do as you say, however—I will look into those I feel I can trust."

Lash shakes his head. "You always were stubborn, Stjepan. At the very least, keep your men close. Sending them after us only muddies the water, and I have enough to worry about with Mercado's men after your daughter."

"They are after my daughter? I assumed he was using her to get to me."

Lash snorts. "I do not know *what* he wants, but I do not think it is you. His men, before I killed them, said he wants her alive. Why, I do not know. Perhaps it is to control you."

"If what you say is true, then would she not be safer at home in my compound, protected by my men?"

"Not if your men are not yours."

"Who can I trust, then, if not the men I have paid handsomely for so many years?"

Lash shakes his head, snarling in frustration. "You are a fool, and I just told Tatiana that you are not a fool. You make a liar out of me, Stjepan."

"Insulting me is not the path to earning my favor."

"I do not *care* about your favor!" Lash snaps. "I care about your daughter's safety."

I touch Lash's thick bicep. "If you know my father," I murmur so only he can hear me, "then you know he must make up his own mind. You will never change his mind."

A disgusted sigh. "Yes, yes. You are right, of course. I forgot what a stubborn old donkey your father could be." He ends the call, cutting short my father's spluttering bluster. He gives the phone back to Tomas. "Go back to him and tell him what happened here. I have not hurt you when I could have."

Tomas, short and wide, tough and dimwitted, nods eagerly. "Yes, yes, I will tell him."

"Come." Lash strides away, and I follow after him.

We round the corner just in time for a city bus to squeal to a halt at a bus stop. Lash and I board, pay the fare, and sit at the back.

A block later, I glance at Lash. "Now what?"

"For your father's sake, I must free my friends. Solomon is not a patient man and will only tolerate captivity for so long. And believe me, when Solomon Cabot runs out of patience, bad things happen." He sighs, rubbing his face with both hands. "The truth is, I have a feeling

Solomon is only here because of me. This worries me. I have a feeling we are only seeing one small aspect of this whole situation."

"Who is this friend of yours, this Solomon?" I ask.

Lash's grin isn't a nice thing. "A ghost. We are all ghosts, Tatiana, me and the men I now consider my brothers."

I consider this for a while, tucking it away with the growing pile of things about Lash that I am trying to process. "And who is Nicolae Dragos?"

He sighs. "That was my name, for a time."

I furrow my brow at him. "For a time?"

A nod and a shrug. "Yes. For a time."

"What does that mean?" I ask.

He doesn't answer right away. "I have had many names in my life. I put them on and take them off like hats. Nicolae Drago is…" he closes his eyes and rests his head backward. "It is the name I wore the longest. I had happiness as Nicolae. The greatest happiness. I also knew the greatest sorrow as Nicolae, as well."

"Will you tell me?" I ask.

He shakes his head, but it does not feel like a refusal. "I would not burden you with such sorrow, Lovely One."

"Yet you carry it alone." For a moment, I see the exhaustion on his face, the old agony.

It is gone as swiftly as it appeared, and his face is an expressionless mask of stone once more. "It is mine to carry."

"Which stop is ours?" I ask, after a long silence.

Lash, eyes closed, just grunts. "We are resting, not traveling. We cannot be snuck upon while seated in the back of a moving bus."

"Oh," I say. "Smart."

A quick quirk of his lips is his only expression. "This is not my first time being on the run." He opens one eye and regards me. "Close your eyes and rest. When the bus stops, we look to see who boards."

And so we passed the hours, dozing between stops. After we ride the bus long enough that Lash feels somewhat rested, we disembark—despite having ridden for a long time, we hadn't actually gone anywhere, since the buses run in a loop. Instead of asking the question I feel percolating in my brain—now what?—I follow Lash away from the bus stop. We cross the street, cut down an alley, cross another street…this is not aimless wandering. Lash going somewhere specific—following smaller one-way side streets and back alleys, places where it is likely we will be spotted by cameras. We walk for ages, it feels like, block after block until my feet ache and my legs protest. Gradually, I recognize where we are: near Tata's compound.

"Lash, we can't get into my father's compound," I say. "It is too well-guarded and too secure."

Lash just shrugs. "Getting in is easy. Getting out with Solomon and his friends without killing your father's men…*that's* the hard part."

I know the security measures Tata has in place: biometric locks, cameras, laser tripwires, regular patrols. Getting in is *not* easy: that is the entire point of the security, is it not?

But then, Lash does *not* seem like your average person, nor even your average operator. For one thing, what did it mean that he has had many names, that he takes them off and puts them on like hats? What is the sorrow he carries? What happened between him and my father?

Why did he reject me?

We are short on time, that much is obvious, and reason enough. But it wasn't that. He didn't act tempted and then stop because we didn't have enough time.

He rejected me. Turned me down cold. Literally pushed me off of him and walked away.

I cannot be what you want. What does *that* mean?

I've never been turned down before. It's not a good feeling and I don't know what to do with it.

I don't know what to do with him.

Am I attracted to him? Or is it merely the feeling that I am safe with him?

I steal looks at him as we walk. He is not a tall man, perhaps five-eight or five-nine at the most, but he is impossibly muscular—massively broad, hard, round shoulders, immense arms, and a thick chest. His long, glossy black hair falls down his back, tangled and in need of brushing. His beard is long and neatly trimmed and clean. His skin is dark olive, naturally dark from his ethnicity and tanned darker yet from a lifetime in the sun.

He notices me looking and arches an eyebrow. "Why do you look at me this way?"

I shrug. "Trying to figure you out."

He snorts. "Good luck with that."

"Why do you say that?"

A shrug. "I am not an easy man to know."

"So I am discovering. You won't tell me anything about yourself."

"No." It is his only response.

I wait until it's obvious nothing more is forthcoming. "Well? Why not?"

"I do not wish to be known."

"Why not?"

A sigh. "There is nothing but pain in my past, Lovely One. I have experienced enough pain to last many lifetimes."

I consider this answer for a long time. "To be alive is to experience pain, Lash. You cannot escape it through isolation. Is that not its own kind of pain?"

He nods. "It is. But I prefer that pain to…." a harsh breath, a shake of his head. "To the pain of loss."

"Who did you lose?"

He doesn't answer, but I see his jaw flexing. He halts, ducking into a doorway. "Wait here."

"Lash—" I start.

He chops his hand downward, silencing me. "This I must do alone. Wait here. Keep a sharp lookout for men you do not recognize. If men you do not recognize approach you, shoot them." He cups his large, rough, powerful hands around mine. "Shoot to kill. If you feel you must shoot, do not hesitate. Hesitation is death."

"O-okay," I say. "Please be careful, Lash."

His smile is gentle. "I will be fine." He gestures at my father's compound. "This is child's play. Your father thinks his fancy electronics keep him safe."

I wonder at that pair of statements, but before I can put together a response Lash is striding away from me, continuing down the sidewalk parallel to the compound. He crosses the street toward the compound and is gone from my sight.

My heart pounds as I shrink back into the doorway, trying to will myself invisible.

It is funny how naked and vulnerable I feel without Lash.

CHAPTER 3

INFIL, EXFIL

LASH

THE COMPOUND—THREE APARTMENT BUILDINGS in a U-shape with a heavy gate across the opening—backs up to an alley. Cameras watch the entrances at each end; it is early evening and the shadows are long. This is the riskiest part of the infiltration, when I stand the highest chance of being spotted. I creep through the deepest shadows along the wall, moving slowly and irregularly. A forgotten second-story window is the biggest security flaw in the system. It is possible that it isn't forgotten, but they merely feel that because it is high above the ground with no easy way to access it, there's no point in alarming it.

They didn't account for one simple thing: this building is quite old, and the bricks are not flush—they protrude quite a bit, and between the abuse of the elements and the wear and tear of the centuries, much of the mortar has worn away, creating an easy path up for someone with rock-climbing experience. I spend a few moments examining the wall, picking out a likely path; I kneel and remove my boots and socks, knotting my boot laces together through the belt loop of my jeans at my back, stuffing the socks into the boots.

And then up. Fingerhold by fingerhold, sometimes supporting my weight by fingertips and a toe—it's slow going, but I'm patient.

Once I reach the windowsill, I use the butt of my pistol to gently crack the glass—small, quiet taps that spread spiderweb cracks across the pane; tap-tap-tap at the top, the bottom, corners, the sides, until the glass is a fragile agglomeration of cracked pieces. Balanced by a precarious toehold, I cannot afford to rush and cause the noise of crashing glass; if I remember correctly, the floor on the other side is tile or marble. I cautiously tap a small piece loose near the bottom edge of the window, pry it free with my fingernails, and set it on the sill. My toe and fingerholds shaking, I grit my teeth, ignore the exhaustion. Free another piece, stack it with the first. Piece by piece, I create a hole large enough that I can snake my arm in and reach the lock, after which it's a simple matter of lifting the sash and climbing in.

Once inside, I close the window once more.

I am in a small, dark, cluttered supply closet—shelves hold boxes of paper towels and toilet paper, cleaning supplies, and the like. I put my socks and boots back on and peek out of the doorway—a long hallway extends in either direction, lined with low-pile industrial carpet, wall sconces at regular intervals shedding orange-yellow light from Edison bulbs.

I watch and wait for several minutes, but no patrol comes by, so I ease out, checking ceiling corners for cameras; through sheer dumb luck, I seem to have emerged in a blind spot. I creep down the hallway, listening for footsteps or voices, scanning for cameras. I spot one as I reach the end of the hall where it turns to the right; the camera watches the hallway, however, and not the stairwell. I shake my head, bemused. A quick scan of the stairwell assures me there is no camera here—once I'm out with Solomon and his companions, I'll have to have a word with Stjepan about his so-called security.

While my recollection of the layout of the compound is hazy, I remember that the security room is in the basement, along with the holding cells.

I descend the stairs, almost missing the laser tripwire along the bottom of the doorway; the door opens into the stairwell, so there is no way to cross the threshold without setting it off.

Tricky.

Once again, pure dumb luck is on my side—the door swings open just then. "This is Lukas," I hear a guard speaking Croatian. "Perimeter check."

I hide next to the door so it hides me as it swings open. The guard is adjusting his gear belt as he enters the stairwell—settling his radio on the belt clip, adjusting the microphone and wire, working the earpiece in place, checking his flashlight and pistol. He doesn't see me because he's not even looking.

Remarkable stupidity and incompetence.

A slow-close hydraulic mechanism allows the guard to reach the next level before the door even begins closing. I step over the tripwire so it only shows a single open-and-close from the guard, pausing just on the other side of the threshold to assess my surroundings.

This hallway is garishly lit by fluorescents, the floor is polished concrete and the walls bare, featureless drywall.

The first door on the right should be the security room. There is a camera watching this hallway, but that won't matter beyond the next thirty seconds.

I hustle to the door to the security room, draw my gun, and enter. Two men sit in front of a display of monitors, but one is watching a football match on his phone with an earbud in his ear, and the other is eating yogurt—neither one has his attention on the screens, or they'd have seen me.

"Forget something, Lukas?" The yogurt-eater says, not looking around. "You always forget something. I swear, you'd forget your head if it wasn't screwed onto your skinny neck."

I press the barrel of my pistol to the back of his head. "Not quite," I say in Croatian. I press harder. "Hands up. Both of you. I don't want to kill you, so just cooperate."

Their hands go up.

"Good." I reach down and retrieve their pistols, stuffing them in my pockets. "Now. Shut down the system."

"He'll still know you were here," the football watcher says.

"I know. I don't care. Tell him I'll call him later, as we've much to discuss." I tap him on the skull with the barrel hard enough to get his attention without hurting him. "Shut it down. Cameras, lasers, everything."

A moment later, the system is off.

"Good. Now. My friends are in the room down the hall, yes?"

"Yes. The next door."

"On the floor, both of you. On your bellies, hands on the back of your heads."

They comply, and I bind their wrists behind their

backs with their own zip ties; I remove a boot and a sock from each man's foot, remove the laces from the boots, and gag each man with his sock and bootlace.

On the desk is a tablet device. I put it in front of one of the guards' faces to unlock it and search it for a layout map; once I find the map, I spend a few minutes studying it and memorizing the best route out—one level up to the ground floor and right out the front door, it appears.

I snatch a keycard on a lanyard from one of the guard's necks and exit the security room, watching and listening for a moment. I hear a merry, tuneless whistling from the far end of the hallway. I close the door. Wait.

The door opens. "Camera six is offline, Anton," a voice says.

"I know," I answer. "I'm working on it."

A pause. "You're not Anton."

I hear the door creak open further, hear his foot squeak on the tile. "Who are you? What are you doing in here?"

I shoot out of the chair and level my gun at him. "Hands up. I won't kill you if you do as I tell you."

His sigh is one of extreme annoyance. "This won't work."

I shrug. "That is my problem. Hands behind your head. On the floor on your belly."

I make swift work of binding and gagging him as I did his comrades and then leave the room yet again.

Here is where I encounter a problem: my keycard does not unlock the door to Sol's cell.

Back to the security room. Ungag one man. "Whose key unlocks that door?" I ask.

He grimaces, spitting to get the taste of his sock out of his mouth. "Stjepan and Igor."

"Where is Igor?"

"Gone for the day."

Fuck.

I re-gag the man and go back to the door, examining it, hoping for inspiration.

Ah!

Since this was, at one point, nothing more than an apartment building, the doors themselves, despite the fancy locks, are simple doors with standard hinges on the outside.

Back to the security room.

"Flathead screwdriver," I demand. "Where?"

One man looks pointedly at a drawer—I open it and find a haphazard assortment of tools—screwdrivers, a hammer, mismatched wrenches, a socket wrench, and an assortment of sockets. I select a flathead screwdriver and the hammer—it's a matter of moments to remove the door, bypassing the lock entirely.

Idiots.

Solomon lays on his back on the floor, one arm over his eyes. The woman—roughly my height, hard-bodied and beautiful—is next to him; they are holding hands, a surprising development.

The other man is an operator—I see it in the way he cracks an eye at me, assessing me with the calm confidence of a man who is sure of his abilities. He is tall, six-four, if I had to guess, and powerfully built with black hair and handsome features.

"Took you long enough," Sol says, grinning at me.

I shrug. "Between Stjepan's men and Mercado's, I have been busy."

None of them are zip-tied—another laughable oversight. Regular prisoners, perhaps, can be left unattended and unbound, but operators like these? Foolishness.

Stjepan, you have grown lax. Did you think I would not come for my brother?

Solomon and the others rise and precede me out of the cell; I put the door back on its hinges, hoping the mystery of their escape will buy us time.

"I assume you know the way out?" Sol asks me.

"Of course." I turn to the woman. "I am Lash."

She nods, shakes my hand. "I know. I'm Scarlett."

I look from her to Sol. "Later there will be time for stories, and I think you have an interesting one to tell."

He nods. "I do. We have to get out of here first, though—out of Zagreb, and fast."

I frown at him. "Why are you here?"

He rolls his eyes. "For you, of course."

I laugh. "You came to rescue me, and now I rescue you. I believe you call this irony." My laughter dies. "Why, Solomon? What is going on?"

"Mercado has Inez."

My blood runs cold. "How?"

"That's a long story," Sol answers. "Short version is, Inez knows him. He's from her past. We have to get the whole crew together and go get her."

I sigh. "Mercado is bloodthirsty and merciless. I do not like her chances of survival if that monster has her."

Sol snorts. "Her chances are better than you think— he wants to play with her. Punish her."

I suppress a shudder. "Even worse. I know what his notion of play entails, Solomon."

Sol frowns at me. "We need to get out of this compound. How the fuck you got in here undetected, I don't know, but they're bound to notice sooner rather than later."

I nod. "Indeed." I extend my hand to the other man. "Lash."

He shakes my hand. "Lorenzo."

"Who are you?" I ask.

"I am Sophia's…." He frowns, shrugging. "I am Sophia's."

"Who is this Sophia?" I ask.

"Inez's real name," Solomon answers. "Apparently."

I absorb this. "Interesting. Clearly, there is much I must be caught up on. For now, however, we must go. You are correct, Solomon—I have kicked the bees' nest, and it is only a matter of time before they swarm. Stjepan is not my enemy, so I will not kill anyone if I don't have to."

I wince, realizing too late my gaffe.

Solomon catches it. "You won't kill anyone…if you don't have to? What about your vow?"

I shake my head. "No time for that explanation, Sol. What I will say, however, is that my vow, unlike yours, does not include the injunction against killing."

Sol frowns. "You're a Broken Arrow."

"I am. Heart and soul."

"But then—"

"Later, Solomon. Later. Tatiana is waiting."

"Tatiana?"

I ignore the question and lead the way to the stairwell. Up to the ground floor, through a hallway past several locked doors, and to the foyer. Three guards huddle together, laughing at something on a phone.

They see us, but too late—I gave Lorenzo and Scarlett the handguns, since like me they have no restriction against killing. Solomon was unhappy to be weaponless but accepted it with only a few muttered curses.

"To the floor," I order in Croatian. "We won't kill you if you cooperate."

"Stjepan knows you are here," one of them says. "He is on his way."

I shrug. "Good. Now he knows the flaws in his security, which are many. Remain still while we leave and you will be unharmed."

Solomon chuckles. "Right out the front door, huh?"

I nod. "It was the closest exit."

We are outside in the night; a taxi passes us, followed by a diesel-spewing bus. The others follow as I head for the doorway where I left Tatiana.

Only...

She isn't here.

A pair of shell casings lay in a pool of blood; the blood points away in a messy trail, as if someone dragged a body.

I follow the trail down the sidewalk, Solomon and the others behind me. The blood trail enters a yawning alley mouth.

"Tatiana?" I call, voice pitched low.

Nothing.

The trail continues, bloody skid marks glistening in the ambient light. I follow it further in—this is a dead-end alley. A heavy male body lies slumped at the end of the alley.

"Tatiana?" I call again.

I hear a whimper.

I look around—a dumpster, overflowing with stinking trash, a pile of discarded boxes and haphazardly stacked pallets, drifts of crumpled newspaper. "Tatiana? It's me—It's Lash." I pitch my voice in a low murmur, in Croatian.

"Lash?" Her voice is tiny, fearful.

"It's me. It's okay. You can come out."

Boxes and newspapers rustle and topple, and Tatiana emerges, a blood-drenched specter.

"Lovely One," I whisper. "What happened?"

She takes a shuffling step, falters, and topples. I catch her and pull her into my arms—she's trembling and hyperventilating.

"He-he-he…" she points at the dead man on the ground. "He—I hesitated. I hesitated."

"Are you hurt?" I ask, scanning her for injuries.

"N-n-no. No. It's his." Her eyes are wet and wide, searching mine. "I hesitated. I hesitated."

I cup her face, smearing blood. "You're alive, Tatiana. He is not."

"I—I—I had to…" she mimes a stabbing motion. "He—he wouldn't die! I—I kept stabbing and stabbing. So much blood—so much blood." She squeezes her eyes shut. "I hesitated. You told me not to hesitate, but he—I didn't see his knife at first. He was going to—he tried to—" she shakes her head. "I fought him, Lash. He was so strong. So big. So heavy. But I fought him. He had a knife and I got it from him and I stabbed him. I stabbed him so many times."

I pull her into my arms, against my chest. "You did what you had to do, Lovely One. Killing a man with a knife is no easy feat."

"So much blood," she whispers.

Muffled gunfire dopplers off the alley walls, and I whirl, putting her behind me, pistol in hand.

Solomon jogs to the alley mouth and crouches against the corner, poking his head out. "Coming from the compound," he says.

I frown. "What? Who would attack Stjepan?"

"Mercado," Lorenzo answers. "We embarrassed him. We got away. He has Sophia, but we took out a lot of his men. His ego cannot allow that."

"I do not see the connection between him and Stjepan. Why Stjepan? Why does he want Tatiana?" I'm asking the questions out loud, more rhetorically than anything, but Lorenzo answers anyway.

"Who knows with Mercado? His distribution network is massive, and he has agents everywhere. If this Stjepan of yours is a major mover in this area, it's likely Mercado is trying to leverage him into service."

I nod, considering what I know. "He styles himself a warlord. Drugs are just how he pays for his real ambition."

Solomon has rejoined us. "So, the real question is do we help out Stjepan? Or do we let his people deal with them?"

I think for a moment. "There is no love lost between Stjepan Juric and me. But, as they say, the enemy of my enemy is my friend."

"No!" Tatiana says. "We should leave."

"Those are your father's men in there being shot," I say.

"My father will not be there."

"They said he was on the way," I say.

"He will know. They will radio him and tell him they are under attack. There is a secret exit to the parking garage.

One or two will stay to distract the attackers while the rest escape."

"You could have mentioned the secret way in," I say, annoyed. "I wouldn't have had to scale the wall like a spider."

"You cannot go in through that way—only out from the compound to the garage. Also, I forgot about it until just now. I've been a little distracted, you know."

I sigh, rubbing my face. "True. I'm sorry." I take her hand. "So, we go. Let your father's men handle their own situation. I feel bad, however—I disabled their security system, so they wouldn't have had a warning."

She just shakes her head. "If my father is in business with a man like this Mercado, then he deserves what he gets."

"Even if that's a bullet to the brain?" I ask.

She shrugs. "He is my father and I love him, but I know very well what kind of business he does. He does not hide it." She looks angry, now. "I have been kidnapped many times because of my father's business, because of his enemies. It is tiresome. Ana and Katya are dead, Georg is dead, and I am being hunted like an animal. I have been forced to kill a man with my hands. So yes, I am angry, and my love for the man who is my father is not stronger than my anger at what the actions and choices of my father the businessman have done to me."

"That is fair," I say. More overlapping gunfire, single shots and automatic bursts. "You must decide what you want to do next, where you will go, and who you will trust. I can deliver you to your father and you can trust him to keep you safe. Or you can come with me—with us."

She frowns, wincing and flinching at the gunfire. "I don't know."

"My goal was always to return you safely to your father. But if Mercado is making moves like this against your father's compound, you may not be safer with him than you would be with me. Which is not very safe—clearly. I have my own enemies and Mercado is only one of them."

Solomon speaks up, then. "Inez mentioned an enemy high up in a government somewhere. I assumed that was Stjepan. He claimed to have trained you, to have made you what you are."

I laugh. "Hardly. I worked for him many years ago, and it is true I learned much while in his employ, but it would not be accurate to say he made me who I am." I shake my head. "And no, he is not the enemy Inez was referring to."

"So…there's *another* powerful figure who wants you dead?" Solomon asks. "Not Mercado, not Stjepan, but someone *else*?"

I shrug. "Yes."

"Who?"

I sigh. "A senior official in Interpol."

Solomon huffs. "Wonderful."

Tatiana leans against me. "Can we leave this alley, please?" She glances over her shoulder at the corpse. "I am not superstitious or religious, but I *feel* him."

"Yes, of course," I say. "I've been in Zagreb for too long as it is. Roberto Pugli, my enemy at Interpol, is an experienced intelligence analyst with decades of experience. He is a top-level administrator now, last I checked, but his contacts cover most of the globe. I am sure he knows I am here."

"Interpol is administrative," Sol points out. "So what

if he knows you're here? He'd have to mobilize local law enforcement."

I shake my head. "It is not so simple. Yes, he can and will send local law enforcement after me, but he knows many people and not all of them operate on the right side of the law. Those kinds of operatives are far more dangerous than the Zagreb police."

Solomon nods, blowing out a breath. "Ah, he's one of those."

"Corrupt, malicious, and cruel?" I say. "Yes. All that and more." Solomon opens his mouth, but I cut him off. "I am certain you have questions, but this is not the time for interrogations. We must flee Zagreb, and swiftly."

"Train?" Solomon suggests.

"Yes, it is best. We can rest and take turns keeping watch."

I look at Tatiana. "Are you able to walk? The train station is some distance from here, but we are not likely to find a taxi at this hour."

She shrugs. "Do I have a choice?"

"Not really." I peel out of my shirt and use it to wipe the blood from her face. Her white T-shirt is splattered with it, as are her jeans and leather jacket. There is nothing to do about that, however. Once I have cleaned the worst of the blood from her face, I shrug back into my shirt—it is now wet and tacky, but that doesn't concern me.

And so we walk—block after block, mile after mile, three killers and an innocent young woman.

CHAPTER 4

FIRST TOUCH

TATIANA

WE CATCH A NIGHT TRAIN TO SPLIT BECAUSE that's the only train leaving at this hour. We get a couchette compartment for the five of us. We each choose a bunk, and within minutes, both Lorenzo and Scarlett are asleep. Solomon and Lash sit beside each other on a bottom bunk, conversing quietly while I try unsuccessfully to fall asleep.

My mind whirls and spins like a child's toy top, spinning and wobbling as it slows.

I close my eyes and see Georg slumped over the hood of my car, sightless eyes staring at nothing while blood spreads in a crimson pool.

Again and again, I see Filip drawing his pistol and casually blasting a hole in Ana's head and then Katya's. I see their heads snap backward in slow motion. I see blood spraying, brain matter spattering.

My eyes wrench open and I stare, eyes burning with exhaustion, at the underside of the bunk above me. I struggle to quiet my mind, and slowly, slowly, sleep begins to pull me under.

In the bunk below me, I hear Solomon whispering to

Lash. I only catch fragments, but it seems as if he is relating the events that brought him to the cell in Tata's compound. I hear exotic sounding places like Quito and San José, and descriptions of gunfights. Lash asks Solomon about Scarlett; I nod off as Solomon relates a story about an operation gone wrong in Venezuela.

Darkness enshrouds me. My feet are heavy, trapped in quicksand pulling me inexorably under. I smell body odor, a rank, thick miasma of rotting onions. A hand closes on my left wrist, and I try to scream, but no sound emerges from my throat.

LASH! The scream echoes in my skull, but my teeth are fused together, my lips stitched shut. I cannot move, cannot withdraw my feet from the sludge encasing them, cannot jerk my wrist out of the painful hold. The scream, my plea for Lash to help me, is stuck in my throat, trapped behind my fused teeth and stitched lips.

Body odor chokes me.

A hand slides up my belly, and then I feel Filip's fingers painfully pinching my nipple. I try to writhe away, but movement is impossible—my limbs are encased in granite, so I cannot push or pull, stand or sit, run or crawl.

Darkness swirls, eddying around me like fog. A big, bulky male figure hulks in front of me, outlined by a murderous red glow. His teeth flash white, all sharp predator incisors dripping blood, and his shaved head writhes with living tattoos, and his hand grows large enough to encompass the entire world as he reaches for me, and I cannot run, cannot run, cannot run.

His hands imprison me, the jaws of a Kraken crunching my bones, pushing me to the dirty wet cold ground; his weight is titanic and immense, and I cannot dislodge him. His breath stinks of beer and meat. His body odor is all-consuming, almost worse than his huge cruel hands scraping my belly as he gropes my breast.

Panic boils in my gut, surging like vomit up to my teeth.

JUST A LITTLE TASTE. The words scratch over my skin, crater in my skull. *JUST A LITTLE TASTE BEFORE I GIVE YOU TO HIM.*

I cannot scream, cannot scream, cannot scream.

He shakes me, rattling my bones. *TATIANA*, he growls, *TATIANA, WAKE UP.*

I cannot wake up, cannot wake up, cannot wake up.

TATIANA.

I try to scream, to run.

He's too strong, too heavy.

I grope for his eyes, trying to punch my thumbs through the soft jelly. Try to knee his crotch. Claw his face. Bite his throat. Snarl like a cornered she-lion.

I feel something cold and hard and slender—a knife. Fumble for it while his hands fumble at my chest, clumsy and cruel.

It's a knife.

I find the small round knob and lever it open and jab it hard, feel skin break and guts puncture. Stab. Stab. Stab.

Fresh hot blood splashes my face and he howls in agony. Rage blazes through me and I cannot stop my hand from stabbing because he's still moving, reaching for me with cold cruel hands that will kill me if I let them touch me, hands that will choke and crush.

TATIANA.

WAKE UP.

WAKE UP.

I'm not dreaming. This is real. I'm not asleep.

I cannot wake up, cannot wake up, cannot wake up.

Stab, stab, stab. Blood splashes, and I stab so hard his soft belly presses hot and wet against my fist where it clutches the blood-slick handle of the knife.

Vomit sears my throat and boils against my fused teeth, stitched lips.

"Tatiana!" Shaking, shaking.

I feel hands, but these are gentle, comforting. Brutally strong and rough with calluses, but they cradle me close and soothe the panic.

"It is a nightmare, Lovely One. You are safe. It's not real."

The voice is beautiful. There's no other word. His accent lilts, curves, dances gracefully across the syllables.

Lash.

Warmth flows through me, washes over me—the comforting heat of safety chasing away the cold of terror.

The blood on my hand drips, drips onto concrete, staining the filthy wet ground.

"Tatiana," comes that beautiful voice once more. "Wake up, Lovely One."

The dripping and drooling of the hot, sticky blood slows, and the darkness around me swirls.

"Tatiana, wake up. You are dreaming."

The knife in my fist loses reality, loses substance. The soft heavy weight of dead, cooling flesh crushing me fades.

"I have you, Tatiana. You are safe now. There is nothing to fear. You can wake up, now. You are safe. It is okay."

A shudder ripples through me; I blink awake. I'm sweat-drenched, fear-parched, terror-drunk. I feel strong hard arms cradling me. Lash's big, firm, broad body shelters me, shields me from the world beyond my narrow bunk. Another shudder wracks me.

"It was him," I whisper. "He was going to rape me. I couldn't stop stabbing him."

His arms tighten. "You did what you had to do, Tatiana. I know it was awful. I am so sorry you had to experience that."

I want to sob, but it's stuck behind my teeth. I can only shake my head. "I keep...*feeling* it."

He pulls me closer yet, and his warmth soaks into me, and the strength of his arms around me breaks the chains of the nightmare. "I know. I know. But it will fade in time."

I breathe out slowly. "Do you still have nightmares, Lash?"

"Of people I kill?" he asks.

I nod.

"No. Not really. I used to, when I was young. For several years, I dreamed of the first time I killed someone. But I have not had that dream in many, many years." A soft sigh. "I dream of other horrors, now."

"Will you tell me?"

A long pause. "Perhaps another time, if you really wish to know. It is not a happy story."

"You said you remember me when I was young."

"Yes."

"What do you remember?"

A thoughtful breath, the gentle rub of his chin on my shoulder. "I remember a summer's day. Where were we? Not in Zagreb. Your father's beach property, I believe. We left very early in the morning. Your mother was still alive, then. Your father carried you to the car and we drove all morning. The sun was bright and warm. I was in the car behind yours. Your father's driver parked and you shot out of the car before it was fully stopped. Your mother shouted at you, something about needing sunscreen, I think."

I smile to myself. "I don't know if I remember that specific day or not, but trips to the beach cottage with Mama and Tata I remember quite clearly."

You were neither a child nor a teenager. I do not remember how old. Perhaps eleven?" A pause. "I was very young, then, myself. Eighteen, I think, maybe nineteen. It was my first job that wasn't washing dishes and sweeping floors. Your father was proud of himself for being so progressive as to hire a *gypsy*." He spits the word so it drips vitriol. "I remember your joy. It was like the sun. I remember envying you. You were so free, so alive, full of so much joy." He's murmuring to me in English, and the foreign rhythm of his words is lulling, soporific.

"I loved the beach when I was a little girl."

"Do you not anymore?"

I shrug, shake my head. "I don't know. I suppose I do. I have not been in a very long time. After Mama died, the beach cottage was too hard for Tata to bear. I don't know if he even owns it anymore."

"I remember you running like an escaped colt. You threw off your shirt and fell in the sand trying to get your shorts off while running. I remember your mother laughing at you when you fell. She caught up to you and slathered you in sunscreen. All you wanted was to get into the sea, but she made you wait until it was dry."

"Mama and her sunscreen," I say, laughing quietly. "I used to lie out on the balcony at the compound and sun myself. I wore my bikini. I wanted so badly to be a grown woman with big breasts like Mama." I laugh again. "Now I am a grown woman, but I still do not have big breasts."

Lash chuckles. "I know how that feels. When I was a boy, I wanted so badly to be tall. I would measure myself every day, hoping for even one centimeter of growth. Even as a teenager, I kept hoping I would have a growth spurt. I would dream of waking up one morning towering over my mother. I never did." The humor drains out of his voice. "You may not have large breasts, Tatiana, but they are perfect. You are the most beautiful woman I have ever met."

"Even though you knew me when I was an awkward little girl?"

"Many years separate the girl you were then from the woman you are now."

"Trips to the beach with Mama and Tata seems like another life," I whisper.

"Truly, it does," he says. "I was not innocent even then, but I had not yet become what I am now."

"What are you now, Lash?" I ask.

I pull away so I can see his face, and his dark eyes glitter in the dim light, and his beard is soft and ticklish against my jaw.

"A ghost with bloody hands," he whispers. "A *mulo*."

"I do not know what that is," I murmur.

"A vampire. Undead. Returned from death to cause havoc."

"You are alive, Lash." I touch his cheek, and the flesh is warm. "You feel my touch, yes?"

I hear him swallow. "Yes."

Warmth, safety, security—these feelings birth boldness, erase the shreds of dreamstuff still lingering in my belly, replacing it with heat and desire.

I curl closer, my hands clasped under my chin, one finger touching just below his lip. I feel his breath catch. Touch my lips to his. "You feel my lips?" I whisper so softly that he must feel the words as much as hear them.

"Yes." It's a breath. "But Tatiana—"

I move my lips on his, and it's not exactly a kiss—more of a hint of a kiss, a promise of one. "Lash, I know."

"You do not. You cannot."

"But I do."

"Remember how I said I was an obsidian blade?"

I nod, moving my lips on his again, relishing the slip and stutter of my lips on his. "I do."

"There is nothing on earth as sharp as obsidian. Not even lasers. An obsidian blade can cut between the walls of cells themselves."

"Truly?" I ask.

"Yes, truly. But obsidian is also incredibly fragile. It can chip and shatter easily if handled incorrectly."

"Oh." I consider this. "You are fragile, then?"

He sighs. "Sometimes I think so. Other times I feel as unbreakable as diamond. The years and the awful things I have done have accumulated upon my soul like the layers of a pearl. Trauma upon trauma."

"The hardest of substances are also the most easily broken when struck at the correct angle." I brush my lips against his, nuzzling his mustache. "None of us are invincible, Lash. We all have pain. You do not need to bear yours alone."

He inhales a short, shuddering breath. Touches his forehead to mine. Lets it out through pursed lips. "Hope is a cruel thing, Tatiana."

"Without hope, what do we have?" I only belatedly realize that at some point we switched to Croatian. "Allow yourself hope, Lash. Reach for something that brings you joy."

A subtle shake of his head. "I do not know how. I have

sheltered my secret heart within a prison of isolation for so long that..." he trails off, shaking his head again, sighing.

"That what?" I prompt.

"I have forgotten what it is to truly feel."

"I am in your arms, Lash. I choose this. I *want* this. I *like* this. I feel safe with you, and I have rarely felt safe. Being my father's daughter has meant I have a target on my back at all times, and I have my whole life. But when I am with you, I know I am safe. I know I am protected. That is how *I* feel." I trail my fingers through his beard, from his earlobe and along his jawline. "How do *you* feel, right now?"

"It is hard to find the words."

I snort. "No, it isn't, Lash. I think you are just afraid of speaking them out loud."

"You demand much of me, Tatiana." He says this in English.

"By asking you to share your feelings? I am not asking you to share your deepest fears or secrets."

"You ask me to unearth my heart. I have buried it, Tatiana. I buried it with my wife. I buried it with my children."

I go still, barely daring to breathe. "Children?" It is a ghost of a question, a syllabic exhale.

"My deepest fears? My darkest secrets? They are deep indeed, and darker than the darkest shadows."

"You had a wife and children?" I ask.

"I did."

"They died?"

"They were murdered. By Roberto Pugli." He pronounces the last name *POOL-yee.*

I cannot get any closer to him while we are both still clothed, but I try anyway, snugging my hips against his, draping my thigh over his, resting my torso on his.

"You don't need to tell me," I whisper. "I can tell that the pain is too great."

"My heart is buried in the earth with Ileana, Leonora, and Leander." I hear him swallow hard. "What remains in here..." he taps his chest over his physical heart, "is nothing but broken pieces, sharp edges, and vacant spaces."

"You are a poet, Lash. Did you know?"

He snorts again. "Language is a beautiful thing. To create beauty and meaning from simple sounds is a kind of magic." His lips touch the top of my head, and he inhales, scenting my hair. "But then, I come from a long line of storytellers."

"You do?"

He nods, kissing the top of my head again. "Yes. My people, the Romani, have always preserved our stories, myths, beliefs, and legends in oral form. We tell stories—all people do. To sit around a fire and spin a tale of gods and men is what makes us human. It is how we understand the world around us. And for my people, it is especially true. We have never had a homeland, and so our stories become our home. They preserve our past, our heritage."

We lapse into silence for a long time, and the gentle rocking of the train lulls me into a drowsy twilight.

"Having you in my arms," Lash murmurs, "feels like... getting a breath of air when you are drowning."

"So keep breathing me," I mumble. "Let me be your breath."

He sighs, a rumbling breath. "Tatiana..."

"Mmmmm."

"It hurts to hope."

"Tata lost his heart when Mama died."

"It is a pain like no other."

"He gave up on himself," I say, struggling to make sense despite how sleepy I am. "In a way, I lost him too."

"Tatiana, I…"

I twist to find his lips with mine, leaving my eyes closed and seeking his mouth blindly. I find it, or he finds mine, or we find each other's. His kiss is slow and sweet, tender and hesitant.

"Just hold me, Lash. I do not ask anything more of you right now." I whisper this against his lips, and I can taste the sorrow on his breath, all tangled up with hope.

He kisses me again, once more so gently I almost wonder if I imagine it, dream it. Only the tingle of my lips tells me it's real.

───── ◆ ─────

I wake to Lash's soft snores against my ear. I leave my eyes closed, hearing Scarlett and Solomon whispering to each other, private murmurs I try not to overhear.

At some point in my sleep I have become wrapped up in Lash on the narrow bunk. His hard thigh is wedged between mine, pressing against my sex. His hand drapes lower on my hip, resting on my bottom, and his breath huffs softly against the top of my head.

I have never felt so safe, so content. I only wish we were alone. The desire I feel for Lash is a simmering cauldron in my belly—I struggle to keep it on a simmer, lest it boil over and push me to act on my desire.

I know he is not ready for that. To push him will be to lose him—he is a ghost of a man, and if I try to cling to him, he'll slip through my fingers.

He rumbles sleepily, shifting. Rolls to his back, bringing

me with him so I'm lying prone on his hard, heavily muscled body. His heart pounds steadily under my ear, and his arms wrap around me, one slung across my shoulders and the other cradling my ass.

I grit my teeth and fight the desire bubbling in my blood. This task is made all the more difficult when he rumbles in his chest again and shifts in his sleep, nudging his hips against mine, pressing his erection against my core.

Morning erections are normal male physiology. I understand this. It is not evidence of his desire for me. I remind myself of this fact, because my heart wishes to believe otherwise. My body yearns to respond.

And it does, despite my best efforts. I lay upon him and breathe, just breathe, but my hips tilt, and press, because the burn in my core, the wild ache of need in my sex is liquid heat that only his touch can extinguish.

I curl my fingers into his shirt to keep them from wandering, from seeking skin, from exploring hardness and flesh. My hips, however...they have a will of their own. They tilt, push, and drive.

He groans again in his sleep and pushes against me. His erection is a thick ridge behind his zipper. The slide of denim against denim is noisy in my ears, and his heartbeat quickens.

"Mmmm." His drowsy growl is rough and quiet.

I know this can go nowhere; I am only torturing myself.

But yet...my face tilts and I seek his skin, find his throat with my nose and lips, taste the pulse at his throat, my fists knotting in his shirt.

He exhales, and his hips push against mine, his erection driving against my sex, making me bury my lips against his throat and mewl as arousal sears through me from core to crown, heart to hands. He rumbles and his huge power-ful hands tense, flex, and twitch against me. Another shift of his hips, another growl, and I can feel him waking. His hands scour my back, roaming from shoulders to shoul-der blades, mid-back to lower back. My breath snags in my throat as he cups my ass, fingers tightening in the swell of flesh and muscle, and then slipping back upward to the gap between T-shirt and jeans. The pound of my pulse becomes frenetic when his hands find flesh, sliding up my spine, carving over bare skin to my shoulder blades and back down, dipping under the waist of my jeans, under the elastic of my panties to clutch hot skin.

I whimper, rubbing against his erection. "Lash," I breathe.

"Mmmm," he murmurs.

I can't help myself. I seek his flesh, his hard muscle, the cut lines of his predator's body. I feel the grooves and ridges of his abs, his ribs, and the fine nerve endings in my fingertips find the raised lines of scars and the hard divots of bullet holes and the smeared smoothness of burns, and the subtle give of muscle.

I look up at him, and his eyes are black holes, voids piercing me with sharp wild life, blazing with desire. I scrape my hands over his pecs, his flat nipples pebbling under my hands, and his grip curls into my ass, and I rub against him; heat billows in my belly, flows with the inexorability of lava, a pyroclastic surge of primal female hunger.

"Tatiana," comes his voice, a growl I feel in my bones, in my sex, in my soul.

I mewl again, rub against him, and his black eyes burn into mine, fiery with fierce need.

"We can't," he murmurs. "Not here, not now, not like this."

I taste the skin of his throat, salty and stubble-rough below the neckline of his beard. "I know," I breathe.

"Never have I wished so badly for privacy," he whispers. "Touching you, feeling the beauty of your body, I can almost forget."

I don't need to know what he can almost forget. The details are irrelevant; the sorrow is all that matters. His heart has calcified in his chest, has become a xenolith.

I dig my fingernails into his chest and find his mouth and I kiss him. He grips my ass so tightly it almost hurts, and he kisses me back, and now finally his lips part and his tongue steals in against mine. I gasp into the kiss as heat pounds in my belly, expanding into my core, making my thighs shake and my breath comes hard and short, and I taste his tongue, his breath; I swallow a soft growl in response to the helpless push of my sex against his erection. He kisses me and kisses me, and my eyes flutter closed, and I grip the huge hard mounds of his shoulders and grind against him.

"Tatiana," he whispers. "Have mercy on me. We cannot."

"I know," I whimper. "But I...I can't not. I crave you, Lash."

I pant into his kiss, and my hips flex in a slow, sinuous writhe, pushing burgeoning heat through my body like a bubble on the verve of bursting.

"It's just you, Lash," I whisper, grinding against him, feeling desperate in a way I haven't since I was a teenaged girl in the back of my first boyfriend's car. "I don't know. I don't know."

Lash rolls me to my back, putting me between himself and the wall, hiding me with the bulk of his body. He leans into me and his palm covers my bare belly, rough and hard against soft skin. I hold his eyes, hold still. The train sways, the *clack-clack clack-clack clack-clack* a muffled metronome rhythm. He dips his fingertips under the button of my jeans, and I reach down, flick open the button, lower the zipper. Beg with my eyes, with the push of my hips.

"Tatiana," he whispers. "We can't. I can't."

"Please," I breathe. "Just...touch me, Lash."

"My hands, my soul," he murmurs, "they are not clean."

I catch his free hand in mine, press his palm to my cheek. Nuzzle his palm, kiss his wrist. Drag his hand to my throat, keeping my eyes locked on his. Guide his hand down to cover my breast where my nipple presses diamond-hard through the fabric of my bra and shirt.

His answering growl is low and hungry and frustrated, and his fingertips steal lower, under the elastic of my panties, scraping sensuously over my skin, and I press my hand over his against my breast and tilt my hips in another silent plea. I feel his middle finger slide to the top of my slit, and then his touch glides down my seam and I whimper.

He presses his mouth to mine. "Hush, Lovely One. You must be quiet. I will not share these beautiful sounds you make with anyone."

I am no exhibitionist; I am a private person. I avoid public displays of affection, much less anything like this. I have never been daring, sexually. I prefer the quiet solitude of my home: lights dimmed, door closed, and blinds drawn so only breath, touch, and flesh remain. I like the mystery of touch in the dark, blind kisses and finding each other without sight, relying on touch and trust.

But with Lash I am different. I know him, down to his soul—I know his sorrow, I know the shape of his torment; I know how deeply he has kept his heart buried, how tightly he locked down his need, his desire. He's an enigma, more at home in the shadows than light.

I do not care who hears.

In fact, what I hear from the bunk above is the sound of kisses, and a soft feminine gasp, and a low male laugh. I hear the bunk shift, creaking. Lorenzo snores on the topmost bunk opposite.

I mate my fingers to Lash's inside my jeans and underwear, guiding his fingers inside me. I hold his eyes, let him see the need bursting through me, the ecstasy of his touch. I push my sex against him, writhe on his finger as it delves inside me.

His brows furrow and his jaw clenches.

"Who is clean in this world, Lash?" I ask. "Who is innocent? I am not."

"But I—"

"I do not care," I whisper. "When we are alone, I will hear your secrets. You can confess to me as if I am a priest, and I will be your penance."

"Tatiana," he breathes my name like a prayer. "Tatiana…"

His fingers move inside me, and the soft wet squelch makes me squirm in embarrassment, but he covers my mouth with his and slashes his tongue against mine and curls his finger inside me. He gathers my wet slick essence and smears it against my clit.

I whimper into his mouth, and my hips lift, my ass tightening as I drive into his touch. "Yes," I breathe. "Lash, please."

"You cannot beg, sweet Tatiana," he murmurs, lips moving on mine. "My control is at the limit already."

I thrust against his finger, yank my shirt up and rake down my bra cup so my breast falls free, and crush his hand against me. He bumps his forehead against mine and growls in short, rough, panting breaths and his finger curls again to gather my essence and smear it against my clit until I'm soaked and dripping, and then he touches the pad of his middle finger to my clit, circling swiftly.

Lighting strikes me at his touch, and he swallows my mewling gasp of pleasure, and his hard hand gives my breast a rough squeeze, and then gentles, and his thumb trips against my thick, rigid, aching nipple and I have to bite down to silence a cry, which shreds past my teeth as a shrill catlike snarl.

Heat smashes through me and stars burst behind my eyes and I grind into his touch and kiss him, shoving my tongue into his mouth.

Ecstasy becomes all-consuming, and I ride his finger to the cusp of climax.

I reach between us and cup his erection over his jeans, and then fumble at his zipper, seeking more, seeking him, seeking his pleasure as the natural mate to mine.

He growls a negative, capturing my hands in his and pinioning them in his fist, preventing me from grasping him. I fight his hold, but he's far, far too strong, and then I'm lost and helpless as my release detonates.

I gasp into his mouth, panting, whimpering, trying to be quiet.

My orgasm spreads through me all at once, a white wave of incandescent heat, and I shake all over, trembling as wild hot pleasure sears through my being. I struggle against his hold on my hands, and he's so strong that I can fight with every ounce of my strength and it makes no difference—I'm helpless, caught in his touch, held and possessed.

I let go.

He takes my tongue and devours my whimpers, touches me through my climax until I'm left shuddering and panting raggedly, a boneless pile of jelly beneath his weight.

Brakes squeal and the train slows, and a male voice squawks indistinctly over the intercom, announcing our arrival in Split.

I wrench my eyes open, meet his. "Lash," I whisper, but can't find anything else to say.

He kisses me again, withdrawing his finger from within me; he zips and buttons my jeans, releases my hands.

"I wouldn't leave you like this," I whisper.

"I don't care. You are all that matters to me." He puts his middle finger into his mouth, and his eyes shut at the taste of me on his finger. "But now I'm going to dream of you. Dream of tasting you, having you on my lips. Hearing you scream."

I whimper again. "Lash, dammit," I whisper. "I want—"

He growls in frustration, rolls off the bunk with abrupt speed, and is out of the couchette compartment before I know what's happened, before I can finish my statement.

CHAPTER 5

FROM THE TRAIN TO THE FERRY

LASH

S O FAR, SO GOOD.

We disembarked the train and left the station together on foot, and now we are walking together down a quiet, tree-lined neighborhood on the south end of Split, near the shore. The sky to the south above the tops of the buildings has that indefinable open quality that says you're near the sea—a deeper blue, perhaps.

Lorenzo is in front, leading us to the ferry that will take us to Ancona, Italy. The plan is to travel as far west as we can by bus, train, or sea within Europe, where security measures are typically less stringent than by air. Eventually, we'll have to find air travel to Brazil so we can join the others in rescuing Inez, but the hope is that between myself, Lorenzo, Scarlett, and Solomon, we can figure out a flight across the ocean that isn't commercial. To achieve that, we must outmaneuver Mercado's forces. I also anticipate a move by Roberto—he's a crafty, cunning man who plans ten steps ahead of everyone else. I know he knows I've surfaced—his network of spies and informants is vast and thorough, and he hates me with a vicious passion. Not as much as I hate him, however. My hatred is that of a widower and a father. He stole my family from me. Stole my life. My identity. I shall take his life before this is over, and then I shall swear the oath I should have sworn when Inez pulled me from the burning wreckage of my former life—the oath to never take a life.

Beside me, Tatiana has been reserved and thoughtful. She steals glances at me now and again, her dark gaze intense and full of private emotion that I cannot quite read.

Scarlett and Solomon walk side by side a few paces behind us, having a quiet conversation.

"Tell me what are you thinking?" I say to Tatiana.

She doesn't answer right away. "The train," she murmurs. "I'm thinking about the train."

"It is on my mind, as well," I say. "*You* are on my mind."

She looks at me. "I don't like how it ended. You walking away."

"I had to."

She shakes her head. "You didn't have to. You could have let me touch you."

"I wouldn't ask such a thing of you in such a public setting," I say.

She snorts. "But *you'll* make *me* come? How is that better?"

I frown at her. "Are you upset with me?"

"A little." She sighs. "I started it. I know that. You woke up to me…" she flushes scarlet, ducks her head. "Acting like a…"

"Like a woman with desires," I finish for her. "There's no shame in it. If there is a better way to wake up, I cannot think of it."

She smirks at me. "I can think of a few ways of waking you up that you might enjoy a bit more."

My breath catches at the implication. "Tatiana, I…" I shake my head. "I guess I do not understand what you are upset about."

"You made me come," she says, switching from English to Croatian—for privacy, I suppose, since we are the only ones who speak it out of the five of us. "And then you walked away. You said you wouldn't share the sounds of my pleasure. I know I wasn't quiet, but I heard them, too." She tilts her head toward Sol and Scarlett, behind us. "So I know they heard us. I heard Solomon…enjoying himself. But you would not let me give you pleasure."

"I am a man," I say. "My release is…messier…than yours."

"Should that not be my choice? Should I not be able to decide if I want to deal with that, and how? My desires do not begin and end with my orgasm, Lash. I desire you. I want to enjoy your body as much as you do mine, but you took what you wanted and then walked away without giving me a choice in the matter."

I frown. "I hadn't thought of it like that."

"I know. You thought you were being…" she shrugs. "I don't know. Noble? But that's not what I want. You physically prevented me from touching you."

"I should never have let things escalate to that point in the first place."

She groans in irritation. "You *still* do not understand, then. *I* escalated things, not you. If that situation made you uncomfortable, blame me for starting it, not yourself for not stopping it. I have never done anything like that, Lash. I am not…like that. I am private. Because of who my father is, I am a pretty public figure in Zagreb. I keep my personal life, my sex life, private. But with you…I didn't care. I knew what I was doing, and I chose not to stop myself. Perhaps I couldn't have. I don't know. I felt desperate. And it's still there, that desperation." She looks at me. "It wasn't sated. If anything, it is only worse."

"I was protecting you."

She nods. "I know. But Lash, I want to be protected from *other* people, not from you."

I walk beside her in silence for a while, thinking, processing. "I understand what you're saying, Tatiana. I will not apologize, because I was doing what I felt was right. But I do hear you, and I understand you." I look at her. "I am confused by all this, Tatiana. By you...and by my feelings for you."

"What is confusing?" she asks.

I shake my head, snorting. "Everything. That I feel anything at all. That part of me has been...dead, I suppose...for a very long time. I never thought it would or could be resurrected. And with you, no less."

"Why me? What is it about me?" she asks.

"Everything. Who you are. Who your father is."

"And?" she presses.

I sigh, running my fingers down through my beard—I badly need a shower, but in such circumstances as these, grooming concessions must be made. I admit, however, that I am a vain man, and to be so dirty, greasy, and unkempt is difficult. I feel uncouth.

"And..." I shrug. "And many things. I am much older than you. I am...I do not like to think of myself as a *bad* man, exactly, but I have done many awful things. I like to think I have only done them to those who deserve it. But then, who is to say who deserves death? I am no god. I worked for your father. He and I have...a troubled and complicated history." I hesitate, and the plunge onward with my confession. "The deaths of my wife and children, the manner and reason…it broke me, Tatiana. It broke me, and I do not know if I can be fixed. But then I saw that vile scum, Filip, dragging you into the hangar, and I knew right away who you were, and I…" I shake my head. "My heart began beating again, metaphorically speaking. I took notice of you. As a woman. You were obviously no longer the girl I knew. But in my spirit, I am still Ileana's husband. I am still Leonora and Leander's father. They are dead and buried, and I mourn them every day. My sorrow, my heartbreak…I fear it is eternal, Tatiana. You are a remarkable woman. Beautiful, strong, and resilient. How can I offer you these broken pieces of myself?"

She looks at me for a long time, silently, her gaze unreadable, searching and piercing. She reaches down, takes my hand, and entwines our fingers. "I am very good at puzzles, Lash."

"But why would you want…" I shake my head and shrug. "I am not whole. I am good at violence, Tatiana, and not much else."

She is quiet again for a while. "Who can explain attraction, Lash? I cannot. I am physically attracted to you. I think you are handsome. I love your hair and your beard. You are fit and strong. But I…I think more than anything, it is the feeling of safety when I am with you. I have been afraid most of my life. There have always been threats, Lash. Tata being who he is and doing what he does, he is always in danger. And so have I been. I've been kidnapped several times. Usually for ransom, or to force my father to do something. While I have evaded rape or torture, the fear is always there. When I am with you, I am not afraid. And that is a feeling I cannot describe, other than a kind of delirious relief, as if I can finally breathe for the first time in my life."

"I will protect you with my life, Tatiana," I say. "As long as I breathe, no harm will come to you."

"I know." She says it as if there is no doubt. "But the question is, do *you* trust *me*?"

I frown. "I…I do not know. Trust is…it is a complicated thing for me." I gesture at Solomon, behind us. "I trust him with my life—he and my Broken Arrow brothers. But trusting them with my life and physical safety is easy enough. They are operators, like me. I know their skills. I have sworn an oath to them, as they have to me."

"But?"

"But trusting them with my safety does not mean I trust them with…" I roll a shoulder, looking for the right word. "With the rest of me, such as I am. They know nothing of me, not really."

"Why not?" she asks.

"Because I was betrayed."

"By whom? How?"

"That is a long, painful story," I say, "And one I have told no one, not even Inez."

She frowns at me. "Who is Inez?"

"My immediate superior in the Broken Arrows."

"And what are the Broken Arrows?"

"A private security company, of sorts."

"Of sorts?"

I nod. "We are unusual, I suppose. All of us operators. Meaning, former black ops specialists for various militaries, except Solomon's brothers, Saxon and Silas. We have all been through unimaginable hell—extraordinarily traumatic events that have left us unfit for society. The Broken Arrows gives us a brotherhood, a community of men who understand each other. We have all taken vows to defend, protect, and serve each other. We work at a night-club and live beneath it. It is a simple, safe life where we can be ourselves with people who understand us."

We have been speaking in English, and Solomon moves up on Tatiana's other side. "What Lash isn't mentioning is that we all swore not only to support and protect each other but also to not take another life, a crucial commitment given our history of violence." He looks at me, and I see the confusion and resentment in his eyes. "Except Lash. Unbeknownst to the rest of us, he didn't have to swear to not kill. And Inez wouldn't say why."

"Because she did not know why," I said. "*I* do not know. Our employer made the decision, and as you know, he does not explain himself to anyone."

Solomon sighs an annoyed huff. "That's a shitty explanation."

"I know, and I'm sorry, but it is the only one I have." I shrug. "I am certain he had his reasons. I wish I knew what they were myself. It is an oath I would swear to right now if our lives were not in such danger. I have kept that oath even though I did not swear it...until now. Until her." I indicate Tatiana. "When all this is over, Solomon, I will take the vow in front of all of you. I will take the brand again if you wish. You are my brothers. That has not changed simply because I did not swear not to kill."

Solomon sighs. "That isn't for me to decide—we'll have to see what the others have to say."

At that moment, Lorenzo, about to lead us around

a corner, jerks back and flattens himself against the wall. "We have a problem, friends."

Solomon and I move up to join him, Sol peeks around the corner, and then I do.

The bus station is just down the street but lined up in front of it are local police, heavily armed and watchful. A young woman and her infant attempt to enter and are searched, the woman's papers checked.

"What do you want to bet they are there for us?" Lorenzo says.

I curse in three different languages. "Only a fool would bet against that," I say. "Their presence is courtesy of Roberto Pugli."

"You're gonna have to explain," Scarlett says to me. "I know Sol has said you're private about your past, and I respect that, I do, but this affects the rest of us, now. So, I think we're owed at least some kind of an explanation. Who the *fuck* is Roberto Pugli, and what does he want with you?"

"I believe I already said—he is a high-level executive at Interpol. He is an intelligence operative by trade but, in reality, he is a much more powerful version of Stjepan Juric." I indicate Tatiana. "Pugli is corrupt, cruel, and evil. He trades intelligence, sells secrets, and facilitates arms deals with terrorists, using his position and influence. He owns many officials across Europe, and has eyes and ears everywhere."

"And what does he have against you?" Sol asks.

"I investigated him," I answer. "I have evidence against him. Enough to bring him to justice." I hesitate, but I know Scarlett is right: I owe them answers. "I brought charges against him. He would have been imprisoned for life had I succeeded, but he…" I swallow hard, fighting the hot lump in my throat, the burn behind my eyes. "He kidnapped my wife and infant children. If I gave him the evidence I had against him, he claimed he would let them go once it was destroyed."

"A man like that doesn't take chances," Solomon guesses.

"No, indeed he does not. I knew it, too. So I…I tried to rescue them. It was…I slaughtered dozens of his men. He had my wife, my children. They were innocent, and he had them. So I…I did what I had to do."

"Of course you did," Sol says. "Who wouldn't?"

I shake my head. "I succeeded…for a while. I tried to get us away, off-grid. I used every favor and contact I had. New identities, a new life. I left Germany, hid my family, and tried to start over working as an investigator for a small police force in Denmark. But Pugli found us anyway."

"Fuck," Solomon says.

I stare at nothing, seeing flames, hearing the screams of my wife. "He captured us. Tied me to a chair and used an ophthalmic speculum to force my eyes open. I was forced to watch as his men locked my wife and infant twins in a room. He himself doused the house in gasoline and lighter fluid, and he himself threw the match."

Silence greets this.

I know I must continue.

"I heard them die. I will forever hear my wife screaming for me to save them. And I could not. I was helpless."

"Lash, Jesus fucking Christ," Solomon says, grabbing me by the shoulders in a rough embrace. "I'm so fucking sorry, brother. That's…I don't have the fucking words."

"There are no words, my friend," I whisper. I look at Tatiana, who is weeping. "That is why I am broken."

"He didn't kill you?" Lorenzo asks.

I shake my head. "No. I had hoped he would. It would have been kinder if he had—which is why he didn't." My eyes burn, and I look away, blinking and swallowing. "He left me alive. Unbound me and left me there to watch the house burn. All I had to bury was a handful of bones. I walked away from everything. Went to the States and…I suppose I was a ghost, then. I found what work I could, usually unsavory jobs for unsavory people. Eventually, I encountered Inez and ended up with the rest of you."

"Perhaps this mysterious employer of yours left you out of the vow against killing because he knew you could never truly find peace until Roberto Pugli has been brought to justice for what he did," Scarlett says.

I nod. "That is my thought as well."

"Do you seek revenge?" Lorenzo asks me, his gaze sharp and watchful.

"Of course." I look away from him. "I have dreamt of it for a long time, but…he is well protected. Insulated. I have formulated many plans for getting to him and killing him, but…my oath to the Broken Arrows took precedence. I could not and would not leave Club Sin to pursue my vengeance. I know well enough that killing Pugli will not bring my family back. Perhaps it will bring me peace, perhaps it will not. But now that I am here in Europe and so close to him, how can I not at least try? But…" I shrug. "Inez is in danger. Her safety is more important. And I still do not know how I would get close enough to Pugli to put a bullet in his skull."

Lorenzo eyes me again. "If it were me, I would not be content with a bullet to the skull."

I shake my head, sighing. "I have dreamt many nights of the punishments I would enact upon him, it is true. Clever, horrible ones. A blood eagle, perhaps. Or cover him in honey and stake him to a fire ant hill, as the Apache used to do. I have realized, however, that to do such a thing would only make me more like him. So no. I will not torture him. I will not murder his family—his wife, his daughters, his grandchildren. They are innocent of his crimes. But he will die. I will look him in the eyes and I will put a bullet in his brain, and I will not take up a gun ever again thereafter."

Tatiana is watching me carefully, tear tracks staining her cheeks. "Lash…my god. How you have suffered." She says it in Croatian.

I shake my head, shrug. "Life is suffering. A mob murdered my parents when I was a boy."

"Murdered by the mob?" Scarlett asks.

I shake my head. "No, not *the* mob, as in your American mafia. A mob. During the revolution in Romania, where I was born. My people, the Romani, were persecuted. We have always been hated and persecuted wherever we went, and we still are. But that was…" I shake my head. "It was a horrible time. Many innocent people were murdered."

"How did you survive?" Tatiana asks.

"Thievery, begging, and starvation." I look at her. "Your father saved me. I left Romania and made my way on foot south and west through what is now Serbia, Bosnia, and Herzegovina, and into Croatia, eventually ending up in Zagreb. Your father hired me to wash dishes and sweep floors in his restaurant. He took pity on me, I think. Why, I do not know. I do not know if he knows why, but he did." I blow out a breath. "Enough story time. Now you know my history." I gesture at the corner, indicating the police presence. "We have to find another way out of Croatia, or we have to deal with them."

Lorenzo meets my gaze. "I think we deal with them. I won't kill police officers unless I have to, but I think we could use them to draw this Pugli out of hiding. Bait him into coming for you himself. You aren't on your own, now. We are with you. We will help you."

"And Inez?" I ask.

"We need a way back across the ocean. But this Pugli is here. He knows you're here. So we may as well make the best of it. Kill him, and then we rescue Inez."

I look at Solomon.

He nods. "I agree. He needs to die. And you know I've got your back, no matter what."

Scarlett smiles at me. "Solomon's loyalty is mine. I'm with you, too, Lash."

Tatiana takes my hand again. "I am not a soldier like you four, but I am with you, Lash, no matter what."

Lorenzo claps me on the back. "So then. We need a plan."

CHAPTER 6

VENGEANCE DEFERRED

TATIANA

IT'S A SIMPLE PLAN, BUT LASH CLAIMS SIMPLE PLANS tend to be the best.

Scarlett leaves the rest of us where we are and goes to do some recon, as Solomon calls it. She returns a few minutes later.

"They've got every entrance and exit covered, unsurprisingly, and obviously we have to assume it'll be the same at the train stations and airports—in Croatia, at least." She shrugs. "There're three or four at each exit. I think we go right up to the front door. Let them see us, recognize us, and then make our move."

The men agree, and we march right up to the four policemen at the main entrance of the bus station.

"Identification," one of them says in a bored voice.

His companion elbows him. "I think it's them," he says.

The first officer glances at his phone, and then at our faces. His hand moves for his radio clipped to his shoulder, but Solomon is faster. Lorenzo, Lash, and Scarlett all act at the same time, drawing their weapons while Solomon pins the first officer's hand and wrestles it away from his radio.

"We will not kill you if you cooperate," Lash says. "Now. Come."

This is all happening right out in the open, brazen as you please. A train roars past with a rapid clack of wheels over wooden ties, and down by the water, a ferry blasts its horn. Bus engines idle with a diesel rattle, spewing clouds of blue exhaust. It is early in the morning, so there are only a handful of people waiting for buses to arrive. Others pass in and out of the shops and cafes occupying the long, low line of buildings that make up the train, bus, and ferry stations.

The men and Scarlett have their weapons drawn but held close to their bodies so it's not immediately apparent to a casual observer what is going on.

"I don't know what you hope to accomplish," says the first officer to Lash, "But you are a fool if you think you will get away with this."

Lash only grins. "I don't want to get away with it." He gestures at the door of a fast-food restaurant. "In there. Go."

We file into the restaurant, which has just opened for the day. A middle-aged woman is behind the counter, wearing one of those silly paper hats, leaning on the counter looking bored.

She murmurs a half-hearted greeting in Croatian, but her eyes flicker to the officers, and the weapons held in plain sight.

"Sit." Lash points at a booth. "Sit, sit." He glances at Lorenzo. "Get us food. We are all hungry. No sense in wasting an opportunity."

"I'll do it," I say,

I go to the counter and order a meal for each of us,

which feels like an odd thing to do while holding police officers hostage.

"Now," I hear Lash say. "Where did your orders come from?"

The first officer, who seems in charge, answers. "The captain."

"Call him," Lash says. "Directly. Only say what I tell you to say."

"I don't know what you hope to accomplish—" the officer starts.

"You don't need to know," Lash cuts in. "Call your captain right now or I'll shoot out your knees. I told you, I have no intention of hurting or killing you, but I will if I must. Look at me and ask yourself if I am bluffing."

The officer seems to arrive at the correct conclusion, produces his phone, finds the correct entry, and places the call.

It rings twice. "Sergeant," answers a throaty, bull-frog voice. "What it is? Why are you calling my personal number?"

The officer looks at Lash for guidance. Lash takes the phone from the officer. "Captain, I am Lash. I believe you have instructions to apprehend me and my companions."

A pause. "I have not heard of Lash. My instructions were to apprehend Nicolae Dragos."

"That is me. Who gave you these orders?"

Another pause. "Why should I tell you?"

"Because you care about the lives of your officers."

A gruff snort. "I suppose I do. It came from the mayor."

"Get him on the line, now."

"It is not so easy, Dragos."

"My name is Lash. Dragos is dead." Lash's voice is

hard and cold. "I do not care if it is easy or hard. Do it or your men will suffer. I do not wish to do that. Do not make me."

"Very well. Give me a moment."

"You have two minutes. Keep this line connected."

A minute or two later, the line clicks. "This is Mayor Puljik. You are the man known as Nicolae Dragos?"

"Yes," Lash says.

"What is it you want, Mr. Dragos?"

"Who gave you my name?"

A pause. "A file was delivered to my office—a folder with information on you. Later, I received a call. The man did not identify himself, but he knew who I was, he knew my family, my address, everything about me. He said you were a terrorist, and he had information that you would be entering my city, and that you should be apprehended."

"And you believed him?" Lash asks.

"Whether or not I believed him seemed irrelevant," Puljik says. "He did not make any overt threats, but it was very clearly implied that I had no choice."

"He has something on you, I assume," Lash says. "Extortion and blackmail are his favorite tactics when he doesn't think bribery will work."

An uncomfortable pause. "Yes, if you must know. I was…indiscreet, and he has photographs. It would ruin me."

"What were your instructions once you had apprehended me?"

"There is a number I was to call."

"And say what?"

"That I had you in custody."

"Give me the number."

"I do not know who you are or who he is. This has nothing to do with me," Puljik says. "But I am not crossing him."

"You are smart. You shouldn't cross a man like Pugli—take it from me. But you aren't crossing him. I want to speak to him." Lash has the phone on speaker so we can all hear.

"Text the number. Captain, withdraw your men."

"I'm not sure I believe you, Mr. Dragos," says the police captain.

Lash gestures at the officer with the gun. "Convince him."

The officer leans over the phone on the table. "Captain, it's me. Please, do as he says. I believe him. Please. Just…just call the men back."

A sigh. "Very well. But if you hurt any of my men—"

Lash snaps over him. "There will be nothing you can do, Captain. I am no better an enemy than Roberto Pugli."

"Just do it, Zoran," the mayor says. "This has nothing to do with any of us. Better we let those involved deal with each other."

A moment later, the radio squawks with a staticky order for the units stationed at the bus station to return to the precinct. Another few minutes later, the phone buzzes with an incoming message.

Lash flips a hand at the officers. "Leave."

Three of them tear out of the restaurant as if they were on fire. The officer at the table with Lash hesitates, however. "My phone?"

Lash arches an eyebrow at him. "I will keep it for now. Tell me the code."

"Six-one-six-seven-seven."

Lash nods. "Be gone. My time is short."

The officer hesitates, and then decides his cell is not worth the trouble—devices are replaceable—kneecaps not so much.

Lash dials the number, and we all sit silently, waiting as it rings.

"Mayor Puljik," comes a smooth male voice, his Croatian passable but heavily accented. "You have Dragos?"

"Roberto Pugli." Lash's voice is dark, heavy, and cold; he speaks in English. "I think it is time you and I put the past to rest."

A tense pause. "Dragos. Is it you?" Pugli answers in English.

"Indeed it is. Did you really think it would be so easy? A few police officers at a bus station? After all these years, you think I have forgotten? You think I have forgiven?"

Pugli doesn't answer right away. "Did you enjoy your little vacation in Las Vegas?"

Lash doesn't seem surprised that Pugli knew where he'd been. "I suppose."

"How do you think this will go, Dragos? I have only grown more powerful since you knew me."

"And no less a sniveling coward who pays others to do his dirty work." Lash's face twists into a rictus of hate. "A pathetic cockroach who murders innocent women and little babies."

Pugli just laughs. "I am a monster, it is true. But a monster you cannot touch. Enjoy your freedom while it lasts, Dragos. I was a fool to let you live. I shall rectify that soon."

It's Lash's turn to laugh. "You think so?"

"We could make a deal, you know. All I want is you.

Your friend? Inez? The man who has her makes me look like…what is it the Americans like to say? A boy scout? I have contacts in the Brazilian Embassy. I can have her free in a matter of hours."

"A tempting thought, but I do not believe you. I am sure you have contacts in Brazil, but they will not cross Mercado, not even for you. Besides, I am not worried about Inez. Mercado does not know who he has captured."

"My sources say he knows quite well who she is."

"You misunderstand me, Pugli. Yes, he knows *who* she is." Lash shakes his head, snorting. "Regardless, no. We both know how this ends."

Pugli laughs again. "I suppose you have dreamed of revenge. Come to Lyon, then, Dragos. You and me, we can have an old-fashioned duel. Ten paces, turn and fire. Hmm?"

Lash snorts. "I think not." He ends the call with a stab of his finger.

I look at him. "That didn't go well."

He looks at me, the rage and hate on his face fading. He shrugs. "It went exactly as I expected. He's not easily baited. I only wanted him to know his attempt to catch me was unsuccessful."

Solomon sweeps a hand through his messy blond hair. "So now what?"

Lash shrugs. "Now I go to Lyon."

I frown. "Why?"

"That is where he lives. That is where his family lives. I'll need leverage if I'm going to get close to him."

Scarlett grunts a negative. "I won't harm innocent people, and I won't be part of it."

Lash glares at her. "You do not know me, Scarlett, so

you can be forgiven for thinking I would harm his family. But *Pugli*, however, doesn't know that I wouldn't. He will assume I am like him—willing to murder in cold blood. I will make him think I will, but no one innocent will be harmed, only held against their will temporarily."

"While you kill him in front of them?" I can't help asking.

"Not in front of them, no." He eyes me. "What would you have me do? It is impossible to get into the Interpol headquarters, at least on such short notice. With several months of prep time, I could accomplish such a thing. But we do not have that time. I know Inez can handle herself, but I also know what kind of person Mercado is."

"Won't he be watching all routes in and out of Lyon?" asks Lorenzo. "Won't he post extra security on his family for just such an eventuality?"

Lash shrugs. "Certainly. We will just have to be smart."

"And do you have a smart idea for how to accomplish this?" Solomon asks.

Lash looks at me. "I do."

I frown at him, puzzled. "Why look at me?"

"Does your father still have that small plane he uses for smuggling?"

I shrug. "How should I know? I stay out of his illegal business." I think for a moment. "I think he might, though. He goes on occasional business trips to places around Europe, and I know he doesn't take public transportation. He is too paranoid for that."

"I will need to borrow it, then," Lash says.

I can't help but laugh. "Then why did we leave Zagreb? If he has such an airplane, it will be back in Zagreb."

He shrugs. "We had to get out of Zagreb before Pugli's men closed in. And your father's."

"Why does my father hate you?" I ask.

Lash shrugs again. "He doesn't hate me. He just…he feels I betrayed and abandoned him after he did quite a lot for me. And that is true, to a degree. He saved my life—gave me work when I was starving and had no future. He taught me many things that I still use to this day. But he began asking me to do things that I simply could not do. He is a complicated man, your father. In some ways, he is good, and kind, and compassionate. He loves you greatly. He is very loyal and generous to those who work for him. But…he is the head of a criminal organization, and he can be incredibly ruthless."

"What did he want you to do?" I ask, fearing I know.

He sighs, finally beginning to eat the food I brought over while he was talking to Pugli; he devours the cheeseburger in a few bites and then answers me. "A certain businessman owed him money. This man wasn't paying what he owed, which was a lot of money—hundreds of thousands of Kuna. Your father wanted me to send a message—the same message Pugli made for me. He wanted me to hold this man's young daughter hostage and take fingers until he paid. I…" Lash shakes his head. "I could not do it. I refused. If there is a fight against armed opponents, I will fight as viciously and mercilessly as anyone, but I could never bring myself to harm a ten-year-old girl, not under any circumstances."

I feel my heart clench, twist. "My father—Tata wanted you to do *that*?"

He nods. "I am sorry, Tatiana, but yes, he did."

"You didn't do it?"

He shakes his head. "Of course not. And that is why your father is angry with me. I left his employ."

I frown. "So? You quit rather than do something awful to an innocent girl."

He nods, but then shrugs and shakes his head. "Yes, that is true. You do not simply *quit* a job like that. I knew many important details about his business and how he operates. I could have gone to the authorities and turned him in to save myself." Another shake of his head. "No, you do not simply walk away."

"So…what? He would have killed you?"

He nods. "Yes, of course. Not he himself, probably, but yes, he would have had me killed."

I push the tray away, my appetite gone. "I knew my father was not always…good. I know the things he does are illegal. Drugs kill people. Guns kill people. I know this. But I guess I never really considered that he would do things like *that*."

"I wish I could protect you from that reality, but I cannot. It is the truth." He looks at me with compassion. "Your father is not evil, but nor is he good. He has done bad things, and that is the reality."

I shake my head. "But…cutting off the fingers of a young girl? He knows that fear! He has had to rescue me from exactly that! How could he do that to another father? So what if he owed him money? Hurt him, not an innocent child."

"I agree with you. I would have not balked at intimidating, threatening, or even hurting the man who owed your father money. He knew the kind of man your father was when accepted the loan. He knew what would happen if he did not pay it back. But the child was innocent."

I squeeze my eyes shut, trying like hell to hold back tears. "It just makes me wonder if I ever knew him at all."

Lash looks at me with sadness and compassion. "Humans are infinitely complicated, Tatiana. We can hold within ourselves an endless array of conflicting feelings and beliefs. Your father loves you. With you, he is gentle and kind. He works hard to take care of you and only ever wanted to give you the best life possible. That is true and not faked. He also can be vicious and ruthless to those who cross him. That too is true, and the two do not cancel each other out. His goodness does not erase the bad he has done, and the bad he has done does not invalidate his goodness."

"That is very hard for me to wrap my head around." I rub at my face with both hands and then use the heels of my palms to wipe away traitorous tears. "I understand being morally gray. But giving the order to chop off the fingers of an innocent girl who could be your daughter because her father owes you money...I do not know if I can forgive that."

Lash shrugs. "I do not say that you should. Why do you think I walked away from him? I could not be part of such a thing. I could not look the other way. And I was unwilling to die for his business and his practices. I have struggled with that since the moment I heard the order. I can comprehend your father, but I cannot and do not justify the things he has done."

"What about yourself?" I ask.

Lash polishes off the last French fry and gathers everyone's trays. "I cannot justify or forgive the things I have done either. That is how I can comprehend your father. I have never intentionally harmed an innocent person, but

I have still taken many lives. I am guilty of being ruthless, vicious, and cold-blooded. I have looked a man in the eyes as he dies with my blade in his heart. What does that make me?"

"Fucked up," Solomon answers. "Just like the rest of us. When you've got blood on your hands like guys—" he glances at Scarlett, "and girls like us do, you're gonna be fucked up. No one is truly and thoroughly *good*. But as an operator, you have to look at your motivations. That's the only way I've ever been able to come to terms with my conscience."

I have a vivid sensory memory of plunging the knife into that man's belly, the soft spring of fat greeting my knuckles, the hot flood of blood over my hand, his quiet grunt of surprise as the blade cuts through flesh, fat, and muscle and into organs.

Nausea rifles through me, bile burning my throat and boiling behind my teeth. I lurch out of my seat and bolt for the bathroom, crashing into the stall just in time to spew out everything I just ate. I hear the door creak open and footsteps on the tile, and a soft touch pulls my hair back as another wave slices through me.

"The first one is the hardest." Scarlett's voice is soft and understanding. "You never forget. Especially when it's self-defense in a situation like that. And no matter how empathetic a man might be, he'll never understand."

Another flash of sensory memory hits—his weight on me as he dies, and he's trying to grab me, grope me, kill me, and I have to yank the knife free and stab him and stab him because he won't fucking *die*.

I retch again, but only bile emerges.

"I kept stabbing him," I whisper. "But he wouldn't—he wouldn't stop. He—he wouldn't die."

"Most people don't understand how hard it can be to kill a human being. TV gets it wrong. People can survive a hell of a lot, especially with modern medicine. And even if you don't survive it, most stab wounds won't kill you right away. Unless you hit them in the heart or sever a major artery like the femoral or the jugular, it can take *a lot* of stabbing to kill someone with a knife." She rubs my back. "You did what you had to do to stay alive, Tatiana. But I know all too well that that doesn't do shit for the guilt. It doesn't take away the memory."

"I keep feeling it," I whisper.

"I know."

"When will it stop?"

"It takes time. You'll think about it once in a while forever. I still remember the first man I killed like it was yesterday. It's not as painful now, but the memory doesn't go away. You just learn to live with it. Remind yourself that you had to do it. Remind yourself what would have happened if you hadn't done it. You gotta argue with yourself a little bit."

"Like arguing with yourself when you try a bikini on for the first time after the winter," I say.

Scarlett snorts. "I guess. I usually have the opposite reaction."

I frown at her. "What do you mean?"

"Being as fit as I am comes with certain downsides in terms of traditional views on femininity. In order to stay at the elite level of fitness my job requires, my body fat stays very low. That means my tits are non-existent. Tiny tits, tiny ass, hard hips. Irregular or non-existent periods.

Hormone issues." She shrugs. "So when I try on a bathing suit, I often have a hard time seeing myself as..." she pauses, swallows. "As feminine. I'm not a girly girl. I'm lean, hard, and mean. It means I'm damn good at my job, but it's hard to feel like a woman, sometimes. I have to argue with myself about it. My femininity isn't defined by my shape any more than someone who struggles with too much weight. As women, we all have image issues. All of us. Mine is just a little non-standard."

I look at her. "I never thought about that."

"Of course not," she says. "Why would you? It's not your experience."

"Thank you," I say.

"Hey, us girls gotta stick together, right?"

"Yes, we do." I rise from the floor and go to the sink, rinse my mouth out. I look at her as I wash my hands. "Can I ask you something?"

"Of course," she says.

"How do I convince Lash that he's allowed to want me? That he's allowed to feel things for me."

Scarlett laughs. "Oh, man. You're asking the wrong bitch, Tatiana. Sol and I are still working that one out. We both struggle with emotional vulnerability. It's tough. I think you just have to be patient and keep repeating the message. Keep showing him it's safe to show you that stuff. Especially after what he told us about what he went through, on *top* of killer's guilt? He's gonna have a hard time. You just gotta give him a safe space to figure out how to get in touch with his heart again."

"He is very resistant."

"Wouldn't you be?"

I nod. "Yes, I suppose I would."

She ducks her head. "I'm still learning how to be the softness Sol needs. It goes against everything my entire life has taught me I need to be."

"What do you mean?" I ask. "The softness he needs?"

She tips her head from side to side. "I don't give a fuck about gender roles or any of that shit. I'm just talking about Sol and me. But what Sol needs is for me to be a woman—his woman. He wants to give me himself—and Sol is all man, right? Big, tough, hard as nails, scary as fuck. He's a killer. He's a fighter. A warrior. But that's not *all* he is, right? Same for me. I'm not big, but I *am* tough and I'm strong. I'm hard, I'm a killer every bit as much as Sol. That's been my life. But with Sol, I can be more. I can be a girl. I can put away Scarlett the operator, the badass boss bitch who can put a bullet in your fucking skull while eating lunch and not lose my appetite. I can be soft. I don't mean physically, but that too—I can be affectionate, tender, all that shit. He *wants* that. He *needs* it. And it took a lot of courage for a man like Sol to even admit that he wants and needs that."

"I suppose I do not understand what you mean when you say softness."

"Let's get out of here," she says. "We'll keep talking, though. We've been in one place for too long."

Since they're the professionals, I let them decide our next move—we need to get to Lyon, according to Lash's plan. But as I listen to them debating our next move and how to get to Lyon and then to Brazil where Sol's and Lash's friend and boss is being held, and I can't help but speak my mind.

"Lash?" I say, cutting through cross-talk as we stand on the sidewalk near the idling busses.

He looks at me. "Yes, lovely One?"

"I'm sorry, but I must ask."

He frowns. "Ask me what?"

"Are you putting your need to avenge your family ahead of your need to rescue your friend?" I rest my hand on his forearm. "This Pugli man. He is awful, and evil. I do not question your need to bring him to justice. But Inez is alive and she is in danger. I suppose what I am asking is if perhaps we should not focus on getting to Brazil and helping her instead of going after Pugli. I know he is evil and needs to be brought down. But Inez is your friend and she needs you."

His face contorts with anger, and he whirls on a heel, stalks away a few paces. His shoulders round with tension, and his head hangs, chin on his chest. "He burned my wife and infant children alive." I can barely hear him, even when I move up behind him, inches away.

"I know, Lash. I'm sorry. I shouldn't have said anything."

He shakes his head. "No. No." He tugs on his beard. "You are right. I am being selfish. I am only thinking about myself."

Solomon cuts in. "He's still a problem, though. He wants you dead, and us by association. Killing him gets him out of the way, if nothing else."

Lash sighs. "But Tatiana is right. I have been focused on the wrong thing. We can just as easily find our way to Brazil as to Lyon. The problem is the same—enemies who want us dead, and will try to stop us and apprehend us. But Inez is alive. Pugli isn't going anywhere, but every minute that goes by is a minute in which Mercado could decide to simply kill her."

"Lash, I—"

He brushes a gentle thumb over my lips, silencing me. "Thank you, Tatiana. I lost sight of what truly matters."

"I didn't mean—"

"I know. I will always mourn my family. And Pugli must come to justice. Perhaps it will be me who does so, perhaps not. But right now, the priority has to be Inez. I owe her my life. We all do." He frames my face in his big hard hands. "I am indebted to you for reminding me what my priorities should be."

My eyes burn again—and god, I'm sick of feeling so damned weepy. "I don't want to take away your revenge, Lash."

He smiles. "But you should. Revenge does not satisfy the soul. It only perpetuates violence. That does not mean he does not deserve a slow, horrific death and given a chance, I will give it to him. But revenge will not bring my wife back. It will not bring Leonora and Leander back. It will not soothe the sorrow I shall always feel. But if something were to happen to Inez because I was chasing my revenge, I would never forgive myself."

Lorenzo claps him on the back. "Speaking selfishly, I am relieved. I am in love with Sophia. Every moment I am stuck on the wrong side of the ocean is agony, because I know far too well what Rafael will do to her."

Lash lets out a growling sigh. "I know, too. I know firsthand. I investigated the disappearance of a German national in Brazil—he was former MAD on holiday in Rio, and he vanished. He was one of ours, so my superior tasked me with finding him."

"And did you?" Lorenzo asks.

Lash nods. "What was left of him, yes. He witnessed

Mercado's men abducting a woman. He stopped them. Mercado had him dismembered while alive."

Lorenzo nods. "Sounds about right."

Solomon clears his throat. "So. How do we get to Brazil? Hop a flight and see what happens?"

"Under normal circumstances, this is where we would call Inez and she would use her resources to procure transportation," Lash says. "But that is obviously not an option. We are on our own. Stjepan's small airplane is of no use to us in this situation, as it cannot make it across the ocean. I do not like the idea of simply entering an airport. Pugli's influence is a problem."

Something snaps past my ear, a hot sharp buzz like an angry bee dive-bombing me. I duck at the same time that I hear a *CRACK*.

Lash's arm smacks into my shoulders and drives me to the ground, knocking the breath out of me. His body covers mine, hot and hard and heavy.

I taste grit. I can see nothing but a narrow slice of sidewalk. I feel him move, and then I hear his gun going off, a deafening bark that leaves my ear ringing.

I hear a pained grunt on my left, hear Solomon shouting, and then Lash's arm scoops me airborne and we're moving.

Lorenzo is covered in blood, his T-shirt is soaked, and his left arm is bathed red, but he's jogging behind us on his own power, a fist pressed to his chest.

Scarlett and Sol bring up the rear, side by side, jogging a few feet, stopping, pivoting, and firing, and then jogging again.

Lash jumps, and we land heavily—his shoulder slams

into my gut and knocks the breath out of me all over again, and I hear gunfire, and screams, and feet pounding.

We've leaped onto a ferry. Lash effortlessly sprints up a steep set of stairs that's more ladder than anything, as if my weight on his shoulder is nothing.

"Get moving," I hear him snap in Croatian. "All possible speed, now."

"But the passengers—" A deep male voice says.

"Will have to wait. Pilot the boat or I'll throw you overboard."

"Put me down," I gasp, wiggling.

He sets me down on my feet, and I bend at the knees and suck oxygen while the ferry pilot pulls away from the pier. The engines roar and the boat rocks as the pilot brings the rear end out.

A few moments later, I feel the boat assume forward momentum.

Something smashes into the glass, shattering it—- someone screams. Not me.

A door slams open, and I see Solomon carry Lorenzo into the cockpit. He's pale and grimacing, fist digging into his shoulder—it looks like the bullet missed anything vital, but he is losing a lot of blood very quickly.

His eyes met mine and he grimaces, probably supposed to be a reassuring smile. "I'll be fine. It went through. Had worse."

And then he passes out.

CHAPTER 7

A CONVERSATION WITH A GHOST

LASH

THE BLUE-GREEN WATERS OF THE ADRIATIC SEA ripple and glint, the brilliant Mediterranean sun shines hot and searing, and the wind blows restlessly. We are in the cockpit with the pilot, making sure he doesn't change course or do anything stupid, like radio the authorities. We reassure him we mean him, the crew, and the passengers no harm—we only need passage away from Croatia.

"This is Ancona line," he says. "It is eleven hour sailing."

"We don't care where you take us," I tell him. "As long as you keep your mouth shut about us. You do not know what happened in Split. You never saw us. Understand? You don't tell anyone on the radio, you don't talk to your crew about us, you don't tell anyone when you get to port, not now, not in fifty years. Yes?"

The captain, an older man, a salty old sailor with weathered skin and white hair and the thousand-yard stare of a man who has seen the infinite horrors of this life, stares hard at us, scrutinizing all five of us as we stand in his cockpit.

He nods after several long moments. "I know nothing. I make mistake, leave too soon. No more job, but I live, hey?"

He produces a first aid kit from a cabinet and shoves it at me with a brusque jerk of his chin at Lorenzo. "He is shooted. Make him better. He die—you put over side. Yes?"

"He will not die," I answer.

He only shrugged. "Do not frighten passenger."

"We will go topside."

He nodded. "Is very long sail. Eleven hour."

So we take ourselves topside while Sol stays with the captain, and I take care of Lorenzo's wound. It is a through-and-through, fortunately, and hit nothing important. I apply pressure dressings to both holes and Lorenzo stretches out across a row of seats. We are alone on the top deck while the handful of passengers on board huddle fearfully in the lower deck, along with the lone crew member. Scarlett stretches out on another row, drapes an arm over her eyes, and is asleep with the speed of a career soldier.

Tatiana watches her lay down and fall asleep almost instantly. "I wish I could do that."

"Do what?" I ask, and then follow her gaze to Scarlett. "Oh, fall asleep like that?"

She nods. "Yes. It usually takes me forever."

"There is a trick to it," I tell her. "It takes a lot of practice, but when you are a soldier, there is a lot of waiting around, and you learn to sleep when you can."

She only nods to this, and I sense the subject change. "Lash, about what I said…"

I take her hand. "Please, Tatiana. Stop." I kiss the back of her hand. "I am grateful. Truly. I was lost in my anger.

You reminded me of my duty—to my brothers and Inez. Not only were you absolutely correct, but it was precisely what I needed to hear. I am indebted to you for having the courage to confront me with a hard truth."

"I just…" her eyes blur with unshed tears. "You deserve the chance for justice. Your family deserves it."

I slide my thumb beneath her eyes. "Tatiana, Lovely One…" I frown, hunting for words. "Justice…Revenge… they will not bring back my wife and children. I do not know if getting revenge will even assuage my feelings. Maybe I would sleep easier knowing Roberto Pugli is dead. But then again, maybe I would not. Who knows? What I know is that I cannot and will not shirk my duty. I will not break the oath I swore to my brothers."

She sniffles, wipes at her face. "I still feel badly. I know it was important to you. I do not want to take anything away from you." She tilts her head back and gives a gruff, frustrated groan. "I am so sick of crying."

I pull her close to me, wrap my arm around her. "It is okay, Tiana."

She shakes her head. "I know. I just…I do not like it. I do not cry almost ever, but…" she huffs a bitter laugh. "Things have been intense lately."

"Yes, just a little."

She's quiet for a moment. "I am going to ask you something. It is quite personal. It is none of my business, but I am going to ask anyway. You do not have to answer."

"Okay. I will answer if I can."

Another brief pause. "Ileana, your wife. What—what was she like?"

Pain stabs my heart at the sound of that name. "Oh, god. Ileana." I lean back in the seat, close my eyes, and think. After a while, I allow the words to pour out. "I have not thought about her, really thought of her, in a very long time. It is hard."

"Lash, you do not—"

"I want to," I interrupt. "I *need* to." I sigh. "What was Ileana like? She was joyful. Always, always joyful. She laughed all the time. It was very easy to make her laugh, and when she laughed, you wanted to laugh with her. It made you feel good. Her hair was like mine, only better. Longer, thicker, glossy as a raven's wing in the summer sunlight. She never cut it, only trimmed the ends once in a while. Sometimes she would braid it, but mostly it was loose. Often, she wore a…" I frown, the word I'm looking for momentarily eluding me—it comes to me in German, Romani, French, Croatian, half a dozen others that I know and have half-forgotten, but its English counterpart avoids my tongue, so I use the Croatian word. "A *marama*. A scarf—that is the word. I could not remember it. She had many of them, in every color and pattern you can think of."

I smile, remembering. "The one she wore the most was…mmm, dark red. There is a word, but I am tired and cannot remember. Dark red, with black designs that looked like commas, you know?"

Tatiana nods. "I know what you mean. I cannot think of the word either, because I do not know it."

"This scarf had little golden coins sewn onto the edges, and they would make music when she moved." I close my eyes and picture her. "She was always moving, and it always seemed like she was dancing to music only she could hear. And those coins would tinkle, tinkle, tinkle."

I lapse into silence again for a moment.

"I said she was always joyful. It is true. But…she would sometimes become very sad. Not often. Only once in a while. But this sadness was not ordinary. It was deep. She would stay in bed for days and do nothing. She would not speak, would not eat, nothing. I could do nothing. It was awful to be so helpless. I could only leave her alone and wait. And then, it would pass like it had never been. It was like the sun came out after days of rain." I sigh. "I thought quite a lot about these sadnesses of hers. And I always thought that it was the price she had to pay for being so full of joy all the rest of the time."

"How did you meet her?" she asks.

"I met her in Munich when I was in the German counterintelligence unit, the MAD. I lived in a small flat in a not very good part of town, but I liked it because it had a small Romani community, and it made me feel more at home. She moved into the flat across from mine, and I was immediately in love." I laugh. "She did not return my love right away. I was very different then. My hair was short, and I had no beard, and I mostly wore uniforms. I did not look or act like Romani. I spoke German like a native citizen. I….it was on purpose. I had been trying to forget my Romani-ness, I guess. After the violence of the revolution and seeing my parents murdered and everyone else I knew either killed, beaten, or chased away from our homes, I…" I shake my head. "I am embarrassed now, but I was scared. I was afraid to be me. To be proud of my heritage. I did not want to be different, to be persecuted and shamed and bullied for my race. I could not escape it, no matter how hard I tried, and I tried *very* hard to seem like just another German. Ileana saw right through it."

Tatiana nuzzles closer. "Of course she did."

I laugh. "Yes, of course she did. She was far braver than I. She was from Hungary, and experienced many of the same things I did. But she did not let them sour her spirit. She did not let them kill her pride in who she was and where she came from. No, she was full of courage and fire and joy. I was not worthy to love her. But I did. And in time she came to love me as well, and helped me find myself."

I glance down at Tatiana, and see a thoughtful expression on her face. "What? I see you thinking very hard. I would know what you think, please."

She sighs. "Maybe it's not for me to say."

"It is."

"I...I am thinking that maybe you have returned to that place. You have not forgotten who you are, I do not think. But it seems like maybe you have let your experiences sour your spirit." She twists to look up at me, dark deep eyes searching and intense. "How could they not? What you went through would kill most men. Yet here you are. I do not fault you, Lash. No one would. But...I wonder what your Ileana would say if you could speak with her."

I feel, again, as if ten thousand volts have shocked me. My instinct is to run, to lash out, to shut down. Instead, I force myself into total stillness; instead, I force myself to examine my feelings with brutal honesty.

The stillness doesn't last.

I gently dislodge Tatiana and stand up, pace across the upper deck to the front and stand at the railing.

What would my beloved Ileana say if she could give me a message from beyond the grave?

"You are a fool, Nico." That was her pet name for me—Nico. *"I am gone. I live on in your heart, but you are still alive. You still walk the earth. You still have a heart. A body. A spirit."*

I know, my beloved. But without you, what am I? Who am I?

"*My Nico. Always my Nico.*" I can almost feel her leaning against my shoulder the way she loved to do as we sipped coffee in the morning and watched the sunrise. "*But Nico, my love…You must move on.*"

I do not know how, my beloved. I am stuck. I am lost.

"*Because you cling to my spirit. You wallow in your grief.*"

My eyes burn.

How can I move on? How can I forget you? How can I allow myself to love another when your spirit walks beside me and haunts my dreams?

"*You will not forget me. But Nico, my love, I am dead. I commune with our ancestors. I cannot be jealous. When I was alive, I was jealous of your time and your attention and your love. But now that I am dead, I only wish for your peace.*"

How can I have peace? The only peace I have ever known in my life was in your embrace.

I hear her sigh—it is a soft breath carried on the winds of the Adriatic. "*Nico, Nico, Nico. You are not looking for peace. You are looking for forgetting. Some men look for forgetting in the bottom of a bottle, but you look for it in self-denial. You deny your brothers the closeness with you which you know they seek. You isolate. You erect walls. You live a sere and spartan life to punish yourself for our deaths.*"

The wind—her breath—snatches away the salt drops leaking from my eyes.

It is my fault.

"*You know it is not. The fault of our deaths lies at the feet of one man, and he is not you.*"

I have not avenged you.

"*Do you think I wish to be avenged? Did I seek vengeance*

against the men who murdered my father and raped my mother and me? No, I did not, Nico. Men like Roberto Pugli will always exist in the world. They always have. Killing him will not bring you peace, my love. It will not satisfy the anger that burns inside you. Would his death be justice? Yes, of course. But what is that, to you? His death will not fill the hole in your heart that my death created."

What can, my beloved? Nothing.

"No, nothing. It is true. No justice, no vengeance can fill the hole. No object, no place." The wind ruffles my hair and beard, and for a moment I can imagine it is her fingers, her lips. *"But no THING is not the same as no ONE."*

I duck my head and squeeze my eyes shut.

Do not say it, Ileana. I would not betray you that way.

"Betray? Nico, you foolish man. I...am...DEAD. You are speaking to yourself. You hear my voice because you have kept me alive in your heart. You cannot betray a dead woman, my love."

So I should let her in? I should open my heart to Tatiana?

Her voice is faint, now. *"My love. Would I not want you to find joy once more? Would I not want you to laugh again? To feel pleasure again?"*

I hear the chime of her scarf on the wind. I hear her laughter. I feel her touch.

I feel her farewell.

Honor me with your life, my love. I am your heart, and hearts are meant to be shared.

Her words are but a whisper on the wind, now, felt more than heard.

I hear Tatiana's steps behind me, feel her presence. "Are you okay, Lash?"

I nod without turning to face her. "Just...saying goodbye."

"To whom?"

"Ileana."

"Lash, I—"

"You asked me what she would say. So I asked myself, and I heard the answer."

Her breath catches on a half-sob, half-sigh. "Lash." She switches to Croatian. "I feel like I am taking things from you. First justice and now your wife."

I answer in English because that is the language I have become most comfortable with. "You have taken nothing from me, Tatiana." I turn and face her, take her hands in mine. "On the contrary. You are setting me free."

She swallows hard, her eyes glistening as they waver, searching mine. "I am being selfish. I...I want you, Lash. I want you to let me in."

I smile at her, and it feels like using atrophied muscles; I lean in and kiss her eye and then the other. "Be selfish, Tatiana. Demand more of me. You will have to be patient with me, but...I will try. I have let the past hold me captive. You have helped me see that."

Her answering smile is tentative and fraught with a myriad of powerful emotions. "I can be patient."

"Tatiana, I..." I close my eyes with a long, slow sigh. "Ileana will always be a part of me. I fear that some part of my heart still belongs to her."

She withdraws one of her hands from mine and cups my face. "Of course, Lash. She was your wife. You loved her. She was taken from you too soon. You should have had a long happy life with her." She steps into me. Her dark eyes search me, pierce my soul. "I do not ask for that part of you, Lash. It is hers. I just...I want the parts of you that can still be mine."

I shake my head. "Why, Tatiana? Why me? Anyone could protect you."

She rolls a shoulder. "Who can say? Who knows why we feel attraction to someone? Who can say why we fall in love?" She grins at me. "Unless you're fishing for compliments. In which case, I can oblige."

I snort. "I am not fishing for compliments. It's just that you are a smart, beautiful, successful woman, and I am a man with a tragic and painful past, and no real ambitions for the future beyond learning to live a life of peace. Death has surrounded me since I was a boy. And the years I have spent in Club Sin with my brothers have been the most peaceful I have ever known, but even those years have been haunted by the deaths of my family. What can I offer you, Tatiana?"

"Yourself. I am not attracted to you for what you can offer me, Lash. What you can offer me is *you*. Your mind, your heart, your body. Protection. Safety. Acceptance." She trails her fingers down through my beard and then grips it in her fist and tugs. "I only want you, Lash. The rest I can find on my own. I have a business and I enjoy running it. I can bring it to the States easily. And to be honest, I think it would be good to get away from my father and his business. I am tired of being afraid of every car that follows me. I jump at shadows because I have had men jump out of them at me and hold me hostage to get money from Tata. I am over it."

"I will always protect you."

"I know."

"I just...I cannot promise you safety until after Inez is rescued. I will have blood on my hands until this is over."

She strokes my beard, tugging it through her fist, combing her fingers through it. "You are who you are, Lash. For better or worse, violence has been a part of my life. That man may be the first person I have killed, but he is rather far from the first I have seen killed. I am not afraid of you."

She takes my hands and kisses the palms, places my hands against her cheeks. "I do not need your hands to be clean, Lash." She giggles. "Metaphorically speaking, at least."

"You are a wonder, do you know that?" I lean in, brush my lips against hers.

She exhales softly as my lips touch hers. "Lash. Kiss me. Please."

So, I do.

For the first time since that awful day, I allow the calcification around my heart to soften. I allow the atrophied muscle of desire to flex, to come alive.

I let out a breath and let my sorrow, which I have held on to so tightly for so long, exhale with it.

I cradle Tatiana's beautiful face in my hands, glorying in the softness of her skin and the anticipation in her eyes. I start small, merely questing my lips against hers. She sighs, and her fingers dimple into my nape, digging in at my hairline, her thumbs grazing behind my ears.

"Lash," she whispers, my name a breath, the movement of her lips on mine. "More."

A deep, wild hunger flickers to life within me, a gaping, yawning chasm of fierce need—cold skin craving the warmth of touch, hard planes craving the softness of curves, the ache of emptiness craving the fulfillment of love.

I twist to press her against the railing and palm the back of her head in one hand, cup her cheek in the other, and deepen the kiss. She whimpers, and her tongue sweeps against mine and her mouth opens, soft and wet and warm and inviting. I can't help but growl in satisfaction and desire, crush my hardness against her softness.

My heart slams in my chest, my pulse pounds in my throat. "Tatiana…my god. What are you doing to me?"

She pulls back and smiles up at me, fisting my shirt in her hands. "Kissing you."

My hands tremble. "It has been so long since I felt…" I close my eyes, shake my head, search for the words. "Anything at all, let alone such a potent desire."

"I never have," she murmurs. "Never. It is a little frightening, is it not? In an exhilarating sort of way."

I've lost track of who is speaking which language. It doesn't matter. We understand each other.

"Yes," I agree. "A little frightening, and a lot exhilarating."

"Kiss me again, Lash. The way you kiss me, I never want to stop."

"I worry about getting carried away," I say. "If we were alone, I never would stop."

She grasps my beard and pulls me back in for another kiss, and this time she cups the back of my head and keeps a tight grip on my beard and sweeps her tongue through my mouth with a soft, delicate moan of pleasure.

My hands take on a life of their own, raking down her waist to grip her hips, and then the taut bubble of her ass. She moans as I cradle her ass, crushing herself harder against me.

Her breasts flatten against my chest, and she is all I feel, all I hear, all I smell, all I taste. Every sense, every synapse is attuned to her.

She pulls away from the kiss, and I feel her smile curve against my lips. She nips my lower lip between her teeth and grinds her hips against mine. "I want you, Lash."

"Tatiana," I growl, panting. "You make me feel like a madman. I am at the end of my control."

She rests her forehead on my shoulder, and I press my mouth and nose into her hair, inhaling her scent. I grunt in shock when she dips her hand behind the waist of my jeans and delves down to cup my erection. "Lash," she whispers. "God. God, I need you."

"Tatiana...we can't. Not here." I grab her wrist but can't make myself stop her touch. "Fuck."

"Where can we go to be alone?" She murmurs. "I need you. I fucking need you like I've never needed anyone or anything. I feel like I might die if I don't have you soon."

"We are on a boat in the middle of the sea," I say. "There is nowhere to go."

Slowly, with obvious and immense reluctance, she pulls her hand out and grips my shirt with it. "Soon, Lash. Promise me. Please."

"Soon," I answer, the word a growl, a hoarse breath. "Whatever it takes, Lovely One. Soon."

"Promise?" She traces my lips with her fingertips.

"I promise. The moment we can steal away and be alone together, You and I, we will..." I shake my head as words fail me. "We shall discover one another."

She huffs a laugh. "I want to do much more than

merely discover you, Lash." She presses her lips to my ear, breathing sensual promises. "I want you naked and all for me. I want to ride you. I want to be beneath you. I want to taste every last inch of you. I want you to come so hard for me that you forget your name. I want you to forget everything but me, Lash. I told you, I'm selfish."

I growl, gripping her ass so hard it must hurt, but all she does is pant with delight and wriggle her ass into my grip. "Tatiana…"

"Lash?" she breathes.

"If I do not let you go right now, I will have you here on the deck of this boat for all the world to see."

Wide dark eyes search and sear, rife with an insatiable need. "Tempting," she whispers. "I've never had sex in public before."

"Tatiana," I breathe, the sound more warning than word.

She only laughs "So serious." She pushes me backward, reaches behind herself and captures my hands, tangling our fingers between our bodies. "Is that better?"

"I would do very bad things to be alone with you right now, Tatiana."

She bites her lower lip and gazes at me. "I know. So would I."

I lead her away from the railing and to a row of seats, sit with my back to the railing, and pull her down between my legs, her back to my front. "If we can't be alone, this will have to do."

She takes my hands and drapes them over her shoulders, clutching them against her chest. Rests a cheek against our joined hands. I feel her breathing slow almost immediately. "It will do. For now."

CHAPTER 8

ACROSS THE SEA

TATIANA

I T IS A VERY LONG, BORING RIDE ACROSS THE SEA; WE are not merely crossing it but sailing far to the north from Split to Ancona, Italy.

Day fades, and the sun sets—and it is one of the most glorious sunsets I have ever seen. I stand at the railing on the upper deck with Lash behind me, his arms wrapped around me, and we watch the huge red sun sink below the waves.

It grows cool, after that, and then cold. We go below, and the handful of passengers shrink away from us, even though we have kept to ourselves and were the ones being shot at. I realize, then, that I am still splattered with blood—it is on my clothing, and I can feel flecks of it when I run my fingers through my hair. And then there is Lorenzo, pale and peaked, his T-shirt stiff with dried blood, bandaged front and back.

I suppose we are a frightening group, especially considering we hijacked a ferry while taking gunfire.

We pass the hours talking. Scarlett replaces Solomon in the cockpit, and then it's Solomon's turn to stretch out on a row of seats in the lower deck, and is soon snoring.

Lorenzo sits in the row in front of Lash and me and he tells us amusing and thrilling stories of his time in the Brazilian military. Lash relates his own stories from his time in the German counterintelligence unit, and some from his time working for my father.

I have a few of my own stories, like the time I was kidnapped by a group of teenaged boys. It was a gang initiation, and they were young, naive, and foolish. They thought waving guns in my face—clearly unloaded, as if the daughter of Zagreb's most notorious gangster wouldn't know an unloaded revolver if she saw one—would ensure my cooperation. One of them tried to flirt with me, another kept threatening to "teach me a lesson," and the third apologized about twenty times.

When my father's men, guided to me by the tracker in my purse, burst into the room and assessed the situation, they all laughed until they cried. The poor boys pissed themselves when they came face to face with Tata's hardened, cold-blooded killers, armed with machine guns.

Lash and Lorenzo laughed—Lorenzo's laugh shifted to a pained groan.

"What did your father's men do to the boys?" Lash asks.

I shrug. "I don't know. Filip took me home, and I did not see what happened. I would imagine they were killed, though. Tata doesn't play games with kidnappers."

Lorenzo sighs. "Unloaded guns. Idiot children playing soldier." He shakes his head, rolling it against the back of the seat. "I experienced something like that once, after I got out of the army. A group of boys, maybe sixteen or seventeen years old. There were, oh, maybe six of them? I owned a pickup at the time. Nothing very nice, just a fourth-hand old Hilux. But these boys thought they could steal it from me, with me in it. They all had handguns and they were shouting and waving them in my face. Not one of them had a magazine in their gun, although I suppose there could have been a round in the chamber." He chuckles and then groans. "Ugh, ow. I gave them a good thrashing and took their guns away. An unloaded gun is only dangerous to the idiot holding it, I told them. If you point a gun at someone, it had better be loaded and you'd better be ready and willing to pull the trigger, or you have no business with a gun."

We doze, chat, and sometimes simply stare out the window at the black water and the starry sky.

Eventually, I doze off, my head on Lash's lap.

I wake up abruptly, and the stars above have been replaced with the amber glow of city light in the distance.

Lorenzo is gone, taking a turn in the cockpit, I assume, and Solomon and Scarlett are sitting with her back to his front, murmuring to each other quietly.

I am alone in the row of seats, my head against the window, pillowed by a folded jacket of some kind, and Lash is nowhere to be seen.

I find him at the prow, watching the lights grow gradually larger. I press myself against his back and wrap my arms around his waist, slide my hands up under his shirt and caress his pecs and abs. "What are you thinking about?" I ask in Croatian.

He shrugs. "The past and the future. What Leonora and Leander would be like, now. Who I would be if…

that…had not happened." His answer is English—we've developed a habit of that, where I speak to him in my native Croatian, and he answers in English, which I comprehend better than I speak. "I am considering how we will get to Brazil. I am thinking that once all this is over with, I will happily swear an oath against killing. I have always felt like I have cheated my brothers. I have the brand, but I did not swear the same oath."

"You have mentioned a brand and an oath before. What are they?"

He turns and pulls up his shirt sleeve so the light from the cabin illuminates the inside of his bicep and the raised tattoo there. Not just a tattoo, I realize—he used the word "brand," and when I touch the stylized broken arrow the skin is raised—the arrow is branded into his skin and then tattooed over.

"What does it mean?" I ask. "And what is the oath?"

"The broken arrow symbolizes the other men and me. We are all warriors, and our experiences have broken us. Before, we were arrows in the quiver of the military. We were weapons. Our lives, our whole purpose was killing—bad people, yes, but still." He lets down his sleeve and turns back to the view of approaching Ancona. "It is layers of meaning. We are no longer arrows. We have chosen a different life. And also, we are all broken in some way. Our employer, who we only know as The Boss, or sometimes The Guardian, rescued us all. We all had enemies who wanted us dead. We had vices, addictions, and secrets. We all have closets full of skeletons, pasts full of ghosts."

"And your boss gave you somewhere you could…not hide, exactly, but just…get away, I suppose?"

Lash nods. "Yes, exactly."

"And the oath?"

He recites. "Once you're in, there's no going back. Never take a life. Loyalty to the brotherhood above all."

"And the others, they all swore that oath. But you didn't?"

I shake my head. "No, I did not. I swore loyalty to the brotherhood, but I did not swear to not take a life. I have never known why. I should have. I often wish I had. Perhaps if I had, I would not have been so consumed with thoughts of revenge."

"Perhaps it was an oversight?" I suggest.

He barks a laugh. "No. Our employer does not make mistakes. Neither does Inez. I took the brand last. It was just me and Inez out in the desert outside Las Vegas. I never told the others that my oath was different. I was... ashamed, I suppose. Confused."

"Perhaps..." I trail off, hesitant to render my guess.

"Perhaps what, Lovely One?"

"Well, I know nothing but what you have told me, obviously, so this is only a guess. But what if he knew you would need to make the choice yourself?"

"What choice?"

"To pursue revenge...or not."

"Huh," he grunts. "You are a wise woman, do you know that?"

"It is the only thing that makes sense to me, that's all. I know nothing of the pasts of the other men. But I do know yours—what you have told me, that is. And if this mysterious man, your employer, does not make mistakes, if everything he does is with intent, then he had a purpose in removing that part of the oath only for you. What other purpose could there be?" I shrug. "He knew that someday you would have to choose to take your revenge against this Roberto Pugli or choose not to. You would have to be free to make that choice, and you would not be if you had sworn an oath not to kill."

He is quiet for a very long time, thinking. "I believe you are correct yet again." He snorts a laugh, shaking his head. "You have upended my entire life and everything I have tricked myself into believing."

"Lash, I—"

He twists in place, silencing me with a kiss. "I am indebted to you a thousand times over, Tatiana."

I shake my head. "There is no debt, Lash. Just…" I trail off, licking my lips. "Just…love me."

His black gaze is glittering and intense. "Tatiana, I—"

It's my turn to interrupt, to silence him with a kiss. "In time, Lash. We just met. I don't expect you to be in love. But that is what I want. It's all I want—for you to love me, someday, if you can." I swallow hard, my damned eyes burning yet again. "I know I cannot have your whole heart. Your beloved Ileana will always have it. But I will accept whatever you can give me."

"You deserve all of someone, Tatiana."

"That is for me to decide, isn't it? If I decide part of you is better than all of anyone else, then what can you say? Nothing. We make choices in life, Lash. You rescued me from Filip. You have protected me. You have shared your heart with me. You have shown yourself to me when I know damned well that you do not do so easily, or indeed at all. So, I choose you. I know my own mind." I lean against him, giving him all my weight, and sling my arms around his neck. "I have often been called impulsive, rash, even reckless. But I listen to my gut, my instincts, and my heart. I rarely listen to my mind, for I know the depths of my ignorance. But I know what I want and I know what I feel." I lean in, kiss him. "So if I choose to accept however much of yourself you can give me, then that is my choice to make."

He holds my gaze for a long time. "I cannot bring myself to argue the point, even if part of me thinks you are cheating yourself. I am a broken man. My heart is in pieces."

"I told you already—I am good at puzzles." I shake my head, and nuzzle his cheek. "Lash, I choose you as you are. Right now. Broken pieces and all."

"I just...I struggle to understand why."

"I don't know!" I shrug, laugh. "I don't know, Lash. The chemistry of love is a mystery, is it not? Why do we fall in love? What causes sexual attraction? Science gives one answer, poetry another. Who knows? I don't. You don't. But I know what I feel and I will not question it." I nuzzle his cheek again. "I have not been through what you have. If you need time to process, or sort through your feelings, or just learn to accept what you're feeling, that's okay. I can be patient. Just don't shut me out."

"I won't shut you out. I can promise you that much."

"Hey, captain says we're gonna be docking soon." Solomon's voice comes from the doorway into the lower deck.

I realize with a start that while Lash and I were talking we'd approached the marina. The lights of Ancona shine brightly against the dark of night.

We gather in the lower deck, away from the small huddle of frightened passengers.

"We have to be prepared for an exciting welcome,"

Solomon says. "We know the captain didn't contact any-one, but our departure wasn't exactly a secret, so we have to assume law enforcement will be waiting for us."

Lorenzo, looking less pale and much stronger, stares out at the rippling dark water for a moment. "What about a lifeboat? Deploy a lifeboat and we find somewhere else to get ashore."

No one disagrees with this plan, so we troop up to the cockpit. When Solomon presents the plan to the captain, the dour, weathered old man just shrugs.

"I have not speak to shore," he grouses. "Is no police."

"*You* haven't," Sol argues. "Someone else back in Split may have."

"Hmmm. Maybe, maybe. You wait. You wait. I call friend." The captain grabs a phone from a cupholder in front of him and places a call.

He speaks rapidly in what sounds to me like a Serbian dialect; being closely related to Croatian, I can follow his conversation, and he is asking if there is anything unusual happening ashore in Ancona.

Pausing to listen, he thanks his friend and ends the call. "Is okay. No police. Maybe people who shooted you in Split," he says, with a shrug, "but no police."

Solomon glances at Lash. "Could you understand him? Is he telling the truth?"

Lash nods and glances at me for confirmation—I an-swer. "Croatian and Serbian are close enough to under-stand. He tells the truth."

The captain looks annoyed to have been questioned, but says nothing.

"I think we chance it," Scarlett says. "I don't like the

idea of being out on the open water in a lifeboat if I don't absolutely have to."

"Agreed," Lorenzo says.

"Agreed," Solomon says.

Lash looks at me and I shrug. "I am not the expert, do not ask me. Like Scarlett, I do not want to be on the ocean in a little boat if it is not needed. But I also do not want to be shot at again."

Lash wraps an arm around my waist. "Unfortunately, Lovely One, it is very likely you will take fire again before all this is over. I will do everything in my power to protect you, however."

I nod. "I know."

When we departed Split, there was only one crew member aboard, the rest were ashore preparing for departure. That crew member, a young man just past his teenage years, wears a thin jacket with the ferry line logo, as well as a hat. He is at the prow with a coil of rope in hand, preparing to dock.

I point at him through the cockpit window. "What if we disguise ourselves?"

Solomon blinks at me. "Why did none of us think of that?" He glances at the captain. "You have extra jackets and hats aboard?"

The captain glares at him, grumbling under his breath in Serbian about stupid, greedy Americans, but he nods, levering himself out of his seat, and hobbling bowlegged across the cockpit to a narrow closet. He rummages in the closet and comes out with five sealed packages. "Is all I have. Very expensive."

I shrug out of my leather jacket, reluctantly. "This is

a very, *very* expensive jacket. Clean it up and you can sell it for a lot of money."

He takes it, turns it this way and that. "Your blood?" He asks me in Serbian.

I shake my head, answering in Croatian. "No. Not mine. He tried to rape and murder me."

He nods. "My wife will clean it up nicely. Maybe you come back and I will give it back to you."

I shake my head. "It's okay. It's just a jacket. We are sorry for causing you trouble. We are not bad people, we are just stuck in a bad situation." I hear Lash giving the others a summary translation of the conversation.

The captain shrugs. "Such is life, hey? Now, you must all leave me alone so I can dock the boat."

We don the coats and hats—the sizes are all over the place, so there is a lot of trying on, shrugging off, and trading until we are wearing sizes close to what fits us. Mine is too large, just like Scarlett's, while the mens' are all too small. Except for Lash's, which is small in the shoulders and chest but long in the arms.

A few minutes later, the boat approaches the dock, and the engines grind noisily as the back end swings in toward the dock. The young crewman tosses the line ashore to a dockworker, who ties it off with expert speed. Before the boat has even settled, Solomon leads the charge, hopping ashore and extending a hand to Scarlett. Lorenzo is next, and then Lash, and Lash lifts me ashore.

It's dark still, the sun having not yet risen. A lone seagull wheels overhead, keening now and again. The marina is empty and quiet. A pair of dim yellow headlights glides along a road that runs parallel to the shore, vanishing into the distance. A dog barks somewhere far away. It's cold, and everything is dew-wet.

"Come on," Solomon says. "Gotta get scarce."

The road nearest the marina, however, is several feet lower than the rest of the city, with another road parallel to one that services the marina; there is no pedestrian access to the upper road, requiring a long walk to where the marina service drive splits off.

Not a soul is visible. The lone seagull is joined by a second, and then a third, and then half a dozen more as the sky lightens.

"This seems too fuckin' easy," Solomon says, scanning our surroundings with one hand in his jacket pocket— gripping his pistol, I assume.

"Maybe they assumed we'd have the ferry take the shortest route across?" Scarlett says.

Solomon rubs his face. "We probably should have. We just wasted twelve fucking hours."

Lorenzo claps him on the back. "I think this was best, my friend. It was unexpected. The time we lost going north we will make up by not having to shoot our way out of Ancona."

"But how do we get to fucking Brazil?" Sol snaps. "I used all my favors."

"After I left the army, I spent some time traveling for fun. I spent a good bit of time here in Italy, and I have even been here, to Ancona," Lorenzo says.

Solomon rolls his hand. "And?"

"Impatient Americans," Lorenzo mutters. "*And...* there is an international airport here, but it only goes direct within Europe, since it is too small for transoceanic flights. To fly direct, non-stop, to South America, we need to get to a major city. Rome, London, Frankfurt."

Solomon nods. "Ah, I see. So the first step is a ride out of Ancona. Bus, train, or car. Public transportation is risky, since Pugli likely has us flagged for detention. How we'll get around that is a question for later."

Lash sighs. "I have an idea for that, but we need to get to Germany for it to work. I have contacts in the German military. I should be able to get us seats on a military flight, but I need to see my contact in person."

"So we steal a car?" Scarlett asks.

"I have enough cash that we could purchase something. It will not be very nice, but it would make smaller the risk," I say.

"You'd be throwing your money away," Scarlett says. "We'd leave it behind when we fly out of here."

I shrug. "It is my father's money."

Scarlett grins. "Well then, let's go buy a car."

Lorenzo guides us deeper into Ancona, which is sleepy but rousing. Cyclists on their way to work zip past us, paying us no mind in our ferry-worker attire. A taxi trundles past slowly, light on, hoping we'd be his first fare of the day. A delivery van beeps as it backs up along the curb next to a cafe; the outdoor seating area is being set up by a pretty young woman, the chairs unstacked and tables arranged just so, while within baristas calibrate the espresso machines, noisily banging the wands to discard grounds.

Lorenzo halts, eyeing the cafe. "We need to eat," he says. "Tatiana, give me your cash, and I will find us a car. Order us food and coffee and I will return as soon as I can."

I sling my backpack-purse off my shoulders and fish the stack of cash out of it, handing it to Lorenzo. He counts it swiftly and hands back a small stack, folding the rest and putting it in his hip pocket; he does all this with his good hand, keeping the wounded one immobile against his belly.

Lash converses with the young woman setting up the outdoor seating area—his Italian, he explains when the woman hustles off to get menus, is far from fluent but he can make himself understood. Moments later, we're seated inside in a back corner, out of view of the street. We get coffee and breakfast, ordering for Lorenzo.

Thirty minutes later, a dirty, rattling, rusty old Lancia sedan squeals to a halt outside the cafe, and Lorenzo emerges. We've all finished eating already and are sipping our coffees while we wait for Lorenzo.

He tosses the key on the table and hands me a much smaller stack of cash. "I got a good deal. We will have to hope we don't get into any high-speed chases, however, since I doubt it will reach ninety-five on its best day." He arches an eyebrow at Scarlett and Solomon. "That is sixty miles per hour, for you Americans and your idiotic imperial system."

Solomon snorts. "Thanks, pal, don't know what I'd do without you." He rolls his eyes. "I may be an American by birth, but I've spent more time outside the US than I have stateside. I'm all for the metric system."

"Same," Scarlett says. "But I am not really an American. I don't know what I am. I spent my career killing for America, but do I identify as an American? I don't know. Part of me still feels like I don't belong anywhere."

Solomon wraps his arms around her, pulling her against his chest—she goes stiff for a moment, frowning, and then softens. "You belong here, my love."

She allows the embrace for a moment and then pushes him away. "Work brain, Sol. Can't do sappy right now."

He just laughs. "Too bad, sweet tits."

She glares at him. "Call me that again and I'll cut your balls off while you sleep."

He just laughs all the harder and kisses the top of her head. She pretends to fight him off, but I can see her trying not to smile.

Lorenzo has polished off his food while this exchange has been going on. He takes a sip of his coffee, grimacing. "Cold." He takes it up to the barista, converses in Italian, waits, and receives a fresh espresso in a paper cup. "Okay, let's go. I know where we are going, so I will drive."

Solomon eyes him. "Sure you're good?"

Lorenzo gives him a flat stare. "Yes. I am sure."

Solomon holds up both hands, palms out. "Hey, man, I'm just asking."

"We are all professionals. You know your limitations. Trust me to know mine."

Solomon nods. "I do, Lorenzo. I wasn't questioning you. I've been shot. The shock can catch up with you at weird times."

Lorenzo sighs, rubbing his jaw. "True, you are correct. I am just fearful for Inez. I need to get to her. I just found her again after many years and I am not going to lose her again."

Solomon grips Lorenzo's shoulder. "We'll get her back, man. she saved my life—all our lives. I owe her. we all do."

Scarlett nods her agreement. "She and I got pretty close back there. Us badass survivor bitches gotta stick together."

Lash claps a hand on Lorenzo's other shoulder. "Inez is important to everyone. But you must remember who she is. It is my feeling that Mercado will come to regret his decision."

Lorenzo nods, snorting a laugh. "That is true. She was content to leave things alone, but Rafael…he does not forget. He is vicious, it is true, and he will do his own killing, but he is not like us. He kills from a position of safety and power. When faced with gunfire, he flees and leaves the fighting to his men. He is a coward and bully. My Sophia will gut him like a fish."

Lash frowns. "Who is Sophia?"

Scarlett answers. "Inez. It's her real name—or her birth name."

Lash's frown deepens. "Sophia. Hmmm." The frown clears, and he shrugs. "It suits her, I suppose. She is still Inez to me, though."

"She will always be Sophia to me," Lorenzo says. He snags the keys from the table, and we head out to the car.

It stinks of cigarettes and engine oil. The exterior is red—or once was, at least, age and weather having faded the paint to a dull, chipped rust color. The interior is plasticky fake black leather, squeaky and uncomfortable. When Lorenzo cranks the motor, it coughs and wheezes like an old man, shudders, and then catches with a belch of blue-gray exhaust.

Solomon laughs, thumping a fist on the roof. "You sure this old beast will make it all the way to fucking Germany?"

Lorenzo laughs. "No, my friend, I am not. But it was the best I could do under the circumstances."

Solomon shakes his head, sliding into the front

passenger seat. "May have to get out and push it up the mountain."

Scarlett grimaces as the engine sputters while idling. "Assuming we make it that far. I'm not criticizing, Lorenzo."

He chuckles. "Believe me, I know. I don't like it either. I managed to get a toolkit included, and I am pretty handy with engines, but without spare parts…"

"We will make do, whatever comes," Lash says. "Let us go. Time is wasting."

I take the middle seat, with Lash on my right and Scarlett on the left, and Lorenzo drives us through Ancona north and west on the E55.

For an hour or so, it's a quiet, easy, and peaceful drive.

And then I notice both Solomon and Lorenzo's shoulders tense up, and Solomon twists to look behind us.

The rest of us do, too—a sleek black BMW is behind us and closing in fast, with two more trailing behind it.

"Too easy," Solomon grumbles. "Fuckin' knew it. Buckle up, boys and girls. Shit's about to get interesting."

CHAPTER 9

ITALY, GERMANY, BRAZIL...AGAIN

LASH

"**L**ET THEM GET CLOSE," I say.

Lorenzo nods, steering wheel gripped in both hands, jaw tight at the pain of using his wounded arm. He backs off the accelerator, allowing us to slow without the use of brakes. The BMW closes on us even faster; the front windscreen is illegally tinted. Half-turned in my seat, I watch the car approach.

"How do we know they're after us?" Tatiana asks.

The timing of her answer is comically perfect: the moment the question leaves her lips, a hand emerges from the passenger window, wielding a pistol.

"That's how," Scarlett answers, glancing at me. "Ready?"

I eject the magazine of my gun, tap it back in, and nod. "Ready. Windows down." We both roll the windows all the way down. "On three. One...two...three!"

In unison, as if we've practiced it, Scarlett and I both twist to lean up and out the windows, facing backward with our torsos half-out of the vehicle. Our pistols crack in synch, and holes sprout in the hood and windshield. The BMW shimmies, the engine billows smoke, and then flat spins ninety degrees and rolls, bouncing. One of the other cars dodges it, but the third car back doesn't, and I glimpse flying wreckage before we speed out of view of the crash. The third car is now fifty-some yards behind us and closing—the powerful roar of its engine is audible with the windows down.

"Two for one," Solomon says, "Good work."

No one celebrates, however; there's still one left. A figure emerges from the passenger window, wielding an assault rifle.

"Fuck," Scarlett snarls. "Down!"

The three of us in back throw ourselves down, and I hear the *rattle-crack* of an assault rifle; metallic thuds echo as a few bullets smack into the body of the car, although most go wide.

I snarl a curse in Romani and then switch to English. "Fucking idiot. Did no one teach you anything?"

I lean out the window, steadying my pistol in both hands, aim, and then cracks off a single shot. Blood sprays, and the shooter slumps to hang half out the window. The body twitches, and then topples out of the window, splatting across the concrete as it tumbles and rolls, rag-doll limp.

Another figure emerges, and, with an annoyed sigh, I repeat the feat, putting a slug through the would-be shooter's skull.

Scarlett eyes me as I sink back into the seat. "Alright then, Annie Oakley."

I frown at her. "I do not know this reference."

Scarlett waves a hand dismissively. "Famous sharpshooter from the American Old West."

I shrug. "Oh. Bah. You could do this. So could either of them," he says, gesturing at the men in front.

"Yeah, sure," Scarlett answers, "But we'd need more than one shot."

I grin. "It helps that I used to practice it."

"How do you do that?" she asks.

Another shrug. "A dummy secured partly out the window of a car. My unit and I practiced it at a remote proving ground."

Scarlett snickers. "That sounds super safe."

I laugh. "It wasn't exactly an approved practice. That was how we filled our free time. Bored soldiers, especially elite ones, will do idiotic things to entertain themselves."

Lorenzo and Solomon both laugh.

"You are not lying, my friend," Lorenzo says. "Wait, they're trying again, the *idiotas*."

With an annoyed roll of his head, I prove that the first two shots were not flukes, nailing the shooter before he can get a shot off.

"How can we get our hands on that car?" Solomon asks. "Without broken windows or bloody seats, preferably. This thing is *not* gonna get us over the fucking mountains, Ren."

Lorenzo eyes him. "I don't know how I feel about you calling me that—only Sophia ever did." he muses thoughtfully. "I could pull over and try to get the driver to come after us. It is quite risky, though."

Solomon watches the side mirror for a moment. "Alright, let's try it. Gun it, Ren. Like we're trying to outrun him."

"And then brake hard," Lorenzo says, finishing the unspoken part of Solomon's plan.

"I don't like this," Scarlett says. "Someone's gonna get shot."

"Gotta better plan, sweet tits?" Solomon asks, winking at her.

She glares at him. "I hope you enjoy your own hand, Sol, because if you keep calling me sweet tits, you'll never get to fuck me again."

Solomon just cackles, monitoring the car in the side mirror. "Okay, Ren. On three, brake and swerve so he misses us. Last thing we need is to get rear-ended."

"I understand the plan, Sol," Lorenzo snaps. "Scarlett, Lash, be ready. The moment that asshole shows his idiot face, kill him."

I look at Tatiana. "When we stop, get into the footwell."

Looking pale and frightened, she only nods, licking dry lips.

"Ready?" Solomon asks the car at large.

"Ready," Lorenzo answers.

"Ready," Scarlett echoes.

"Ready," I say.

Tatiana doesn't answer, just slides down into the footwell and shrinks herself into the smallest ball possible, hands over her head. I glance down at her and she gives me a shaky smile and a thumbs-up.

"Now!" Sol barks.

Lorenzo slams on the brakes; tires squeal and the car lurches and fishtails, swerves, and then momentum goes haywire as we go into a spin. Tires squeal again—not ours, but our pursuer's. I feel our car tip precariously as we come to a stop, nearly toppling over, and then we come to a rocking stop, facing backward.

Silence.

"Not yet," Lorenzo murmurs.

I can't hear past the slam of my pulse in my ears.

"There—he's getting out," Lorenzo says. "Now! Go! Go!"

I shove open my door and kneel in the opening, aiming through the V of the door and the car body. Scarlett does the same. The BMW driver shoves open his door and scrambles out, leveling an assault rifle at us. He doesn't even have time to get off a shot though—Scarlett and I light him up, blasting round after round at him. He jerks and twitches as the bullets smash into him, and his shirt spreads red. He staggers, drops his rifle, and then hits his knees, frowning in confusion. Topples forward and plants face first on the road.

I grin down at Tatiana. "Got him, Lovely One. It is safe to sit up now."

"Lash, you're bleeding!" Tatiana says, panicked.

I touch the side of my face.

She dabs at the side of my face, and I make a *huh, weird* expression when her fingers come away bloody.

"He must have nicked me," I say. "It is nothing."

"You are lucky," she tells me, touching the side of my head near the top of my ear. "Very, very lucky. A hair's breadth more and it would have gone through your brain. "

I pull her into my arms, kissing her forehead. "I am well, Tatiana. Are you hurt?" I touch a few red dots on her face. "You are scratched."

"The glass," she says.

I nod, twirling a finger at her. "Turn your head upside down and shake."

She swiftly unbraids her hair and flips upside down,

shaking her head; when she's done and flips back upright, there's a sprinkling of glass shards on the ground at her feet.

"Do not touch your head until you have washed your hair," I say. "There will still be some tiny pieces against your scalp."

"Here," Scarlett says. "Let me re-braid it for you." She makes quick work of a tight braid, and Tatiana thanks her, gingerly smoothing her hand over her scalp, wincing and yanking her hand away.

Solomon drags the corpse off the shoulder and into the vineyards that line the highway for mile after mile, rifling through the dead man's pockets. He comes up with the key fob for the BMW and another handgun with a pair of spare magazines.

Blood paints the outside of the car, long sprays of it in overlapping Rorschach patterns, but the vehicle is otherwise undamaged.

"Not much we can do about the blood," Solomon says. "But at least this thing won't die on us halfway up the fucking Alps."

Lorenzo shakes his head with a disgusted sigh. "Let's see you find a better vehicle at six o'clock in the morning in a city you do not live in for only a few thousand euros."

Solomon just laughs. "Buddy, I'm not shitting on you. I couldn't have done better. I just do *not* want to push a thirty-five-year-old car across the goddamn Alps."

Lorenzo mutters something under his breath in what I assume is Portuguese, and Solomon responds in the same language.

"I forgot you speak Portuguese," Lorenzo says, finally laughing.

Solomon claps Lorenzo on the shoulder. "Ren,

buddy, we're in a high-stress situation. Tempers flare, we both know that. It's all good. Let's get this shitshow on the road so we can find Lash's contact and get our asses across the pond."

Lorenzo nods, rubbing his face. "You must forgive my temper. I am not a patient man under the best of circumstances, but right now I am exhausted, wounded, and most of all worried about Sophia. I am not myself."

"Like I said, it's all good. Nothing to forgive." Solomon climbs behind the wheel. "I'll drive. You can navigate."

Scarlett slides into the seat behind Solomon, Tatiana takes the middle again, and I'm on the right side. This car is brand new, a top-end 8-series with luxurious leather seats and every amenity.

"I see how it is," Lorenzo jokes. "I drive the shit box, and you drive the Bimmer."

"Yup," Sol says, putting it in gear and nailing the accelerator; the powerful motor sends us rocketing forward, fishtailing wildly before he gets it under control. "Jesus. *This* is what I'm talking about. Ride to Germany in style, motherfuckers."

Scarlett reaches forward and touches Solomon's shoulder. "Are you good to drive?"

He glances back briefly. "I'm good. Why?"

She shrugs, sitting back. "I mean, it's been a bit of a whirlwind. What was it, just a few days ago you were a prisoner in the fucking jungle? And we've been on the run ever since."

Tatiana looks from Solomon to Scarlett with interest. "The jungle?"

And such is how we pass the time on our drive— Solomon and Scarlett relating their wild, hair-raising adventure in the jungles of South America, with occasional input from Lorenzo.

Solomon drives for three hours, and we stop for fuel and food, at which point Scarlett takes the wheel for another stretch. We make another stop to stretch our legs, and then I take the last stretch of driving into Germany; my contact is at the Ramstein Air Force Base.

It's the middle of the night by the time we get to Ramstein; I know my contact lives on base, but whether or not I'm able to get in touch with him is another story.

We approach the gate and are stopped at the guardhouse by an eager young American private. We have no active military ID, no paperwork, and no official business, so getting in to see my contact is going to require some finagling.

I've always been able to find him because I was either stationed there myself or was active military with high enough clearance that I could just drive onto any base in Germany.

It's a different story, these days.

"I need to see Oberstleutnant Nils Weissmann," I say. "Find him, wake him up, and tell him that Leutnant Nicolae Dragos is back from the dead and here to collect. Use exactly those words. Repeat them back to me please, Private Larimer." *LOYT-nahnt.*

He blinks at me "Um."

I put the snap of authority into my voice. "Repeat the message, Private—*now.*"

He blinks, stammers, and then goes to attention. "Find Oberstleutnant Nils Weismann and tell him Leutnant Nicolae Dragos is back from the dead and here to collect. Sir." *OH-burst-LOYT-nahnt.*

"Very good, Private. Get moving—we do not have all night."

He double-times it back into the guardhouse, dials a number, and lets it ring. A transfer, and a second, and then a long wait. I hear him speaking, passing along my message in a mix of English and halting German, and then he hangs up and returns to my window.

"He is on his way, Leutnant Dragos," he says. "You'll have to wait here—I'm not authorized to allow you in, sir."

"I understand," I say, using the imperious tone of dismissal common among officers and noncoms. "That will be all."

The private salutes, I salute back, and then he goes to stand outside the guardhouse at attention.

"What is it you're here to collect?" Solomon asks me.

"An old debt," I answer. "Nils got himself into trouble—gambling and drinking. He was a talented young noncom on a bad downward spiral. For reasons that were never entirely clear to me at the time, I stepped in and helped him get out of debt, helped him quit both drinking and gambling, and he soon got promoted above me. We were in different units—I was in counterintelligence, and he's in transportation and logistics, which is why he will be able to help us. He is, last I knew, a liaison between NATO, the US Air Force, and the German Air Force. He should be able to get us on a flight out of Germany on a C-130 or something."

Fifteen minutes later, an SUV with bright white LED headlights halts on the other side of the gate; the driver's door opens, and a tall, slender figure emerges and strides with confident, military precision toward us.

I recognize Nils' gait as he approaches my side of the BMW.

He leans into my open window. "This is illegal tint, Leutnant Nicolae Dragos." He's a very tall man, almost as tall as Rev, with a shaved head, a short, neat blond beard, and brown eyes.

"It's a...loaner, Oberstleutnant Weismann," I answer.

He grins, tapping the insignia on his uniform. "It is Hauptmann, now, as a matter of fact." *HOWPT-mahn.*

"Ooh, very fancy," I say. "Hopefully that shiny metal on your collar means you can help me and my friends."

Nils peers into the car, assessing my companions. "I can help, but you'll have to tell me the truth, Nicolae," he says in German. "What do you need, and why is it so important that you show up here in the middle of the night, especially after disappearing the way you did?"

"Let us in, give us somewhere to rest, and I'll explain everything," I tell him. "But you know damned well I wouldn't be here like this if it wasn't important."

Nils nods. "Very well," he says, switching back to English. "It is good to see you, Nicolae."

I shake his hand. "Truly, Nils, it is good to see you, too."

He waves at Private Larimer. "Let them in, please, Private." He turns to me. "Follow me. You can stay with me for now."

A few minutes later, we're parking outside the DRC and following Nils inside. At this hour, all is still and quiet. His quarters are small and spartan.

"It's this or pay for lodging," he explains. "But I assume you're contacting me because you need to get out of the country undetected, and I've got a flight leaving tomorrow. Once I know more about your situation, I can arrange logistics for you."

We find seats wherever we can, which mainly means the floor, although Nils insists Scarlett and Tatiana take seats on the bed.

Once again, we find ourselves relating the events of the past few days—I know Nils well and I trust him, so I explain the situation with Roberto Pugli, and thus our need to get to Brazil quickly and off-book.

Once the whole convoluted, multi-faceted story has been related, Nils spends a few minutes thinking. "Quite a situation you've gotten yourself into, Nicolae. My girlfriend is a senior intelligence officer. Obviously, there's much she cannot share, but I do know she has been investigating reports of a corrupt official within Interpol—that's all I know, but it is likely the same person."

"I have evidence, Nils." I look down, struggling with my emotions. "After...what happened, what he did, I...I took the warning. I let him think he'd destroyed all the evidence I had against him—and I *did* give him all my original copies. But I am no fool—I have backups hidden. But I lost my appetite for justice. I was so..." I let out a shuddering breath, and Tatiana rubs my back, "so broken that I just didn't care anymore. But now, I care. Get me in touch with your girlfriend, Nils. If she is investigating Roberto, then my evidence could be vital."

He nods. "I will tomorrow. Now that you've gotten me up, I might as well get to work putting together your trip to Brazil. I assume Manaus will be acceptable?"

"Of course, my friend. Wherever you can get us. We are all rather resourceful."

"Well then, I'll get to work," he says. "Please, however,

stay here. I cannot have you five wandering the base. You know this."

"We have been traveling for a very long time, Nils. We are ready to rest. We drove straight through from Ancona."

"What is that, twelve hours?"

"More, with stops."

He pushes on his knees to stand up. "I'll let you rest, then. I'll come back for you in a few hours, get you some food, and go from there."

I stand up and embrace him. "I cannot thank you enough, Nils."

He grins, slapping me on the back. "Nico, my friend, you saved my life and my career. I will be in your debt forever. This is just a down payment."

"You've made good on it, Nils. I am proud of you."

He ducks his head, grinning, and then bids us all goodbye and heads out.

Within minutes, we are all asleep, crashed out on the floor and bed and wherever we can stretch out. So tired are we that even the floor feels comfortable.

———— ◆ ————

Nils' girlfriend is several years older than him and of a higher rank—she's attractive, a short woman with dark brown hair and pale blue eyes and a no-nonsense demeanor. Nils introduces us, explains to Major Lisel Neufeld my connection to and experience with Pugli.

She scrutinizes me and then nods; we're in a conference interview room somewhere in the bowels of an administrative building. "Your evidence," she asks. "What is it?"

"Footage of interviews with eyewitnesses, documents showing the paper trail connecting Pugli to payments, bribes of government officials, and an audio recording of Pugli himself giving an order for the assassination an upper level admin at an American embassy—the individual in question had stumbled across Pugli's interference in some kind of operation that would have exposed him."

"The unsolved murder of Jeffery McCann," she guesses. "You have evidence of this?"

"And much else besides."

She frowns at me. "And you have been sitting on this for this long?"

I glare at her. "He burned my family alive in front of me, Major Neufeld. What would you have done?"

She sighs. "I cannot say—who could guess how they would react to such trauma?" She taps the table with a pen. "You have access to this trove of evidence?"

"I can tell you how to. It is in a storage locker in a train station in Berlin." I give her instructions on how to retrieve the evidence. "All I ask is that you make damned sure that monster is brought to justice. You have to be *absolutely* certain your case is airtight, Major Neufeld. If it isn't he will weasel his way out of it, and if that happens, you and everyone you care about will be dead within seventy-two hours."

She nods, seeming unfazed by my warning. "Believe me, I am well acquainted with how Pugli does business, Mr. Dragos." She rises and we shake hands. "If the evidence is what you claim, it should be the nail in the coffin for Mr. Pugli. I am only one member of a multi-country, multi-agency task force investigating his operation. We have enough evidence as it is to put him away, but we have been looking for that one thing to make sure there is no possibility of error or escape."

"Well then, my evidence should be that," I say. "And I can guarantee you, all of it will be admissible. I made sure of it."

———— ◆ ————

Nils arrives at the god-sized hangar in his personal SUV a few minutes after the rest of us, his uniform crisp and perfectly creased.

I shake hands with him, and then I gesture at the huge aircraft. "So. All is arranged?"

He nods. "Yes. You will land in Manaus, and the next day, a helo will take you wherever you need to go. You will make one stop en route."

I arch an eyebrow at him. "Oh?"

"I have a contact just outside Manaus. He is not always on the right side of the law, but he is a good man. He will provide you and your friends with weapons. I cannot supply personnel—that would attract attention I do not think you want, but I can provide transportation and weapons." He claps me on the back. "I owe you, Nicolae. My life and my career, I owe you."

I return the back-slap. "We are even now, Nils."

A snort. "No, my friend. We will never be even. But this is a start."

I shrug. "If you say so. I am grateful. My friends are grateful."

He embraces me. "I'll go over things with the pilots once more, and then I have a meeting to get to." He hesitates. "It's good to see you back among the living."

I return his embrace. "It is good to be back. Take care of yourself. Visit me in Las Vegas."

"How will I contact you?" he asks.

"I will get word to you."

He nods, waves, and goes to speak to the pilots.

Thirty minutes later, we're strapped into jump seats of a C-130J headed across the Atlantic. It's another long, boring, uneventful leg in our crazed trip across the globe. The C-130 takes us to Manaus, Brazil. We're bleary-eyed, jet-lagged, and disoriented. Only a few days ago—how many? I can't remember—I was on a jet leaving Las Vegas. Since then, I've been to Zagreb, taken a train to Split, a ferry across the Adriatic, drove to Germany, and now flown back across the Atlantic to Brazil; Solomon, Scarlett, and Lorenzo's adventure has been similarly complex, so by the time the C-130 touches down at the AFB in Manaus, we're nearly zombies. Nils' arrangements include off-base lodging under some very thin fake identities for all of us, but a little palm-greasing of the right people and judicious use of Lorenzo's contacts in the Brazilian military gets us to our rooms without issue.

Scarlett and Solomon have one room, Lorenzo another, and Tatiana and I have our own.

Which means we are alone together at long last.

My exhaustion burns away the moment Tatiana shuts the door, and the look in her eyes tells me everything I need to know about her state of mind.

CHAPTER 10

RELEASE

TATIANA

SILENCE REIGNS FOR A LONG, FRAUGHT MOMENT. Standing with his back against the hotel room door, Lash's dark eyes are fixed on mine

"Are you tired, Lovely One?" he asks, slipping the do-not-disturb sign on the outside of the door, sets the chain lock, and then stops in front of me.

"Yes," I admit. "But I couldn't sleep now if I tried."

He prowls closer to me, a faint smile curving the corners of his lips. "I know the feeling."

Desire burns in my belly, but other sensations clamor just as loudly, if not louder. "Lash, I—"

He takes my hands in his and walks backward, pulling me after him—to my surprise, we pass by the bed and make for the bathroom.

"I know what you need, Tatiana," he says. "A long, hot shower."

I groan at the thought. "That sounds like the best idea ever."

He grins. "You only have to decide one thing."

"And that would be what?" I ask.

"Do you want to shower alone, or would you care for company?"

"I wouldn't mind company," I murmur, feeling excited and shy and eager and hesitant all at once.

"I was hoping you'd say that." He takes my arms in his big, hard, strong hands. "Let me take care of you, Tatiana."

I lean my forehead against his chest. "Okay."

"Come." He tugs me by the hands to the bathroom. "Just relax, now. I will see to everything."

"What about you?" I ask.

He smiles. "I haven't forgotten what we talked about. But Solomon and I, and the others, we are professionals. We are used to this—long hours without sleep, endless travel, boredom on long flights, crossing time zones. You aren't. Let me take care of you for now. There will be time for everything else later. We meet with the others at noon tomorrow."

I nod, my eyes burning, even though I also feel oddly wired. "I feel a little delirious."

"That is to be expected, after all the thousands of miles we have traveled in the last few days, especially considering all the stress and adrenaline." He brushes a thumb over my cheek. "Just let me care for you."

I nod, sighing. "Okay."

He helps me slip out of the ferry logo jacket—the hat I discarded in the junker car the moment I sat down; I hate wearing hats. Next, he kneels and unties my boots, loosens the laces, and helps me out of my boots and socks. My heart pounds with increasing vigor as he stands up and reaches for my shirt, I lift my arms over my head. He peels my shirt off, tosses it aside. Unzips my jeans, frees the button. Tugs them down, crouching to lift one foot and then the other to tug the legs free. Now I am shivering in front of him in a rather unsexy pair of black briefs and a white sports bra, goosebumps pebbling my skin, nipples hard, breath coming in short, nervous pants.

He twists the shower on and turns it to hot, and within seconds the stream is steaming.

He rubs my arms. "Cold?"

I nod.

He searches my face. "Nervous?"

I shrug, hesitate, and then nod. "I don't know why."

"There's nothing to be nervous about, sweet, beautiful, courageous Tatiana Juric. It's just you and me. Whatever you feel comfortable with and no more." His voice is gentle, his touch soft as he rubs my arms.

"I'm not nervous as in scared," I say, taking his hands in mine. "More nervous just because we're finally alone. Not nervous, I suppose, just...nerves."

Steam swirls in the small bathroom despite the drone of the vent fan. Lash slides his hands down my arms one more time, and then to my waist. Hesitates at my back, below my bra strap. His eyes meet mine, seeking my consent. My answer is to lift my arms—my breath catches as he peels the undergarment off, and my breasts ache, heavy and turgid, my nipples erect and sensitive.

He kneels in front of me, pressing kisses to my belly, my diaphragm. His hands caress over my bottom and then hook in the elastic at my waist. His beard is ticklish, and soft and scratchy at the same time. I cup his face as he slides my underwear off, leaving me naked and shivering and breathless.

"So fucking beautiful," he murmurs, almost to himself. He curses so rarely that it's almost shocking to hear it.

"You don't curse very often," I say.

He shrugs, sitting on his heels as he gazes at me, taking in my curves, my bare flesh, his hands raking up my belly to cup my breasts. "No, I do not."

"Why?"

A shrug. "Habit?" A frown. "It is more than that, I guess. My parents were devout Roman Orthodox Christians. They never cursed and were adamantly against me cursing. I suppose I choose not to curse as a way of honoring them, even all these years later."

"It's a simple but beautiful way of remembering them, Lash."

He smiles, standing up. "You are shivering. Get in, get warm."

"Not without you," I say. "I am not so tired that I don't want my turn."

"Your turn?" he asks, smirking.

"Yes, my turn. You've seen me in varying stages of nudity already, and I have barely gotten to see you shirtless. It's my turn."

He holds his arms out to the sides. "I am yours to command and control, in that case."

"Command and control, is it?" I say, feeling the rippling of desire surging through my body, searing away the exhaustion—temporarily, at least.

His only answer is to wait silently for me to decide what I want to do.

Shirt first, obviously. And my god, the man is ripped. Smooth brown skin wrinkled and rippled with scars telling the story of a lifetime of violence, and the heavy, lithe muscles of a trained predator. Anvil-slab pecs, brawny arms, thick, veined forearms, shredded abs. My mouth goes dry at the sight of him, all the moisture in my body traveling south.

He kicks off his boots and socks, and then I open his black jeans, lowering the zipper. The organ I had such a woefully brief encounter with springs into the V of the opening, pressing against the fabric of his underwear. I help him out of his jeans; such is my impatience to see all of his glorious body nude that I can't wait for him to toe off his jeans before I shove his black boxer briefs past his hips.

The cock that is revealed leaves my sex aching with anticipation—it's the most beautiful thing I've ever seen. Long, thick, and straight, straining, veins standing out…

"Lash, my god," I whisper. "you're incredible."

He seems uncomfortable with my praise, only shrugging in response. "Tatiana, I—"

I step into the shower, hissing as the scalding water streaks onto my shoulders—I adjust it to a temperature living creatures can withstand. Once it's piping hot but tolerable, I move under the spray and pull Lash in after me. He closes the curtain, and now the world shrinks down to just the two of us, the stream of hot water, and our naked bodies.

Nerves, fear, exhaustion, everything fades. All that matters is him.

Greed for his body surges through me; I twist so he's under the stream, freeing his hair from the ponytail and then running my hands over his shoulders and down his pecs.

"Tatiana," he murmurs. "I am supposed to be taking care of you."

"You are," I answer, letting my hands slide down his waist to cup the hard bubble of his ass. "This is what I need. Giving me what I want *is* letting you take care of me."

He snorts. "That's not exactly what I meant."

I shrug. "I know what you meant. And that will happen. Eventually."

"Eventually?" He echoes, making it a question.

"Eventually." I step closer, so the tips of my breasts brush his chest, and I loosely clutch his cock in both hands. "I have other plans first."

He throws his head back at my touch, groaning. "Tatiana, fuck."

"Talk to me, Lash."

He hisses when I stroke his length. "I...It has been a very long time since I was with anyone."

"You've been celibate ever since...then?" I ask.

"Yes." There's a whole world of emotion in that one word.

"That's okay," I tell him, leaning into him to steal a kiss. "I'll use your own words, Lash—just relax and let me take care of you."

"How did the tables get turned?" he asks.

"I told you—giving me what I want *is* taking care of me. I enjoy being taken care of, Lash. I like letting you meet my needs. But I have other needs, and right now those are front and center."

"It is hard for me to be selfish," he says.

"Then don't think of it as being selfish," I respond, stroking him again. "Think of it as...as giving through receiving."

"That feels a bit convoluted." He opens his eyes and watches my hand slide down his length. "God, Tatiana. The way you touch me."

"What about it?" I ask, using a hand-over-hand stroke to make him dip at the knees, groaning.

"It feels so good." He grunts, then, bucking into my hand. "*Too* good."

"No such thing as too good," I tell him. "Just enjoy it. You said you were mine to command and control? Well, this is what I want. I want to touch you, Lash. I want to feel your body. I want to watch you lose control. I want to make you feel so good you forget everything."

He dips at the knees as I slowly caress his length, now one hand and then two, now pumping and then twisting at the top. "Tatiana, fuck. I...god. Oh—god."

"What, Lash? Tell me what you're thinking."

"It feels so good I almost feel guilty."

I touch my forehead to his, whispering. "Lash, you're allowed this. It's okay to want it. It's okay to let yourself have it. It's okay to let yourself have *me*."

"I've denied myself emotional peace and physical pleasure for so long, it's hard to remember how to feel otherwise."

"You start by trusting me."

He trembles. "Tatiana..."

"Call me Tati."

His breath comes in short, gasping pants. "Tati...I... oh—Tati, I can't—"

"Feel it, Lash. Enjoy it. Let go. Give me you. All of you." I nibble at his earlobe, breathing the words in his ear. "Let go for me, Lash. Just let go."

He sags backward, and I turn us so his back is to the wall, the spray hitting my back and bottom as I press him against the wall of the shower. He pulses in my hands, and his hips push into my touch—he's close.

"Tati—Tatiana...oh god."

I nip his lower lip, and he turns his face to mine and then we're kissing, and he demands my tongue and thrusts into my hand.

Fuck, I want him inside me, but I know it's been so

long he won't last much longer; besides, I'm not on birth control, and the condoms are in my bag back in the bedroom. He needs this first release now, with no expectations, no pressure to perform.

Just pure pleasure.

A reminder that it's okay to want—to have.

He groans, and the groan turns to a growl, and he thrusts into my fist.

Almost.

"Come for me, Lash," I whisper in his ear. "Show me. Let go."

I feel his knees buckle, and his hands wrap around my ass and dig in hard, gripping me as he reaches his climax. He's grunting through gritted teeth, driving into my fist.

"Oh god, Tatiana—" he gasps. "I'm coming—I'm coming. Oh god, Tatiana…Tati…"

He spurts a thick, hard stream of cum over my hands as I stroke his thick, pulsing length with both hands; another stream jets out of him, this one splashing onto my belly and his.

I drop to my knees and the shower stream beats hot on my back and shoulders. I rake my fingernails down his chest and wrap my lips around his cock, and he shouts in shocked ecstasy as his next spurt sluices into my mouth and down my throat—I take as much of him as I can, and he groans, growls, his hands clutching the back of my head.

I moan at the taste of him, running one hand up his torso, relishing the hard furrow of his abs and the powerful solidity of his chest. My other hand wraps around his base and I pump him hard and fast, and he sags, dipping at the knees as he unleashes another hot salty stream of cum.

I let him pop free of my mouth, rise to my feet, and

stroke him, nipping and nibbling kisses to the corner of his mouth. He huffs gruffly, nearly collapsing as his knees try to give out.

When I can milk no more of his release from his slowly slackening length, I let him go and turn him beneath the shower stream.

He tilts his face up the water, eyes closed, luxuriating in the heat, a contented, sated smile on his face.

He allows himself that for a moment or two, and then his eyes snap open, and a hungry grin blossoms on his features. "My god, Tatiana," he whispers, awe in his tone. "That was…"

"Just the beginning," I finish.

"Indeed. Just the beginning. Now, my sexy, beautiful Tatiana, now it is *my* turn."

And again, he surprises me. His strong, clever fingers do not find my tender, sensitive flesh, his mouth does not find my aching nipples.

No, instead, with exquisite tenderness, he washes me. He frees my hair of the braid, tips my head back, and rinses my hair, using the detachable wand to thoroughly rinse any stray glass shards from my scalp. After carefully running fingertips over my scalp to ensure the glass is gone, he shampoos my hair, kneading and massaging my scalp, lathering the thick glossy length of my black hair. He rinses it, works conditioner into it, and then gently but thoroughly scrubs my body with the bar of soap. He takes his time, not just lathering me with the soap, but using it as an opportunity to learn and caress my body, to memorize my curves.

In some ways, this is more intimate than sex.

I soak in the hot stream and close my eyes, giving myself over utterly to the worshipful way Lash's strong, callused, gentle hands carve over my curves. They cup and weigh and squeeze my breasts; roll and pinch and twist my nipples until I gasp; they grip and knead and pet my ass; they slip down my thighs and palm over my calves and scrape up my hipbones. He massages my back and shoulders, slides soapy hands with slow, reverent affection up my belly and over my breasts again, hungry, greedy eyes roaming, devouring.

"Lash..." I whisper. "I need you." I grip his beard and tilt his face to mine, moving my lips on his as I murmur. "Please."

He uses the wand to rinse me off and shuts off the water. He steps out, opens a towel, and I step into it. Wrapping it around me, he dabs, scrubs, and pats me dry, all while dripping wet himself.

Brusquely drying himself, he drapes the towel on the edge of the tub and turns to me.

He takes the towel from me, tosses it aside; I shiver, but not from cold—I'm flushed with anticipation, shaking with barely restrained desperation for Lash.

He scoops me up and carries me into the bedroom, places me on the bed, and crawls up after me. His hair is long and black and glossy and damp; his skin is flushed with desire; his eyes dance and glint with arousal. He hovers over me, and his mouth finds mine. I gasp into the kiss, and then cup the back of his head and mewl softly when his tongue carves through my mouth and dances with mine.

"Lash," I whisper again, saying his name as a prayer, as a plea.

He kisses my chin. My throat. My breastbone, and the tender path between my breasts, and then my belly.

"Oh god, please," I whisper, letting my hands rest on his damp head, guiding him to where I so badly want him.

He gives me what I want, the soft friction of his beard against the tender silk of my inner thighs delicious and heady, his tongue hot and clever against my clit. I moan and whimper, bucking my hips to ride his mouth, and his powerful hands drive up my thighs and cover my breasts. Climax rises inside me, a hurricane of sensation centered on my core, and I cling to Lash as it builds and builds. He seems to know my body as if it were created especially for him, slowing his touch when I need a break, renewing his fervor and speed to bring me back to the edge, slipping two curling, questing fingers inside me when I need that touch, need something inside me.

"Lash!" I cry, as orgasm swells and rocks through me. "Oh god, oh god, Lash!"

He guides me through it, tongue swirling and probing, fingers driving and sweeping. I come and I come, riding a wave of climax that leaves me screaming and shaking, weeping and trembling.

My purse is on the bedside table—when he finally allows me to quake down from the peak of climax, I grab it and rummage blindly in it until I find the string of condoms. I rip one free, tear it open with my teeth.

Plucking the ring of latex from the package, I grip his erection and caress him until he groans and his hips begin to buck. I roll the condom onto his thick length and then pull him toward me.

"Come here," I murmur, "make love to me."

He twists, his hard, muscular, broad body levering over me. I open my thighs for him, curling my legs around his ass and pulling him close. Reach between our bodies and find his hardness waiting for me. He braces his hands beside my face, long black hair a shampoo-scented curtain. His dark eyes blaze with emotion, searching me.

I fit him to my entrance, and my mouth drops open, quivering as he spreads my sex apart with his thick cock. "Lash," I whisper. "God, yes."

Raw emotion ravages his face, and I don't need him to explain what he's feeling—he wears it openly for me, letting me see everything: need and desire, desperation and hunger, fear and nervousness, sadness, even; love.

"Tati," he breathes. "Tatiana."

I meet his gaze and let the pure joy I feel wash over my expression. "Lash."

His eyes shimmer. "Nicolae," he whispers. "I think perhaps Lash can return to the shadows whence he came."

"Nicolae," I say, rolling my hips in small circles with him notched just barely inside me.

"Nico," he breathes, eyes squeezing shut, a tear slipping down one cheek, disappearing into his beard. "Let me be your Nico."

He is laying his ghosts to rest. Burying the past. Stepping into the future.

I tilt my hips, taking him fully inside me. "Nico," I whimper, my own eyes shining wet and locked on his. "Nico. My Nico."

He groans, burying his face between my breasts. I hold onto his head and meet his thrusts, and our bodies move together in a union of joy and ecstasy. His thrusts grow faster and harder, and I cry out each time he drives home inside me, and I clutch at his ass with my legs, holding onto his head with both hands as he arches and bows his spine with each ravaging thrust. He lengthens above me, and my legs fall apart and I draw my heels up against my ass and accept with eager panting cries the hard, fast, driving wonder of his cock as it fills me, withdraws, fills, withdraws.

"Tati," he growls. "Come with me."

I fit my fingers to my clit and circle, and my cries grow desperate. "Nico! I'm going to come, Nicolae. I'm going to—right now."

"Tati," he gasps. "Tatiana, oh god, oh god, Tatiana!"

I feel him release inside me, his thrusts wild and rough, and I come through it, weeping and whimpering and wailing as wave after wave of orgasm washes over me, slashes through me. My hips tip and tilt, drive and circle as I come, desperately thrusting against him.

Slowly, we drift down the other side together, panting and sweating. Lash—Nicolae—gives me his weight, resting his face against my breasts as I roam his shoulders and back with my hands.

"Nico," I breathe.

"Tati…" He whispers, his voice shaking and fraught. "Tatiana, I…" I hear throat-shredding raspy hoarse agony in his voice. Wonder. Embarrassment.

I push at his heavy shoulder, and he rolls to his back, turns his face away from me. I lean over him and kiss his cheek. He doesn't respond, but his shoulders lift and fall, and then shake.

"Lash—Nicolae. Look at me, please." I cup his cheek, the one pressed into the pillow away from me.

He growls, gruff and harsh, a ragged negative. "A moment."

"No. No." I straddle him and crush my body against

him, take his face in my hands and force him to look at me. "Nico. It's *okay*. You can trust me with this, too."

"I am unmanned, Lovely One." His voice is so ragged it hurts my heart to hear, shredded as if he swallowed razor blades.

"No, my darling." I don't know where the term of endearment came from—I am not one to use such terms. "You are a man, and men feel things. Men have emotions—strong ones. Feeling them and letting others see them is not weakness. It is not unmanly."

"I do not know why I am..." he shakes his head, unable to even say the word.

"Crying, Nico. You are crying, and it is okay." I turn his face to mine. Kiss his cheeks, and taste salt. "It is okay. Do you really think I would reject you for crying? That I would stop being attracted to you? Do you think me so weak and shallow that a strong man showing emotion after such beautiful vulnerability would turn me off?"

Slowly, he turns his face to mine, wet eyes cracking open as he fights for breath, for calm. "No—no. But, I..." he shakes his head, sighing. "I don't know."

"Talk to me, Nicolae." I sit on his belly and hips, the slimy cold wetness of the condom against my buttock—I barely notice and care even less. "Tell me why you weep."

"Catharsis," he says, using the Croatian word rather than English—I don't think I would have known what the English word meant. "I...it's also sadness."

I wipe at his cheeks with my palms. Kiss them. Kiss his eyes, softly, delicately. "Tell me," I whisper.

"I...I have clung to Ileana's ghost for so long. Clung to the grief. The anger. Thoughts and dreams and plans for revenge. I vowed I would not cut my hair or beard until

Roberto Pugli was dead by my hand. But you…" He sits up on the bed and now I am sitting on his thighs, facing him; he caresses my shoulders, my cheeks, and brushes my damp hair away from my cheeks. "You changed everything. Changed me. Has it even been a week? I don't know—time has distorted since I woke up in that Zagreb Hangar. I thought I would be lost without revenge to drive me, but I…letting Major Neufeld take the case and bring him to justice according to the courts of law rather than the law of the sword…I feel free."

I swallow hard. "I have said before that I was worried you would feel I was taking something away from you."

"You did. I was holding onto an anchor chain, and the anchor was hurtling to the bottom of the sea, taking me with it. You pried my fingers from it and showed me the surface. Helped me swim upward. And now I can breathe. Now I can see the light." He cups my face in both hands. "Tati, I…" a shake of his head, his eyes watering again. "I have also had to let go of Ileana. Of Leander and Leonora. I have not been living—I have been wandering the earth as a half-ghost, one foot in the grave with them, waiting for the chance to kill Pugli and join them in Heaven."

"Oh, Nico," I whisper, a tear slipping down my cheek.

He catches it with his thumb. "No, Lovely One. Do not weep. They are not gone—they wait for me in Heaven, or wherever and whatever comes after this life. They…" He touches a closed fist to his chest. "They live on with me. I remember them. I love them. But I…my Ileana would want me to live. She was jealous of my love while she was alive. If I spoke to a beautiful woman, she would be jealous, even though she knew I was loyal to her and in love with her. But you asked me what she would say if she could give me a message from the grave, and I know now what she would say. She would tell me to choose life. To choose love."

I can only shake my head and let tears fall. "I don't want to be selfish, Nico. But I am. I want you to love me."

"I do." He says it simply, with a shrug, clear-eyed and confident. "She would want me to love you. To let you love me. To be happy. To find joy again. To find pleasure." He exhales through pursed lips. "That is part of why I was crying. I felt guilty for a moment because it felt so good—*too* good. I have denied myself that connection with other humans since she died. Hugs. Hand holding. Sex. All of it. And then with you, it…we…" he swallows hard, shakes his head. "I let myself have you, let myself feel what I feel for you, and…" he trails off.

"You can tell me anything, Nico. Even if it is hard or uncomfortable."

He nods. "I know. You are strong and brave." He smiles at me, but it fades quickly, becoming an emotional, thoughtful, complicated expression. "I was young when I met Ileana. We were young and passionate. Our relationship was… very physical. I had other lovers or partners before her, but not many, and they weren't very good. With Ileana, it was magical. And I think that when she died, it was a very large factor in why I clung to grief for so long, why I refused to allow myself to even wonder what could be…" he pauses, sighs, and continues. "Was fear. Fear that…"

He can't seem to finish.

"That no one and nothing would ever compare to what you had with her," I finish, guessing at the rest.

He nods. "Precisely. How could it? How could anyone understand me the way she did? How could I ever feel such magical ecstasy with anyone else? How could I ever love anyone else? It seemed impossible, and futile to even wonder, to even try. It seemed too painful to even consider. I refused to entertain the possibility."

"But?" I prompted.

"But then you came along. You opened my eyes to possibilities. The ghosts of my past do not threaten you. I can show you my grief and it does not turn you off or overwhelm you. You softened my heart and breathed life into me. And now…" he rests his hands on my thighs, and then cups my bottom, and his eyes rake over my breasts on their way to piercing me, searing me. "You have shown me that I can feel that magic again. I wept because it was such a relief. I also wept with guilt, because it was…the pleasure I felt with you was as great as I remember. You are you, not her, and it is different with you in ways I cannot put into words. I just…I felt guilty for feeling such pleasure. It felt like a betrayal, almost. That I could move on. That I could find love. That I could feel such incredible pleasure with someone else."

"That is understandable," I say. "You are allowed to feel anything you feel, Nicolae, and I just…I suppose I hope you will share those feelings with me, whatever they are—good, bad, scary, exciting, complicated…everything."

He cups my breasts and lets them fall. Thumbs my nipples until they ache and I gasp. "I will, Tatiana. I will share myself with you."

I sigh, eyes closing at the pleasure of his touch. "Oh, Nico. Nico." I open my eyes and look deep into his. "Is it crazy? That I could love you already?"

He shakes his head. "I will not always talk about her this much, but…when I met Ileana, I knew I would love her. And I did. I knew I was in love with her within a few days of meeting her. I waited to say so for an embarrassingly long time because I did not know if she felt the same way. I told you, she took a while to come around to accepting me, and even longer to accept her feelings for me. But I knew." He touches my mouth, tracing the bow of my lips. "I only say this so you know that I believe you *can* love someone right away. The heart is a mystery, Tatiana. But that is my experience."

I close my eyes, sighing as he caresses my breasts, thighs, buttocks, face, arms—everywhere. "I want you again, already, Nico."

His lips touch my chin. My mouth—I tilt my face to turn the touch into a kiss. "Aren't you tired?" he murmurs.

"Bone-tired. But I won't be able to sleep until I am sated."

"And what will sate you, Lovely One?"

I grin, shrugging. "I don't know. Right now, the way I feel? Nothing. I need you, Nico. I fucking need you so bad it feels like madness."

"Then let me clean up and come back to you, and we will see what we can do about curing your madness."

I sling my leg away, slipping off of him. "Let me do it."

I strip the condom off him and take it to the bathroom, wrap it in toilet paper, and discard it. Wetting a washcloth with warm water and squeezing it out, I bring it to the bed and clean his cock. I toss the wet cloth into the tub, and by the time I return, he has fallen asleep.

I laugh to myself, and curl up on him, nestling against his chest. He curls an arm around me instinctively. I bring the blankets over us, and despite my claim from a moment ago, I fall asleep.

CHAPTER 11

A LIGHTNESS OF BEING

LASH

I WAKE WITH THE DAWN OUT OF LONG HABIT.

For the first time since Roberto Pugli's merciless, evil eyes bored into mine as he threw the match, I wake with a lightness in my soul; a lightness, as in the absence of weight; a lightness, as in the presence of light.

The light of attention, affection, and love finally illuminated the shadows which have haunted the vacant, echoing spaces where my heart should be.

I linger in bed, caught in the drowsy quasi-wakefulness that comes after a restful night's sleep. And I realize, only as I drift toward full wakefulness, that I have not truly rested since the death of my family either.

I open my eyes—gray dawn light filters through the gapped curtains; the hotel room is a carbon copy of every middling quality hotel room in every developed country in the world—ugly thin beige carpet, ugly sheer drapes, and ugly white scratchy bedding, an aging TV, and a sad little Keurig coffee machine.

I roll to my side. Tatiana is still sound asleep, her slender form turned away, the blanket draped over her hips and tucked under her arm. She lets out a little snort, a sigh, a pause, and then a deep breath sucked in fast and let out slowly.

My hands twitch, longing to caress her tender skin and soft curves, to know the pleasure of her touch again, but I know she needs her sleep. I slip out of bed, dress, and steal silently out of the room in search of real coffee, and perhaps something to bring back for breakfast. I take the elevator down to the first floor. The doors slide open; on the wall opposite the elevators is a large mirror, in which I see my reflection.

I do not recognize myself.

It's a moment of disorientation—a mini existential crisis. Who am I? Without the haunting horror of what happened, without the driving rage of revenge, who am I?

Lash no longer.

He was a creation born out of sorrow—a vow of revenge, a new name, a burial of everything I was with my family; a vow, too, to not cut my hair or beard until Roberto was dead.

The man in the mirror is…Lash.

My hair is past my shoulders, nearly to mid-back, thick and glossy black, albeit with a strand or two of silver at the temples. My beard is that of a wizard, long and thick and bushy, tapering to a point at mid-chest.

Who am I?

Who do I want to be?

I am free of my rage—Roberto Pugli has had a vise grip on me for so many years, and by letting go of the drive to kill him myself, I am free of his control over me.

I am free of the ghosts of my past. My beloved Ileana is at rest. My sweet, innocent baby son and daughter are resting with their mother. I will always miss them. Always grieve them. But I cannot live in thrall to their wandering spirits any longer.

I must find a new way forward.

With Tatiana.

As Nicolae.

Nicolae Dragos was vain. He visited the barber twice a month, kept his hair short and neat, and his beard closely trimmed. This vagabond wizard look no longer suits me, I think.

Time to make one last symbolic gesture of release—cutting away all that remains of Lash.

So, I get a cab to a nearby store and buy a grooming kit—clippers, scissors, and a comb, as well as some beard oil and hair pomade. Back to the hotel, where I find a decent continental breakfast on offer; I prepare two coffees and two bagels liberally smeared with cream cheese, and bring everything upstairs.

It's a tricky juggling act getting the door open with everything in my hands, but I manage it. Once inside, I discover Tatiana is still asleep—she must be very tired or a heavy sleeper, for I wasn't exactly sneaky on the way in.

Funnily enough, it's when I sit on the edge of the bed to remove my boots that she wakes up. She rolls over to her back, blinks blearily at me, smiles softly, sweetly, and then stretches prodigiously, yawning and shuddering. The blanket slips off, leaving her naked body bare.

I growl in wordless appreciation. "Beautiful Tati. So damned beautiful."

She smiles again and crawls across the bed to lay her head in my lap and gaze up at me. "Where'd you go?" She sniffs the air. "Coffee?"

I chuckle. "Yes. Coffee, and a bagel."

She rubs my crotch. "You're the best."

"It's only coffee."

She shakes her head. "No, Nico. It's the simple gesture that you went and got coffee and a bagel for me."

"It's nothing," I insist. "Just coffee and a bagel from the lobby."

She rests her head on my thigh, smiling lazily and lasciviously at me. "Just let me be grateful, will you?"

"Very well, then," I say, snorting a laugh. "You are most welcome, you sexy, naked, wonderful woman, you."

"Sexy, naked, *and* wonderful? All at once?" Her fingers drift up my thigh to the closure of my jeans, flipping it open and tugging down the zipper.

"Those are just the descriptors that came to mind first. I could fill an ocean with words to describe you. I am fluent in several languages, and passable in several more."

She tugs at my jeans—more of a gesture than a real attempt to pull them off. I lift up and slide my jeans and underwear off, and then rip off my shirt.

"My god, you're so fucking hot," she whispers, almost to herself. To me, then. "I'm listening."

"Beautiful," I say in English, and then start listing descriptors in every language I know. "Sexy. Alluring. Intelligent." More English. "Talented. Hardworking. Wise." Croatian. "Arousing. Tantalizing. Bold." Romani.

She gathers my cock in her hands, gazing up at me as she strokes me to aching arousal.

"Sensual. Strong. Resilient." Italian. "Bold. Powerful. Insightful." German. "Creative. Driven. Compassionate." Russian.

"I only know Croatian and English," she murmurs,

"but I like hearing you say sweet things to me, no matter the language."

She licks her lips, eyes glinting and aroused, and then takes my cock in her mouth and drives down, and a groan escapes me. I let her back away, suckling around my glans greedily for a moment, and then slide her lips back down around me. When I feel arousal surge and boil in my balls, I gently guide her away.

"Tati," I whisper, "I need to be inside you."

She sits up, breasts swaying, hair loose and wild, eyes shining with need. "Then take me, my Nico."

My Nico.

It stings for a moment, hearing that phrase again. But then the sting morphs and becomes pain—the kind of pain that comes after a good workout, an ache that tells you you're alive. And then the pain morphs once more and becomes…joy.

Relief.

Love.

"Say that again," I say, stretching across the bed to snag a condom. I open it and roll the condom on.

Sitting up with my feet on the floor, I reach for her. Tatiana slides a leg over my hips, gliding astride me in a smooth, lithe, sensual movement. She tosses her long black hair over one shoulder and sits up on her knees, reaching between us to grasp my cock, notches me at her entrance and lets go.

"Take me, my Nico."

My eyes burn and water. "Again. Just—just the last part."

Understanding floods her features. "My Nico."

I surge upward, gripping her hips and pulling her

down onto me. I cry out with a loud, rough bark of ecstasy as her tight hot wet pussy swallows me whole, takes me home. "Tati!" I rasp. "My Tatiana."

She sinks onto me until her ass smashes flat against my hips and thighs, and I ache from being so deep. "Nico— my Nico. Mine."

"I never thought to hear that again," I whisper.

She wraps her arms around my neck and presses her lips to my ear. "Does it hurt?"

I shake my head. "A little, at first." I pull away, brush her wild loose hair out of her face. "It's yours, now. *I* am yours, now."

She writhes on me, driving her hips back and forth, rocking my cock inside her until I growl with the unutterable intensity of it. "My Nico." She nips my earlobe. "I love you, Nico."

Wonder floods me, and I thrust up into her, hard, while crushing her down. Ecstasy and love war within me, fighting for my breath, stealing my words. I wrap one arm low around her waist and the other around her shoulders, clutching the back of her neck. Our eyes are locked, hers glistening and mine wide. She grinds on me slowly, clutching the back of my head, gasping and huffing.

"Tati," I whisper, overwhelmed and overcome as I feel her reach the cusp of orgasm; mine is near, and I roughly grip the crease of her hips and thrust madly. "I love you."

She pants raggedly in my ear. "Harder, my Nico. Take me."

My rage has been bottled up for so long, my needs repressed, ignored, denied. I have lived a half-life for too long.

With her whispered demand, she grants me yet another layer of freedom.

I stand up and stride across the room with her, press her back to the wall beside the bathroom door. I grip her ass cheeks in my hands and bury my face in the side of her neck and scent her skin and taste her flesh and growl as her nascent orgasm causes her walls to clutch and clench around me.

"Take me, my Nico," she whispers yet again, whispering hot words directly in my ear. "Fuck me, my love. As hard as you want. As hard as you can. Give me everything, Nicolae. *Everything.*"

I groan a ragged growl and thrust into her. She rakes her fingernails up my back and keens in my ear. "*YES!*"

The clawed fingernails, the cry of encouragement—it unleashes something inside me.

"Tati," I whisper. "Mine." It's a growl.

"Yes," She gasps. "Yours. Take me. Show me how I'm yours."

I thrust into her rough and hard. She cries out, a sharp wail of pleasure. Again—and she whimpers again.

Tatiana clutches the back of my neck with one hand and slips the other between us, finding her clit and giving herself the edge she needs to orgasm with me.

I lean back to give her hand room to move, holding her weight in my hands, and I let go. Abandoning all restraint, I give her every last shred of myself. I drive relentlessly into her and our bodies meet with loud wet slaps, and she shudders all around me, sinuously arching and writhing, screaming as she comes. I feel my own release smash through me and stars burst behind my eyes and heat floods through me and everything clenches and I roar and bellow, fucking her without restraint, and she screams "*YES! YES! YES!*" while holding onto me and raking her fingernails into my shoulders and meeting every one of my rough, slamming thrusts with her own, rising and falling onto me, using my shoulders for leverage.

I come for an age, and she matches me, meets me there, coming so hard she weeps uncontrollably, sobbing breathlessly.

When at long last we are done, she collapses forward against me. "Bed," she breathes. "Take us to the bed, Nico."

I take us back to the bed and sit down, and then lay back, and she sits on top of me, above me, keeping me buried deep inside her sweet, perfect sex.

She gazes down at me, tears staining her cheeks, flyaways sticking to the tears, breasts heaving with ragged breaths. "Fuck, Nico. That was…"

"Something I have never, ever, *ever* experienced before," I finish.

"Me either."

"God, I love you." She smiles at me, and then my bag from the store catches her eyes. "What's in the bag?"

I grin up at her. "Something I was hoping you would help me with."

"Anything."

"I want you to cut my hair."

She blinks. "What? C-cut your hair?"

"The last of Lash must vanish," I say. "I vowed to not cut my hair or beard until I had killed Roberto Pugli. But I have released that vow. I have turned over my evidence against him to an investigator in Germany who has an iron-clad case against him. My evidence will only add to the burden of proof weighed against Pugli and he will be brought to justice for his crimes, not just against me, but many, many others." I rake my hand through my hair, and then through my beard. "So now, I cut my hair and trim my beard."

She touches my jawline. "So you won't completely shave?"

I laugh. "My god, no. I haven't fully shaved since I was old enough to grow a beard. I will still have a beard, just not this wizard thing," I say, flipping the end.

She laughs. "Okay, okay." The laughter fades. "But, Nicolae, I am not a barber."

I shrug. "That does not matter. Back in Las Vegas, my brother Rev's woman cuts hair for the others. Apparently, she used to do that for her father and brothers and now the other men have her cut their hair. So you will just cut off the length for now and Myka will fix it when we return to the States, if necessary." I search her face, her thoughtful expression. "Are you changing your mind about moving to the States with me?"

She shakes her head. "No!" She smiles, shaking her head again. "No. Not at all. I just...I realized I don't know much about your life there."

"Well, we, the Broken Arrows, provide security for a secretive, exclusive nightclub called Club Sin. It is...well, it is a rather wild place full of debauchery and mayhem. Our job is to keep everyone safe and make sure that everything happens with the fully informed and sober consent of all parties. We work there, and we live in what amounts to an underground bunker beneath the club. It doesn't feel like a bunker, however. It just feels like...well, somewhat like a university dormitory, perhaps. We work nights and have days to ourselves. Until recently, we never left the club because we all had enemies who would kill us if we did. But now those enemies are sorted out and things are changing. I think all of us will continue living under the club for a while yet, though. None of us will give up that camaraderie."

"But I will be able to come and go? To operate my business?"

I smile at her. "Of course, my love. You are not swearing an oath to anything or anyone. You are simply choosing to live with me."

"And there are others? Other women?"

I nod. "Oh yes. Several. Rev has Myka, Kane has Anjalee, Chance has Annika, Silas recently returned from Boston with his lovely Naomi, his brother Saxon at nearly the same time with Terra, and now Solomon has Scarlett."

"And you have me."

I nuzzle her cheek. "Just so."

She trails her fingers through my beard. "Well, as long as you fully understand that I have absolutely zero training or experience in cutting hair and that I am not responsible if you end up looking like shit, then let's do this."

"You will do fine," I reassure her. "We will leave enough length for Myka to work with. But, just to say, Ileana used to cut my hair, and I know what to do, I just cannot do it myself."

She shrugs, laughing. "You are crazy, asking me to do this. But okay, Nico. As you wish."

"It is not so hard, I promise. It will not be complicated."

And so we leave the bed. I put on underwear and she opts for only my T-shirt, which doesn't quite cover the lower swell of her tight, plump, beautiful ass. I carry a chair from the desk into the bathroom while Tatiana unboxes the kit and plugs in the clippers.

I face the mirror, letting out a quick sigh. "First the beard. Cut it an inch or so below my chin with the scissors."

"You are nervous," Tatiana points out.

I shrug, nod. "A little. It is a big change. It represents turning over a new page in the book of my life."

"You don't want to wait? Have your friend Myka cut it properly?"

I shake my head. "No, no. I want you to do it." I grip my beard in my fist and pinch between my index and middle finger below my chin. "Cut between my hands.

She brings the scissors closer and then hesitates. "Are you sure?"

I laugh. "Yes, Tati. I am sure."

She sucks in a breath, holds it, and then cuts through my beard.

My hand comes away clutching six inches of beard. I hold it up. " There, you see? Not so hard."

She looks at me. A slow grin spreads across her face. "Wow. You…it is different, good, but it will take some getting used to." She runs her fingers over my jawline. "I think I will quite like it."

I indicate the clippers. "I will trim it properly once you have finished with my hair. Now, create a ponytail and cut the long part off."

She grabs the comb and pulls it through my hair, straightening and neatening it, and then pulls it into a ponytail in her fist at the top of my head. Another moment of hesitation, her eyes on mine in the mirror, and then she snips through the thick mass of my hair.

I blow out a breath as the remainder falls loose, shapeless and blunt. I run my fingers through it, shaking my head and moving it around in an attempt to come to grips with the newly weightless feeling.

Tatiana covers her mouth with her scissor-holding hand, eyes wide. "Nico." She shakes her head. "It looks awful. I mean, you're still handsome, but..."

I laugh. "You aren't done, Tati. Now the clippers."

I show her the correct guard—the longest one, since my intention is to leave it long enough that Myka will have length to work with.

"This will give it more shape. Just run the clippers through my hair." I smile at her, hoping to reassure her. "And remember—it is just hair. It will grow back even if something were to happen. Which it will not. So just breathe, alright?"

She nods, sighing nervously, and then turns on the clippers. She runs them over my head from front to back, and chunks of my hair topple to my shoulders and the floor. Top, left side, right side, and back. She shuts off the clippers and drags her fingernails backward over my scalp from forehead to nape.

"So?" she asks. "Okay?"

I nod. "You are doing wonderfully. So good that I think we can continue."

"*Continue?*" she squeaks. "Nico, I am *not* good at this."

"Sure you are. Look!" I turn my head side to side. "It looks good so far, yes?"

She shrugs. "I mean, yes. I suppose."

I choose the next guard, remembering with painful, bittersweet clarity how Ileana used to do it. "Now this one, but only on the sides. Hold the longer part of my hair to one side and go first down, and then up." I drag my finger along my hair to show her the line. "You want to make a sharp line just here, on both sides and around the back. You see?"

She nods, licking her lips nervously. "Yes, okay."

With a sharp exhale, she wiggles the guard to make sure it's secure and then turns the clippers back on. She does as I instructed slowly and carefully, biting the corner of her lower lip with each pass of the clippers.

"There," she says. "Good?"

I nod, checking side to side, running my hand over the sides and through the length on top. "Perfect. See? We won't even need Myka." I switch to one last, shorter guard for the areas above my ears. "Now, this goes from level with the tip of my ears to about here," I say, drawing a line about halfway up.

This part is quick, and when she's done, she covers her mouth again. "Nico!" She shakes her head in wonder. "You are like a different man! I barely recognize you!"

"But you still think I'm sexy, yes?" I ask, smirking at her reflection.

"Once you get that hair off you, I'll show you how sexy I think you are." She runs her fingertips through my hair and down my jawline. "I can't believe I did this."

"Not as hard as you think, huh?"

She shrugs. "No. But I think anyone with training would probably have some thoughts."

I laugh. "Of course. But I do not need a two-hundred-dollar haircut, Tatiana. This is exactly what I wanted."

In fact, I barely recognize myself. I still need to clean up the shape of my beard, but...I look like Nicolae Dragos once more. Lash is truly and forever gone.

"My god, it feels strange," I say, passing my hand over

my scalp, expecting still to feel the long locks slip through my fingers, finding instead the soft fuzz and short locks.

She exhales again, nodding. "It will take some getting used to, that's for sure. You are a beautiful man, Nicolae." She leans on me from behind, arms slinging around my shoulders. "It makes me feel good that you trusted me with this."

"Of course I do, Tati." I stand up and turn in her arms. "Now. I will clean this up. You have coffee and eat."

Once I've cleaned up the hair as well as I can without a broom, I rinse off in the shower, re-washing my newly shorn hair, and then I style it and put oil in my beard. Clean and feeling like a new man, I sit beside her on the bed, and we drink our coffee and eat our bagels in companionable silence.

Every so often, I catch her glancing at me, frequently seeming surprised. But then, when I use the bathroom and catch a glimpse of myself in the mirror a while later, I am surprised at myself.

The man in the mirror is a stranger to me. It has been...how many years? Six? Seven? It is hard to remember. I have been with the Broken Arrows for three years...I think...and I wandered the earth aimlessly for two or three years before encountering Inez. So yes, six or seven years.

In those years, I have changed. Crow's feet crease the corners of my eyes, where before they were laugh lines. I am leaner in the face, my jawline sharper, my eyes deeper. I look harder. Older.

If I look closely, I can still see the Nicolae Dragos I remember, he's just...older and harder.

In short order, it is time to meet the others on the base for our departure to Colombia. Tatiana and I, having been up early anyway, are the first to arrive at the specified hangar near the specified runway on the Manaus airbase. An aging but well-cared-for Huey is on standby outside the hangar, the pilot and co-pilot going through pre-flight.

A few minutes later, a vehicle brakes to a precise halt near the hangar, and Solomon, Scarlett, and Lorenzo emerge.

I feel for Lorenzo—he has a faint limp from a previous injury, and his arm is in a proper sling against his torso. He has his color back, however, and despite the limp strides with confidence and determination toward the Huey.

He reaches me first, eying me. He nods. "Looks good. We are ready?"

"Thank you, and yes." I pause, waiting for Solomon and Scarlett to reach us so I only need to update everyone once.

Solomon stares at me for a long time. "Damn, dude. You clean up good." A shake of his head. "I seriously didn't recognize you at first."

Scarlett snorts. "I just met you, so I wouldn't have known you from Adam."

I glance at Tatiana, let out a sigh, smiling at her. "It was time. I am letting go of the past." I look back at my friends. "Which means I am putting Lash to rest."

"Nicolae Dragos," Solomon says. "I heard Nils use your real name."

I nod. "Yes. Nicolae is the name of my birth. I adopted the moniker Lash after my family was murdered. Nicolae was dead with them, so I became someone else. I am no longer that man, however. I have resurrected Nicolae

Dragos." I pass my hand over my hair and jaw. "Which also meant this."

Sol pulls me in for a resounding embrace—I go stiff for a second, unused to such physical affection from my brothers in the Arrows, and then I force myself to loosen and return the hug. "Does this mean you'll stop being so damn mysterious and standoffish, now?"

"Who is mysterious and standoffish?" I say, faking a blustery offense.

He grins, shoving me away playfully. "Right, right. Not you, certainly. I mean, it's not like I've known for you three years and am just now finding out your real name and literally *any* details about your past."

I wince, letting the playful bluster go. "I am sorry, my friend. I felt...I long assumed I would find a way to get close to Pugli, kill him, and die in the process. I saw no point in getting close to people who would just lose me when I died."

"So when you were pushing us to hunt down Pugli, you always assumed you would get killed?" Scarlett asks, frowning. "What about the rest of us? What about Inez?"

I shake my head. "I cannot excuse that. I meant to send you all on without me at some point or leave you in the night to finish the job. But I..." I look at Tatiana. "I was shown the error of my ways. I now see a better path."

She sighs, her expression full of understanding and sympathy. "I get it, Lash...or Nicolae, I guess I should say. I lost everyone I ever cared about. I lived my life assuming I'd die sooner than later and not caring. And I found someone who showed me that life is worth living. So... yeah. I get it."

The helicopter is starting, now that the pilot and

co-pilot have finished their pre-flight checks. The rotors begin to spin, slowly at first and quickly speeding until they're a blur of black overhead.

At that moment, Solomon's burner rings. He puts a finger in one ear and the phone to the other. "Yeah?" he shouts. Listens. "Leaving Manaus now. Tolemaida Airbase. Right. Yeah, we've got Lash. No, we've got firepower covered. See you soon."

He ends the call, shoves the phone in his pocket, and then twirls his finger over his head. "Let's bug out!"

We board the helo, strap in, don headsets, and then we're airborne, at last en route to springing Inez from the clutches of the world's most dangerous cartel warlord.

This should prove to be most entertaining.

CHAPTER 12

THE GANG'S ALL HERE

TATIANA

OUR RENDEZVOUS WITH NILS' CONTACT IS BRIEF, a liaison of less than five minutes in a clearing outside a village in the rainforest some twenty miles from Manaus. The contact is a local from a native tribe who emerges from the forest as we touch down. He is short, slender, and hard-eyed, lugging two huge black duffel bags, staggering under their weight. Solomon and Nicolae leap out of the helicopter and jog to meet him, taking the bags from him. He nods, waves, and trots back into the jungle.

Once airborne, the men open the bags and examine the contents.

Solomon hoots with excitement as he lifts a strange-looking assault rifle from the bag. "A Steyr-Aug. Where the fuck did that little dude get this shit?"

Lorenzo snorts. "You would be surprised. He was probably holding them as a favor to someone. Currency means little to him, so he will likely receive compensation in the form of goods he and his tribe will find useful." He pulls another gun out. "This is excellent gear, however. Lash, you owe your friend Nils a huge debt of gratitude."

Despite growing up around guns, I know very little about them, as far as makes and models go, but the men and Scarlett seem very pleased with the contents of the bags—ten assault rifles, the same number of handguns, several boxes of ammunition of assorted sizes, magazines, and clusters of grenades and flashbangs.

We spend the rest of the flight loading bullets into the magazines. I am shown how to do it, and which bullets go into which magazines, and I spend the rest of the flight slotting cold brass shells into hard plastic magazines.

Solomon receives a text message with a specific location where we will meet the rest of the Broken Arrows—a large field on a hilltop overlooking a river. The rainforest has been clear-cut and burned here, and I notice that Lorenzo in particular is looking around at the devastated landscape below us with sorrow and anger.

As the helicopter touches down, Lorenzo is the first out, an assault rifle slung on his back, and a few grenades clipped to a bandolier, along with spare magazines. Large yellow construction machines sit parked in a row at the edge of the far side of the field, perhaps half a mile away.

Ignoring everyone, Lorenzo marches across the field, a grenade clutched in his hand.

"Oh, shit," Solomon says, watching. "He's gonna blow that shit up."

Nicolae, with anger suffusing his handsome features, spits on the ground at his feet. "Good. It won't stop them, but it's something. This is evil, this destruction."

Solomon nods. "It is," he says. Movement catches his eye—a caravan of battered SUVs emerging from a two-track path in the forest close to where Lorenzo has reached the equipment. "Oh, hey, here come the guys. Let's go, ya'll. Double time."

Nicolae and Solomon carry the bags on their backs, their arms hooked through the handles. We jog across the field—footing is treacherous, the ground lumpy and rough, with rocks and roots and stumps littering the brown soil. The SUVs, four of them—all old, battered Land Rovers— cut a wide circle and stop facing the path from which they emerged. Doors open and five massive men get out.

We reach them a moment later, and Solomon in particular is greeted with rough, energetic, hyper-masculine hugs, full of backslapping, laughter, and playful fighting. Two men seem especially happy to see Solomon, both of them tall, lean, and hard, one with blond hair like Solomon's, and the other reddish like sun-burnished copper.

Nicolae, close to my side, murmurs to me. "Those are his brothers. Solomon has been missing for some time. Well before I got hijacked to Zagreb." He entwines our fingers and kisses the back of my hand. "I shall make introductions once Lorenzo has finished his act of protest."

I look across the field to see Lorenzo jogging across the line of machines, yanking pins free and tossing grenades into the tracks, engine compartments, and cabins. Once the last machine has received an explosive, Lorenzo pivots on his heel and sprints as hard as he can toward us, his rifle clutched in his hands. He gets perhaps a hundred meters before the first explosion sends him sprawling in the dirt. He hits the ground, rolls, and springs to his feet, turning to walk backward so he can watch the rest of the explosions—*BOOM...BOOM...BOOM...BOOM*! Parts fly and burning diesel fuel sends black clouds of angry smoke spewing into the sky.

The machines are wreckage now, little more than charred hulks of scrap metal. He nods once and makes his way more carefully across the field to the line of vehicles. The explosions, naturally enough, dominated everyone's attention. Now, it's time for introductions.

Solomon takes the lead on this. He claps a hand on Lorenzo's good shoulder. "Lorenzo, meet the crew." He points to each man in turn. "That big motherfucker over there is Chance. The almost-as-big motherfucker next to him is Rev. Beside him is Kane. These two knuckleheads are my younger brothers, Saxon and Silas." He squeezes Lorenzo's shoulder. "Everyone, this is Lorenzo. He's our South American guide and translator, and he and Inez are…I dunno. Something."

Rev, a massive, muscular, brown-skinned man with a short, black-haired mohawk, frowns. "Inez is something with someone?"

Lorenzo chuckles. "Indeed. She and I have an extensive history."

Rev snorts. "I always sort of assumed Inez just appeared on the earth one day, fully formed and scary as fuck. Hard to imagine her getting all cozy with anyone."

Lorenzo laughs again. "That is an understandable notion, Rev. Sophia is…rather unique, shall we say."

"The fuck is Sophia?" Rev asks.

"That is the name she was born with," Lorenzo answers. "Any more is her story to tell, however, not mine, so please do not ask. I won't betray her trust."

"Just as soon interrogate a cobra," Rev mutters. "The woman scares me."

"That is wise," Lorenzo says.

Solomon wraps an arm around Scarlett. "This is Scarlett Gutierrez. She was in the CIA with me, and she sprang me from the jungle."

Saxon grins at his brother—Saxon is burlier than his brothers, with a nasty scar running down the side of his face, and blond hair shaved on the sides and back, left long-ish on top and swept diagonally backward. "Somethin' tells me you're leaving some shit outta that little summary, bro."

The other brother is tall and lean with clean-cut good looks and coppery hair. He slugs Solomon's arm. "Yeah, like all the good details."

Solomon snorts, shoving his brothers away from him. "Back off, you damn cavemen. Yeah, yeah, we're together." He indicates them both. "I hear the two of you came outta shit with women of your own. We'll shoot the shit once things go back to normal."

The brothers nod and drop the subject.

The huge man, Chance, frowns at Nicolae. "Wait, hold the actual fuck up. Lash? Shit, brother, I didn't even realize that was you. Goddamn, son."

Nicolae grins. "A lot has happened since I got on the plane." He rubs the back of his head, feeling the fuzz there. "I will fill you all in at a more appropriate time, when we are all together, as Solomon has said. But what you must know for now is that my name is Nicolae Dragos. Lash was a...a persona, I suppose."

No one speaks for a moment or two—they all seem stunned.

"Nicolae Dragos," says the man named Kane.

He is not especially tall, around six feet, but mon-strously muscular, wider than two of me across the shoulders and chest, with arms and legs like tree trunks, his hair cropped on the sides and tied back in a long po-nytail. He wears a black-and-white checkered scarf around his neck, the kind of thing men from Middle Eastern countries wear—at least, on the news I have seen.

"It's a good name, brother," Kane says. "Nice to finally meet the real you. Cut looks good, too."

Nicolae grins at me. "See? You did a wonderful job."

I blush, shrugging. "It was nothing. You told me what to do," I say in Croatian.

Rev looks from me to Nicolae. "Who's she? And what language is that?"

"She is Tatiana Juric, daughter of the man who hijacked my flight—I worked for him, many, many years ago. She is Croatian. And we are together."

Rev juts his chin in the direction of our joined hands. "Figured. Glad for you, brother."

Kane frowns. "Her dad gonna come lookin' for her?"

Nicolae shrugs. "I do not think so." He looks at me.

"I should call him soon," I say in English. "I am upset with him right now, but he is my father and I love him, and he will be worried. We did sort of disappear from Zagreb."

Solomon claps his hands. "Okay, gang. Introductions have been made, environmental protests have been conducted, and reunions had. Let's get this shitshow on the road. I'm not sure if we're rescuing Inez from Mercado or the other way around, but either way, I'm not leaving her with him any longer. Lorenzo, this is your show, bro. Take us in."

Lorenzo rolls his injured shoulder, wincing, and then nods. "We're about nine or so hours from his compound. Last intel I had on his operations there, he retained somewhere between twenty and thirty men on-site—hard, bad men, ex-military, and mostly special forces. They are heavily armed and well-trained, and their orders are to shoot on sight anyone who has not received clearance from Mercado himself. He can field another thirty or forty men from a nearby village, perhaps twenty minutes response time." He pauses, thinking. "His estate is walled all the way around, topped with razor wire, patrolled, and alarmed with state-of-the-art security."

"Fuckin' lovely," Kane says. "This'll be a real fun fuckin' party."

"Indeed," Lorenzo answers. "It is a fortress. Ingress will be difficult at best. We will need to come up with a plan before we attempt anything, or we will only get ourselves slaughtered."

"So we're ten people against potentially as many as seventy?" Saxon says. "Fuck, man. We don't need a plan, we need a fuckin' Apache."

I raise my hand. "I do not know if you should count me. I am not trained like the rest of you."

Nicolae glances at me. "You cannot sit this one out, Lovely One. I will do everything I can to make sure you are safe, but once we have Inez, we will have to exfil and bug out very swiftly."

I frown at him. "What is 'exfil' and 'bug out'?"

"Oh. Military terms. Exfil means get out of the combat zone, and bug out means get away, as in go home."

I let out a shuddery breath. "I will do what is needed, Nico. But I am afraid."

The big man, Chance—seven feet tall and as broad and dense with muscle as Kane—gives me a reassuring smile. "Sweetheart, we're all hardened combat vets, and even we get scared. We'll take care of you."

Scarlett comes up beside me and slings an arm through mine. "I got you, chica. You and me will fuck up some thugs. If you can gut a rapey motherfucker with a knife, you can pop a few in the fuckin' skulls."

I sigh and shake my head. "I sell clothing. My father is the popper of skulls, not me."

She grins. "Well, chica, you do what you gotta do. But I'll be with you the whole time."

Solomon meets my eyes. "If Scarla says she's got you, you're safe as houses, honey."

I frown at her. "Scarla?"

She shrugs. "Nickname." She touches the long, nasty-looking scar running down the side of her face, a near mirror to the one on Solomon's brother Saxon's face.

"Ah. I see." I nod. "Well. I know how to shoot a pistol. I will do my best."

Scarlett pats my back. "All any of us can do."

Lorenzo puts his fingers to his lips and lets out a piercing whistle "We must go. My Sophia has been in Rafael's hands for too fucking long as it is. I will drive the lead. We stop for no one and nothing but to refuel as necessary."

Kane pats the tailgate of the nearest SUV. "Got that covered. We got jerry cans full'a fuel in each Rover as well food, water, and med kits." He juts his chin at Nicolae. "I assume those bags have the bang-bang goodies in them."

Lorenzo nods, sighing in relief. "Good. Very good. Yes, we have plenty of guns and ammunition. We are as prepared as we can be. Now, we get to the compound and figure out a plan that will hopefully get us all out alive."

It's a bouncing, jouncing, teeth-rattling ride through the jungle. I've long since lost track of what time it is; time distorts. We've always been here, in the jungle, on these hard bench seats, hot and sweaty and jarred by ruts and hillocks and thrown to either side as we swerve to avoid potholes that could swallow the compact cars so prevalent in my native Europe.

We stop after a few hours to stretch our legs and refuel. Scarlett pulls me after her off the trail and into the rainforest just out of eyesight of the small caravan. She shows me how to use her trench knife to dig a pit at the base of a tree, lean back against it with my pants and underwear around my ankles, and pee without splattering myself. She even has a small package of biodegradable wet wipes that get buried once we're done.

As we walk back, she hands me a pistol. "Pull the mag and put it back."

Understanding her intention of assessing my familiarity with the weapon, I eject the magazine and tap it back into place.

"Good. Put it away and draw it," she instructs.

I tuck it in my waistband at the small of my back. Pause, hands at my sides. Draw, assuming the basic triangle pose taught to me by Anton, the instructor at the gun range.

She nods again. "Good. How accurate are you?"

I shrug. "Okay. I can hit the target, but I am not an expert."

She smiles at me. "That's okay. No need to be an expert. What you need to know is that if you're gonna draw that gun and point it at someone, you gotta be ready to pull the trigger. And you can't hesitate. If you know you gotta shoot, then draw, aim, and fire. Don't think, just do it."

I nod, a memory of being attacked in the alley in Zagreb flashing through my mind. "Lash—Nicolae, I mean—said the same thing. I…" I shake my head. "I didn't listen. I was in that alley by myself. And that man walked by. He saw me. He started walking toward me, and I was afraid. I could feel that he meant nothing good for me, but I…I didn't see if he had a weapon, not until it was too late. I didn't even draw my gun. I…it is embarrassing, but I lost it in the struggle. He got close, and then he had a knife, and I fought him. I remembered some things I was taught about defending myself from big men with knives." I shut my eyes, stopping to lean against the smooth bark of a tree. "I still don't know how, but I got the knife from him and I stabbed him and I stabbed him and I stabbed him, so many times I stabbed that man, and he kept—he wouldn't—he just *would not* die."

She rubs my shoulder blade. "A horrible way to get your first kill. Knife work is messy and intimate. And yes, it's very, *very* hard to kill someone quickly with a knife. There are only a few places on the human body where you can cut or stab someone for an instant or nearly-instant kill. Human bodies are complicated. We can be very fragile and we can also take a shocking amount of damage and survive."

I let out a breath and shake my head. "I just want this to be over, Scarlett. I sell clothing. All the guns and the shooting and the killing, I…I never wanted any of it. That is my father's world, not mine. I did everything I could to live my own life, to be separate from my father and his stupid, awful business."

Scarlett pats me again. "I know. I wish we could get to the good stuff, too. But in shit like this, the only way out is through."

I push away from the tree, hearing the SUVs cough and bark and rattle to life. "Does it get easier? Killing people, I mean."

Scarlett shrugs. "Unfortunately, yes. You're never not afraid before a battle, though. But the first few kills? You *always* remember them. The rest, not as much. When you've spent as much time downrange as I have, you kinda block it out when you're not doing the job. Otherwise, it'll just... fuck you up. Probably a lot like cops, medics, and ER docs and nurses. You can't think about it when you're not doing it. You can't think about the shit you did, the shit you had to see." She moves behind me and puts her hands on my shoulders, affectionately and gently guiding me back to the road. "Hopefully you'll never have to know whether or not it gets easier. Hopefully, we'll get Inez back, and we'll all go live happily ever after in good ol' Las fuckin' Vegas."

I laugh. "I sense perhaps you are being sarcastic about Las Vegas."

She barks a laugh. "Yeah, just a little. I fuckin' *hate* Vegas. It's hotter than Satan's ball sack, there's no nature, and everyone is fuckin' crazy, desperate, and stupid. And also, fuck casinos. Noisy, smoky, lightless, soulless hellholes of addiction and desperation. Fuck Las Vegas."

I laugh. "I see. But yet, despite feeling this way, you are going to move there with Solomon?"

She sighs. "Yes. Yes, I am. I love him, and that's where he has to be for now. I'm gonna take the brand and the oath and become a Broken Arrow. And hopefully, I won't have to leave the Club."

We reach the road and the caravan, piling into one of the Land Rovers—Solomon drives and Nico is in the front seat beside him, so we slide in behind them.

Into the jungle we go, sweating, bouncing, and avoiding thoughts of the future.

I am roused from a fitful, restless half-sleep when the caravan halts and the engines turn off. I blink awake, peering around—it's pitch-black outside beyond the windows, and for a moment or two, all is dead still and silent. After those moments of silence, the night creatures of the jungle come to life once more, croaking, whirring, chirping, hissing, and rustling.

The whole team circles up in the road in the yellow bath of the lead SUV's headlights; flying insects flutter and swarm.

Solomon seems comfortable taking the lead, and the others seem content to let him. "We're two miles from the compound, according to Lorenzo."

Lorenzo shrugs. "As close as I can estimate, at least. Probably a little more, as it is better to be farther away than closer."

"So, my thinking is we send a few of us out for recon," Solomon says. "Get the lay of the land, sniff out patrols, and see if we can get eyes on the compound itself for some intel so we can make a plan."

Lorenzo scans the group. "I think it should be myself, Scarlett, and Lash—sorry, Nicolae."

"Reasoning?" questions Kane.

"Very simple. We three are not bound by the oath against killing," Lorenzo answers. "And we need the patrols neutralized, not just incapacitated. We can't afford some hard-headed asshole waking up and giving us away."

Nicolae's hand goes to the back of his neck at Lorenzo's words.

Rev is the first to speak, after a long, stunned silence. "Wait…*what*? Scarlett and Lorenzo, you're not Arrows. No brand, no oath, so I get it. But Lash? What the *fuck*, dude?"

"I had hoped to avoid this conversation till after," Nico says, sighing. "But we may as well get it out of the way. Yes, it is true. I took the oath of loyalty to the Broken Arrows, but our employer did not, in my particular case, demand the oath against killing. I did not know that was unusual until after I joined you, for one thing, and I was not given reasoning, for another. I took the oath that was asked of me. If it had included the injunction against death, I would have sworn to that. I did not ask for that exception. I never saw a point in telling you. I worried it would only muddy the waters, or cause resentment. Which I can see it has."

Rev shakes his head. "Not resentment, man, just…I dunno. Maybe a little. We've all had to do this shit with one hand behind our back, so to speak. It's a lot fuckin' harder when you can't kill 'em."

Nicolae nods, shrugging. "I know. When we have the luxury of time and safety, I will tell you all the backstory which will explain, I believe, why I was not required to take that particular oath. For now, we have work to do. I am your brother. I will live for you, fight with you, and die for you if required. And when this is all over, I will take the oath again, with a new brand to mark the occasion."

Rev nods, satisfied with the answer. "Well then, let's fuckin' go."

Nico rummages in one of the duffel bags and produces a suppressor for his pistol, which he screws on. From the other bag he finds a long knife with a black, serrated blade; he whips off his belt and fixes a holster for his gun on one side and the knife and sheath on the other, and puts the belt back on. Once more into the bags, coming out with a thick black bulletproof vest. He slots magazines into the front of the vest, and then grabs one of the assault rifles; his has a short, thick barrel, which he explains is a built-in suppressor. Thus armed and armored, he is ready to go.

I catch his arm. "Nico, please be careful."

He grins, confident, cocky even. The hard, angry, closed-off mask of Lash is gone, leaving only the charming breeziness of Nicolae. "This is what I do best, my love."

"What, exactly?" I ask.

He gestures at the surrounding jungle. "Infil, recon, target elimination, and exfil, without being seen."

He catches the back of my neck and pulls me to him, crushing my body against his and slashing his mouth over mine in a hot, demanding kiss. "Stay close to the others while we are gone. Listen to them when they give you instructions. And above all, do not—"

"Hesitate," I say, overlapping with him. I kiss him again, rubbing my hands along the hard line of his jaw. "I learned that lesson."

His expression darkens. "I am sorry you learned it the way you did."

"I will not make that mistake again." I scratch his jaw. "I like this. The new you—I like him."

He looks away, thinking. "I am not so sure it is a new me."

"It must be, Nico. The old you died. Then, you were Lash. Now you are Nicolae again, but what made you Lash is not gone. Nor is what has remained of the old Nicolae. You are a bit of both. A new you."

He shifts his gaze, considering, then looks back at me. "You are not wrong."

Lorenzo and Scarlett are similarly armed and attired.

"We have to go, Nicolae," Lorenzo says. "My gut is telling me time is short."

Nico kisses me once more. "See you soon."

After a brief murmured conversation, Lorenzo stalks forward down the path, Scarlett cuts to the right into the jungle, and Nico goes left.

Chance sees me staring after Nico and comes to tower over me. "He'll be fine."

I nod. "I know. I still worry."

His huge, heavy hand rests on my shoulder for a moment. "I'm glad he found you. He's different. Better."

"I am glad, too."

He nods. "Well," he sighs. "Now we wait."

CHAPTER 13

DUPED

LASH

I CREEP THROUGH THE JUNGLE, PAUSING TO LISTEN every few steps. So far, only jungle noises. Orienting myself in the dark is tricky; my HK MP5SD does have a flashlight on the lower rail, but I'm hesitant to use it unless absolutely necessary—it sort of does away with stealth if you give yourself away with a light. I test my steps before I commit to them and keep my head on a swivel. It's a long, slow walk, but eventually I see a dim glow in the distance and head for it.

I reach the edge of the forest and crouch just inside the tree line, assessing what I see. The bag of goodies Nils' contact provided also contained military-grade comms, and I key the mic and whisper into it. "Nicolae, in position. Holding and waiting for patrols."

Lorenzo and Scarlett echo my message.

There is a good hundred yards of clearing between the wall of the estate and the tree line, with a wide grassy swath between. Floodlights at the base of the wall shine bright lights at regular intervals, illuminating the gleam of the razor wire along the top.

Several minutes after I reached the tree line, a patrol

of four men saunter around the far corner. They carry sub-machine guns, wear body armor, and have comms. They mutter to each other, and one of them barks a laugh. Occasionally, the man on the outside sweeps a flashlight across the lawn. These are not bored, idle guards, these men are alert and know their job.

"North side," comes Lorenzo's whisper. "Four-man patrol leaving the main gate on foot. Approaching my position."

"East side," says Scarlett. "Four-man patrol going from the south wall to the north."

"West side," I say. "Four-man patrol going south to north."

"Stand by," Lorenzo mutters. A few minutes later he whispers into the comms again. "They meet at the gate and go back the other way. Nicolae, circle to the south wall. That may be our way in."

"Copy," I respond. "Moving."

I slip further back into the trees and make my way along the west wall. Once I'm facing the south wall, I crouch and watch until the patrol appears. They round the west-south corner and halt in the middle of the south wall. They stand in a line abreast, waiting and watching until the east wall patrol rounds the corner. The two patrols converse for a few moments in voices too low for me to make out, and then the west side patrol resumes their track to the gate.

"They stagger the patrols," I whisper. "West patrol reaches south first and waits, east patrol reaches them and they wait there together, and then west patrol moves out, and *then* east."

"Shit," Lorenzo mutters. "How long is the south wall unguarded?"

"Stand by," I answer.

I watch the patrols through two more cycles, timing them. "Two minutes max between patrols at the south wall."

"Patrol nearing my position," Lorenzo whispers, so quiet it's barely audible. A few minutes later, he's back on the comms. "They go about half a click down the road, stop, turn around, and then split at the tree line. Two go east along the perimeter, and two go west. I think they make a circle to the south, meet again at the north, and repeat."

"Copy," I say; Scarlett echoes me.

"Let's watch a few more minutes to confirm the pattern. Meet back at the caravan in ten," Lorenzo says.

Scarlett and I both confirm his order. Sure enough, a few minutes later, two men approach my position, walking parallel to the tree line. They shine lights into the trees and scan the lawn as they walk. I shuffle backward and find a spot to hide behind a wide tree, peeking out every few seconds to assess their progress. Once it's clear, I slip back to the edge and watch them. As Lorenzo suspected, the two patrols meet in the middle of the south side, converse, and then go back the way they came. Lorenzo confirms they pause a few minutes at the gate and then start the pattern all over again.

Once I'm certain we have the patrol patterns established, I make my way slowly and silently back to the Land Rovers. Scarlett and Lorenzo appear almost at the same time as me.

Solomon flicks the headlights back on—while they

waited for us to recon, they turned them off and waited inside the vehicles.

"We didn't make contact," Lorenzo says. "It was to observe and report only. They have three patrols—one from the north gate to the south wall and back, another on the opposite side, and a third that goes down this road half a click and then around the perimeter."

"What's the wall like?" Kane asks.

"Fifteen feet or so, topped with razor wire. Probably a shit load of electronic security measures inside, as well as more patrols," Lorenzo answers.

"So, what's the plan?" Saxon asks. "Sounds like they got their shit locked down pretty tight."

"The south wall is unguarded for about two minutes," I say. "If we can find a way over the wall and the razor wire, that's our ingress point."

"Big if," Silas says.

"What if we pick off the patrols?" Rev suggests. "Get their attention."

"Kicking the nest doesn't seem like a good plan to me," Chance says. "We're outnumbered."

"Any tools in those bags?" asks Kane.

Silas roots through both and comes up shaking his head. "Nothing for wire. No rope, either."

"Shit." Solomon turns away from the group, thinking. He comes back, pointing at Rev. "I think we have to go with his idea. But we don't pick them off one by one. We do it all at once, in sync. It'll have to be you three again. Once we're inside, the rest of us can and will incapacitate, but until we're in, we can't risk accidental detection."

"So we take out the patrols, and then what?" Kane asks.

"Fake 'em out," Chance suggests. "Toss some grenades over the south wall to get their attention while everyone else breaches the gate."

"What do we know about the gate?" Silas asks.

"Not much," Lorenzo answers. "I couldn't risk getting close enough to assess."

"We do have breaching explosives," Silas says.

"So we take out the patrols, pull their attention to the south wall," Lorenzo says, putting the plan together. "Breach the front gate. Infil, find Inez, and fight our way out."

"I'm just gonna say this because someone has to," Saxon says into the ensuing silence. "I'm not sure how realistic it is to think we can accomplish this without killing anyone, even by accident. We all know that once a pitched firefight starts, you take the shot you get. You can't wait for a perfect target. This is already damn near a suicide mission."

Rev clears his throat. "I don't disagree. I'll do everything I can to keep that oath, but if it's my life or one of yours on the line, I'm doing what I gotta do, oath be damned. I swore that oath and I fuckin' meant it, but not at the expense of the lives of the people I care about."

"Word," Saxon says.

Solomon scans the group. "I think we all agree. We keep our oaths, but if it comes down to dropping a motherfucker to save a life or stay alive, do it."

"Agreed," Chance says.

"Same," Kane adds.

Silas frowns and then shrugs. "I don't see another way. Don't give a fuck what it takes, I'm going home to Naomi."

Everyone assents to that.

"But listen to me," I say. "Please, do not throw away your vows lightly. I know, this is easy for me to say as I have not sworn that oath. But it means something. If you must break it, then so be it. But do not look for excuses."

There's no verbal response to this, but I see everyone nodding, thinking.

"So," Solomon says, clapping his hands to get our attention. "Teams. Scarlett, Tatiana, Kane—you take out the south perimeter patrol. Lorenzo, Silas, and Saxon, west side. Lash, Chance, Rev, and I will take the gate. Stay on your comms and wait for the signal from me." He waits for questions. "Once the patrols are down, Scarlett, Tatiana, and Kane, you throw a bunch of grenades and flashbangs over the south wall. Maybe just flashbangs, honestly—we don't know the layout of the interior, so we don't wanna cause destruction when we don't know where Inez is being held."

"Copy that," Kane says. "Flashbangs only."

"Once we have the distraction, my team will breach the gate and the rest of us will infil."

"We'll be a ways behind the rest of you," Scarlett says. "We gotta circle from the south."

"That actually works out," Solomon says. "You can be rearguard, make sure we don't get surprised. Maybe post Tatiana at the gate watching for reinforcements."

Tatiana looks frightened but determined. "I can do that."

"Good." Solomon scans us again. "Any questions, comments, or concerns?"

Silence.

"Everyone knows the plans?" he asks.

We all do.

"Alright then," he says. "Let's go get Inez."

Tatiana crosses to me and hugs me. "I am frightened, Nico."

I breathe in her scent. "I know, Lovely One. But you will be okay."

"I wish I could go with you."

I sigh. "I know. But it is better this way. If I am with you, my focus will be on you. And my focus is needed elsewhere. Scarlett will not let anything happen to you. Nor will Kane."

Kane gives her a reassuring smile. "No worries, baby girl. We got you."

Scarlett meets my eyes and nods, then pulls Tatiana away. "C'mon, it's time to move. You're a badass, Tatiana. You've got this."

Tatiana nods, lets out a harsh sigh, and then shoots me one last longing look. "I love you."

"I love you as well," I answer. "See you on the other side."

Scarlett, Kane, and Tatiana filter into the forest and are soon gone. Within seconds, everyone else is vanishing into the jungle.

Chance, Solomon, Rev and I make our way along the narrow path in a V formation. Once the lights of the compound are in sight, we inch carefully forward until we can almost see the compound itself.

The dirt road is narrow, the jungle forming a thick canopy of foliage over our heads, blocking out the sky. Ahead, we can see the whitewashed adobe walls lit by the floodlights. The gate is high, arched, and of black metal. If I squint, I can almost make out movement within. We only have to wait a few minutes before the perimeter guards meet where the road exits the rainforest and move up to the gate. They stand there for a few minutes, watching, talking, and smoking cigarettes, and then they start their walk this way.

They walk four abreast, chatting in low tones in Spanish, assault rifles hung on their shoulders. They are alert but not expecting trouble. After all, who would be so foolish as to assault Mercado's home compound?

Solomon uses hand signals to direct me and Chance to one side and him and Rev to the other. More hand signals indicate that I take point on the elimination. I acknowledge and prepare.

Clipping my MP5SD to my vest, I draw my pistol, check the load, check the suppressor, and then crouch in wait; Chance looms behind and above me, a mammoth, watchful shadow. The dim light from the courtyard behind the approaching patrol casts long, faint shadows of each figure along the low, narrow path. Insects whirr and chirrup; an owl hoots in the distance. I hear their voices first, occasional desultory mutters, and then the crunch of their boots on the hard-packed dirt road. They scan the road and the edges with their flashlights; one of them sweeps the beam of his light across the path and then lifts his fist to call a halt, crouching and focusing on something in the path—a boot print.

Time is up.

They are a little over fifteen meters away, so not close, but within range even with a suppressor. I shift my weight so I am kneeling with one knee in front, brace my elbow on my knee, and draw bead on the farthest guard. Inhale, hold my breath.

POP-POP.

He drops, two red spots blossoming on his forehead.

Before the others can figure out what's going on, I shift my aim to the next.

POP-POP.

POP-POP.

POP-POP.

Each man drops silently, crumpling heavily to the ground as if a puppeteer had cut their strings.

I wait a moment or two, listening for an alarm, and then key my mic. "This is Nicolae. Gate and perimeter patrol neutralized. Proceed with east and west patrol neutralization."

"Copy," Lorenzo and Scarlett say at the same time.

Chance and I each grab a guard and haul them off-path, and Solomon and Rev do the same, bringing their corpses to the opposite side. I grab the walkie and earpiece from one of the guards and clip it to my belt, running the earpiece up under my vest—I'll have to be careful about which mic I'm keying, but it will be helpful to hear what they are saying.

The four of us jog up the path foursquare, slowing when we near the opening of the clearing around the compound. We split again, kneeling in the dense undergrowth just off-path and inside the tree line.

"Nicolae—you eliminated all four guards?" Scarlett asks.

"Affirmative," I respond.

"West patrol approaching our position," Lorenzo says.

I can see them from here, small black dots skylined against the white adobe wall, bathed in floodlights.

A few seconds later, Scarlett comes on the radio. "East patrol approaching."

"On my signal," Solomon says. "Hold—hold—"

He's watching the east side, and glancing at me every couple of seconds. I give him a hand signal, and he nods. "Now—now—now. Neutralize."

Lorenzo, Scarlett, and I carry suppressed MP5s, making the sound of gunfire almost indiscernible from this distance. The only noise is a faint click of the bolt and a soft WHUMP, barely audible beyond a short distance.

The outermost guard's head jerks sideways and blood sprays in silhouette. Before the other two can react, even to shout, Lorenzo is moving in a fast tactical crouch, firing as he moves, dropping the other two a split second later.

"All targets neutralized," Solomon reports. "Hide the bodies and converge at the gate. Scarlett and Tatiana, prepare to deploy flashbangs."

Everyone replies with a "Copy," and within a minute or so, we're approaching the gate from oblique angles, staying out of eyeline in case there are guards within the courtyard.

"Ricardo, report," comes a gravelly male voice in Spanish in my stolen earpiece.

I key the team comms. "I have one of their radios, Sol," I say. "They are asking for a report in. Ignore or respond?"

"They're about to know we're here, so ignore," he answers.

"Ricardo! Report now!"

We're crouching in clusters on either side of the gate, waiting. I hear boots on gravel, and the same voice now echoing in both my ear and in the earpiece simultaneously. "Ricardo? Mateo? Alvarez?"

"Deploy," Solomon orders.

A few seconds later, there's a loud *BANG!* from the

far side of the compound, and the boots sprint away, the voice shouting.

"We're under attack! All units, we're being breached at the south wall. Luis, Andre, Carlos, gate. Everyone else, south end."

"Breach the gate," Sol orders.

Kane moves in front of the gate and applies the breaching cord to the hinges and lock. Before he can fire it, though, he curses and ducks back around behind cover.

"Contact," he hisses.

"Light 'em up," Sol snaps. "Oath-holders, center mass shots only."

Kane, Silas, and I move in unspoken unison, rolling out in front of the gate. Another series of loud bangs erupt from the south end in quick succession, accompanied by automatic weapons fire.

"Who are they shooting at?" Saxon asks across the line.

Three men approach the gate at a jog—they see us a split second too late; their rifles are lifting as we're firing. Silas and Kane do not have silenced weapons so their shots are a giveaway.

"Contact at the gate," someone says on the enemy line. "Shots fired at the gate."

"Breaching," Kane grunts into the mic.

We all turn away and cover our ears; the detonation of the charges is deafening, even with our ears plugged. The gate creaks and then topples inward. Ears ringing, we roll around into the opening in double file, sweeping the interior of the courtyard.

The compound covers several hundred acres. The main house sits on the far rear of the property, barely visible from the gate. A long, low garage parallel to the west wall just inside the gate, and a two-story guard barracks is along the east wall opposite the barracks. Three black Suburbans are parked on each side of the courtyard, facing inward. Smoke billows skyward from the south wall, and a confused overlap of chatter in Spanish fills the comms line of my stolen earpiece—orders, questions, curses.

Perhaps two minutes after the first flashbang went off, a new voice fills the channel, this one sharp, pissed off, and authoritative. "What is happening? Antonio—status report."

It's Mercado.

"I am not sure yet, sir," Antonio says. "Flashbangs at the south wall but no contact. Patrols are unresponsive. I'm getting reports of a breach at the gate. I am on the way there to assess."

"I want every available man inside the residence, NOW," Mercado snaps. "Call in for backups from the village, ASAP." The last word is pronounced in English, military-style—*AY-sap*.

"Yes sir, right away," Antonio says.

"They're calling all units inside the residence," I say across our line. "Mercado is here, he's pissed, and he's calling for reinforcements. We are officially on the clock. We are fucked if we are not gone by the time the reinforcements arrive."

"We're gonna have to fight our way in and out," Saxon says. "Shit's about to get hot."

"Lash, Ren, Scarla—you're point," Solomon says. "We stick together for now."

"Copy," Lorenzo and Scarlett answer, once again in near unison.

We're passing through the courtyard in a tight double-file line. Now that Scarlett and Tatiana have stopped throwing flashbangs, the compound is oddly silent once more.

I feel a hand on my shoulder—Scarlett. Lorenzo moves into position on the other side of Scarlett, and the others readjust the formation into an inverted wedge, with Tatiana at the back.

"Tatiana is staying with us," Scarlett says. "It's too risky for her to wait at the gate alone."

"Copy," I mutter. "Moving."

We surge forward through the courtyard, making no contact. The main house is a massive, distant shadow, three sprawling floors with an east and west wing framing the center. A mile-long, ruler-straight driveway runs from the courtyard to the gate flanked on both sides by towering trees. Off to the west, half a mile distant, is the moonlit silhouette of a huge stable.

Panting from the mile run, we pause at the base of the steps, staring up at the monstrous house. Built of white marble and roofed in scalloped slate tiles, the house is ornate, with Ionic columns holding up the portico over the front porch, which doubles as a balcony overlooking the compound. The grass island at the center of the circle drive is an ornate marble fountain—a reproduction of something from Roman antiquity, most likely. A trio of glossy black Range Rovers are parked in a line in front of the house, and sixty or seventy meters to the east of the house, perched on the wide rolling lawn like a hungry insect, is a Soviet gunship helicopter.

"Kane," Solomon says across the line, "take out the helo. In fact, you and Silas take out the Suburbans back by the gate. Except one, if you can find keys, so we can make a getaway."

"He'll have them tracked," Kane says.

"I can find the tracker and get rid of it," Silas says. "Not a problem."

"Go," Solomon says.

The walls encircling the compound must encompass several miles of perimeter to enclose this much area; it's easily a mile from wall to wall east to west and roughly the same north to south. The hacienda sits in the middle of the compound toward the south wall, on a slight rise.

Figures move in the beams of headlights over near the stable—more hands hurrying to obey Mercado's call to defend him at the main house.

"Contact west," I say. "Targets mobilizing at the barn."

"Copy," Solomon says. "Saxon, Chance—they've only got one route here. Take them out."

"Copy," they both say.

A huge explosion rocks us, and we watch as the gunship bursts into flames. Seconds later, a much larger, brighter blast follows as the fuel ignites.

Without a word, we all break into a run—that explosion will have gotten Mercado's attention for sure. We reach the line of Range Rovers and take cover behind them, pausing a moment to catch our breath.

Tatiana is behind Scarlett on my right, holding her pistol in both hands barrel skyward, finger outside the trigger guard, panting and looking scared but calm.

Solomon gives the signal to move, and Scarlett taps Tatiana on the shoulder and repeats the signal; Tatiana nods and follows as we slip around the SUVs and head for the front door.

"Assume contact on the other side of the door," Solomon says. "Rev, kick it in."

"Copy," Rev mutters.

I put my hand on Rev's shoulder and follow him up the wide but shallow marble stairs. As we reach the door, I check my mag, charging handle, and fire selector switch, making sure everything is ready for action.

Rev does the same, glances at me, and receives my nod.

With a deep breath and a sharp exhale, he nods once to psych himself up, and then takes a big step backward and lunges forward, planting his boot right next to the door handle. It splinters but holds; he swivels out of the way of the door, anticipating a barrage of gunfire that never comes. After a short wait, he boots the door in the rest of the way. The doors burst inward with a crash, slamming all the way in, hitting the wall on the inside, and shuddering to a halt.

I shuffle past Rev, sweeping the vast foyer with my barrel—acres of polished, black-and-white marble tiles in a checkerboard pattern gleam, lit by a crystal-dripping chandelier. A suit of medieval armor stands on a pedestal in the center of the foyer, wielding a polearm. Twin staircases curve up to a second story landing in graceful, mirrored arcs on either side of the foyer, with more suits of armor marching along the wall from the stairs to the front door.

Beyond, looking beneath the second-story landing, glimpses of the kitchen—marble counters, the same checkered floor, and glass doors overlooking an expanse of verdant green lawn.

All is silent.

"Foyer is empty," I report across the channel. "No signs of life so far."

"Search the house," Sol orders.

Something doesn't feel right. It is based on nothing but instinct, a niggling in my gut. This has been too easy.

I glance at Rev, who is scenting the air like a wolf, eyes narrowed, rifle at the ready. He shakes his head. "Negative," he says into his mic.

"Repeat," Sol says.

"Negative," Rev says again. "This feels wrong."

"I agree," I say. "Something does not feel correct."

A pause. "Pull back to the circle," Solomon says.

Rev and I jog outside and to the circle where everyone else is gathered.

"Explain," Solomon says, rifle hanging from his shoulder, hands hooked into the neck of his vest.

I shrug. "It feels wrong. In there, I mean. It's too easy. They know we are here. Rafael called for all units to the house, and we're just going to walk right in? It feels like a trap."

Lorenzo growls. "I agree. Rafael is clever. He will have expected us. He likely knows of our escape from Zagreb and Pugli's men. Also, my intel says that he does not usually keep prisoners at the house."

"Where, then?" Kane asks.

Lorenzo points at the barn. "There."

"But Inez is no ordinary prisoner," Scarlett says.

Lorenzo shakes his head. "No. But then, he did not apprehend her out of revenge. He needed information from her. And there is only one way to get information out of someone like Sophia Sousa."

"Sophia Sousa?" Chance rumbles. "That's her real name? I like it."

"She will be pleased," Lorenzo says, his voice dripping with sarcasm.

"What information?" Rev asks.

Lorenzo sighs. "She will not like that I have shared this, but it was going to come out regardless." Another sigh. "She has a son—Rafael's son. She fled with him and placed him with a woman. She ensured she never knew where he was. Rafael is thinking of the future—of his legacy. He had another son with a different woman, but a rival killed them, so now he looks for his son with Sophia so he can make him the heir to the Mercado empire. He will not rest until he has what he wants. He knows that while she may not know where he is right now, Sophia can find her son. So the only question," Lorenzo says, "is how long Sophia can hold out. How much torture she can withstand. She will never give him what he wants—never. But he will not accept failure. So either she will break or she will die."

"And the point you are making is that he will not torture her in the house?" Kane asks.

"Correct," Lorenzo answers.

"But can we afford to make that assumption?" Solomon asks. "Time is wasting. We're here. Our entire plan was based on assaulting the main house."

"No, our plan was based on getting inside the compound and finding her," Lorenzo replies. "I do not think she is in the house. I think Rafael gambled on us assuming that, and probably that we would get their comms. If we search that house, we walk into an ambush."

Solomon glances across the compound at the distant bulk of the stable, then at the house. "Fine. You know Rafael, we don't." He circles his hand over his head and then points at the barn. "Double time it, folks."

We form a single file line that spreads out as we run across the lawn toward the barn, Lorenzo in the lead and Chance bringing up the rear—Chance can plod along at a jog for a very, very long time, but he will never be a fast runner.

Rev falls in beside me. "I don't like this, Lash. Sorry, Nicolae. That's gonna take a minute to get used to."

"I agree," I say. "This feels like a fishing expedition. Mercado is clever. He is usually several steps ahead of his enemies, which includes US intelligence. Something is amiss." I grin at him. "You can call me Nico, if you like. It may be easier."

"Alright then, Nico." He slaps me on the back. "Good to have you back. Gotta say, brother, it's great to see you and Tatiana together. You seem...lighter. I dunno if that's the right word."

I nod. "It is as good as any. I do feel lighter."

A couple minutes later, Sol calls a halt as we near the barn. It's dark, all exterior lights off except one, on a pole near the large sliding doors, casting a wide pool of yellow light on the white gravel. It is too still, too quiet. In a distant paddock, horses cluster together, heads down as they sleep, a couple of them laying down—it's hard to get a good count in the dark from a distance, but it looks like at least a dozen horses, if not closer to twenty. Which means the barn is likely empty—they put all the horses out to pasture to protect them from the anticipated gunfight. We're at the apex of a slight rise, looking downward toward the barn, kneeling or on our bellies as Solomon scans the barn with the scope of his rifle.

"Cameras at the corners," he whispers. "Nicolae— take 'em out."

I spot the cameras, glowing red with infrared. *Pop—Pop*.

"Advance," Sol whispers.

So far, this has not gone as we've anticipated. My gut roils with unease. There's something we're missing, I just have no way of knowing what until it happens.

And that's how people get killed on ops.

We advance to the side of the long structure, pausing to catch our breath as the rest of the team assembles. Using hand signals, Solomon indicates that half of us should go around the rear, and the other half around the front; I'm with the half hitting the front, along with Chance, Rev, Silas, and Kane, while Saxon, Solomon, Lorenzo, Scarlett, and Tatiana go around the rear.

I take out another camera and then aim my rifle at the smaller human-sized door beside the large double sliders. Chance kicks the door in and swings out of the way.

BOOOM! The blast of a shotgun is a deafening concussion, accompanied by the rattle-sprinkle of buckshot pellets punching holes through the walls.

"Fuck," Kane snaps, dancing away from the wall, clutching his left tricep.

There's no time to worry about him—it's a minor injury at worst and Kane is tough. I took a few flashbangs as we left the circle—I arm one and toss it in through the open door. I turn away, close my eyes, and plug my ears as the device goes off with a bang deafening even with my fingers in my ears, and blinding even with my eyes shut and my body turned away.

The second it goes off I'm in motion, surging through the doorway, stepping through and then sideways in a low crouching shuffle. I see a figure in the swirling smoke, dazed and disoriented—male, with a rifle.

I drop him with a pair of slugs through the skull, step over his body and catch up the shotgun—an excellent operator-grade Binelli.

He has a bandolier of shells which I also claim and sling over my torso.

I let my MP5 hang behind me and proceed through the gloom of the stable. The pungent smell of hay and manure and horse is thick and close; the lights are off, only the open door shedding light into the interior—all I can make out are shapes. I see the bars of horse stalls on either side, an intersection at the center of the structure faintly illuminated by the red glow of an exit sign. I hear the slam of a door being kicked in, the concussive chatter of an assault rifle opening up on full auto, abruptly cut off.

The five of us make our way slowly and cautiously down the stable hallway, sweeping each stall as we pass them. To the right of the intersection at the center of the barn is the vast, echoing space of an indoor arena. To the left, a short hallway leads to a closed doorway; on the left side of the hallway is an open stall for bathing and grooming the horses, while a darkened room on the right holds the bulky shadows of saddles and tack. More stalls march down the stable beyond the intersection, and large double sliding doors, a smaller human-sized door beside them; the smaller door is open and shedding ambient light from outside. The shadows of our team loom large on the stable floor as they enter the barn and head this way, scanning the stalls as they pass.

Solomon assesses the intersection, and then juts his

chin at the arena, glancing at Lorenzo and me. "Check it out."

"Copy," I mutter.

Lorenzo and I move in silent tandem toward the arena; it is not pitch black, having narrow, rectangular windows running the perimeter along three walls just below the roofline. The ground underfoot is soft, fine, dense dirt, compressing silently under each step. I click on the flashlight on my lower rail, indicating with hand signals that Lorenzo should go left while I go right. The arena must be at least ten thousand square feet of open, echoing space; in the middle are the shadowy shapes of dressage and jumping practice elements. Lorenzo and I make a quick circuit of the space, sweeping our beams across the middle, and then return to the team at the intersection.

Solomon eyes the doorway at the end of the lefthand hallway. "Well, I guess we go there."

"I will continue to take point," I say, trotting to the door.

It is thick metal, windowless, with a numeric keypad lock. I check the knob, just in case, but it is, in fact, locked.

I look at Lorenzo. "I will breach. Cover me."

He nods once, assuming a ready stance, aiming at the doorway from an oblique angle so anyone shooting through the opening will miss him. The others press against the walls, waiting. I thumb a new shell into the Binelli, rack the slide to eject the spent casing, and then blast a round through the lock—*crump-BOOM*! The lock disintegrates and the door squeals on its hinges. I shoulder it open and pivot to lean against the frame, dropping to a knee as Lorenzo sweeps from the inside right corner across the space to the inside left corner behind the door.

We're in another hallway, this one short and more like an office than a barn, with polished concrete floors and drywalled and painted walls. There are four doors, two on each side of the hallway. First on the right side is an empty bathroom, first on the left is a storage closet; second right leads to a large, industrial kitchen with acres of dully gleaming stainless steel, and opposite the kitchen is a den, with a big U-shaped sectional facing a massive TV. On the coffee table in the center of the sectional's open space is a clutter of empty beer bottles, half-empty liquor bottles, overflowing ashtrays, baggies of cannabis and cocaine, and boxes of ammunition and empty magazines. One of the ashtrays holds a still-smoldering cigarette butt.

"Well, they *were* here," Solomon says, eying the smoldering butt. "And recently."

"What did we miss?" Silas asks.

Lorenzo is back in the doorway between this section and the stable, spinning in a slow circle, his gaze thoughtful.

"What, Ren?" Sol says.

A shrug. "I do not know. But they are here somewhere. I can feel it."

"Okay, I believe you," Solomon says. "But where? We've searched the barn. No upstairs, no obvious basement."

"No," Lorenzo says. "It would not be obvious, would it? It isn't a basement, it is a cellar or a dungeon. It will be hidden."

"So we're looking for a trap door?" Saxon says. "That changes things. It won't be in the arena or the stalls. Tack room, maybe? Our barn at the estate we grew up on had a small cellar below the tack room. Dad hid the trapdoor beneath a fancy-ass rug, because the motherfucker was a bougie-ass dick."

Lorenzo strides aggressively toward the tack room and flips on the light—saddles rest on racks on the walls and on sawhorses here and there, with bits and bridles and halters hanging from hooks. Wide, deep wooden chests line the walls below the hooks and racks, and a large, expensive Persian rug covers the center of the floor. Lorenzo grabs a corner of the rug and tosses it, revealing a trapdoor. I help him pull the rug out of the way, and then he grabs the ring, pausing with a glance at me. I brace the shotgun in my shoulder, aim it at the door, and give him a nod. He jerks, but the door must be locked from below. He backs away and turns aside as I rack the empty shell out and blast a round through the handle. Lorenzo snags the gaping hole and heaves the heavy wooden door upward and drops it; I scan the opening with my flashlight.

A staircase, very steep, almost a ladder. Darkness below.

With a bracing exhale, I drop onto the stairs into a crouch and bend, tilting my shotgun sideways to sweep the light beam across the space: cinderblock walls, bare concrete floor, spiderwebs in the rafters, exposed electrical and plumbing; a long, wide corridor running the footprint of the stable. Bare lightbulbs dot the ceiling at regular intervals, turned off. A closed door here, a slightly ajar one there. Piles of random junk are scattered here and there— discarded building supplies, old saddles and pieces of tack, and agricultural tools and implements I cannot identify. Lorenzo follows me down, followed by Saxon and Rev; Lorenzo and Saxon search the lefthand corridor, and Rev and I the right. We creep silently for the nearest door, left slightly ajar. Rev takes up position on the hinge side while I wait by the latch side, switching back to my MP5; Rev shoves the door open and bolts backward out of the way; just in time, too.

Gunfire is a sudden barrage of noise and light and chaos, slashing through the dark silence. Rounds smash through the wall where Rev had been standing. If he hadn't expected exactly that and moved, he'd be dead.

I have one flashbang left, but I opt to preserve it, along with my pair of frag grenades. I use the bright spear of muzzle flash to pinpoint the shooter and send a trio of rounds just above the muzzle flash. They smack wetly, and the shooter collapses with a soft grunt.

Rev sweeps into the opening and rakes his beam across the room, momentarily blinding the three other occupants. He drops one with a pair of rounds to the chest—he's wearing a vest, so the shots aren't lethal; my follow-up slug to his skull is. The other shoot is quick to drop to a knee and rip off a short burst at Rev. He's too quick, the rounds going wide, and Rev doesn't miss, putting three more rounds to center mass, and I drop the third with a round through the throat, finishing the second shooter before he can recover.

I hear gunfire, a shout.

Tatiana screams; more gunfire. Scarlett shouts something, and then Solomon.

Cursing in Romani, I bolt out of the room. At the far end of the other corridor, Sol and Scarlett are pulling an enraged Tatiana out of a room, screaming and kicking.

A powerful hand grabs my arm. "We gotta clear this room, Nico," Rev growls in my ear. "You gotta trust them for a second."

Cursing again, I stomp across the hall and kick in the closed door, a rash, foolhardy action.

Something smashes me in the chest, knocking me backward several feet and crushing the breath from my lungs. I crash to the ground and crack my head on the floor, and stars whirl behind my eyes.

Rev steps over me and his rifle barks in a quick series of three-round bursts. He stares down at me as I blink and gasp. "Rookie mistake, Nico."

I nod, my mouth working as I struggle to catch my breath. That was stupid. I know better: don't rush is rule number one of room-clearing. I catch a sliver of oxygen and then manage a deeper breath, and then finally my lungs catch up and I gasp, gag, and cough. I hear groaning and gasping—the same noises I'm making. I grab Rev's proffered hand and accept his help up to my feet, struggling to pull a full breath. In the room, several men lay writhing and gasping and coughing on the floor.

Pissed off at myself, I switch to the Binelli and finish them off with a rapid sequence of blasts.

Rev chuckles as I exit the room. "Alright, then." His humor fades immediately. "You alright?"

I nod, pushing on my chest to check for tenderness, wincing and hissing. "Yes, I do not believe anything is broken."

More gunfire, a few quick bursts. At the other end, Scarlett has Tatiana pressed up against the wall, speaking to her intently. I jog down the corridor to them.

"What is it?" I demand. "What happened?"

Scarlett meets my gaze, indicating the room I saw them dragging Tatiana from. With a heavy heart, I enter it.

Hanging from a hook in the ceiling by thick, rusty

chains, shoulders dislocated, bruised, beaten bloody, tortured, and left to bleed out is Stjepan Juric—Tatiana's father.

"Fuck," I snarl.

Solomon reenters. "Punishment for letting us get away, I guess."

"That must be what the shooting was after we left—Mercado sent men to make sure we were finished off," I said, "and when they discovered we were gone, they took Stjepan instead."

Sol just nods. "No sign of Inez. We've searched the whole barn."

Kane pokes his head in. "Lorenzo took Sax, Chance, and Si back to the house to look there. But I think we were played. He took her—probably waited somewhere he could see us within walkie range and left a few sacrificial lambs to make it convincing."

Solomon rubs his face. "Goddammit. God *fucking* dammit."

"I knew this was too easy," I snarl. "Lorenzo will be fit to be tied."

"Let's go help them search that big ass house, just in case," Kane says.

I nod, exiting the room. Tatiana surges past Scarlett and slams into me.

"Why?" She sobs against my chest. "I don't understand. Why?"

"He allowed us to get away. Mercado does not tolerate failure." I let out a sigh, stroking her hair. "I am so sorry, my love. I am sorry. He did not deserve to die."

"Not like this," she murmurs. "Not like this."

"We have to go, Tati. We can't stay here. Mercado's men might return."

She shakes her head. "We cannot leave him here, Nico. We can't."

"We cannot bring him all the way back to Zagreb, either. It is simply impossible."

Despite my words, I lower Stjepan from the hook, unchain him, and put him over my shoulder. He is not a light man, but I am strong, and it is for my Tatiana, so I do it without complaint.

Sniffling quietly the whole way, Tatiana accompanies me to the main house, where Lorenzo is waiting near an idling Suburban with a murderous expression on his face.

One by one, everyone else files out of the house, morose, pissed off, and defeated.

Solomon is the last one out, carrying a small tablet.

When Silas saw me coming with Stjepan on my shoulder, he went back inside and came out with a flat sheet and some bungee cords; he places the flat sheet on the ground and helps me wrap Stjepan in it, securing the sheet around his cold and stiffening body, and we place it in the back of the Suburban.

Once this is done, Solomon hands me the tablet without a word. Tatiana moves to stand beside me, her lovely face tear-tracked and sorrowful. I click the button on the top right end of the device and it comes to life without a passcode; an upward swipe opens it to a video. When I press play, the blur on the screen resolves into Rafael moving into the frame.

"Welcome, friends," he says with a winning grin. His English is absolutely flawless—if I didn't know better, he could be a third-generation Colombian-American, raised speaking English as a first language. "By now, since you are viewing this recording, you have discovered that you are not as smart as you thought. In fact, you have the lovely Sophia, whom I believe you know as Inez—" he reaches off-screen and jerks Inez into view, "to thank for the fact that you are still alive. I could have had you all killed at any time, but I am only interested in one thing, and Inez, my lovely and loyal wife, values your lives, so she gave me what I want."

I pause the video, sighing as I curse under my breath in Romani.

Lorenzo spits in the gravel at his feet, cursing floridly and extensively in Spanish, English, and Portuguese. "Fuck," he snarls, in English, after pausing for breath. "She gave him up."

"Her son?" Scarlett asks. "I can't believe she would do that, even for us."

Lorenzo shakes his head. "I don't know. I do not know. I would not think so either, not after everything she did to see him safe from Rafael. But you are her responsibility, and she takes that very seriously."

"Something's off, though," Solomon says. "Keep watching."

I tap the screen to play it again.

Inez is in awful shape—her face is bruised, bloody, and swollen, with cut lips, black eyes, a visibly broken nose, and a vicious gash to her left cheekbone. The camera pulls back and it becomes clear they did more than just hit her—she's been tortured. Lorenzo collapses to his knees in the gravel, keening a guttural cry like a trapped panther. He rockets to his feet and moves to smash his fist into the side of the suburban, but Chance dodges in front of Lorenzo and takes the blow to the gut. Lorenzo shouts something unintelligible in Portuguese, shoving at Chance, who barely moves.

"You need your hands to save your woman," Chance murmurs. "Need to hit something, hit me. I can take it."

Lorenzo shakes his head, the fight leaching out of him—he collapses again, this time bonelessly, and Chance catches him.

"We'll find her, Ren," he murmurs. "She's the toughest bitch this side of Hell, and we both know it."

Lorenzo finds his feet after a moment, swiping at his nose with his wrist, nodding. "Sorry. I'm—I am sorry, I—"

Chance's mammoth arms pull him into a crushing hug. "No apologies, bro. We all know exactly how you feel. We've all had our women in danger. We'll stop at nothing to get her back, even if we have to wade into fuckin' hell itself."

"He fucking *tortured* her," Lorenzo hisses, his accent thicker than I've ever heard it. "Beat her. Cut her. Pulled out her fingernails. I…I fucking—when I get my hands on him, no death will be too fucking slow for that—that…" he shakes his head. "I do not have the word for what he is."

Solomon moves to Lorenzo's other side. "You gotta keep watching, man. She's giving you a message. You gotta watch."

Lorenzo takes the tablet from me and plays the recording again.

"Look at her eyes," Solomon says. "Watch."

She's blinking strangely, I realize. Too fast or too slow, and in a strange rhythm.

"Oh, fuck," Kane says. "Morse code!"

"What?" Saxon asks. "She's blinking in Morse Code?"

"Yeah," Kane says. "I read about this on Reddit once.

There was this POW in Vietnam. They made him make one of those propaganda videos, you know? He was saying what they told him to say, but he was blinking a whole other fuckin' message in Morse Code. Can't remember what the message was, but it doesn't matter."

"So, who knows Morse code?" Lorenzo asks. "I did not know she knew it."

"Inez is a deep well of mysteries," Silas says. "None of us really know her. Shit man, you don't know her—not all the way. You knew the woman she was. The woman she still can be, and still is in some ways, but she's also totally someone else."

Lorenzo waves this off with a disgusted sigh. "I know you are right, but psychology is meaningless to me right now. What the fuck is she saying? That is what I need to know."

Solomon brings up an internet search on the tablet. "Here we go. We need a notebook or something."

A few minutes later, Solomon has transcribed the Morse code alphabet onto a notebook page. Then he rewinds the video and plays it frame by frame, writing down the pattern of Inez's blinked message—it's a slow, painstaking process. Once the message has been written down in Morse Code, Solomon and Scarlett work together to translate it.

Finally, Solomon smacks the page. "Inez, you clever fuckin' bitch."

"What?" Lorenzo snarls, snatching the notebook, and reading out loud. "R knows who not where. Name is Lorenzo Oliveira." Lorenzo chokes, here, voice shaking. "He is in—shit. Shit! What does this say, Solomon?"

Sol peers at it. "Man, she's spelling the name of

a town I've never heard of in Brazil, and she's spelling it Morse fucking Code." He checks the notes. "Looks like…S-U-R-U-C-U-C-U."

Lorenzo growls, rubbing his face. "That's not what you wrote here. This is gibberish." He holds up his hand, head hanging. "I apologize—it is not your fault. I have heard of this place—it is a very small place, barely a village on the Corumbá River, south of Brasilia." He scrubs his face. "The message concludes—'R will find L. You find first. Forget me. Get L.'"

Silence.

"She named him Lorenzo," Lorenzo whispers. To the group, then. "We must go, now. I will arrange transport to Brasilia." He looks at Tatiana. "I will also make arrangements for your father. I am sorry for your loss."

Tatiana, tears streaking anew down her face, meets his gaze. "This Rafael or Mercado, or whatever he calls himself—he owes us all a slow death. It is a tragedy we cannot kill him more than once."

"Facts," Saxon says. "Let's find keys for these slick-ass rides and get the fuck to Brazil, ASAP."

"Agreed," Silas says. "I don't like feeling like I fucked up and failed. This motherfucker is gonna die."

Lorenzo says nothing, but the venomous fury on his face says it all.

CHAPTER 14

LITTLE LORENZO

TATIANA

LORENZO ONCE AGAIN USES HIS EXTENSIVE network of contacts—we trade Rafael's Range Rovers and the Suburban for seats on a Colombian Army Chinook headed to Manaus for a joint training exercise. True to his word, he also secured a plain pine coffin for Tata's body and a flight back to Zagreb.

It's hard to fathom that my father is gone.

I have been through quite a bit in my life as the only child of a notorious gangster who also happens to be an elected official. But nothing could have prepared me for the devastating shock of walking into that room below Rafael's barn and seeing my father's broken body strung up like a side of beef.

I do not understand why. The others have explained it—Tata was supposed to keep Solomon, Scarlett, and Lorenzo captive as leverage to make Inez do what he wants. Lash too, I suppose—the redirection of that jet and the capture of Solomon and the others were part of the same plot.

But why kill Tata? Surely he would have continued to be valuable to Mercado? Apparently not.

I am truly adrift in the world, now. My business is me. I am the CEO, founder, president, COO, CFO, everything. Katya and Ana were my primary employees, and now they're gone too. Georg. Tata. Mercado has destroyed my life from the inside out, and I'm not sure he even realizes it.

I'm just collateral damage, something he doesn't give two shits about.

I spend the flight to Manaus stewing in my grief and my rage.

All this for…a single child?

The boy's life undeniably holds value. But…how many people have to die for Mercado to get what he wants? The death toll has to be in the dozens at this point, with many more to come before it's over.

When the helicopter lands on the base in Manaus, I am delirious with exhaustion, boiling with impotent rage, and gutted with grief. Nico wraps an arm around my waist and guides me down the ramp and across the tarmac—a van is waiting to take us across the airfield to a different runway, where a twin-engine prop plane is being prepared for takeoff.

I groan as we pile into the aircraft, the weapons and other gear stowed in the duffel bags once more. "I feel like I have been traveling forever," I mutter to Nico in Croatian, too tired and emotional to bother with English.

"I know, my love," he says. "It has been a lot."

"I was so mad at him for…being what he was, I guess. But now…" I shake my head, blinking back tears—I've cried more on the flight here than in the last several years combined. "I just…he's gone, and I…I guess I feel lost, even though I spent my life as an adult trying to get away from him and his effect on my life."

"Mercado is a singularly destructive force in this world," Nico says. "Everywhere he goes, everything he does, he leaves a wake of destruction and death behind him."

"Can you explain something for me?" I ask.

He shrugs. "I can try. If I can, I will."

"You all refer to him as both Mercado and Rafael. Which is his name?"

"Rafael is the name he was born with—Rafael Sousa. Mercado is his business persona. Very few have even heard the name Rafael Sousa. Many know the name Mercado— it is at once his name and the name of the cartel he runs, his operation as the king of cartels. So, people will say 'Look out, be careful, Mercado is coming,' and they mean Mercado's men, not he himself. They say 'You do not want to cross Mercado,' and they mean both the man and the organization. But when *we* say Mercado, we mean the man, Rafael Sousa."

"Oh. I see. And Inez?" I ask. "I've heard her called two names also."

He chuckles. "It is sort of a thing for us, it seems—assuming new identities to get away from the past. I was born Nicolae Dragos, and when my family was killed, I chose the name Lash. Scarlett, according to what I have overheard, also has a name she was born with, different from Scarlett."

Scarlett is sitting in front of us, dozing. "I was born Maria Rodriguez," she says, without turning or lifting her head. "I'm from Panama, originally."

Nico laughs, rubbing his face. "I didn't realize I had switched to English. I am exhausted and disoriented."

I rest my head on his shoulder, laughing. "I didn't either."

Scarlett snorts. "He speaks to you in English, and sometimes Croatian, and you almost always speak to him in Croatian when it's just the two of you having a private conversation. But then other times, you switch back and forth at random."

"Anyway," Nico says. "Inez, too, has a past she sought to escape. I have not heard the whole story, however, but from what I gather, she was married against her will to Rafael. So legally, her name is Sophia Sousa."

Lorenzo is behind us. "She was born Sophia de Silva. Her father was the original kingpin of the cartel Rafael took control over. He married Sophia against her will—the details of that are not my story to tell. This marriage cemented his place in the cartel as Sophia's father's right-hand man. Once the marriage was done, Rafael killed Bruno de Silva, Sophia's father, and took over. The de Silva cartel was already immensely powerful, and Rafael, working under the name Mercado, expanded the cartel's sphere of influence through a variety of means. He bribed officials, courted the favor of generals, took over smaller competing cartels by force and absorbed them into his operations. For the larger cartels he didn't want to go into outright war with, he used assassination to remove the cartel heads and installed people he controlled or who were loyal to him. Once his empire was big enough, he then began using more direct methods to assume further control. Now, he controls nearly the entire flow of drugs, guns, and humans into and out of South and Central America. That is Mercado. That is the man we seek to kill." Lorenzo sighs. Continues. "He is also a cold-blooded sociopath who delights in torture and murder."

"Lovely," I murmur. "So we are fighting a sadistic Goliath."

Lorenzo snorts. "No, Tatiana, we are fighting Goliath and the entire Philistine army."

"So how can we hope to succeed?" I ask.

Lorenzo doesn't answer immediately. "He cannot bring the entire force of his empire to bear against us all at once—it is spread out across Brazil, Colombia, Venezuela, and Mexico, not to mention all the other smaller countries in between, in a terrorist cell-type structure. He has eyes and agents everywhere, not just in Latin America. What works in our favor, however, is that he is intensely paranoid. He only trusts a very small circle of people, and his personal bodyguard is also a relatively small force because he trusts no one. So despite the size of his empire and the personnel and resources he controls, he is only surrounded by a very small entourage of assistants, lieutenants, and guards."

"Oh," I say, "so as long as we can stay close to him, we stand a chance?"

"More or less, yes," Lorenzo answers. "I have my own network of resources and contacts in governments and militaries in Brazil and Colombia, and those are people I know for a fact are not owned by Mercado."

"And do you have a secret name, too?" I ask.

He laughs. "No. I am only Lorenzo Oliveira Araujo, as I have always been."

"Lorenzo Oliveira," I say, remembering Inez's message.

He lets out a long, shaky breath. "Apparently she gave him my name. I am a little angry with her for not telling me that. It was also perhaps a little foolish to give him my name—Lorenzo is not a very common name over here. It is an Italian name, but my mother read it in a book and decided she liked it."

I turn to look at him over the back of my seat. "Is it possible that he is not Rafael's son, but yours?" I ask.

Lorenzo shakes his head. "Very, *very* unlikely. I...we only had a little time together before we were discovered, she was punished, and I was forced to escape with my life. No, the timing of her pregnancy does not align with our time together. I think she gave him my name out of love, and so no part of Rafael would be applied to him other than the unfortunate fact of his genetics."

Solomon speaks up, then. "I thought she said she didn't know his exact whereabouts."

Lorenzo shrugs. "She doesn't—not exactly. Surucucu is probably a last known location or general area." He growls. "I don't think she factored in Rafael being able to use us as leverage. She could and would have endured any torture without a word, but trapped between loyalty to us and love for her son, she was left with no good options."

"Are we really going to go after her son rather than her?" Solomon asks.

Lorenzo lets out a long breath. "For now, yes. She would murder us all herself if we rescued her and not her son. Once we have him and get him to safety, we get Sophia."

"Now that he has a name," Scarlett asks, "Does he even need her?"

"That is an excellent question," Lorenzo answers. "And I do not know. He is unpredictable—part of being a sociopath, perhaps."

"So for now, we focus on getting little Lorenzo to safety," Chance rumbles.

"Yes," Lorenzo says. "That is what she will expect. And we must all remember that this is Sophia. I do not think any of us can appreciate how dangerous she is. She went willingly into the lion's den, knowing full well what she would endure."

"You think she's playin' possum?" Kane asks.

Lorenzo shrugs. "Possible. If by playing possum you mean biding her time until she unleashes herself upon Rafael and his men, then yes."

"How will she know?" Saxon asks.

Lorenzo shrugs again. "I am not certain, but I have a feeling that when Rafael discovers we got to his son before he did, his reaction will be…intense, to say the least. If I had to guess, that is how she will know. Which means that we cannot fail to get to him first."

"Motherfucker outsmarted us once," Rev growls. "Not fuckin' happenin' again."

"Facts," Saxon says. "I just hope Inez leaves some of Rafael for us."

Lorenzo's laugh is deep and dark and wicked. "I do not. As much as we all have reason to hate him, none of us as much as she. And trust me when I say the death she will give him will be one for the ages."

I shudder. "Perhaps I am weak, but I do not think I should like to see that."

Nico kisses my temple. "It is good you do not. I do not wish for you to become like us."

"You may not be some vanilla virgin," Scarlett says, "but you're still a helluva lot more innocent than the rest of us. And in my book, that's a damn good thing."

I shake my head. "I do not know, Scarlett. I think seeing my father like that erased the last of my innocence."

Nico sighs. "Perhaps. Just do not become so accustomed to seeing and dealing with death that it no longer affects you."

I can't think of an answer to that, so I let my eyes droop closed and let the drone of the engines lull me to a fitful sleep.

I wake as we prepare for landing. It's a smooth touchdown and a short taxi. Waiting for us on the tarmac at the airfield in Brasilia is an ex-military troop transport—a huge vehicle with a single bench cab and an open-air bed with benches on both sides facing inward.

Chance groans when he sees it. "Fuck, man. I thought my days of climbing my giant ass up into those things were over."

Lorenzo laughs, clapping him on the shoulder. "I am sorry, my friend. It was the best I could do on such short notice."

Chance chuckles. "Nah, it's fine. We'd be fucked without you. I'm just not as agile as I was back in the day."

"Who is? Time waits for no one." Lorenzo rolls his shoulder and flexes his leg. "Once upon a time, I would barely feel these. Now? I am not as invincible as I used to be."

One by one, we all climb into the back of the transport, Lorenzo driving and Kane up front with him.

It is a long, slow, winding journey through rolling hills, flat grasslands, wide fields, and patches of forest, gliding along paved highways and bouncing over rutted dirt tracks. Immediately outside of Brasilia, the traffic is thick, but the further south we go, the more rural the landscape and the fewer cars we pass.

Lorenzo consults a navigation app on his phone now and then—it cuts in and out of service as we pass through dead zones and areas of reception, but after about two hours we begin passing the occasional residence and other signs of habitation. And then suddenly we're at a crossroads, and Lorenzo seems stumped.

He picks a fork, and we end up in a…I'm not sure what to call it. A neighborhood? Sort of? Cobbled together houses, repaired and rebuilt endlessly, serviced by dirt roads and surrounded by scrubby yellow grass lawns, all of it nestled in the U of a dense forest, with a vast, flat, open savannah forming the open part of the U-shape.

Faces peer from windows, curious and wary. At one home, a hunched old man hobbles out, leaning on a cane, and glares daggers at us. Here, Lorenzo brakes to a squealing halt, leaves the engine idling with a noisy diesel clatter, and approaches the old man. They converse for a few minutes, the old man gesturing eastward with his cane. Lorenzo shakes the man's hand with a warm, grateful smile. As Lorenzo saunters with a slight limp back to the truck, I see the old man glance into his hand, and then shove that hand into his pocket.

"Alright, friends," Lorenzo says, climbing up to stand in the open door of the cab, addressing us all. "We have a lead. There's a condo building east of here, and I am told that a young boy named Lorenzo lives there, or did recently."

Returning to the fork in the road, we take the opposite

path. Although newer than the houses in the other area, the condo building is in serious need of repair. A yelling, screaming cluster of children ranging from toddlers to young teens ramble the sparse, yellow grass and dirt road around the condo building, kicking and chasing a football around. They don't seem to be playing a game by any rules that I can see beyond getting the ball and keeping it as long as possible.

Lorenzo parks the truck again and hops down—Solomon joins him, and together they spend a few minutes talking to the kids. As the conversation continues, Lorenzo, almost absently, toes the black-and-white checkered ball toward himself and skillfully juggles it from foot to knee to chest to head, turning it into a game of keep-away while he asks his questions. After a few minutes of this, he seems to have gleaned the information he seeks and gestures for us to follow him into the building. Kane shuts off the motor and we all pile out and follow Lorenzo. Inside, the floors are covered in thin, tattered, and stained blue carpet. It stinks horribly, as well, some miasma of indeterminate origin, and is sweltering hot. Lorenzo leads the way up the stairs to a unit at the far end of the third floor.

He scans the group and then gestures at me. "Will you accompany me, Tatiana? We need to present an unthreatening face. This will be an unexpected and frightening process, most likely, and you will lend warmth and openness. Everyone else is rather terrifying, for a young boy especially."

I shrug. "Alright. You will have to translate for me, though."

"Of course." He rests a friendly hand on my shoulder. "All I really need from you is to smile and be kind and reassuring and calm. I am an old soldier, Tatiana so my bearing is not always…approachable for women and young children. You are here to soften things a bit."

"Are you saying I'm not soft and approachable?" Scarlett asks, deadpan.

Lorenzo just laughs. "No, Scarla, you are not."

She covers the scarred side of her face with one hand. "How about now?"

Lorenzo snorts. "I think I will stick with Tatiana. The rest of you, keep watch. We cannot be sure Rafael's men will not arrive while we are here."

Lorenzo knocks on the door while everyone else takes up positions at the window, on the stairs, and at the doorway.

After a moment, Lorenzo and I hear locks scraping, and then the door swings open inward. On the other side is a woman about my age or perhaps a few years older. She has brown skin and black hair in a loose bun with blunt, squared-off bangs, large silver hoop earrings, and long, pink press-on nails. She's wearing cutoff denim shorts and a pale green tank top, her large breasts braless, and a bit of a belly. She is suspicious and wary.

Lorenzo addresses her in rapid Spanish, but all I can make out is the name Lorenzo Oliveira. The woman stares at him silently for a moment and then shuts the door.

Before the door closes all the way, Lorenzo says something that I think must be "Wait!" He pulls his phone from his pocket and brings up a photo—it actually looks like he took a picture of an actual printed photograph with his phone.

This time the woman does respond with a terse question; judging by her tone, she's asking what he wants. She points at the others visible from her place just inside her condo, asking another question.

Lorenzo answers, but she doesn't seem to find his answer satisfactory. She moves to shut the door on him again, and again he blocks it with his foot, speaking more forcefully this time.

Angry now, the woman snaps at him, shoving him and kicking at his foot simultaneously. Unfortunately for her, Lorenzo is huge and powerfully built, and he's wearing heavy boots while she's barefoot, so Lorenzo doesn't go anywhere, and she hops backward, hissing and dancing as she clutches at her toes, cursing at him.

"CONTACT!" I hear one of the men shout from the door of the building. "Three SUVs and a technical."

Lorenzo grabs me by the arm and shoves me into the woman's condo, yanking his pistol from the back of his waist. The woman is yelling, hauling on his arm, and gesticulating at me. When this doesn't work, she lets go and darts into her kitchen, emerging with a massive kitchen blade.

Lorenzo holds his hands out toward her, trying to placate her, but she ignores him, approaching him with the knife in a posture that suggests she's no novice to a knife fight.

Gunfire erupts then, coming from the front of the building—a burst of automatic weapons fire.

The woman screams, running to a back bedroom with the knife clutched in her hand. Lorenzo follows her, and I follow him. The apartment is low-ceilinged, with yellowing drywall and cheap laminate floor, a sliding glass door to a postage stamp balcony shedding the bright hot Brazilian sunlight. The bedroom is tiny, with a narrow bed, posters of famous Brazilian footballers on the wall and thin, dirty beige carpet on the floor. A boy of about ten sits on the floor at a mound of LEGOs. As his mother bursts in wielding a knife, he drops the pieces in his hand and stares at her.

"Mama?" he queries, confused more than concerned.

Lorenzo fills the doorway, pistol in hand, and the young boy shoots to his feet and puts himself between his mother and Lorenzo, chin high, eyes blazing and defiant. More gunfire erupts—only a handful of seconds have elapsed from the first burst, and now the boy takes notice, turning to look up at his mother.

Lorenzo says something in a low, comforting tone, pointing toward the noise with his gun. I wriggle under his arm, offering mother and son what I hope is a reassuring smile.

"It's okay," I say in English. "We are here to help you."

Lorenzo translates, and I put myself between him and the mother and son. The woman responds, and I wait for the translation.

"She wants to know who is shooting and why we are here," Lorenzo murmurs to me.

"What have you told her?" I ask him.

"That I'm a friend of Sophia's, and that we need to get her and her son out of here."

"Seems like a lot more than that was said, Lorenzo."

"Yes, but most of it was her being suspicious and telling me to leave, and me trying to explain."

I give him a droll look. "Lorenzo, you are a big scary man showing up out of the blue talking about this boy's birth mother, telling her she needs to go with you. And then there's shooting. Of course she's going to be wary and protective."

The woman snaps something.

"She wants to know what we are saying."

I shuffle toward her, hands out so she can see I am unarmed. "You adopted Lorenzo from this woman, yes?" I ask, holding out my hand to Lorenzo; he puts the phone in it with Inez's photo on screen.

Soí," she says. "And?"

I point toward the gunfire. "There are bad men out there who want to steal Lorenzo from you."

"Who wants to steal him? Why?" she asks, through Lorenzo.

"Do I tell her the truth?" I ask him.

"Yes, it is best, at this point."

So, I tell her, having to get closer to hear her over the back-and-forth chatter of the gunfight—deafening, terrifying.

"Lorenzo's father is Mercado," I explain, speaking slowly with pauses for translation. "I know you must have heard of him. He is a very evil man. He wants to make Lorenzo the next Mercado."

This gets her attention. "Mercado is the devil." She dry-spits on the floor and makes the sign of the cross. "My husband was killed by Mercado gangsters. He was doing nothing—shopping for food for dinner. Someone who angered Mercado was there, and they shot him, and my husband was in the way. They did not care. They are monsters."

I point in the direction of the gunfire. "That's them out there, and my friends are holding them off."

She looks at her son, and then at me. "He is the son of the devil?" She clutches her son to her chest with her free hand, the knife still at the ready.

"But he was raised with love," I say. "His mother—the

woman who bore him, she will not let him become like Mercado. She sent us to protect you."

The woman's gaze goes distant. "She was hurt and afraid. She gave me a lot of money, but told me to be very careful with it. Never tell anyone how I got him." She snaps her gaze back to me. "Why does Mercado want him now, after so many years?"

"I do not know for sure. I heard that he had another son who was killed. He needs an heir to give the Mercado empire to, so he decided he wants it to be his son."

The woman presses a kiss to little Lorenzo's head, her eyes thoughtful. She shakes her head, mouth still pressed to her son's head. "He is my son. I do not care who his father is, and I will not give him back to her. He is mine."

Lorenzo steps forward then, addressing; after, he tells me what he told her. "Sophia is not trying to take him back. She wants you both to be safe. That is all."

The woman stares hard at Lorenzo. "Are you lying to me?"

Lorenzo shakes his head and meets her gaze without wavering or looking away. "Sophia went through a hell you cannot ever imagine to give that boy a safe life away from the world he was born into. She gave him to you to protect him, to raise him, and to love him. You have done this. Now, you must trust Sophia. You must trust us. We will keep you safe until Mercado is no longer a threat, and then we will help you find a new place to live." He thumps himself on the chest. "I was there. I saw what she did, what she went through. I helped her escape and I helped her get a new identity and papers for him. I will help you again when this is over. For now, you must come with us and let us protect you."

The gunfire stops abruptly, and Solomon and Scarlett find us—Scarlett is splattered with blood, her face, hands, and chest painted with it. They both have assault rifles held casually across their torsos.

"Threats neutralized," Solomon says. "But we gotta go. There'll be more."

"Everyone okay?" Lorenzo asks.

Solomon nods. "These guys must have been the B-team for some local gang. Couldn't hit the broad side of a barn with a shotgun from point blank range if their lives depended on it."

The woman and Little Lorenzo have backed away from the bloody specter of Scarlett. I move away from them and toward the pair, speaking in a low tone, trusting Lorenzo to translate.

"We really need to leave now, okay? Pack some clothes and your most important belongings—only things you can carry."

"Will we come back?" The woman asks.

I can only shrug. "Truthfully, I do not know. All I know is that more bad men will come looking for you, and soon. Belongings can be replaced—your lives cannot."

She lets out a shaky breath and then turns to face her son in a crouch, murmuring to him in Spanish. He nods, eyes wide and constantly flicking back to Scarlett."

Lorenzo eyes her. "Maybe you can clean up a bit? You are scaring the boy."

Scarlett rolls her eyes at him, but heads into the bathroom across the hall. "Oh, well shit. No wonder the poor kid looks like he's about to shit himself."

"*Exatamente*," Lorenzo mutters, more to himself.

A few minutes later, the woman—whose name I still

haven't heard—has a duffel bag and a backpack as well as her purse, and Little Lorenzo has his own duffel bag and backpack. They follow us out of the building and stop at the top of the steps, staring. The parking lot is littered with bodies, and one of the SUVs is smoking from the hood.

Kane trots down the steps after us. "Did a quick check of the facing units. It doesn't seem like anyone got hit by any strays or ricochets. They're pissed and confused, though. We're gonna have cops on our ass if we don't get the actual motherfuck out of here."

Solomon claps him on the shoulder. "Good news. Thanks, Kane." He raises his voice. "We need to split up. Take the intact SUV. Nico, Tatiana, Rev, Kane—you take the technical. Nico, I want you on that fifty cal. You so much as *smell* anyone on our six, light 'em the fuck up. Everyone else, in the SUV."

The technical, it turns out, is a pickup truck with a giant machine gun mounted in the bed. The pickup is an older model four-door pickup with ripped and filthy cloth seats, trash cluttering the footwells, and stinking of cigarettes and body odor. Rev and Kane take one look at the interior, at each other, and then say, "Oh, fuck no," in unison. Within seconds, they've tossed the trash into the backseat of one of the shot-up SUVs. That done, Kane takes the driver's seat, glances at me and points at the front passenger seat while Rev sets up in the back seat, laying not one but two assault rifles beside him, along with several boxes of ammunition and a handful of spare magazines. Lash climbs into the bed and immediately goes to work checking the machine gun, testing the movement of the action, running his hands over the belt of bullets, testing the range and smoothness of the tilt and swivel. He crouches and goes over the spare belt of ammunition and then rises and readies the weapon. That done, he takes a seat in the bed and slaps the side a couple times.

The others load into the SUV, Lorenzo behind the wheel; a few moments later, we're heading north. The troop transport we took here has been shot to hell, the tires flattened, the engine filled with holes, and all the glass shattered, which is why we had to split up.

Rev hands me a box of ammunition and several empty magazines. "Tatiana, if and when shit starts to pop off, you're my reloader, yeah? Your job is to make sure I'm never out of fuckin' bullets. When I run out, I'm gonna say 'reload.' That's your cue. When you hear that word, you hand me the other rifle." He passes one of the guns to me and then leans over the console, pointing at a particular button near the handle. "This is the mag release. Press it and the mag will drop out. Slide in a fresh one—*tap* gently it to make sure it's in place. *Do not* whack it, that's TV bullshit and you'll cause a jam. So. I say 'reload' and we switch. Then, while I'm shooting, you put in a new mag and refill the empty one. Got it?"

I nod. "Yes, I understand. I am familiar with pistols as my father made me practice with him at the shooting range once every week for my whole life, and I do have *some* experience with bigger guns like this one."

He nods. "Good. Let's practice. Safety on?" He watches as I check the safety, nods again when I am sure it's engaged. "Okay. Reload!"

I pass him the gun but fumble it in my haste. "Shit," I say in Croatian and then address him in English. "I am sorry. Try again."

"This is why we practice," he says. "Remember—slow is smooth and smooth is fast. Don't try to hurry."

"Slow is smooth and smooth is fast," I repeat. "Okay."

He hesitates, puts the gun to his shoulder, and then down. "Reload!"

I exchange with him, this time focusing on smoothness rather than speed, and it works perfectly. The exchange goes well, and I release the magazine, pick up another full one, slide it in, and tap it home. We exchange again, and I switch mags again. We practice the exchange several more times until it's smooth. I glance at Nico through the rear window and find him watching me. He gives me a smile and a nod and then goes back to scanning our back trail.

The first hour is uneventful and boring, passing cars and fields and forests and the occasional town or village.

And then it happens.

A caravan of four SUVs, black Suburbans identical to the ones in the compound, pass us heading south. They see us, and brakes squeal as they make hurried U-turns. Nico keys his radio, and I hear his voice through the window and from the radio sitting in the cupholder in front of Kane.

"Contact! Four hostile vehicles."

"Copy," comes Solomon's voice. "Engage. Weapons free."

"Alright," Rev says. "Let's fuckin' go, boys and girls."

Nico is on his feet at the big machine gun, and the weapon is belching fire and noise, and the whole vehicle shudders and rocks with the recoil. Rev twists in the seat to lean through the open window, tucks his rifle to his shoulder, and opens fire, adding to the deafening barrage of gunfire.

Nico's first burst walks rounds toward the enemy

vehicle, sending chunks of road spraying everywhere, and then the rounds smash into the SUV's hood and shatter the windshield. White smoke billows from the hood and the big vehicle wobbles, spins sideways, and then flies into a barrel roll. The vehicle behind it swerves and barely avoids it, only to meet Rev's bullets, which pock the hood and put spiderwebbing holes in the glass. Nico sends another burst at them, and the glass shatters and red sprays, but the vehicle continues after us. Someone in the Suburban returns fire, and I see the metal of the bed pock and dent and divot inches from Nico, and then the rear window shatters. I duck, screaming, as more rounds thunk into the console inches from me. Nico fires another burst and these rounds smash into their hood, loosing a cloud of white smoke, and the vehicle wobbles, brakes, and fishtails.

Rev doesn't let up, pouring fire into the vehicle even after it has halted, and I catch a glimpse of crimson spray. His weapon clicks, and he passes it to me, shouting "RELOAD!"

I trade with him as we practiced, put a new mag in the weapon, and spend the next few moments thumbing shells into the plastic magazine.

"I think I might've killed someone just now," Rev says, conversationally.

"But you don't know," Kane answers, "So don't fuckin' worry about it. This is survival, bro. Mercado can send a fuckin' army after us."

Two down, two to go. The other two have closed the gap, and now men are leaning out of both rear windows of the lead SUV, their rifles chattering—their shots go wide, although one smashes the side view mirror on the driver's side.

Nico fires another long burst, pauses, and fires again, but the Suburban swerves just in time and the rounds hit the vehicle behind them—tires pop, the hood sprouts holes, smoke billows, and that vehicle brakes and spins to a halt. The Suburban swerves, narrowly avoiding oncoming cars. The shooters open fire at the same time, and several rounds walk with vicious violence up the bed and into the seat next to Rev, into the console, and into the radio, smashing it to splinters. I duck instinctively—a round punches through the headrest where my head was moments before, and then through the windshield. Nico's weapon barks, and the technical shudders with the recoil, and Rev fires as well. More rounds clank and thunk off the side of the truck, and glance off the roof.

And then Rev grunts in pain, pulling himself into the cab with a string of curses. "Fuck, fuck, fuck, shit, fuck. That fuckin' hurt, you fuckin' twat." He's bleeding from the arm. "Goddammit. Lash, finish them off, for fuck's sake!"

"How bad is it, Rev?" Kane asks, without turning to look.

"Had worse," Rev answers, peeling his shirt off with a wince and grunt. "Through the bicep."

Nico loads a new belt into the gun, he racks the action, and pours another long burst at the final Suburban— the shooters are reloading as well. Nico is faster, and his rounds smash through the driver's side of the glass and send a cloud of red mist up to paint the interior—the vehicle swerves, tilts, and rolls; an oncoming car avoids it, but another isn't so lucky, causing a pileup.

The sudden silence is strangely loud—the only sound is the whistle and roar of the wind through the windows.

Rev rips a strip from the hem of his shirt and ties

it around his wound, gripping one end in his teeth and yanking it tight until he grunts in pain. That done, he sags against the seat, panting.

"Getting shot fuckin' sucks," he mutters.

"Yeah, it definitely doesn't tickle," Kane answers. He looks at me briefly. "You good?"

I finger the hole in the headrest, feeling shaky. "That one was close."

Kane touches a hole in the dashboard—that round nearly hit him as well. "Yeah, that one almost had my name on it."

I hold out my hand, which trembles uncontrollably. "I cannot stop shaking."

He nods. "Adrenaline. It'll pass. Just focus on breathing." He reaches out and squeezes my shoulder. "You did good, Tatiana, real good."

Rev squeezes my shoulder as well. "Yeah you did. Good job, darlin'."

I give them each a weak smile, and then look at Nico through the now-shattered window. He's leaning against the back of the cab, a hand pressed to his hip.

Blood streams down his thigh, and he slumps slowly to his butt in the truck bed.

"Nico!" I cry, scrambling over the console and leaning through the rear window frame. "You're hit!"

CHAPTER 15

SNUGGLE-FEST

LASH

I GENTLY BUT FIRMLY PUSH TATIANA BACK INTO THE cab and away from the window frame. "You will get cut."

She resists. "Nico, let me see."

"There is glass in the frame, Tati," I growl, the pain making me snappy. "I am fine. It glanced off my hipbone. The bone is not broken. I am not seriously wounded. It is merely painful and bloody."

She slides down to the bench, worry painting her features. "You have to put pressure on it."

I chuckle. "It is not my first time being shot, my love."

Rev tears a wide swatch from his already torn shirt and hands it to me. With no other materials to create a pressure dressing, however, I will have to hold it in place, so that is what I do. I press the makeshift bandage against my hip, hissing as the pressure sends a sharp lance of pain searing through me.

"Good, bro?" Rev asks, his voice tight with pain.

I extend my fist to him. "I will be fine. You?"

He taps his knuckles against mine. "Straight through

the muscle. Could be better, could be worse. Have to see if I can manage a rifle or not." He winces. "Later, though."

Solomon's voice crackles from the radio. "Good work, guys. Anyone hurt?"

Kane thumbs the radio. "Yes, but not bad. Rev took a round through the bicep and Lash took a glancer off the hip."

"There's a med kit in here," Sol says. "Need it?"

Kane glances in the rearview mirror. "You guys need a med kit?"

I grunt as I shift positions. "I could use a pressure dressing."

Kane relays the message, and Solomon answers after a minute. "We got one. Pull up alongside and I'll toss the kit."

"Copy," Kane says.

Once oncoming traffic has cleared, Kane accelerates up alongside the Suburban. The rear driver's side window rolls down and Solomon hangs out the window, a large red soft-cover med kit in his hands. Kane inches closer until the vehicles are less than a foot apart, and Solomon tosses the kit into the truck bed. I slap it down out of the air and pin it to the bed with my hand before it can bounce out, and then Kane drops back and pulls in behind the other car again.

I open the kit one-handed, rifling through it until I find the pressure dressing. I rip open a thick square of gauze with my teeth, slap it against my wound, and then wrap the stretchy ACE bandage around my torso and tie it off—the little pins won't hold well enough under movement. This creates pressure against the wound, helping it absorb and clot so I lose less blood.

"Hey, can I see the kit when you're done?" Rev asks. "This shirt is soaked through already."

I pass the kit through to him, and he folds a gauze square into a smaller, thicker rectangle, and uses another ACE bandage to compress it in place, and we both let out identical grunting sighs.

"Never thought I'd miss a long, boring shift at the Hel Gate," Rev says, referring to the heavily guarded and secured entrance to Hel, the ultra-exclusive brothel that's part of Club Sin. "I'm outta practice with this shit."

I laugh. "I agree. Now that I have experienced a life of peace and boredom, the action of firefights is much less appealing."

"I used to live for this shit," Rev says. "Now, I just wanna get home and veg out in the common room with Myka."

Tatiana, who has been loading the empty magazines, glances at Rev. "Tell me about Myka, please, Rev?"

He leans his head back and sighs. "She's...fuck, I don't know. Everything. She came from a super conservative Christian family. No cursing, women couldn't wear pants until she was, like, a grown-ass woman and decided she didn't agree with that rule. Church on Sundays and Wednesdays, no dating, only courting with chaperones."

Tatiana laughs in disbelief. "That sounds horrible."

Rev barks a laugh. "She'd agree, Tatiana."

"Please, Rev, call me Tati or Tiana."

"Tiana, like from The Princess and the Frog," Rev says, laughing again.

Tatiana frowns. "I do not know this."

"Disney movie," Rev answers. "That is where a princess has to kiss a frog to turn him back into a prince. Only, in the Disney version, she turns into a frog instead of him turning back into a person."

Tatiana snorts. "Rev, why do you know this?"

He sighs. "Myka has siblings with kids. We visited over the holidays and they tied me to a chair, forced me to watch Disney movies, and put a bunch of makeup and shit on me."

Tatiana snickers, covering her mouth. "And you allowed this?"

He grunts an affirmative. "Hard to say no to half a dozen half-feral little girls when they're climbing on you and begging you to play with them."

I grin at him. "Sounds like good practice for the future."

Rev scrubs his face with a blood-stained hand, smearing blood on his forehead, nose, and cheek. "That's what Myka said. I'm not sure I'm father material, though. Kids scare me. They're crazy, sticky, smelly, strange, unpredictable, and fragile. And I'm a fuckin' soldier. What the fuck do I know about raising a kid?"

I reach through the empty window frame and rest my hand on his shoulder. "I felt the same way when Ileana first told me she wanted to get pregnant." At his quizzical expression, I sigh. "Oh, right, I haven't told the rest of you. I was married. I had children,—infant twins. A corrupt Interpol official I was investigating at the time kidnapped me, tied me up, put a device on me that forced my eyes open, and made me watch as he burned my wife and children alive."

Rev doesn't answer for a while. "Fuck, man. Jesus Christ. No wonder you kept that shit tight."

"Indeed," I mutter.

"You kill the motherfucker?"

I grunt a negative. "He is too well-placed. And I...I was too much of a mess for many years to put together a proper plan, and then I encountered Inez and joined you all."

"But you're going to."

I shake my head. "I gave the evidence I had against him to an agent investigating him. He will pay within the justice system. My need for revenge was eating me alive and preventing me from having anything like a real life. Now that I have released that desire for vengeance, I am free. I am no longer the angry ghost I was for long. I am Nicolae Dragos, and I have a future."

Rev is quiet for a while. "You're a better man than me, brother. Not sure I could let that go."

I reach in and grab Tatiana's hand, squeeze it. "It was Tatiana who helped me see a better way. She set me free."

Rev nods, eyes closed. "I feel that. Myka saved me, too."

"Anjalee forced me to face my past," Kane says. "A lot like you, Nicolae, I was hogtied to past mistakes. Lived half-dead, consumed by guilt. She made me face myself and the shit I did. I got forgiveness, and I forgave myself."

Tatiana clutches my hand, kisses the back of it. "I think I will like these women."

"I know you will," I respond.

Tatiana lets go of my hand and squeezes Rev's shoulder. "Rev, if my father can raise a child, so can you. He is... he *was*—a" she clears her throat and starts over. "He was a criminal. A bad man who did bad things. And not always to bad people. He had bad things done to innocent people to send messages. But he loved me, and I never doubted that." She jostles him. "And Rev, you seem like a good man. I do not know you well yet, but that is the feeling I get. If you and your Myka have children together, I do not doubt that you will be a fine father."

Rev covers his face. Sighs heavily. "I...fuck. It's just fuckin' scary—the whole concept. Myka is the best thing that ever happened to me. But bringing a kid into it? I never had parents. I'm still figuring out how to be a good partner for Myka. She's a grown-ass woman. She can tell me what she needs, what I did wrong. A kid can't. What if...what if I lose my temper?"

I swallow a hot lump in my throat. "Rev, my friend. If you think loving Myka is rewarding, children are even more so. I only was able to be a father to Leonora and Leander for a very short time, but they..." I squeeze my eyes shut, grateful for the wind that snatches the tears away. "They lit up my life in a way I have not experienced before or since. It is a thing that is unique to being a father, I think. The love you instantly feel for them...it changes you."

Tatiana and Rev both reach out and comfort me, and I grab each of their hands with mine, unashamed of my sorrow—if I cannot share it with the woman I love and a man with whom I have shed blood, then...who?

"I'm so fuckin' sorry for what you went through, Nicolae," Rev says. "No one should experience that."

I nod, too overcome to speak. Instead, I squeeze his hand and let the sorrow flow out of me.

The moment it passes, I feel a lightness I haven't known in years, as if a physical weight has been lifted from my chest.

"Look at us, bonding and shit," Rev says.

"Consider me part of that snuggle fest back there," Kane says.

Rev leans forward and rests a hand on Kane's shoulder, and now we have a four-way thing going on, Tatiana to me and to Rev, me to Rev and Tatiana, and Rev to Kane.

Rev lets out a long sigh. "Thanks, guys. Guess me and Myka gotta talk when I get back."

———◆———

We arrive at the Brasilia airport with no further incident. Lorenzo called ahead to a friend in the Brazilian government and got us entry into the private flight section of the airport, so we were not subject to security—obviously a necessity considering the weaponry we carry.

A small single engine prop plane is being readied by an older man with weathered skin and gray hair, wearing dirty jeans and a dirty white tank top.

We all pile out of the vehicles; I climb out slowly, wincing.

"Uh, Ren?" Sol asks, eying the plane. "We aren't all fitting in there, buddy."

Lorenzo shakes his head. "No. We have to get Lorenzo and Beatriz somewhere Mercado can't get to them, at least until we take care of Mercado and rescue Sophia."

"So you're sending them...where?" Sol asks.

He shrugs. "I have a friend in El Paso who works for border control. I was thinking I would send them there. Mercado can reach across the border, but not easily."

Scarlett chimes in, then. "I have a better idea. You have your friend get you guys across the border, and then I'll have *my* friends take you to a safe house I know of in

Houston. We'll put them in protective custody, basically, but off-book. Once shit has settled, if she wants to, we can bring Beatriz and Little Lorenzo wherever she wants to go."

Lorenzo nods. "I like this plan. Let me talk to her and see what she says.

What follows is a very animated conversation between Beatriz, Lorenzo, and Scarlett. Obviously I cannot follow any of it, but Beatriz does not seem happy, and neither does Lorenzo.

"Yo, yo, yo!" Solomon shouts, silencing everyone. "*What* is the fuckin' issue here?"

Scarlett answers. "Beatriz doesn't like the plan *at* fuckin' *all*."

Solomon rolls his eyes. "I do speak a little Spanish, you know. So yeah, I caught that."

"I do not speak Spanish, and I caught that," Tatiana says.

"She does not trust us," Lorenzo says. "More accurately, she does not trust our friends in the States. She says if she lets us put her in protective custody, she is afraid she will never be free again. She says the only way she will go along with it is if I go with her."

"Well that's fuckin' tricky," Solomon growls. "You've been invaluable."

"I know," Lorenzo grumbles. "I don't like it either. But I know Sophia well enough to know what she would tell me to do."

Sol nods. "She'd say you need to keep Beatriz and the kid safe and trust us to rescue her."

Lorenzo growls a sigh. "So, yes. That is what she would say." He scrubs the back of his neck. "I can still provide assistance remotely. Call me and I will do what I can over the phone."

The pilot finishes his preflight check and shouts something in Portuguese, Lorenzo shouts something back, then turns to the group. "So it is decided. I will go with Beatriz and Little Lorenzo and get them to safety in the United States. Scarlett, contact your people in Houston and send me the details when you have them."

Scarlett nods. "Will do." She extends a hand to him. "It's been fuckin' real, Ren. You're a hell of an operator."

Lorenzo shakes her hand and then pulls her into a hug, a backslapping, one-of-the-boys sort of hugs. "You are a fearsome warrior, Maria Consuela Rodriguez. I am proud to have fought beside you. We will see each other again soon."

Scarlett nods, swallowing hard, and backs up. "Fuck off with the emotional shit, asshole," she says, her voice tight. She gives him a two-finger salute. "See you soon, Ren."

Then it's Solomon's turn, and he and Lorenzo embrace, even more roughly, and then push each other away to grip forearms.

"That boy doesn't deserve any of this," Solomon says. "Keep him safe. Her too."

Lorenzo nods, his expression ferocious. "I will. He is a good boy." He shoots a glance at Scarlett. "It has been good for my soul to watch you and her find your love. It gives me hope that Sophia and I can find that for ourselves."

Solomon claps him on the arm. "You will, brother." He pulls up his sleeve and shows Lorenzo the brand. "And when this is done, you and Scarlett can take the brand and become Broken Arrows with the rest of us. You're one of us now, Ren."

Lorenzo hesitates. "It would be an honor to be oath-bound with all of you. But this is not goodbye, only farewell for now."

The pilot shouts again, and Lorenzo gives him a thumbs up.

"We must go. The pilot is impatient. it is a long flight to El Paso." He scans the rest of us. "I will see you all soon. Rescue my Sophia. Please. I have lost her twice. You *must* find her."

Chance steps forward. "No fuckin' doubt, man. Inez saved us all. She made us Arrows. We'll pull Mercado's world down around his fuckin' ears or die tryin.'"

We all add our voices to Chance's reassurance, and then Beatriz, Little Lorenzo, and Big Lorenzo climb into the little aircraft. We move out of the way as the pilot taxis to the nearby runway, pauses for clearance, and then takes off.

Once the airplane is out of sight, we circle up.

"So," Saxon says, breaking the silence. "There goes our guide. We have no fuckin' clue where Mercado took Inez. Two of us are walking wounded. We won't all fit in that Suburban and the Technical is shot to shit."

Silas slugs his brother in the arm. "Helpful assessment, Sax. Thanks for that."

"Oh fuck off, Si," Saxon snarls. "Gotta face facts so we can plan accordingly."

"Right, because you're the tactical genius of the family," Silas shoots back.

"Shut the fuck up, both of you!" Solomon yells. "You two are like toddlers, sometimes. Jesus."

"He's not wrong though, Si," Rev says. "Shit is pretty hairy right now. We need a plan."

Silas turns away, passing his hand through his air. "Fuck. Sorry, Sax. I'm fuckin' exhausted and I miss Naomi. And honestly, I'm over this shit. It's fuckin' stressful."

Saxon laughs. "All good, man. I feel ya. I used to live for this shit, and now it's like…" The humor saps out of him abruptly. He shakes his head. "I guess now that I've got something—some*one*—to live for, I find myself caring a whole fuckuva lot more whether I live or die."

"We were talking about that on the way here," Kane says. "I'm over this shit. Ready to stand around with my thumb up my ass in Club Sin, watchin' dumb fucks get fucked up."

Sol nods. "I think we all feel that way. All the more reason to get Inez, take out Mercado, and go home."

"So, how do we find her?" I ask. "Mercado has many resources. They could be anywhere by now."

"Rafael is paranoid," Scarlett says. "According to what Inez and Lorenzo said, at least. He wouldn't go just any-where. He'd go somewhere he feels secure."

"Another house?" Rev asks. "Motherfucker has more money than god. He's *got* to have property somewhere else."

Solomon snaps his fingers, pointing at Rev. "That's it! Lemme call Ren real quick." He dials a number and puts it on speaker.

Lorenzo answers after two rings, his voice muffled and nearly drowned out by the roar of the propeller. "You are calling me already?"

"Where would Rafael go?" Solomon asks. "He's

paranoid about security. He wouldn't just drive aimlessly around the Brazilian countryside."

"Ah, this is true, yes." A moment of silence as he thinks. "Perhaps the old de Silva estate. I will send you the coordinates. It is the most likely possibility."

"Thanks, Ren."

"Of course. I will find the coordinates and send them to you."

A few minutes later, Solomon's phone dings with an incoming message. He puts the coordinates into the phone's GPS app and spends a moment or two examining the results.

"Well," Solomon says, "it's a big fuckin' place outside Rio de Janeiro. Set on some pretty wicked elevation, with only one route in or out. No walls, but the location they chose meant they didn't need them."

"So, another suicide mission assault," Chance grumbles. "Sweet. Love that for us."

"And since Inez *is* the mission," Rev adds, "we don't have oversight."

"No point bitching about it," Kane growls. "Let's just figure out a fucking plan and go. He had to scramble to get the fuck outta dodge before we hit him, so how likely is that he has a full roster with him?"

"No way to know what he can pull off last minute," I say. "I think our only option is to go there, do some recon, and devise a plan from there. We have zero intel at this time, so any plan would be riddled with flaws."

Silas points at me. "Lash is right." He furrows his brow. "Sorry—Nicolae.

I wave him off. "It will take time. Also, you are all my

brothers, so call me Nico. But Lash will work fine if you forget."

"I agree," Solomon says. "But the issue we face now is that Rio is a long ass fuckin' way from here." He manipulates his nav app. "Sixteen-plus hour drive."

"We are at an airport," Tatiana says, gesturing around us. "Surely there must be a way to find a ride on an airplane."

"We have to assume Mercado has commercial flights monitored," Solomon answers. "Plus, we'll need our gear. We can't exactly assault without weapons."

At that moment, a compact pickup approaches from the service drive and halts next to our huddle. "I am a friend of Lorenzo Araujo," the driver says—he's a good-looking man of about thirty, with slicked back black hair, a friendly smile but cold eyes; he's wearing Brazilian army fatigues with lieutenant's bars. "He mentioned you may need a ride to Rio."

When none of us answer, he just laughs. "I grew up with Ren in the favelas of Rio. I owe that man my life, and I would do anything for him—and that includes his friends. He told me to tell you that Sophia's life depends on a quick reaction, so shut up and trust me. Me meaning me, not him."

Saxon grunts. "Don't see a choice. What kinda ride you talkin' about, amigo?"

"I am a pilot. I am flying a small transport into Rio, but I have room for a few stowaways." He checks his watch. "I have to be wheels up in twenty, so we must go quickly. Come, follow me, *Sí*?"

Solomon shrugs. "Alright, ya'll. You heard the man. Let's fuckin' go."

Seated among crates and stacked pallets of supplies, we are all clustered and huddled together. Tatiana sits beside me, her head resting on my shoulder. Nearby, Solomon and Scarlett murmur to each other. The others, professionals that they are, stretch out and catch some sleep.

I know Tatiana is not asleep—I know by her breathing, but also I can feel her sorrow like a palpable thing, a cloak resting on her shoulders.

"Perhaps this is a stupid question," I whisper to her in Croatian, "but are you okay?"

She gives a half-lift of her shoulder. "I am still processing the fact that he is really gone. It was just so unexpected. Seeing him like that, Nico…" she shakes her head and turns her face into my shoulder, silently sobbing. "He was all I had. Mama has been gone for years. I never met any of my grandparents—they all died before I was born. I am an only child. The only other people I know are Ana and Katja and Georg—sweet old Georg. And Filip killed them all. It's just so senseless, Nico."

"Hey," I whisper. "I know it is not the same—he was your father. But you are not alone, Lovely One. You are allowed to grieve."

She nuzzles her mouth and nose into the side of my throat, and cups my opposite cheek. "It is very hard to understand so late in life that my father had such a dark side to him he never allowed me to see." A sigh. "It makes grief difficult. I love him. He took care of me. He did his best to protect me. I never, ever doubted that he loved me. But…I went through some very traumatic things because of who he was and what he did for a living. I often hated him for it, even as I loved him. It was very complicated, and now that he is dead, my feelings are even more complicated."

"That is understandable, my love. But…well, I am no expert. But we can hold very complicated emotions within ourselves simultaneously. You can hate what he did and the choices he made and the effects they had on you while also loving the man as your father." I turn my face to kiss the top of her head. "We humans are complicated creatures, Tati. We are fragile yet resilient, wildly intelligent yet extraordinarily stupid. We can love and hate in equal measure, and sometimes those two feelings can be almost indistinguishable. I suppose what I am saying is that there is no right or wrong way to feel."

She lets out a long sigh, her breath washing warm over my neck. "I am so tired of traveling, Nico. I have long since lost track of how long ago it was that I met you in that hangar, and it feels like we have done nothing but fly and drive and run and hide and plan and fight. We barely eat, barely sleep. And all I want is to be alone with you. To have you all to myself."

"It is almost over, Tati. But I do agree—this has been a very overwhelming series of events."

Her voice, already a murmur, drops to a whisper only I can hear, and I have to strain to hear her. "Nico, I need you. We only had those few short hours together—and I honestly don't even remember where we were or how long ago that was. Days? Not even a day? I don't know. I just know I fucking need you, Nico. I have so many feelings and I just—all I want to feel is you inside me. I want to forget everything and everyone else. All the death, all the danger, all the adrenaline. It's done something to me, I think. I have always enjoyed sex, but now, it is a *need*. I have tried to keep it reined in because we are never alone. But Nico, my love, I feel like I am losing my mind."

I let out a rough sigh. "Oh, my sweet Tatiana. My emotions have been through a maelstrom since I met you. I feel like I have been turned inside out and upside down, like I have been broken open and my insides washed out with a firehose. But through it all, you have been a constant. Sweet, and loving, and kind, and understanding. Challenging me to see the truth, to let go of the past, to reach for a future I thought had died long ago. I truly did not know it was possible to come to love someone so powerfully in such a short period of time."

Her soft sigh is a hot breath on my cheek. "Oh, my Nico."

For a split second, I almost hear Ileana's voice as Tatiana says those words, the way Ileana said them—*oh, my Nico*—on a sigh, her sweet breath on my cheek, fingers in my beard. I am disoriented for that split second. But then it passes, and Ileana is gone again.

She lives on in my heart, but her spirit is finally at rest because I have learned to release her. She was not haunting me—I was clinging to her ghost.

I am alive. Tatiana is alive. We are together. That is what matters.

A welter of feelings rushes through me, fills me, percolates in my soul—things I have been setting aside so I can focus on the mission at hand.

Chief among them—desire.

"My god, Tati," I breathe. "What I wouldn't give to have even five minutes of privacy."

She giggles breathily. "Five minutes? Nico, my love, that isn't nearly enough for what I have in mind."

"I know," I murmur, chuckling quietly.

She snuggles closer to me, and her hand comes to rest, almost by accident, on my groin. "Couldn't we find somewhere on this airplane to be even sort of alone?" She whispers. "I need you, Nico. I need to feel *something*, anything—*anything* but this…this…I don't know. I don't know."

I groan. "This is a small cargo plane, Tati. Anywhere we go, we can be heard."

"I can be quiet."

"Fuck," I hiss in English, then revert to Croatian. "How am I supposed to resist you?"

"You aren't, silly. That's the whole point."

I stand up casually and make a point of stretching as if working out the kinks in my muscles and the stiffness in my joints—and it is not an act. After a moment, Tatiana does the same. I find a path to the tail end of the transport, swinging my arms and lifting my knees high, rotating them outward to stretch my hips—the wounded one protests the action, the bruised bone aching and the torn flesh and muscle screaming. It hurts like a motherfucker, but it won't limit my mobility too much, even if only because I won't let it.

I pace back toward the nose, stepping over my sleeping compatriots—Chance cracks one eye open, watching. When Tatiana makes her way toward the nose and disappears behind a tall stack of strapped-down crates, I catch a smirk and a wink from Chance before he tilts away and drapes a heavy arm over his eyes.

Need swells in me, then, as I follow her behind the stack.

CHAPTER 16

A STOLEN MOMENT

TATIANA

IT DOES FEEL LIKE A KIND OF MADNESS, THIS DESIRE within me. Is it masking my sorrow? Is it a response to the constant brushes with death? Or just a normal craving for intimacy with the man I am falling in love with?

The spot I chose is as ideal as you could ask for in a situation like this. We are in the farthest back right corner against the bulkhead between the cargo bay and the cockpit, in a cozy little alcove created by tall stacks of crates and pallets piled high with supplies shrink-wrapped in thick plastic.

I know this is a little reckless, but I have been pushing down and ignoring my needs ever since that too-short night in the hotel…wherever the hell that even was. Germany? Brazil, somewhere? I don't know.

Nico slips his short, broad, densely muscled frame through the narrow gap between a five-foot-high stack of crates and a pallet. I sink to the floor, my eyes locked on his, and drag my shirt and bra up to free my heavy, aching breasts. Nico's eyes flare, raw hunger suffusing his features.

"Fuck, Tati," he breathes. "So beautiful."

I reach for him, and he whips off his shirt, folds it, and

uses it to pillow my head as he lays me backward. Soft lips find hot flesh, and a sharp line of arousal sears through me as he suckles my nipple into his mouth. I bite down on my lip to stifle the moan.

He captures my mouth with his, devouring my gasp as he fondles my breasts, tweaking and twisting and pinching my nipples until I'm writhing and panting into the kiss.

Levered over me, bracing his weight on one hand, he tugs open my jeans and greedily shoves his hand under my panties, finding my sex wet and hot.

I have to bite down on my lip so hard it hurts to silence my whimper when his fingers delve inside me, and then my jaws clench so hard my molars ache when he smears my essence over my clit and circles me there as his lips tug at my nipples, one and the other in turn.

I catch at his soft, short, hair and hold his nape as he plies my breasts with kisses and licks, nips and nibbles. With my other hand, I seek his skin. Find it between his shirt and jeans. Fumble at his zipper. Eager and impatient, I get his jeans open and plunge my hand beneath his underwear and find him hot and hard and ready for my touch. He growls softly, and I put my other hand over his mouth, hushing his quiet groans as I stroke his length thumb and forefinger first, gliding my touch down his erection.

It's a race, then—and he's winning. His fingers ply my core with deft touches, pressing against my aching clit with just the right pressure, with perfect speed, until I'm panting raggedly through my nose, my gaze fraught with aroused wonder as I stare up at him.

I arch up off the floor as the first waves of orgasm shudder through me, and I clutch his cock with spasming, greedy fingers, tasting copper as I bite my lip to keep from shrieking as my climax rips me to shreds.

God, this man knows me so well. He knows how to touch me, knows my body, knows my needs. When I start coming, he continues touching me exactly in the way that got me there, and when I buck upward and shudder, he speeds up until white stars burst behind my tight-shut eyes, and incandescent heat builds beneath and behind my belly, expanding outward and overtaking every part of me.

I writhe upward, pushing into his touch, and his mouth covers mine, and his tongue drives between my teeth, and I can't breathe and couldn't scream if I wanted to, can only shake and shudder as I come. The hot hard length of his cock in my hand is an anchor point to reality, mooring me to earth—without it, I feel like I could be flung free of the earth to float away into nothingness. But I don't. Instead, I cling to his cock and stroke it from tip to root and back up, squeezing as waves of ecstasy crash through me.

He rumbles softly, a chest-sound. His fingers slow, and I float back to earth, panting quietly but rapidly.

I feel him throbbing in my grip. I know he's close. I break the kiss, smiling up at him as I caress his length faster and faster.

He braces both hands beside my shoulders and he starts to push with helpless need into my hand.

"Tati," he whispers. "You must stop."

"Never," I whisper back. "Lay down."

Moving gingerly, he rolls to his back. I tuck his t-shirt under his head and hold myself above him as he was above me moments ago. His hands carve up my belly to cradle my swaying breasts, and I gasp at his touch.

"Tati," he breathes. "You don't have to—"

"Shut up, Nico," I interrupt. "I love you but shut up. I know I don't *have* to. I *want* to. I *need* to. We can't make love—not here, not now. But I can do this. And I want to, so I'm going to, and you're going to lay there and let me."

"Yes ma'am," he answers.

I sit on his knees and carefully work his jeans down past the bandage over his hip wound—he wrapped the bandage around his belly at an angle. Once his cock is bared, I waste no time. I slip my hands under his shirt and explore the hard wonderland of his muscled torso and kiss his belly, his navel, avoiding the wounded area. He gathers my hair in his hands and piles it on my head and holds it there, cradling my head in his powerful hands. I stretch myself out, sitting on my heels and reaching up his body to toy with his hard flat nipples while I kiss my way down to his erection.

"Tati," he breathes.

I take him in my mouth, lips stretched wide to wrap around his thick organ, tasting salt and skin and the distinctive tangy, smoky musk of his pre-cum.

His fingers dimple into my scalp, and apply the gentlest amount of pressure, encouraging me to take more of him. I eagerly oblige, swirling my tongue against his hot flesh, tasting his veins as they stutter against my tongue, until I've taken as much of his considerable length as I comfortably can.

He arches, hisses, and drops back to the floor. I slide my mouth up his length and bob around the plump, round head, tasting his pre-cum as it leaks out of him, and now he lets out a low huff, and then a teeth-clenched grunt as I give him my mouth in long, slow drives from the soft, springy tip down as far as I can and back up—every time I reach his glans once more, I give him a few short fast bobs, and then a long swallowing slide.

Bob, bob, bob…slide.

Again and again.

He clutches at my head and pressures me downward, thrusting into my mouth with a tightening of his ass muscles, panting raggedly now. He groans when I take him as deep as I can and bob there, my mouth and throat suckling around him—I reach up and slap a hand over his mouth, stifling another groan. He huffs into my hand, gasping as he thrusts harder, nearing climax. I let his cock pop free of my mouth and caress his hot, spit-slick length, and then suction my lips around his tip and bob there, just above my stroking hand. Hissing through gritted teeth, Nico thrusts helplessly, desperately. I bob on him faster and faster now, and plunge my fist around his root with hard, twisting strokes. Grunting once, a rough snarl in the back of his throat, he palms the back of my head and holds tight, pressing me gently downward. I accept the guidance and take more of him, gliding lower and lower, shortening the strokes of my hand as I gulp and gasp around his cock.

Now.

I feel him cut loose all at once. There's barely time to prepare for it, so sudden and fierce is his release—I think it surprised him, as well. He grunts into my palm and I taste his cum as he floods my mouth with it, and I swallow greedily, backing away to suck around his head and jack his hot, throbbing length as hard and fast as I can.

He comes and comes, writhing and desperately growling, gasping, and grunting through his orgasm, his sounds muffled by my palm. At long last, his release slows to a trickle and then subsides altogether. When I know he's done, I let him go and tuck him back into his jeans and do him back up, and then he hauls me up his body and cradles me to his chest.

"Tati," he whispers.

I touch his lips. "I know. Me too."

"You don't know what I was going to say," he protests.

I nuzzle his jaw with my nose. "Sure I do. That was amazing, and you love me, and you can't wait to get me alone again so you can fuck me until I can't take anymore."

He huffs a laugh, his belly and chest bouncing. "Pretty much, yes."

I kiss his cheek, put my lips to his ear. "I love you, Nicolae Dragos. I need this to be over so we can hole up in a room somewhere for a week straight and have sex and eat carryout and watch stupid television together."

"We are nearly there, I promise." He turns his face so our lips meet. "You amaze me, you know that? All of this was thrust upon you, and you have dealt with everything that has been thrown at you with barely a word of complaint. You have adapted as needed, and you always pull your weight, which is especially impressive in a situation so far outside your comfort zone."

My heart swells at his praise. "I just don't want to be a burden. I don't want you and your team to have to carry me through this."

"I am proud of you, Tatiana. Truly."

My nose stings and my eyes burn, and my god I'm so sick of crying, but even though Tata loved me, he rarely praised me or told me he was proud of me. He was generous with hugs and affection, frequently told me he loved me, but being praised and told that he was proud was a rarity. So hearing it from Nico…

It makes me cry, but a good kind of cry.

I lose track of time after that, dozing in the warm comfort of Nico's strong arms. I'm woken when the world tilts.

"We're landing," Nico murmurs to me. "Better go back with the others."

I hum a sleepy affirmative as I sit up and stretch. We both get up and put our clothes in order and then rejoin the others near the tail of the airplane. No one says anything about our reappearance, although Chance and Nicolae exchange looks.

"We're a very close-knit group," Nico murmurs to me. "And we live in close quarters. No one will say anything, and if they do, it will be good-natured teasing." He indicates the three brothers, Saxon, Solomon, and Silas, who are huddled together talking in low tones and laughing. "Those three are all in brand new relationships, too, so if anything, they're probably jealous that I get to sneak off with you for some private time."

"I am not sure I would want someone I love to be involved in this if it wasn't necessary," I say.

Nico nods. "I understand that. I would spare you all of this if I could."

I sniff a laugh. "What is ironic about that is even though this is frightening and exhausting, I have found you because of it, so even if I could go back and avoid it all, I am not sure I would." I sigh and shake my head. "I wouldn't want Tata, Georg, Ana, and Katya to die, though. Ana and Katya especially. They were young, smart, innocent girls with their whole lives ahead of them. They'd never done anything to hurt anyone. Killing them served absolutely no purpose whatsoever."

"I do not know if I have said it, but I am truly sorry for all the loss you have endured, Tatiana my love," Nico says.

I don't know what to say to that other than thank you, but I'm saved from having to reply when the pilot sticks his head out the cockpit door. "We will be landing in a moment, my friends. Hold on to something, please."

We all brace ourselves against crates and pallets and find handholds. Without windows, however, there is no way to know when we will touch down, none of that increasing sense of speed as you approach the ground. There is only the faint sense of movement, a gentle side-to-side rocking as the pilot feathers the controls, and then a sudden jarring bounce and a loud bark of rubber tires on the tarmac, another smaller and gentler bounce, a third touchdown without a bounce, and then we're flung forward as the pilot brings the aircraft's speed down.

Several minutes of taxiing and waiting, and then we're greeted by the hydraulic whine of the ramp lowering, and brilliant Brazilian sunlight slices through the relative gloom of the cargo plane's interior.

We all file out of the cargo bay and into the blazing heat, stretching and flexing. Once the pilot has finished his post-flight duties, he joins us on the tarmac in front of a massive Quonset hut hangar, from which streams a gaggle of workers with forklifts and dollies and such, ready to unload the cargo.

The pilot holds up his clipboard. "I have to oversee the unloading so I must stay here, but Lorenzo arranged for a vehicle for you." He grins sheepishly. "It is…well, you will see. But it is the best that could be done on short notice. Once you have finished with it, just leave it any-where. If it finds its way back to me, then good. If not?" He shrugs. "Oh well."

We all shake his hand and thank him, and then follow his verbal directions to where the vehicle is parked in an out-of-the-way alley behind a dusty, forgotten old hangar on the edge of the airfield.

It's a battered, rusty old passenger van, the kind with several rows of benches and a sliding door on the righthand side. Once white, it is filthy, covered in dirt and rust, and, somewhat concerningly, bullet holes.

Rev whoops when he sees it, bizarrely excited. "Chance, what does this piece of shit remind you of?"

Chance frowns, and then his face clears into laughter. "Fuck me, I'd almost forgotten about that op. Jesus, what a hysterical clusterfuck that was."

Solomon arches an eyebrow. "Care to share with the rest of the class?"

"I'm driving," Rev says, slinging himself behind the wheel. "Chance, you got shotty, just like old times."

"Fucking church vans," Chance mutters. "Rev, bro, you are way too fuckin' excited about this."

We all pile in, with Solomon in the middle of the sec-ond row so he can direct Rev. Once we're away from the airfield and on a two-lane highway, Rev tells the story.

"So, a couple years after we made Recon, we were sent on this op in the Congo. The actual details of the op are classified, obviously, but suffice it to say the whole thing was a goddamn shitshow from the jump."

I lean closer to Nico. "I do not know what many of these words mean. Recon, classified shitshow, from the jump."

"Recons are a special forces group in the Marine Corps," Nico answers in a murmur. "Classified means only certain people are allowed to know about it. Shitshow just means a messed up situation. From the jump means right from the start."

I nod my understanding and tune back into Rev's story.

"...So we were supposed to be protecting a CIA asset. Intel was that it was gonna be a nice, easy, boring op. The asset was supposed to meet us at a certain place and time, and we were gonna escort him to some other location. Even we didn't know too many details, just 'get this person from point A to point B and don't let 'em get fuckin' killed.'"

Chance cackles bitterly. "Man, that shit was FUBAR'd the second we were boots down."

Nico mutters to me, "FUBAR means 'fucked up beyond all recognition.'"

"So worse than a shitshow," I say.

Rev hears me and glances at me over his shoulder. "Yeah, babe. We got a whole system of describing the levels of fucked-up-ness in the military. It started out a shitshow and went FUBAR real goddamn fast."

"It was not a simple escort mission, I assume," I say.

Chance belly laughs. "No ma'am, it most certainly was not."

Rev picks up the thread. "The second we got off the plane, I knew shit was gonna get hairy. We were supposed to have a real fuckin' ride. A HUMVEE or a Jeep, a Suburban, fuckin' *anything* that wasn't a rusted-out bucket of bolts. But some pencil-pusher decided to save a few bucks and put us in a church van like this one, only way older and way shittier."

"Why do you call it a church van, please?" I ask.

Chance answers. "Oh, well, in the States, vans like this are often used by churches to transport kids or whoever from the church to some activity or something I dunno, I never went to church. " He laughs. "Honestly, I just know they're called church vans."

"Oh."

Rev thumps the dashboard with a huge fist. "Man, that van was the sorriest fuckin' piece of shit I've ever seen. It was literally held together by duct tape in some places. It had no A-C, and this was fucking Africa. Windows didn't roll down either. The engine had been replaced by some tiny little four-banger that was barely able to get the god-damn thing moving. Floorboards were so shot I coulda Flintstoned that fuckin' thing." I don't bother asking what a four-banger is, or what Flintstoning means—the point is that it was a terrible automobile.

"The squeal of that engine," Chance groans, laughing. "You could hear it from a mile away."

"Second issue was the asset was a legit dumbfuck. Like, listen, most dumbfucks in this world aren't actu-ally stupid, they just don't always think things through or make good decisions. But this dude, he was..." Rev shakes his head, laughing. "He not only got the day and time of the meet wrong, he was in the wrong place. At the wrong time on the wrong day. Once we were boots down, we had no communication with anyone, so we had no way of getting in touch with anyone to let them know the asset never showed. Our hostel sprang a leak the second day and all our shit got soaked. And then, once we finally made contact with the idiot fuckin' asset, a big ol' fight popped off and we couldn't go anywhere—couldn't get out of the city, couldn't leave our leaky fuckin' room. So finally, middle of the night, we packed our sopping wet shit and piled in that cosmic joke of a van, and we booked it outta there. But the fuckin' thing was so goddamn loud between the squealing belt and the missing muffler that we got made before we'd gone a mile and had to shoot our way out."

Chance snickers. "And that little fuckin' asset, man. Dumb as a post. We were behind cover, right? Hunkered down behind this old piece of wall, who knows how fuckin' old that shit was. And this dipshit kept poppin' his head up to see what was going on. He didn't speak dick for English and none of us spoke his language, and again, some pencil pusher decided we didn't need a fuckin' interpreter."

"It was an actual literal miracle he didn't take one to the head," Rev says. "It was pop goes the weasel with that guy. We'd shove his head down and get off a few shots, and then he'd crawl somewhere else and pop right back up, like duhhhh, please shoot me."

"Dude was stupid," Chance says.

"If he was so stupid, why was he an asset?" I ask.

Chance and Rev shake their heads, guffawing in laughter. "That right there is the million dollar question," Chance says. "Why the actual mother*fuck* would you send a whole-ass Recon unit all the fuckin' way to the Congo with no comms to mission control, no ride, no oversight, and no interpreter to protect a so-called asset who couldn't find his own ass if you gave him a map and a goddamn flashlight? Like, what possible value could someone as empty-headed as that dude provide to the CIA? And why the Congo? A billion questions and no answers."

"Every time I see a white church van," Rev says, "I think about that op. I think about that pipsqueak of an asset just *trying* to get himself killed."

Kane launches into an even funnier story of a mission he went on, which featured a runaway cow and a very angry farmer. All the way to our destination, then, the team regales each other with stories, and it seems to be a competition to see who can get the most laughs. The stories get increasingly ridiculous, to the point that I eventually lean into Nico again.

"Are these stories true?" I ask. "Some of them seem… quite implausible."

Nico laughs. "They're probably sixty or seventy percent true, ten or twenty percent heavily embellished, and the rest is made up."

"Why?"

He shrugs. "Time-honored tradition among soldiers, my love. You tell stories to pass the time. Life in the military is a lot of waiting around, so you find ways of entertaining yourselves and each other. You sleep, play cards, read books, write letters, and tell stories to make your friends laugh. Especially if you're about to go into combat."

"And lying and embellishing the truth is part of it?"

"Sure. If your friend tells a funny story, it is an unspoken rule that you or someone else has to tell a funnier one. It's just the way it is. And in order to make it funnier, you make things up. Everyone knows it's all bullshit, or mostly, but it's for fun. Later, you might talk to your friend who told the story and get the truth from him." He shrugs. "It is the way of things with men like us." Scarlett, behind us, clears her throat. "My apologies, Scarlett—guys and *girls* like us."

She leans forward onto the bench-back between us. "By the way, Tati, it's more like fifty percent true and fifty percent made up or embellished. And anything that Sol tells you, probably all bullshit."

Solomon hears this and holds up both middle fingers without turning around. "Heard that. And that's just not true. Now Scarlett—*she's* a real bullshit artist."

We have been traveling away from Rio de Janeiro and into increasingly rugged terrain. The road switches back and forth as we climb, and the engine is groaning as if in agony. Solomon consults his phone and then leans forward. "Should be a turnoff up ahead, Rev. Pull over. We're getting close—less than three miles to the estate."

Rev nods, and sure enough, we round a bend and the road widens, the shoulder infringing into the forest to create a place where you can pull over or turn around. Rev pulls over and stops, shuts the engine off and rolls down the window.

Sol consults his phone again. "So, we're gonna have to send a couple people to do some recon. Get the lay of the land, check out possible approaches, see how many tangos Mercado has, and if possible, get eyes on Inez." He glances at Nico. "Lash—Nico, I mean. You and me. Yeah?"

Nico nods. "Very well, then. Let us recon."

And yet again I have to sit idly by and watch as the man I love strides boldly into danger.

CHAPTER 17

THE ASSAULT

LASH

SOLOMON AND I WALK CASUALLY DOWN THE middle of the narrow dirt road for the first mile or so, chatting easily in low tones—the kind of idle chatter meant to pass the time on a march that soldiers have engaged in since humans first began forming armies.

It's a damned hot day, the air close and thick and humid, the sky heavily laden with dark, angry gray storm clouds that rumble and flash but hold their rain. The dirt under our feet is fine and dust-like, accepting our prints silently.

About halfway into the second mile, Solomon holds up a fist, calling a halt, and crouches, frowning. "So far there's only been one set of tire tracks, which I can only assume are recent, right? I mean, it rains here just about every day, which is gonna wash away older tracks." He indicates an array of boot prints. "Looks like four guys come this way, stop, and turn around."

"We are, what, a mile, a mile and a half from the estate?" I ask.

He nods, glancing at his phone. "About that, yeah."

"Then we had better get off the road," I say. "This is

a recon mission, so we cannot afford to risk encountering them."

"Agreed," Solomon says. "You wanna stick together, or separate?"

"I think it will be more effective if we split up. We will cover more ground that way."

"Alright, then, I'll go right, you go left. Meet back here in thirty?"

"Excellent," I say.

I slip into the dense undergrowth, wishing I had a machete even though I know using it to clear a path would only alert any scouts or perimeter guards of my presence. No, I just have to do it the hard way. Ducking and twisting under low-hanging branches, stepping and climbing over fallen trees and tangles of branches, I make very slow progress. The undergrowth is amazingly dense, forcing me to go around dense clumps of flora. More than once, I duck under a fat, drooping leaf and dislodge a trapped palmful of water, which douses my head and runs down my back, making my shirt stick to my body.

Thunder grumbles threateningly, and lighting prowls across the sky restlessly; the scent of petrichor is thick in the air, and I know the deluge is imminent.

Only a handful of minutes later, the rain comes. It's just a noise at first, a *tick-tap-hiss* of plump raindrops on the canopy above, slow and desultory, just a few bold drops exploring the path past the foliage to the thirsty roots beneath the soil. And then a few more drops find the way down to plop onto my skull and dance upon my back and shoulders. And then, between one step and another, the sky unleashes a wet hell of rain so torrential it's a silver curtain encasing the whole world. Within seconds, I'm soaked to the bone, and the sound of the rain is nearly a roar.

Which is how I almost ruin the whole plan—I can't hear them as I approach them, and so I almost stumble directly into the laps of a pair of scouts angling my way toward the road. I only see them when they're a few feet away, and the only thing that saves me is the fact that they're too busy trying to get their rain slickers on to notice me.

I throw myself to the ground and roll into the lee of a fallen tree and then shimmy further under it. The earth is pungent, the wet, rotting bark even more so, a sweet, thick smell. Something small and hard wriggles under my palm, and something else tickles over my scalp. I shudder as the insect—which I can only hope is not something venomous—crawls down my neck and, thankfully, over my shirt rather than beneath it.

The sentries get their slickers situated, grumbling in Spanish about bullshit perimeter assignments.

They continue past my hiding place on their way to the road—I assume they're making a wide circuit around the estate, looking for...well, exactly what's happening.

"Contact," I whisper into the mic. "Two tangos heading your way through the jungle."

"Copy," Solomon whispers back. "Do not engage."

"Roger," I answer back.

Once they're out of sight, I wait another minute or two, and then crawl out of my hiding spot; if possible, I'm even more soaked after laying under the log like that. Funny how you think you're as wet as you can get, and then somehow you get even wetter.

Moving slowly and pausing to listen, now, I continue my path through the jungle, and encounter no one else.

Ahead, I start to see evidence of the forest thinning, and I slow my pace even more, eventually finding a spot where I can see the clearing ahead. The forest thins and then stops, becoming a hillside covered in low, dense growth of creeping vines and dense shrubs and ferns.

The hill slants sharply down into a deep ravine, which creates a remarkably effective natural barrier. While I could hit the other side of the hill with an easy underhanded toss of a stone, the sides are so sheer crossing it seems nearly impossible—I'd be almost climbing a nearly vertical face through dense undergrowth. The other side is a steep-sided plateau a few hundred feet high, an island-like miniature mountain in the middle of the jungle.

I watch for a while—on top of the plateau is the estate itself, a sprawling, single-story hacienda-style mansion, whitewashed adobe, and red terracotta roof tiles. I see figures pacing the perimeter of the plateau; after ten minutes of watching, I count eight men in pairs at regular intervals. As advertised, there is only one approach to the hacienda from the east.

I leave my spot and move east, well inside the tree line, moving slowly and cautiously, listening every few steps. Another patrol approaches me from the east, heading west; they're running concentric perimeter patrols. Again I have to wriggle my way underneath a hollow created by a fallen tree, curled up in the depression where the root ball ripped out of the earth. More creepy crawlies across my skin and over my head, including a massive, venomous centipede. I have no choice but to risk detection by throwing it off of me; getting bitten by something venomous would be catastrophic right now.

I fling the gigantic, palm-length centipede away from

me into the underbrush; the rustle-thump of it hitting the ground catches the attention of the patrol; being hidden a few feet below ground level and shrouded by the dirt-clumped tendrils of the roots, I cannot see them, but I hear them whispering to each other in Spanish. I hear their steps approach my hiding spot. I hold my breath and close my eyes, not daring to so much as blink for fear that they'll see the whites of my eyes. I hear them shuffling their feet in the dirt, muttering about it just being a forest creature, and then they move away. I continue to hold my pent-up breath with my eyes closed until the sound of their passage is gone, and then I slowly release the pressure in my burning lungs.

Easing myself upright, I climb out of the hole and crouch on the edge, watching and listening. When I'm satisfied the patrol has moved on, I key my mic. "A second patrol closer to the estate, moving east to west."

"Outer patrol and inner patrol?" Solomon says.

"Affirmative."

"Copy." A pause. "I count four patrols of two men each in the estate itself."

"Confirmed—that's my count, as well," I say.

"Let's head back," Solomon commands.

"Negative," I respond. "Need a closer look at the approach."

"Copy."

So I steal back toward the road and halt in a crouch when it's within view—I wait and watch for a few minutes and then make my way parallel to the road within the trees. The approach to the estate is not good news.

It's a short bridge—the plateau the estate sits upon is actually an island, so to speak. I'd assumed there was a natural land bridge where the ravine was broken up by an intersecting ridge or something, but no.

The bridge is only thirty or so feet long, but it creates a natural choke point. Guards are posted on either end, and on the estate side of it is a fenced-off holding pen with a heavy-duty gate manned by more guards.

This is not good.

I creep back into the trees and make my way to the meeting point, where I find Solomon.

"So?" he asks. "What's the approach like?"

"Not good, Sol," I answer. "Not good at all."

I give him a thorough description of what I'd seen—the bridge, the holding pen, and the eight armed guards, two posted at either end, two in the middle, and two at the gate on the far side of the pen.

When I'm done with my report, Solomon lets out a growling sigh. "Fuck."

"Yes, indeed," I answer. "This is going to be very difficult and very hazardous. When we encountered no patrols and so few guards at Mercado's home, we should have known something was amiss."

Sol nods, scrubbing his face. "Yeah, we were a tad... confident."

I snort. "I believe you mean to say arrogant."

"Yeah, maybe," he says. "But I feel like that's not without reason. We are all the best of the best, Nico. We can do this."

I wipe rain out the rain out of my eyes. "I agree. We just need a solid plan."

"Let's get back to the others and come up with one, then." Solomon claps me on the shoulder. "C'mon, brother."

We double-time it back to the others and report our findings. For a few moments after our report, everyone is silent, thinking.

"And that's not counting however many guys he may have inside," Kane muses. "A fuck-load of tangos."

"So then, is this just a straight-up frontal assault?" Rev asks. "I mean, the ravine, the bridge, the pen...fuck. This is gnarly. Mercado is nobody's fool."

"No, he is not," I say. "I do not think that simply attacking the bridge is going to work. There are too many of them in a defensible position. They can just drop back to the estate and pick us off as we attempt to cross the bridge. We need to distract them. I think our plan last time was effective. Pick off the perimeter patrol as a distraction."

"Is scaling the ravine totally out of the question?" Chance asks. "I mean, I know *I* fuckin' can't—I'm too goddamn big to sneak up the side of anything. But Lash, you and Scarlett are sneaky and agile. You could go up the back and do some silent elimination to even the numbers a bit and then create a distraction while we hit the front."

I look at Scarlett, but she just shrugs. "I didn't see the ravine, Nico did. If he says it's scalable, I'm down to give it a shot."

I consider what I saw, sighing. "It is...possible. It will be a physically demanding climb—it is steep, with dense undergrowth. To climb it without being seen or heard..." I wince, shaking my head. "It can be done. But it is not without great risk, and will be quite difficult."

Scarlett just shrugs again. "Hey, I'm not scared of hard. Maybe you guys can take potshots at them just to draw their attention away from us."

"And then," Rev adds, "while you two are sneaking

around doing murders and creating a diversion, the rest of us take the bridge."

Chance eyes his best friend. "Doing murders?"

Rev chuckles, shrugging. "Heard it on some video Myka watched. Thought it sounded funny."

Scarlett snickers. "I like it. C'mon, Nico. Let's you and me go do some murders." She holds out her fist to me, and I tap mine against it.

"Everyone on board?" Sol asks.

Tatiana raises her hand. "Um. What about me?" She scans the faces of the group. "I don't want to stay here, but I am not like you. I do not have your training or your experience. If I go with you, I am afraid I will be a liability. You cannot afford the distraction of having to babysit me."

Solomon frowns at her. "You aren't wrong. It's not a good idea for you to stay here by yourself, I agree. But you're not trained in assaults like this. I'm not worried about babysitting you, per se, more than just that I don't want to see you get hurt or killed." He holds up a finger. "Wait, hold on."

He goes to the back of the vehicle, rummages in the gear bags, and comes up with a sniper rifle. "We're looking at pretty short distances here, and despite the rain, there's not much wind. Would you feel comfortable using this from the tree line?"

Tatiana takes the rifle from him and ejects the magazine, checks the bolt action, replaces the magazine, points it away and peers through the scope, and then angles the barrel down with a nod. "Yes," she says. "I can do that."

I smile at her encouragingly. "I will help you find a good spot."

She gives me a small but determined smile and a nod. "That would be good. Thank you."

Sol claps his hands. "Alright. Scarlett, Nico, Tati, you'll need a head start. Get going while the rest of us gear up."

Solomon gives Tatiana a small box of ammunition and a couple of spare magazines; Scarlett and I check our loadouts, and then the three of us move into the forest and head for the estate.

We find a spot to hide while the patrols pass us by, and then continue. Tatiana, after the second patrol passes out of earshot, frowns at me. "What about them? Won't they hear my shots and come looking for me?"

Scarlett and I exchange looks, and then I nod. "Yes, you are right. Scarlett and I will eliminate them."

I scout the tree line around the path, looking for a good angle on the gate and bridge where she will be well hidden. After several minutes of hunting, I find a thick tree with a four-way fork where each trunk is fat and sturdy. I climb up and test it out, checking the sightline and positioning. Satisfied, I bring Tatiana to it. I crouch on the ground in the position she'll need to assume in the tree, showing her how to support the barrel on her forearm braced over her knees.

"As Sol said, there's little wind and the distance is only a couple hundred yards, so you will not need to worry about windage or drop calculations. Just put the crosshairs on your target and squeeze the trigger. You have range training, so I know you can do this."

She nods, her expression a fierce frown. "I always liked rifles more than handguns or assault rifles. I can do this, Nico. I will make you proud."

I cradle her face in my hands. "I already am, my love.

You are brave and resilient. And if for any reason some-one in the estate spots you and starts shooting at you, get down and find a new spot. Even on the ground, lying down. In fact, it may be a good idea to change locations every few shots, anyway. Keep your earpiece in. If someone says overwatch, that's you. Aim for center mass, not the head. Reload *before* you run out."

She lets out a sharp breath with a firm nod. "I understand."

I kiss her. "It is okay to be afraid. But you will be fine." I pull back. "You have a pistol and spare mags?"

She nods. "Yes."

"Good. Keep your head on a swivel. We will take out the patrols before we go down the ravine, but do not as-sume you will be alone out here. Make sure you see who you are shooting at before you shoot, if anyone approaches you—it could be one of us." I let out a breath. "Okay. You can do this. I love you."

She swallows hard, eyes watering. She closes her eyes tight, breathes deeply a few times, and then opens them, the tears unshed and glistening on her eyelashes. "I can do this," she repeats. "I love you, Nico." She pushes me back-ward. "Go. No more advice. Just go before I lose my nerve."

Scarlett watches her scramble up the tree and unsling the rifle from her shoulder, assuming the position I showed her, settling in.

Tatiana sees us watching and shoos us away with a flap of her hand. "You two have a role to play. Go. I will be fine."

With one last look over my shoulder, I force myself to walk away from her yet again, knowing I have no choice but to trust that she can take care of herself.

Scarlett bumps me with her shoulder. "You snagged a good one, my friend."

"She continues to amaze me," I say.

"I suppose it helps that she grew up with the father she did. Someone else may not do as well as she has," Scarlett says. "She's smart, brave, and learns fast."

I just nod. "Let's get this over with. I am tired of this jungle."

Scarlett snorts. "Buddy, you have no fucking idea. I already hiked halfway across the goddamn Amazon looking for Sol, rescuing him, and then escaping with his ass. And now here I fucking am, a-*fucking*-gain, in the goddamn jungle. I swear to god, if I never see this place again, as beautiful as it is, it'll be too soon."

"We are nearly there," I assure her. "Let's find these patrols and take them out."

We find the outer ring patrol easily—they're at the road, smoking cigarettes under the shelter of a tree, looking pissed off and miserable. Scarlett and I drop them with a single round to the forehead each and then pull their bodies into the brush.

The inner patrol requires more searching, however, and we stumble upon them, quite literally, by accident. They see us first and one actually manages to get his AK-47 up to bear, but I'm faster, and he drops. Scarlett takes out her man a split second later, and since we're already well off-path, we leave them where they lay. I take a radio and earpiece from one.

I key our comms. "Overwatch in place, outer patrols eliminated. Beginning our descent."

"Copy," Solomon says. "When you begin your ascent, we'll get their attention."

It is extremely slow going, sneaking down the ravine's face. It's steep, and the undergrowth is wickedly dense. Branches catch on our clothes and weapons, scratching our faces and hands. After what feels like an eternity, we reach the bottom, panting, sweaty, and covered in scratches. We take a moment to catch our breath and then approach the ascent.

We stand side by side, peering up.

Scarlett wipes her forehead. "Fuck that, man. Down was hard enough. We have to go up *that*?"

It does look much higher and steeper from here.

She rolls her shoulders and exhales. "Alright, well, nothing for it but to get after it."

We're at the rear of the property, with the lights a dim yellow glow far above us. The sound of a radio crackling reaches us, and then a voice, too faint and muffled to make out—I hear it on my radio, though.

"They're trying to contact the patrols," I say into the mic. "We're beginning our ascent."

"Copy that," Solomon says. "Wait for us to start shooting and then start up."

"Roger," I answer.

"Overwatch, pick a target and when you hear us start shooting, take your shot, and then fire at will," Solomon says over the radio.

"Okay," Tatiana answers. "Um, roger. Should I say roger or copy?"

Solomon's voice is amused. "It doesn't matter as long as you acknowledge somehow. We just use the terms we're familiar with."

"Okay," She says, and leaves it at that.

A few seconds later, I hear a three-round burst and

a faint cry of pain. That first burst sets off a barrage as the crew unleashes hell from across the ravine. The return fire is immediate and heavy, with overlapping silences as our side finds new positions to make it seem like there are more of us than there are.

CRACK! Tatiana's rifle speaks, a loud, sharp report layering over the chatter of the automatics.

"Overwatch, call out your kills," Solomon commands. "Just say confirmed kill or something like that."

"Okay," she murmurs into the radio. *CRACK!* "Confirmed kill. My first was a kill also."

"Two for two," Scarlett remarks to me. "Not bad."

"Ascending," I say into the radio. "I hope she remembers to change locations." The last part was just to Scarlett.

We begin our grueling climb. The grade is only a few degrees off vertical, so we have to pull ourselves up by branches and bushes, some of which come loose as we pull, necessitating a scramble to keep from toppling backward.

CRACK! "Three," Tatiana says.

More automatic fire. Chatter crackles from our comms as the team coordinates movement. Panicked chatter swarms the enemy comms—they have no idea how many there are, and the chatter is mostly concerned with trying to locate the sniper.

"You are doing excellent work, overwatch," I say. "They are afraid of you."

"I've got four tangos making a break for the bridge," Rev says. "Overwatch, take them out, and fast." I worry that they're expecting too much from Tatiana.

I can just barely see the far side of the bridge from my location, and I pause to watch. I see four figures sprinting, stopping, and sprinting down the length of the bridge.

CRACK!…CRACK!…CRACK!…CRACK!

"Four confirmed," Tatiana says.

The four figures are now slumped on the bridge in a line.

"Damn, girl," Chance says. "That was some stellar fuckin' shooting."

"I suppose I should be grateful my father insisted I shoot every week," she answers. "I never in a million years thought I would be doing this."

Scarlett and I are only halfway up. She taps me. "We gotta move. Eventually, someone is gonna get across that bridge."

"You are correct," I answer. "We must double time it."

Up is much, much harder than down. My lungs burn and my legs ache, and my hands and forearms sting with a crisscross of scratches. There is nothing else to do, however, but keep going. The whole plan relies on us, so we must simply grit through it.

It is an agonizingly brutal climb to the top. We reach it at long last, and slump, huffing and puffing, in the brush just below the rim, waiting for the patrol to pass before emerging so we aren't surprised by them.

Once they pass us, we slip out onto the short, rain-slick grass behind them. With a glance at each other, we count to three and then put slugs through the back of their heads and then topple them down the ravine— the bodies flip and bounce and roll with a series of loud crashes.

Which no one notices over the gunfire.

We jog forward and encounter another pair approaching us—they see us and immediately open fire. We both go prone the second we see them raising their AK-47s; their rounds go high and ours do not.

"They scaled the side!" someone shouts on the enemy comms. "Rear of the property." The speaker calls out half a dozen names and tells them to handle it.

"It's working," Solomon reports. "Half a dozen tangos just peeled off and headed your way."

"I have reloaded and I am moving locations," Tatiana says.

"Copy," Solomon says. "Be quick. We're going to assault soon and we'll need you. Keep your scope on us and watch for anyone approaching from behind or on our flank. Use the clock—do you know it?"

"Yes. Twelve o'clock is front, six is rear. So I would say bad guy on your four o'clock or something like this, no?"

"Use the word tango," Sol says. "Otherwise, yes."

"Tango? Like the dance?"

"Correct."

"Roger."

Scarlett and I sprint for the hacienda's wall, following it forward toward the entrance. A large air conditioning condenser hums noisily. We take cover behind it, and I peek around the side—three male figures jog this way, carrying assault rifles.

We wait until they're nearly on top of us before we send bursts in tandem over the top of the condenser. They're thrown backward by the impacts, momentum making them topple and roll awkwardly. The chatter on the enemy comms has ceased abruptly, which means they've likely switched to a new channel. I ignore that as we continue toward the main entrance of the house. We reach the front corner and halt, I peek around the side and assess.

The gate is no longer manned, and the bridge is littered with bodies. Tatiana's rifle cracks again, and again. An assault rifle on this side chatters.

"I am taking fire. Moving," Tatiana says.

I peek out and see the flash of muzzle burst. I put three rounds a few inches behind the burst and hear a soft grunt.

"Approaching the bridge," Solomon announces. "Overwatch, do you have eyes on us?"

"Not...yet," she puffs. "One...moment."

Several figures rush out of the entrance of the hacienda, kneel at the gate of the pen, and open fire. Our side returns fire, but everyone's rounds go high or wide.

"In...position," Tatiana says, out of breath still. "I see you."

"We're taking fire," Solomon says.

"I have them," Tatiana answers.

Scarlett and I trade glances, and then roll out from behind the cover of the corner, opening fire. The figures twitch and spin and lurch as our rounds hit them, and then the rifle cracks and another one falls backward. We retreat back behind the corner. A minute or so later, there's the crump of explosives as the bridge gate is blown open.

The rain has let up, finally, leaving the air a bit cooler and noticeably less humid, with a soft breeze blowing. It is fully night now, the last of the daylight having bled beneath the horizon. I peek out and see our crew jogging across the blacktop that leads from the bridge in a straight line to the courtyard of the hacienda.

I hear the crackle-chatter of an assault rifle behind me and something hot snaps past my ear. I spin and drop to a knee, jerking Scarlett down with me. The other three tangos must have circled the structure looking for us; only the fact that the shooter had poor aim saved my life. Bullets buzz and snap and whine, and we crabwalk behind the AC unit—thunks and dings echo as rounds hit the unit. One punches through and I hear a crunching grind as the unit shuts down.

They have us pinned down, working in trained concert to keep suppressive fire directed at us. "Overwatch, do you see us? Behind the A-C unit."

"No, I do not have an angle from where I am."

"Okay," I answer. "Stay where you are, then."

I have one grenade clipped to my vest. I meant to grab more but forgot—a foolish thing to forget in a situation like this. But, one is enough for now. I pull the pin, peek around the side to judge the distance, and then hook-toss the grenade.

While it is in the air, they pour more fire at us, and a round punches through the A/C unit and hits me in the vest. Its momentum is slowed enough that it only feels like being kicked by a horse rather than punched by a god. My chest will be a mess of bruising, later.

I'm thrown backward to my back, left gasping and blinking at the cloud-dark sky, hearing gunfire and voices in my ear.

Crump-BOOOM!

The grenade detonates with an earth-shaking roar, and the gunfire goes silent.

Scarlett's face swims into view above me. "You good, bro?"

I grab her hand, let her haul me up to my feet, and then bend over to suck in oxygen, nodding. "Took one to the vest. I am okay."

After another moment or two to catch my breath, I

reload and follow Scarlett around the corner. We're just in time to join the rest of the team at the gate as Kane places the breaching chargers on the gate. The explosion shakes the ground, and the gate flies apart with an ear-piercing shriek of protesting metal. Solomon is first through, and we form up on him.

The courtyard is wide and blacktopped, and empty of cars. All is peculiarly silent.

"Not saying this has been easy," Kane mutters, "But this feels too easy yet a-fuckin'-gain. Something's up."

I sweep the roofline but see nothing. Ahead, the main doors into the hacienda stand closed. Solomon approaches, standing to one side. Chance approaches, rears back, and kicks it open, ducking out of the way the second the door splinters open.

Just in time—gunfire blatters concussively, and we all throw ourselves to the side as rounds chainsaw across the ground and bite into the doorway and shatter glass.

Rev lobs a flashbang inside, and we all turn away and plug our ears—the detonation leaves our ears ringing and white lights dancing in our vision. Kane fills the doorway and his rifle barks in a series of three-round bursts.

He gestures at me and at the doorway, indicating I should precede him through.

Scarlett grabs my shoulder and follows me through the doorway; several bodies lay writhing on the floor, bleeding from legs and shoulders onto the elaborate blue, white, and yellow Spanish-style tile of the foyer. Inside is cool and airy, the walls more white-washed adobe, with nooks built into the walls housing vases and other decorative knickknacks.

The foyer opens to a wide, high-ceilinged hallway

extending left and right, arches marching in both directions. Directly opposite the foyer on the far side of the arched hallway is an open-air courtyard with a blossoming orange tree heavy with fruit, the tree surrounded by elegant wrought iron benches; small, low-to-the-ground lights bathe the tree in a soft amber glow. To the left, the hallway leads to the library; to the right, the kitchen and den.

"Must be in the basement," Saxon says.

"Find the basement, then," Solomon orders.

We split up into pairs and clear the house—other than the small contingent left to die in the foyer, there's no sign of anyone else.

"Found it!" Silas calls out over the comms. "Kitchen."

We all converge on the door, which is locked.

Chance chose the Benelli shotgun I claimed, and he uses it to blast open the door. Gunfire echoes and slugs splinter through the lintel and doorframe and chew at the ceiling. A round hits Chance in the chest and knocks him backward, and that backward stumble saves his life as another buzzes through the air where he was.

He drops to a knee, hand on his chest, gasping.

Saxon, Silas, and Rev all fill the doorway, pouring fire down the stairs.

"Well, fuck," Saxon growls. "He ducked into my round and took it to the fuckin' head, the dumbfuck."

"I think that was mine," Silas argues.

Solomon whacks them both. "Shut the fuck up, both of you. He's dead. Let's move on. We gotta find Inez and get the fuck out of here." He rests a hand on Chance's massive back. "You good, man?"

Chance nods, straightening to stretch his torso, wincing. "Good. Let's go. Fuck these fuckers."

The stairwell abandons the Spanish Hacienda style in favor of modern, utilitarian plain white drywall and simple wall sconces.

Down we go, Saxon in the lead, now, with Silas on his left and Sol on his right in a tight triangle formation. The stairs go down to a landing, where the shooter now slumps over himself, drooling blood from a hole in his forehead into his lap. Blood is splattered on the wall, sprinkled with pink chunks. At the landing, the stairs turn left and descend again, reaching a squeaky, black-and-white checkered epoxy floor and drop-tile ceilings with LED lights. A bar runs the length of the basement on the right side, with the usual assortment of basement features—a pool table, couches, and a gigantic flat-screen TV.

A door on the left is closed—Rev stands beside it, and Chance kicks it open. A bathroom, empty. Another door leads to a wine cellar—a brick barrel vault ceiling with built-in wooden racks containing hundreds of bottles of wine. Solomon grabs one and appraises it with a critical eye. "Expensive."

Saxon snorts, rolling his eyes. "You think a man who spends thousands of dollars a year just in rubber bands for his cash is gonna have cheap-ass fuckin' wine? C'mon, bro."

"Shut the fuck up, ass-wipe," Solomon says without looking at his brother. "We're missing something."

We search the basement again, but there are no other doors. Scarlett and I do another search of the main floor again, this one more thorough, but it turns up nothing except expensive taste.

"There is something happening in the forest," Tatiana says across the comms. "It sounds like a helicopter."

"From the *forest*?" Sol asks.

"Yes, from the forest. To the behind of the house."

"I found a secret door," Silas says over comms. "In the wine cellar."

There's a lot of shouting from the basement, none of it over comms—Scarlett and I run downstairs, caroming off walls in our haste.

We stumble into the wine cellar, where a section of the brick wall pivots away to reveal a small chamber lit by a single naked bulb.

Suspended by chains from the ceiling is Inez.

Her face is a bloody mess, she's naked, bruised, and limp. Her toes brush the concrete floor as she sways and twists slightly.

We're all huddled just inside the chamber, silent.

Rev is the first to move toward her, his hand shaking as he presses his index and middle fingers to her pulse point at her throat.

One eye snaps open, blazing black, and she levers upright, bare, bloody legs wrapping around Rev's throat—the move is faster than a cobra's strike.

"It's—me—" Rev gurgles, patting her thigh. "Inez—Inez! It's me."

Her swollen eye blinks, seems to clear, and then she abruptly releases him. "Took you long enough." Her voice is a hoarse, gurgling, lisping rasp.

CHAPTER 18

RESCUED

TATIANA

I SLOWLY SCAN THE ESTATE IN A CRISSCROSSING pattern, watching for movement. So far, nothing. My stomach is in knots as I try to not think about how many people I've killed so far.

No time to think about that. Focus.

The sound of the helicopter has been steady for a minute or two, and I still can't identify where it is, the sound dopplering off the ravine walls and muffled by the forest.

I'm not in a great position, lying prone in the brush at the tree line, looking into the courtyard outside the front door at an oblique angle. I can see most of the courtyard, all of one side of the house, and all of the bridge. Nothing moves.

A sound reaches my ears, faint, beneath the chopping of the helicopter—a rustle. A whisper.

Shit.

I lay the rifle down and get out my pistol—Tata taught me to always check a gun before I try to use it, so, as quietly as I can, I check the magazine, ease it back in, click it in place as gently as possible, and then thumb back the hammer. Roll to my back, aiming down my body.

I key my mic. "There is someone in the woods near me," I whisper into the mic.

"Say again?" I hear Solomon say—it sounds so loud in my ear, now that I have to be quiet.

"Enemy," I hiss. "Nearby."

"Nico is coming. Do what you gotta do. Don't hesitate."

I click the mic button, hoping it will serve as acknowledgment; the rustling is closer now.

I hear voices—whispering in Spanish. Closer. Closer.

My heart pounding, I wait, listening, motionless.

"*Ella esta' aqua' en laguna part,*" the voice says.

"*So,*" Another voice answers.

Two of them, it sounds like, unless there are others not participating in the conversation. The rustling becomes footsteps in the undergrowth, and then I can see the branches moving as they approach my position as if they know exactly where I am.

I hold my breath now, gun braced in both hands, arms outstretched along my body—I am proud, perhaps inordinately so, of how steady the barrel is, considering how hard my heart is hammering in my chest.

A burly arm sweeps aside a clump of ferns; I aim inwards of the arm and squeeze the trigger three times in rapid succession, controlling the kick the way Tata taught me. A wet, wheezing cough, and a short, stout man topples forward, eyes blinking at me in shocked confusion.

Something niggles in my gut, whispering that I should roll over a few times. I don't question the feeling and roll to my left. The gun digs into my gut as I roll over it, and a branch pokes me in the face, but I ignore all that and roll again. The blinding flash of a muzzle precedes by a fraction of a second, the concussive rattle of a machine gun spraying bullets where I'd been, thumping wetly into the man I just killed. Laying on my side, I shrink into a small ball, gun held close to me now, waiting. Another burst of gunfire echoes, rattling and chattering, and dirt sprays and leaves thwack and bark splinters as the shooter fires indiscriminately, spraying side to side.

I wait.

Hold my breath.

A whipcord-lean figure steps over the body of his friend, gun held at his hip, sweeping the area where I'd been laying.

He sees me lying in the undergrowth and swivels to bring his rifle to bear, but he's too slow. My first bullet punches through his biceps, spinning him to one side, and my second tears through his throat, splashing red down his front in spray and then in riveleting buckets. My third bullet smashes into his chest, the bone cracking wetly as a red blossom spreads dark on his front.

He sinks to his knees, dropping his gun and clutching at his throat as if to hold his blood in.

His eyes glaze over and go sightless, and he slumps forward at an angle.

Running steps crunch and crash through the forest, but I hold my fire, remembering Solomon's word of warning, and his promise that Nico was coming to me.

Sure enough, Nico's face breaks through the branches, painted with worry. He skids to a halt in the wet, slippery carpet of rotting leaves, staring at the two dead men.

"I heard the shooting," he pants in Croatian. "I was afraid for you, but I should have known better."

I'm shaking now, eyes wide, hazy with tears. Nausea

roils through me, and I close my eyes to combat it, breathing through the acidic burn of bile as it rises in my gorge, swallowing hard against the surge of vomit.

But with my eyes closed, I see the men I killed with the rifle—heads jerking as my bullets splat open their skulls like watermelons.

I roll to my hands and knees, still clutching the pistol in one hand, and spew vomit across the forest floor. I hear his feet, feel his presence, and then he's kneeling beside me, hand on my back.

"It is over now." He murmurs this in Croatian. "It is all over."

"Hel-helicopter?" I pant.

"Mercado got away." He sounds furious about it. "There was a secret tunnel. The helo took off while you were having your shootout."

Another flash flood of images assaults me—blood spraying, Tata's broken body, the man I stabbed and his blood hot on my hands. Vomit hits my teeth and I have no choice but to let it out, spine arching upward as I heave.

Spitting and wiping my lips on my sleeve, I sit on my heels. "Inez?"

"We have her. She's alive. Not in great shape, but alive."

I notice him rubbing at his chest. "Are you hurt?"

He shakes his head. "Took one to the vest. I am well." He sits cross-legged in the wet leaves and pulls me onto his lap. "You were amazing. You do so well, Tati. You are a miracle. I love you so much."

I bury my face in his throat, letting my emotions wash through me. "I hate killing, Nico. I *hate* it."

"Good," he whispers. "You should."

"It was so easy with that rifle," I whisper. "Too easy."

"I know," he mutters.

"If Mercado is still out there, then it isn't over," I whisper.

"No, it's not totally over. But this part is. We have to get Inez medical treatment. We have no way of knowing where he went, but we'll find him. Inez isn't going to let him get away with what he did to her."

"She is in bad shape?" I ask.

He nods. "She was badly tortured. We arrived just in time to save her life, though. He was about to kill her. We arrived, and he was forced to flee instead."

I do not know how to reply to that, so I say nothing. After a few moments of Nico holding me in silence, He lets out a sigh and kisses my temple. "We must go, my love."

I nod and clamber to my feet, retrieve the rifle where I left it, sling it over my shoulder, and then follow Nico back to the road and the van. Nico climbs behind the wheel and we drive down the road, across the short bridge, and into the courtyard. He bleeps the horn a couple of times.

The big double front doors slam open and Chance emerges in the headlights, his expression grave and furious. In his gargantuan arms, he carries a limp figure wrapped in a blanket. I scramble out of the front passenger seat and open the sliding door so Chance can slide onto the first bench, resting against the far side with Inez in his arms.

She moans softly. "Ren? Where's Ren?"

"Keeping Little Lorenzo safe," Chance answers. "He and his…" he trails off, unsure how to finish.

"Mom," Inez finishes. "She's his mom. I was his mother, but she is his mom." She has a faint accent.

"Ren figured you'd want him to protect Little Lorenzo and trust us to get you. He wanted to be here, though."

Another quiet groan of pain. "He…fuck." A hiss as she tries to sit up.

"Inez," Chance growls. "Relax. I fuckin' *got* you, Boss."

"Not…weak," she says, her voice a whisper—but a snarled predator's growl.

Chance actually laughs. "Boss Lady, you're as far from weak as a human being can get. You were tortured half to fuckin' death. You're allowed to hurt."

"But I have to—"

He cuts her off. "You have to rest and recover so you can fuckin' murder Rafael or whatever the fuck his bitch-ass name is. Not one of us will have any less respect for you because you let *us* take care of *you* for once."

I hear her breathing hard. "I couldn't escape. He is no fool. He fears me. He—he made sure there was no way."

"He should be afraid of you," Chance says.

"It hurts, Chance. Everything hurts."

"I know, Boss. Just try to breathe. We'll get you a medic asap."

"I was afraid. He was about to kill me."

"Been there. We all been there. Bein' afraid when you're face-to-face with death is fuckin' normal. You're still the baddest boss bitch in all the land."

She sniffs a sort-of-laugh. "Don't—ow. Don't make me laugh. Ribs hurt."

"Sorry."

While they talk, the rest of the team loads into the van. I'm on the edge of the first bench nearest the door, and when the last of the team has found a seat, I drag the sliding door closed. The figure in Chance's arms is hidden from me, swaddled in a thick indigenous tribal-style blanket so all I can see is a hint of black hair and a smooth brown forehead, blood-smeared.

Small, rust-crusted hands tug the blanket down from her face and wide, deep, dark black eyes regard me with open curiosity. "You are with Lash." It is not a question.

I nod. "Yes. Nico and I are together."

Her eyes widen. "Nico?"

The man himself leans over the back of the bench, reaching down to grab one of Inez's hands. "I have told them everything. Lash is no more. I am now Nicolae—Nico."

Her eyes flick to his hand on hers, narrowing for a moment as if in warning, and then she lets out a breath with closed eyes and puts her other hand on top of his, squeezing. "Nico. That's good." She looks at me again. "And who are you?"

"Tatiana Juric," I answer.

"Juric…"

"Stjepan Juric was my father." My voice cracks.

"Was?" She looks at Nico.

He nods. "Mercado captured him and tortured him to death for letting Solomon, Scarlett, and Lorenzo escape. For letting me spring them free." He glances at me, then back at her. "And also because he wanted Tatiana for himself, which I also prevented."

"Tell me everything that has happened," she commands, the snap of authority clear in her voice despite the quietness of her tone.

Rev is driving again, pulling around the courtyard. Inez glances through the window at the house—which is remarkably beautiful, I must admit.

"Wait," Inez orders. "The house. Burn it down."

Rev brakes to a halt and Kane and Saxon hop out with

a grenade in each hand. They disappear into the house for a few minutes and then emerge at a run.

"Go, go, go!" Kane barks. "'Bout to be a big-ass bada-boom."

Rev guns the engine and the back end fishtails on the wet blacktop, stutters, and catches, and then we rocket forward. I watch through the back window, waiting for the explosion.

There isn't one explosion, though. There are several in a row—four smaller ones in rapid succession: *boom-boom-boom-boom* in the wings and center of the structure. These smaller explosions shatter windows and blow out walls. The last explosion, however, is a different beast entirely. This one rattles the windows of the van, and the shockwave makes the bridge sway precariously and the back end of the van leaps skyward as we cross it. The center of the house bellies outward and the roof pops off in a shower of red tiles; fire billows hungrily from the windows, licking and spreading eagerly.

"Shoulda blown up his other house," Saxon grumbles. "Motherfucker."

Inez grunts in pain as she grabs the bench back and hauls herself upright to watch the house burn as we drive away from it. Once it's out of sight, she slumps back down against Chance's chest.

She sighs in exhaustion. "Nothing personal, Chance, but I wish you were Lorenzo."

"I know, Boss Lady."

"Now," she says. "Tell me what's happened since I let Rafael take me."

Solomon, Scarlett, and Nico take turns relating the events from Zagreb until we arrived in South America, and then Silas, by some unspoken agreement with the others, relates their side of things—getting the call to assemble everyone and get down to Brazil ASAP, meeting up with us, and everything up to now.

Once she's caught up, Inez spends a few minutes in silence, thinking. After a while, she lifts up awkwardly to look at Nico over the back of the bench. "You gave up going after Pugli to come after me?"

He sighs, nodding and shrugging. "That is correct, to a degree. It was not solely for you, however. Tatiana helped me see that my thirst for vengeance was hobbling me. I let it go so I would have space in my soul to love her. Hatred and vengeance were consuming me. But also, yes, I came for you. I felt my loyalty to you was more important than revenge, and I could not do both."

Inez peers at me through heavy-lidded eyes. "You are a miracle worker, Tatiana Juric. You brought a dead man back to life."

I can only shrug. "I...I suppose I saw beneath the shell that was Lash to the Nicolae within. And selfishly, I wanted Nicolae for myself, not Lash. I love him. It is strange and unsettling to feel such powerful love so swiftly, but I cannot deny what I feel."

"We are all beneficiaries of the courage of your love," she says to me. "I am sorry for the loss of your father. But now you are one of us. You belong with us."

I frown. "Must I be branded as well?"

Inez sniffs a quiet laugh. "No, that will not be necessary. Unless you wish to—but it is not something anyone can be compelled to do. You must truly desire it for yourself."

I can't help the sigh of relief. "I do not mind swearing

an oath—and I would gladly swear an oath to never kill anyone again. I have had my fill of that. But I do not much care much for the idea of being branded or tattooed."

Nico smiles at me. "No brands or tattoos for you, my love. But if you wish to take the oath when Lorenzo and Scarlett do, you may, of course."

Inez frowns up at him. "Lorenzo's going to take the brand?"

Nico shrugs. "I believe so. I thought I heard him say something about it. I could be mistaken—it has been a very…busy and chaotic and exhausting few days." He frowns. "How long has it been since the airplane was re-routed? I cannot even remember." A shake of his head. "Anyway. Yes, I believe Lorenzo wishes to take the brand. We have all grown to admire and respect him. We could not have succeeded in this without him."

Inez nods. "I would like that."

Chance makes a wordless rumbling sound—a sigh or growl, or something of both. "You need to rest. Be a bit of a journey to get you to a doctor."

"No," she murmurs. "Get me home. No doctors here. Rafael is still out there. This is not over until one of us is dead, and he knows I will need attention. I will live until we reach Las Vegas. Just get us there."

"Boss Lady," Chance starts. "You're in bad shape. You need—"

"*No!*" She snaps. "The club! That's it. Straight there. No doctors, no medics. Just…home." Her tone softens. "I know my body. I know my limits. You must trust me."

Chance grumbles quietly again. "Only cause you're the boss."

"Damn right, I'm the boss. You know better than to argue with me, you big lunk."

Chance just laughs. "Yeah, yeah, you're the boss. Now shut up and rest."

———— ◆ ————

The ride back to the airfield is quiet—we're all beyond exhausted. Once there, Inez uses Solomon's phone to call Lorenzo.

It rings four times before he answers. "Sol. How did it go?"

"It's me, Ren," Inez says in a low, shaky voice. "You're on speaker."

"Take me off speaker," he says.

She does, and now we can only hear her side. "Yes... Ren, come *on*...fine. Yes, I miss you as well. I know—I *know*. No, no doctors until we're back at the Club. I already had this argument with Chance. I'm not having it with you." A long silence as she listens to him. "Good, that's good. No, it would not do anyone any good for either of them to speak with me. Perhaps once this is all truly over....because he *escaped*, Ren. He's still out there. And you know as well as I do that he will not stop until I am dead or he is." She listens again and then sighs heavily. "I cannot give you those words right now, Lorenzo. But I do care for you. If all goes well, we will be in Las Vegas late tomorrow. We will see. Yes, if you could get us an off-book flight to the States, that would be best. I'll call you again as soon as possible. Very good. You as well. Goodbye."

She hands the phone back up to Solomon, who is sitting in the front passenger seat next to Rev. "He is calling in one more favor to get us home. We will have a long wait ahead of us, but we all need rest, anyway."

Lorenzo calls us back an hour or so later and informs us that the next flight back to the States from here isn't for another forty-eight hours, so we should find rooms nearby.

This is welcome news to me—I could be tempted to do something violent for a hot shower and a real bed. Inez pulls some strings with someone in the US Embassy in Rio, and we are provided with rooms in a hotel in downtown Rio. These rooms are a far cry from the mid-level one we had in Manaus, or wherever that was. The room provided for Nico and me is a massive suite with a sitting area furnished with expensive leather couches, a full bar, a huge bathroom with a rainfall showerhead, and a king-size bed with a comforter so thick it almost swallows me when I flop down onto it on my back.

I snicker a laugh as Nico sits on the bed beside me.

"What is funny, Lovely One?" he asks, his voice flat with exhaustion, his face pale and drained.

"I am just realizing that I am somewhat spoiled. My thought, as I see this room, is that we have finally gotten a *real* hotel room."

Nico snorts. "You are the daughter of Stjepan Juric. He always liked the finer things in life, so of course he would spoil his only child."

I turn to rest my head on his lap. "After Mama died, he only spoiled me more, as if to make up for her loss and his own absence due to his work demands. But yes, I have acquired his taste for the finer things in life."

He sighs. "I do not know that I can provide that for you, Tati. I have never been a wealthy man, and to be very honest, I do not care to be. I wish to have enough that I need not worry, but that is about all."

I reach up and caress his jaw. "I do not care, Nico. I know how to make money. I will provide that for us." He opens his mouth to protest. "You will love me. You will take care of me. But I will also love you and take care of you. It will go both ways."

He pulls me onto his lap and draws us up to the head of the bed, knocks away the blankets, and tugs them over us, cradling me on his chest.

His heartbeat *thump-thump—thump-thump—thump-thump*s me to sleep.

CHAPTER 19

AN INFINITE MOMENT

LASH

I GRADUALLY RISE FROM SO DEEP A SLEEP THAT I AM disoriented at first, unsure when and where I am. Sunlight is bright and warm, and I feel heavy-limbed. A soft female snore huffs adorably nearby, breath hot on my back.

At first, for the briefest of moments, I think it is Ileana, but then memory surges through me, awareness returning, and there's another brief, inescapable moment of sorrow. I allow myself that moment, breathing through it, letting myself miss her. There is a twinge of guilt at this, as if I am betraying Tatiana, but I push that feeling away, knowing my Tati would not begrudge me a moment of missing Ileana.

The moment passes, and Ileana's ghost fades into the ether. Tatiana is spooning me from behind, her knees tucked up behind mine, hips to my buttocks, breasts against my back, forehead and nose against my shoulder blades. Her hand has found its way up under my shirt and curls against my stomach.

For a measureless time, I drowse there in the bed with her, not quite asleep nor awake. The sun is warm, bathing me in yellow heat, and Tatiana is soft against my back, the rhythm of her breathing lulling me into a trance-like state. Time ceases to exist, and I luxuriate in the warm contentedness of the infinite moment.

At some point, Tatiana's hand twitches against my belly. She snuffles, delicately rubbing her nose against my back. Makes a soft, wordless sound in her throat as she drifts up toward wakefulness. Then she yawns, stretching, arching her breasts and belly against my back, pulling at my stomach.

"Hi, baby," she whispers in Croatian.

"Good morning," I say, also in Croatian. "Or at least I think it is morning. I am not sure, and I must confess, I do not much care."

"Me either." She nuzzles the back of my neck. "I slept like a dead person."

"So did I."

For a moment or two, we linger in the sweet, wakeful silence together. And then Tatiana groans. "My god, I have to pee so bad. I do not want to get out of bed right now, though."

I can only laugh. "Unfortunately, I cannot help you with that," I grumble wordlessly. "Of course, now that you said so, I realize I have to go as well."

She laughs, kisses my shoulder, and rolls away. I stay as I am, hearing her pee and wash her hands. She climbs back under the covers and snuggles up against me once more. "Your turn. Hurry up and come back to me."

I take care of my bladder, wash my hands, and rinse out my mouth with water and the complimentary mouthwash. I'd fallen asleep in my clothes, and now I strip out of them—Tatiana's clothes lay in a pile on the floor near the toilet, and the knowledge that she is naked under the blankets sets my libido on fire.

Our little rendezvous in the back of the cargo plane was fun, and satisfying for what it was, but nothing can sate my ravenous hunger for Tatiana, my insatiable need to make love with her.

Her eyes blaze brightly as I swagger back to the bed—the need in her eyes fills me with pride that she wants me, needs me. She has the blanket pulled up to her nose, so only her eyes, nose, and the top of her head peek out, but the brilliant fervor in her eyes follows my every step, lingering on the sway of my cock as it unfurls with every step closer to her.

When I reach the side of the bed, she tosses the blankets open, revealing her nude form. She is posed perfectly, a goddess made of flesh—head resting on one hand, hair spread around her in a crow-black curtain, on her side with her knees slightly bent, her other hand draped down her thigh. Her bust, waist, and hip form the loveliest, most mouth-watering curve I have ever seen, and my cock jerks to a painful erection.

"So fucking beautiful," I whisper in English.

Her smile is shy and pleased at the same time, and she reaches for me, fingers curling around my cock as her eyes lock on mine. "So are you, my mighty warrior." She continues in Croatian, and even the sound of her voice in her native language turns me on.

She pulls me toward her, and I kneel on the bed. Brace on all fours above her and dip down, claiming the plump wet softness of her mouth. She opens for me with a groan, and her tongue rakes through my mouth. I shift my weight to one hand, tangling my tongue with hers, and find her center. She's wet and warm for me, slick and soft and waiting for my touch.

I fit my middle finger along her seam and drag it upward to the turgid nub of her clit—she gasps into the kiss. I delve my finger into her sweet, wet, waiting channel, dive deep, withdraw, smear her desire over her clit again. I'm rewarded with a quiet whimper and a twitch of her hips. I do it again, and now the hip twitch becomes a thrust. Her fist plunges down my hard length, and I groan, circling her clit with my finger; we groan together, Tatiana arching up into my touch while I push into hers.

"Nico," she whispers. "Please. I need you inside me, my love."

"Condom," I growl.

"Purse," she answers in a whisper, pointing at the leather backpack-style purse she's managed to keep hold of all the way since Zagreb.

With an inventive string of curses in Romani, I roll off the bed and go to her purse, on the small table behind the couch in the sitting area. I find the string of packets, rip a couple off, and tear one open with my teeth while I hurry back to her. I roll it on as I kneel on the bed, and then she grabs my sheathed cock and pulls me to her. She guides me to her entrance, notches me between her lips, and takes me inside her, all in a single, fluid movement, lifting her hips to push against me, taking me deep. Her legs wrap around my back and she pulls me down to claim a hot, wild kiss.

"Love me, my Nico," she breathes, the words felt on my lips as much as heard in my ears. "Love me with all of you."

I cradle the back of her head and neck in my hand

and push deeper until our hips bump together and our bellies touch. "Tati, my love."

She groans as I fill her, head tilting backward as the ecstasy consumes her. She levers her hips against mine, arching into me, taking me, gasping at the slick hot slide of my cock through her quivering wet sex. She pulses around me, edging toward release already. "Nico, my love—more. Harder."

"Come for me first," I say, my thrusts slow and measured.

She shakes her head. "Need it. Need you."

"Touch yourself," I tell her. "Let me watch you come while I'm inside you."

She drops her legs to the bed, as I lift up to sit tall on my knees and drape her heels over my shoulders. She gasps, eyes flying wide as I push inside her at a new angle and drive deep. "Ohhh, fuck, Nico. *Yes.*"

"You like it like this?" I ask.

She pinches a nipple with one hand and fingers her clit with the other, and now her hips begin to buck against mine with increasing speed, and her cries of pleasure come faster, louder, and more shrill as she ramps up toward the peak of climax.

I resist the urge to let go, to join her in release—I keep my thrusts slow and measured. She pushes against me with a loud whimper, spasming as the first waves of release smash through her—I grit my teeth and clench all my muscles to keep from coming with her. I'm not ready yet. I need more; she needs more.

"Nico, oh god—oh god," she gasps. "Oh god, I'm coming. I'm coming so hard!"

She cries out, then, fingers flying, hips grinding

against me, taking me in a ravaging glut of wild thrusts. I'm on the verge of releasing against my will when she finally subsides from the peak of ecstasy, panting, whimpering.

"Nico," she breathes. "You didn't—did you come yet?"

I shake my head. "Not yet."

"But...why? I want you to."

I grin down at her. "Oh, I'm going to. But I want you like *this*." I pull out of her, roughly flipping her to her belly.

She shrieks with shocked laughter at the unexpected move, playfully pretending to try to get away, crawling on all fours, giggling wildly when I wrap an arm around her thighs and yank her backward to me. Still laughing and breathlessly panting with eager need, she keeps pretending to try to get away. I hold her in place, grip my cock in my fist and push between her thighs, dragging the tip against her clit. She jerks at the sensation, still hypersensitive from having just orgasmed, laughter fading as need takes over.

She nudges me to her slit and feeds me into her pussy—we both groan in unison as I slick deep inside. "Ohhh *fuck*, Nico."

I roam my palms up her spine and rake my nails down her back, grasping a handful of each plump ass cheek and spreading her apart so I can push deeper. Her groan goes ragged and her upper torso sags against the mattress even as her back half stays upright.

"My god, Nico," she gasps breathlessly. "Yes. Just like this. Fuck me, Nico. Fuck me as hard as you can. I want it. I want you. I need you to fuck me until I forget who I am."

Her words are the catalyst I need, the permission required to throw off my restraint. I grip her round, beautiful ass and thrust into her slowly, exploratory, questing, testing. Her shriek of ecstasy is wild and unfeigned, and the sound of it is like jet fuel on the fire of my need.

I growl as heady, delirious need smashes through me, nearly undone by the sight of my beloved Tatiana on her hands and knees for me, perfect ass lifted high, sweet pussy taking my cock, her cries of joy loud in my ears as I pound into her.

"Harder, my Nico!" She begs. "Harder. Fuck me. Please fuck me, Nico."

God, her pleas ravage me. Undo me.

I snarl like a wolf and slam into her, the slap of her ass against my thighs a loud wet smack.

"*YES!*" she screams. "*YES!*"

I bellow, then, shouting wordlessly as my own orgasm boils in my balls, sending white heat shearing through my being as I let go, let myself take her with everything I have.

It's a mad race to climax, then, and I feel her pussy quaking and clenching, and she gasps and shrieks and screams as I slam into her without reprieve. The harder I fuck her, the louder she screams, the more unabashedly she chants my name.

I feel it hit me all at once, and I have no chance of holding this one back—I do not even try. I know she feels me let go as well because her cries go breathless and her pussy spasms around me as if my orgasm is a trigger for hers. We join with a cracking slap of flesh, and my release is a hurricane within me, my eyes clenching shut and dizziness washing through me and heat blasting and ecstasy building to a crescendo as we move together, come together.

The crashing rush of orgasm is slow to subside, and I keep thrusting into her, and she whimpers with each slow hard thrust, gasping each time I fuck deep. At long last, I'm done, and I give her one last slow thrust, and then I pull out. She gasps at the loss of me, flopping over on her back. She lurches up, grabs me by the neck, and hauls me down, cradling my head on the soft silky slope of her breasts. I both hear and feel her heart hammering in her chest, smell the musk of our sex, taste the sweat on her skin.

"Tati," I whisper, when I am once again capable of forming words. "Did I hurt you?"

Her answer is a bark of laughter, surprised and sarcastic. "Did you *hurt* me?"

I rest my chin on the narrow slice of skin between her breasts and gaze up at her. "I could not control myself at the end."

Her smile is loving and amused. "Nico, my sweet, darling man. I *begged* you to fuck me as hard as you can." She caresses my face. Feathers fingers through my hair. "You gave me exactly what I asked for—a good, hard fucking."

I let myself rest there on her chest, eyes closing at the tender bliss of her affection. "I just...I love you so much. I want to take care of you, protect you. I never want to hurt you."

Her tender touch skates through my hair, over my nape, my shoulders, my upper back, and then traces the corner of my jaw, the shell of my ear. The side of my nose. "Oh, my sweet Nico. Did it sound like you were hurting me?"

"No."

"What did it sound like?"

"Like you loved it."

"Because I did. I loved every second. I *crave* you, Nico. I want more of you, always." She tilts my face up and takes my mouth. "I can't get enough of you. I'm still shaky from the last two orgasms and I already want you again."

I chuckle. "I may need a moment or two to recover."

"Bo," she teases. "I need you *now*."

"Then how about…this?" I growl, and slip down her body, kissing her plump firm breasts, the soft flat field of her belly, and then finally the honey-sweet nectar of her sex.

"Oh god," she gasps. "That would be—you can— oh, fuck, *yes*, Nico. *Please*."

I taste her, devour her. She wraps her strong thighs around my neck and pins me there, grinding against my hungry mouth as I work her clit with my lips and tongue. Her hands grasp at my hair and claw at my shoulders, and then she clutches my head in her hands, keening wildly as she reaches orgasm in seconds. I wedge a hand under her body and slip two fingers inside her, giving her something to squeeze around as she comes, and now she grinds and rides my face and fingers.

She comes fast and hard, and her cries of ecstasy bleed into overwhelmed sobs, the two blurring until I can't tell if she's sobbing or screaming or some combination of both.

I keep her coming until she goes limp, legs falling apart, and she pushes me away. "I can't, I can't—no more. No more, Nico. I can't come anymore right now. I'll die." She pulls at my shoulders. "Hold me, baby."

I crawl up and gather her in my arms, and we breathe together.

Eventually, we both fall back asleep.

——— ◆ ———

When I rouse again, I'm spooning her. Her soft slender warm body is nestled against mine, my hand cradling her breast, with her hand over mine. She stirs. Exhales softly. Wriggles, waking.

As I drift toward a more fully wakeful state, I become aware of my hard-on, which is nestled between the globes of Tatiana's ass. The erection is an ache, one that I suddenly cannot ignore now that I'm aware of it.

Tatiana, still half-asleep, turns her face to the side, touching her lips to mine. I rumble a happy, pleased, aroused groan as her soft wet lips slide against mine. She tilts her hips, rubbing against me as she becomes aware of my erection as well. Her lips fuse with mine, and I steal my hand down between her thighs and swirl a fingertip against her clit. She twitches, whimpering into my mouth. I kiss her, tasting her tongue, her lips, and feather soft, slow touches to her clit, unhurried and lazy. She starts to pant, mouth dropping open to freeze wide against mine, and she pushes the taut, plump softness of her ass against my cock.

I feel Tatiana's fingers on my hip, and then she has my hard, aching length in her fist and she's pumping me behind her back, caressing me while gasping as I circle her hard little clit.

And then I'm inside her. There's no warning—she tilts her hips and all at once I'm buried to the hilt inside her wet heat and she's pulsating around me, slick and tight. I groan and nip her lower lip, thrusting against her, pushing deeper. She flexes her hips to meet my thrust, and then she grabs my hand and moves it to her breast, and while I cup and knead and caress the tender weight of her breast, I feel her fingers moving on her clit. I plunge deep and then pull back, and she strokes my length, slick with her essence, as I pause before driving back in.

"Nico," she keens, breathless and fraught, panting my name like a prayer.

She pivots her hips to force me deeper inside her, lifting her upper thigh so she can reach between us and cup my balls as I move inside her, buried fully within her and pushing deeper, and deeper, aching to be as united with her as I can be, desperate to feel more of her. I wrap my whole being around her, clutch at the hot firm weight of her tits and press my belly to her back and my hips to her ass and thrust deeper and deeper, and she gasps my name, chanting, praying, crying, keening, calling.

She caresses my balls with one hand and swirls her clit with the other, thrusting raggedly back against me, and now her body begins to quiver and shake as her orgasm burns inside her, building and building to a frenetic crescendo of gasping shrieks and shrill breathless whimpers.

"Nico, Nico, oh god, Nico," she gasps, her head thrown back against my shoulder and her mouth seeks mine as she chants my name as a plea.

My own climax swells, and I drive into her with

mounting desperation, heat and pressure shattering inside me, bursting within every synapse, every cell of my being—all of me is attuned to her every breath, every movement, every gasp, every whimper and whine, every thrust, and I know when she reaches the verge of climax. I feel it in the way her whole body tenses, in the way her panting moans become sobs, in the way her walls clamp down around my cock, in the way her whole body spasms as the waves of ecstasy shudder through her.

"Come with me, Nico," she pleads. "Now, my love. Come with me."

I roll to my back with her on top of me and pull her thighs up against her belly, spread wide open, and sink my teeth into the tense ridge of her shoulder muscle and gasp and growl as my orgasm ramps up toward release. Tatiana, still sobbing and spasming around me, sweeps both hands down to where we're joined, fingers smearing over my slick cock as I glide in and out of her, cupping and massaging my heavy, aching, swelling, pulsing balls—now with one hand, now with both, caressing my cock and my balls at the same time.

"Nico," she pants, turning her head to whisper into my mouth, "Please. Come for me. Come inside me. Fill me, my love."

Slower, now, but harder, sliding out slowly, pausing to feel her cup and caress and tease my length, and then drive into her more slowly yet, not stopping when I bottom out inside her but continuing to push deeper until she cries out—and then I withdraw again and repeat the process, drawing out the moment of orgasm.

It smashes through me all at once, ripping me apart from the inside out, white heat blasting through me from balls to brain, stars bursting behind my eyes, and I lose all control, pace and rhythm and technique abandoned as I give her what she's begging for. I come hard, crying out with a guttural shout, and push my heels into the mattress as I fuck my beloved Tatiana without restraint. She wails with ecstasy, my release triggering another for her, and now she clutches my cock with her walls until she's so tight around me it's nearly painful, and she's weeping and sobbing and wailing as I pound into her with a symphony of wet slaps and ragged shouts. I come and I come and I come, and she takes it all and when I slow, she massages my balls and caresses my cock where it's not buried inside her, teasing another spasming burst from me.

Subsiding together into stillness, we pant in unison, gasp in synch. I feel the wet warmth of my release slipping out of her, and only then realize that we'd forgotten something rather important.

"Tati," I whisper, panicking. "I'm not wearing a condom."

She twists to kiss me, cupping my balls and tenderly massaging them. "I know."

"I'm sorry, my love, I—"

She nips my lip to silence me. "I *wanted* it like this. I needed you. Needed to feel you bare. Nothing between us."

"But you're not...are you on birth control?"

She shakes her head, teasing my lips with hers, a smile curving her lips. "No."

"Then..." I start.

She slides up to let me slip out of her, groaning as she loses me, and then turns to kneel above me, black hair a curtain around our faces. "Then, Nicolae, my love, I will happily, eagerly, and joyfully bear your child." She flattens against me, giving me all of her weight, and her sex is wet against my belly, breasts smashed flat between us. "There is nothing that would bring me more joy than to fill our lives with a child. I know—it is madness, considering how short a time I have known you as an adult, but I know my heart, my love. *You* are my heart. You are my life. My future."

My eyes burn, and she kisses them softly, with exquisite tenderness. I cup her bottom and tell myself to breathe. "Tati, I—"

She cradles my face, and kisses the corner of my mouth. "I am not afraid. I am not worried. I am happy." She nibbles my lower lip. "Now. Tell me what *you* are feeling, Nico, my love."

"So many things. I wouldn't have thought, even two weeks ago, that I could ever..." I huff, fighting for composure. "That I could ever feel this way again. So loved, and so full of love. I would never have thought that the idea of—" My breath leaves me in a ragged rush as the words abandon me. I try again. "I was so...happy and proud to be a father, Tati." Tears flow, and I cannot stop them; she doesn't shush me or wipe them away, just rests her chin on her folded hands on my chest and gazes at me as I weep, love and acceptance and understanding written clearly on her lovely face.

"So proud," I whisper. "So happy. I didn't feel ready, but I was happy. I had everything, Tati. And then it got taken away from so fucking brutally, and I..." I swallow, shake my head. "I never thought to have that feeling again. And it scares me how much I want it."

"I want it too, Nico."

"How can you be sure? What if—what if this is just... adrenaline and danger making us feel this way?"

She sniffs a laugh, dismissing and unworried. "Do you really believe that?"

"No," I breathe, blinking hard. "No, I do not."

"Neither do I, you silly man." She wipes at my cheeks, then, smiling, tears of her own gleaming in her eyes like diamonds sparkling in the sun. "I have had boyfriends and lovers. I have lived with men. I am not a child, Nicolae. I am a woman. I know my heart. I know myself. I have even loved before—young love, foolish, infatuated love, but still a kind of love. And *this*, Nico…" she shakes her head.

Her gaze bores into mine, intense and demanding truth, searing away the lies and doubt and fear, leaving only the purity of what has grown between us since I opened my eyes to see her in that hangar in Zagreb, shirt torn open, fear in her eyes, tear tracks staining her cheeks.

"This, with you?" She licks her lips, shakes her head again. "It is…pure. It's wild. It's powerful. It's *real*, Nico. Who can say how love forms, hmm? For some, it builds over years. For some, it's like a dandelion, bursting to life faster than you'd believe, popping up seemingly overnight, and then fading to nothing, blown away by a gentle breeze. For others, it's…comforting and gentle. For Mama and Tata, it was like that. Soft, sweet, and gentle. It wasn't intense, but it was no less powerful for all that. And you and me, Nico, my love, it's…all of that." She cups my face and searches me intently. "We have lived a lifetime together in the last few days or weeks or however long it's been. I do not doubt my heart, and I do not doubt yours."

"My god, Tatiana. You are the bravest woman I've ever met. So courageous, and so fierce. The way you love me, it's like the sunlight when I have been lost in the cold shadows for so many years."

She buries her face in the side of my neck. "I guess I feel like everything I've been through in my life has been for a purpose—for this, for you. There have been so many times that I've wondered why this has to happen, why I have to go through that—growing up my father's daughter, being kidnapped, seeing people killed, I hated it. I wished so many times that…" she huffs. "I hate saying it now that he's gone, but I often wished I had a different father. One who wasn't a gangster. But now, it all makes sense. I'm not afraid. I mean, I have been afraid, but I know I can handle things. My life has made me strong. It's prepared me for this. For life with you. So I can be the woman you need."

"You are." I swallow hard, gazing at her, knowing the love I feel for her blazes in my expression.

She lets out a long, contented sigh, and then wiggles her sex against my belly, smearing wetness. "Take me to the shower," she commands, whispering the words in my ear as a hot breath. "And let me fuck you again."

"As you command, my love. And with a will."

CHAPTER 20

FIREFIGHTS, NICKNAMES, AND SORE VAGINAS

TATIANA

I DON'T THINK I'VE EVER HAD SEX AS MANY TIMES AS Nicolae and I did in the forty-eight hours we spent in that hotel room in Rio. We order room service and eat it naked on the bed. We shower together and make love in the shower—Nico turns me to face the wall and frames me from behind, slides inside me, and fucks me roughly, with delicious power, his strong hands gripping my hips and jerking me backward into his thrusts.

We drowse in the bed watching an old action movie badly dubbed into Portuguese, and wake up in the middle of the night, restless and unable to get back to sleep.

We crack open a bottle of whiskey from the bar and get tipsy together, and I push him onto the carpet and ride him until my breasts ache from bouncing so wildly, edging us both to the verge of climax and then stopping with his cock buried deep, teasing us away from the edge, and then fucking him to the edge again—when he finally comes, it fills me and surges out of me and coats us both in the sticky smear of our mingled essences, requiring another shower.

We make love slowly and sweetly the next morning, order breakfast, sip coffee, and make plans for the future—mainly the logistics of migrating my business to America.

That day is much the same as the one before, full of sweet cuddles and kisses, rough and indelicate fucking, slow and deliberate lovemaking, whispers and cries, shouts and wails, groans, whimpers, moans, laughter, tears…

By the time we fall asleep late on the second night, I am thoroughly sore, sated, and happy. And if I'm not pregnant, it'll be a statistical miracle, considering we never used a condom again. Some may say it's foolish, reckless, even irresponsible to throw myself so fully into love with Nico when we've only really known each other as adults for a handful of days, but I don't care.

As I told him, I know my heart. I know what I feel, and I know it's real. I know that giving Nico a child would be the greatest privilege of my life.

I don't need months or years with him to know that he is my life, my future, and my everything; I don't need to wait to know that I will marry him, that I will bear his children—now or weeks or months or years from now—and we will be deliriously happy. We will argue, of course, and I'll want to throttle him for something stupid, and I'll make him angry and we'll sort it out and have wild makeup sex.

For the first time in my life, I know that I'm where I need to be, with the person I'm meant to be with.

I know things may not be totally over yet, but no matter what happens, Nico is my everything.

I'm almost glad Filip did what he did, that he brought me to that hangar. I'm not glad that so many people I care about died for the idiotic plans of selfish people, but I am happy with how things turned out.

I mourn my father, of course. I mourn Ana and Katya

and Georg and Tata. I will miss Zagreb and the beauty of the Croatian seaside. I will miss Low Town and High Town, and trains across Europe from one pop-up to another. But in exchange for all that, I gain friends—brothers and sisters. I gain a family, a big one, and a wild and strange and dangerous one. I gain a home. I gain a husband.

We wake early on the third morning, my head on his chest, his heart thudding steadily under my ear. Sunlight shines on a few strands of my hair that I shed last night, draped across his chest. On a whim, I make sure he's awake and watching, and then I twist the strands of my hair, wrap it around the ring finger of his left hand, and knot it.

"Be my husband, Nico," I whisper, holding his eyes. "As soon as possible. I don't care about rings or churches or anything. I just want to know you're mine forever."

He doesn't reply immediately, but the brilliant hot joy in his eyes says all there is to say. When he does speak, it's to whisper "Yes" into my ear—first in Croatian, then English, then Romani, and then in every other language he knows.

And that is how I find myself engaged to Nicolae Dragos.

Minutes later, there's a knock on the door. I tuck the sheets in my armpits while Nico shrugs into a hotel robe and answers the door.

The whole crew barges in, bringing with them several room service trays piled high with bagels, croissants, muffins, bacon, scrambled eggs, hard-boiled eggs, steaks, sausage, fruit, yogurt parfaits, and several silver pots of coffee. And just like that, our quiet engagement is suddenly a noisy, raucous, impromptu gathering. Everyone talks over everyone else, laughing, teasing, and telling more of those ridiculous fables. Someone flipped the lock to prevent the door from closing and latching, and at some point in the festivities, Inez shuffles in, wrapped in a robe, looking bleary-eyed and irritated. She stands behind the couch, breathing heavily, both eyes black and blue and green and yellow and swollen, nose crooked, lips puffy, cheeks cut and scabbed, standing stiffly with one hand bracing her ribs.

For a moment, no one speaks.

"Well?" she demands. "One of you assholes pour me coffee."

It's Nico who moves first, filling a white mug for her. "Here, Inez, sit on the bed with Tati."

Inez nods, shuffling carefully over to the bed and gingerly slides in beside me. I toss the blankets over her lap and wedge a pillow behind her, and she settles back with a sigh.

"Thanks," she says with a sigh. "I forgot how much torture sucks."

"No shit," Rev growls.

"Facts," Solomon adds.

Has everyone here been tortured?

"Would you like some food, Inez?" Kane asks.

She sips from her mug, nodding. "Please. I'm fucking ravenous. Fucker didn't feed me."

Slowly, the noise level returns to where it was before Inez arrived—loud. She sips and nibbles, taking it slow while she watches the men—and Scarlett—joking and ribbing each other.

After a while, she turns to me. "So. Tatiana Juric."

"Inez," I say. "Or is it Sophia? Lorenzo only referred

to you as Sophia, but in this group, I know old and new names are a sensitive topic."

She snorts. "I have not decided yet. I am Sophia to Lorenzo because he has never known Inez. I am Inez to them because they never knew Sophia. And the two are not…it is a hard thing to know how to merge them." She smiles at me, a quick tilt of her lips, so brief I almost miss it. "Let's just go with Inez, for now. I will need time to learn how to be Sophia again."

Scarlett overhears us and leaves the group of men to climb up on the bed, sitting cross-legged facing us with a bagel in her teeth and a slice of bacon in one hand and coffee in the other. She balances the coffee on her knee and sets the bagel on the other, nibbling on the bacon.

"Not again," she says to Inez.

Inez frowns. "Hmmm? Not again what?"

"You're not ever gonna be Sophia *again*. That's what I've come to realize since we talked last, on that boat." Scarlett must be referring to a conversation I know nothing about. "I am not Maria again. I'm not Scarlett anymore either. I may take up the name Maria again, once I take the brand, but it'll be…" she shrugs, shakes her head. "A bit of both, I guess."

Inez nods, sighing. "You're not wrong, of course." She peers out the window for a moment, frowning. "I think…I think Lorenzo and I have some…unfinished business to attend to before I can go there. Before I can see Sophia in myself."

A long silent moment passes between us three women.

"And before that can happen," Inez says, "Rafael Sousa must die."

Scarlett rests her hand on Inez's knee. "And for *that* to happen, *you* need to heal."

Inez's eyes blaze. "Fuck that. He won't rest and neither will I. I'm not going to just go back home to the club and act like things are back to normal when Lorenzo is in some safe house and Rafael is out there plotting my death—all of our deaths."

Our conversation has caught the attention of the men, and Solomon leaves the couch he was lounging on and enters the room, leaning against the doorway with a mug in his hands.

"But we can't just hang around Brazil waiting for him to show up, either," he says. "We have no fucking clue where he might've gone."

Inez rubs the bridge of her nose between forefinger and thumb, sighing. "Yes, yes, you are right. We have to find him. Or bait him into finding us."

Chance stands in the doorway next to Solomon, resting a thick forearm on Solomon's shoulder. "And not for nothin', boss, but some of us, like Sol, here, have been on the go for fuckin' weeks. This whole goddamn shitshow started when Sol went missing, it just…blew up into something a fuckuva lot bigger than any of us expected. We aren't saying give up and go home, but…maybe go home and catch our breath. See our ladies, reassure them we're all alive and in one piece. Regroup and come up with a plan."

Inez nods. "You are right, the both of you." Her eyes harden. "But I do dearly wish we could destroy his compound before we leave Brazil. He is dangerous all the time, and while I recognize that angering him might be foolish, I think to destroy that place would infuriate him to a degree that he might start making mistakes."

Solomon grins, sliding his cell from his pocket and dialing a number. He puts it on speaker and moves to perch on the edge of the bed next to Inez. It rings twice.

"Sí, Solomon?" Lorenzo's voice says after a couple of burbling rings.

"Hey, bud, you're on speaker with the whole gang," Sol says.

"Hello, everyone." His voice drops. "Sophia, *meu amor*."

Inez winces. "Ren."

He just chuckles. "Still shy about it, eh? No worries. I will be bold enough about our love for us both."

"Ren," she starts, and her tone suggests a scolding to come.

He interrupts. "I know, I know. It's okay, *amor*. I understand." A sharp, short sigh. "So. What do you need? Your flight leaves in a few hours—I have a driver from the embassy coming to pick you up soon."

"We were wondering if you had any favors left in your pocket," Sol says. "Big ones."

Lorenzo sighs. "I have leveraged most of my connections and resources, unfortunately. I could maybe start owing someone favors, I suppose. What is it you need?"

Inez takes the phone. "I want to blow up his house, Ren. We burned down the other estate, and now I want to destroy his. I want him to know it was me."

Lorenzo whistles low. "That is a big ask, *amor*."

"I know."

He clicks his tongue, a thoughtful noise. "Hmmm. It would need to be done off-book and in a way that does not put those who do the destroying at his mercy." Another musing click of his tongue. "It would be simplest to drop a bomb on it, of course. But a flight and munitions of that sort…it is a big expenditure. Hard to write that off."

"I do not care how it is done, Ren. All I care is that it sends a message that he is not untouchable. Drop a bomb, send a team to blow it up or set it on fire, what-the-fuck-ever." Her voice drops, becoming vicious and intense. "He must suffer before I kill him, Ren. You know the monster he is."

"I do."

"If you could see me, what he did to me…"

Lorenzo's voice is thick and shuddery with emotion. "Be glad I cannot. I would drop everything and hunt him down."

"I know, I know." She sighs. "I need you where you are, Ren. Protecting my—protecting Little Lorenzo."

Ren chuckles. "It is funny that we have all been calling him Little Lorenzo in English. His mother, Beatriz, she calls him Reninho. Basically it means Little Ren." He pronounces it *Ren-IHN-yo*.

"Guess who just got a new nickname?" Solomon says, laugh. "Reninho and Big Reninho."

Lorenzo cackles. "That is stupid. Big little Ren makes no sense. I thought you were fluent in Portuguese."

Solomon just laughs again. "I am. But it's funny. Big Reninho."

"No." Lorenzo says it flat—no discussion necessary. "I will do some thinking and make some calls. Sophia, *meu amor*—"

"Ren, stop," Inez snaps. "Not now. Please. You must give me time."

"When you have watched Rafael bleed out, you

mean," Lorenzo says, not without some bitterness. "Then you will let yourself love me."

Inez sighs. "Perhaps I do mean that. But also, I am a very private person and this is not a private situation. You are on speaker phone."

Ren sighs. "Of course, you are right. I'm sorry, *meu*—Sophia. I understand. Do what you must. I will see that Rafael's estate is destroyed even if I just go there and burn it down myself."

"I know you will," Inez answers. "I trust you."

"At least there is that," Lorenzo says with a sigh. "It is a start."

"Lorenzo," Inez snaps.

He just laughs. "I have loved you since the moment I saw you, Sophia Bruna Santos de Silva. I have waited a very, very long time to be reunited with you, and yet you keep slipping out of my fingers. You must indulge me at least a little bit."

Finally, Inez's voice softens into something like tenderness. "I know, Ren. I know. Soon, okay? I promise, you will have me to yourself very soon."

Silence. "You do not make promises, Sophia."

"This, I do."

Another silence. "*Eu te amo. Conversaremos em breve.*"

Inez's eyes squeeze shut, hard, and she shakes her head, clutching the phone until her knuckles turn white. "*Te*—" her teeth click together. "Talk later, Ren. Goodbye."

She tosses the phone to Sol, levers awkwardly and stiffly off the bed, and limps out of the room—I think under other circumstances she'd have stormed out angrily, but in her current state, a pained, limping shuffle is the best she can do. She does manage to slam the door so hard it shudders, hitting the lock latch and shivering back open.

"Sophia?" I hear Lorenzo's voice say from the speaker.

Solomon clears his throat. "She's gone, man. Thinkin' maybe it was too soon for 'I love you.'"

Lorenzo just chuckles. "She knows I love her. She has fought it from day one. Even as a teenage girl, she was prickly and difficult. But, much like the cactuses of your Southwest deserts, beauty blooms among the thorns."

Solomon snorts. "Well, now that poetry hour is over, we gotta get ready to go and you gotta call people about blowing shit up."

"You are just jealous that you do not have my sensitive nature," Lorenzo teases.

"Yeah, I'm just a brutish American," Solomon drawls. "Talk later, Ren."

He taps the screen to end the call and shoves the phone into his pocket. "Alright, then, boys and girls. We've got a plane to catch back to the good ol' U-S-of-A. Get your shit together and meet in the lobby in thirty." He points at Nico and then me. "That means the fuck-fest is over, you two."

I blush furiously and duck my head, cheeks burning, embarrassment blazing in my gut. "Sol!"

He chuckles. "I'm teasin', babe. Mostly. Our ride is gonna be here soon, though."

"You didn't—hear us, did you?" I ask.

Kane splutters a laugh. "Half of fuckin' Rio, heard you, darlin'. And I gotta say, it's good to see a smile on our boy's face."

I look, and Nico is grinning—beaming, really. "Nico, they're teasing me!"

He comes over to the bed and kisses the top of my head. "Yes, they are. In this group, you must give as good as you get. It is meant with love."

I glare at Kane and Solomon. "You two are just jealous. You do not have your girlfriends here to have a two-day fuckfest with."

Solomon smirks at Scarlett. "Oh, I dunno. I wasn't exactly twiddling my thumbs."

Kane snickers. "You would be correct in my case. But you oughta know, Anj and me's room—" he pauses, frowning. "Anj's and mine? Anj and my? I don't fuckin' know. Fuckin' bullshit grammar. Whatever. Point is, our room is next to his, so you'll get an earful when we get back—trust that, baby girl."

"Anj's and my room," Silas says. "It would be Anj's and my room. Split it up—Anj's room and my room. Anj's and my room."

Kane flips him off. "Thanks for the lesson, Professor Cabot."

Silas returns the gesture. "No problem, *dropout*."

"You dropped out too, dipshit," Saxon snaps.

Kane's eyes narrow, and I think the exchange could have taken a turn for the ugly, but Solomon steps between them. "Okay, we have officially spent way too long in close quarters. Let's get our shit and get home."

He shoves Kane and Silas for the door, one hand on each of their backs. Silas reaches around Solomon's back and slugs Kane in the arm. Kane returns the favor, but he's so much bigger than Silas that his playful punch sends Silas stumbling sideways.

Silas rights himself, laughing. "Oh, yeah? Wanna play it that way, you big gorilla?"

Once they're out in the hallway, he launches himself at Kane and puts him in a headlock, and the two men wrestle their way down the hallway...until a door opens and someone shouts something in very loud, very angry Portuguese.

I hear Solomon scolding them before Nico moves the latch to let the door close and lock.

"When did Solomon become our leader?" he muses out loud as he comes to sit on the bed near my feet. "It just sort of...happened, and no one seems to question it."

I shrug. "You are all army men. You look for a leader by nature. With Inez having been a prisoner, you all needed someone to lead. Solomon assumed the role."

Nico nods. "Yes, this I know. It is more curiosity that it was Solomon who assumed the role. We are all capable of leadership. We have been leaders at one point or another. But in this, Solomon seemed to just naturally take the position. There wasn't any discussion, either. It is curious." He tugs at the sheet tucked in under my armpits so it comes loose, baring me for him. "Now. We have thirty minutes and nothing to pack. What shall we do?"

I laugh, playfully trying to drag the sheet from his grip. "Nico, no. I am sore. I hobbled to the bathroom like an old woman."

He laughs as he yanks the sheet away entirely, crawls onto the foot of the bed, and grabs my ankle, hauling me to him. "Sore? Where?"

"You know where!"

He raps his knuckles against his temple. "I must be suffering from amnesia, because I seem to have forgotten. Perhaps you fucked the brains out of me, hmm?" He kisses my ankle. "Is it here?"

I fake glare down at him, playing along. "No."

He kisses the inside of my knee. "Here?"

I shake my head. "No, not there either."

He kisses up my thigh, and I find myself breathing hard in anticipation. His lips touch the silky flesh just beside my sex. "Here?"

"Nearly," I breathe. "But...not quite."

"Mmmmmm," he hums. "I seem to remember...ahhh yes. I know—it is here!" He kisses my pussy, tongue slithering in, breath hot.

"Yes," I gasp. "There."

"Then if you are sore, I shall kiss it all better."

And he does. Slowly, as if we have all the time in the world, he brings me to orgasm using nothing more than his lips and tongue, making me cry out loud as if I was not just teased for having woken half of Rio de Janeiro.

When I'm left panting and limp, he rises from between my thighs, wipes his mouth on his forearm, and then presses a kiss to my lips.

"There. All better?"

I nod, delirious. "Yes...all better." He slips off the bed, removing the robe as he reaches for his clothes, discarded and forgotten for the last forty-eight hours. "Wait, where are you going?"

He grins. "Getting dressed. We have a plane to catch, my love."

I roll off the bed, stumbling on jelly legs, and then lurch unsteadily toward him. "Perhaps I am not as sore as I thought."

He groans as I caress his hard length. "Tati, we really do have to go."

I grin at him, bracing my arm around his shoulders as

I lift on my toes, notch him at my entrance, and lower myself onto his cock. "But Nico, sweetheart, we both know how fast you can be when you want to."

He frowns at me, or tries to. "Are you implying that I am not lasting long enough for you?"

"No, darling," I whisper, wrapping one thigh around his hips—he catches my intent and lifts me. "I am saying exactly what I said—we both know that you can finish quickly." I put my lips to his ear. "Which is what I want. How fast can you finish, Nico?"

He walks with me to a bare stretch of wall next to the bathroom, presses my back to the cold hard wall, kisses me so thoroughly I'm left gasping, my lips swollen. And then he nails me to the wall, fucking me with delicious, ravaging, powerful thrusts—relentless, almost savage. He's done in a matter of a couple of minutes, filling me to the brim with his hot release.

Panting raggedly, he slumps against me, breath hot against my chest, holding me pinned against the wall, his cock still buried inside me.

"There," he growls. "What about that?"

I scratch his back, nibbling his earlobe. "Perfect," I whisper. "But you may have to carry me to the lobby."

He pulls away to gaze at me, love written in every line of his face. "I'll carry you to the ends of the earth, my love."

I cup his face. "I know." I pat his arm. "Let me down. I need to clean up and get dressed."

When we arrive in the lobby, Kane, Silas, Saxon, Chance, and Rev are already there, sipping yet more coffee from lidless paper cups, standing in a circle, all in the exact same pose: burly arms crossed over big, hard chests, coffee cups resting on a bicep, legs planted wide. Noticeably absent are Solomon and Scarlett.

They arrive only five minutes before the driver is scheduled to be here, both of them not exactly hiding the glow that I'm sure Nico and I must also be sporting.

Solomon and Nico get coffee and join the circle of men, and Scarlett and I take seats on a nearby couch. We both sit down somewhat gingerly.

We trade looks and then burst into laughter. She leans close and whispers in my ear. "Walking bowlegged?"

"What is bowlegged?" I ask.

She stands up and pushes her knees apart as if she is sitting a horse. "Bowlegged."

I flush. "Oh." I snicker. "Yes. *Very.*"

She holds a fist to me, and I tap my knuckles against hers, feeling awkward and silly doing so. "Same, girl." She sits beside me and whispers again. "Sol and I have had a lot of sex over the years, but the last two days?" She wipes pretend sweat from her brow. "Girl, my cooch is gonna need a *minute.* We were *busy.*"

A strange warmth fills me, a frisson of excitement or happiness, and it takes me a minute to understand what it is—where it comes from.

Scarlett, being extraordinarily perceptive, notices. "What?"

I shrug. "I just…nothing."

She bumps me with a shoulder. "Nah, nah, nah. None'a that shit. Out with it."

"I just…I've had employees I was close to—" I swallow hard. "Ana and Katya. They were killed at the beginning of this, when I met Nico. But I've never had…friends.

A girlfriend." I look at her. "You are my friend. It is...a new feeling."

She blinks hard, looking away and up at the ceiling, shaking her head. "Shit."

"Scarlett, what? I—"

She bites her lower lip, scrubs her eyes with the heel of her hand. "No, I'm good. I'm good. I just..." she gives me a bright but watery smile. "I've always been one of the guys, you know? Dick jokes, roughhousing. Coed locker room because I'm the only girl, not just in the unit but the whole fuckin' section. I've never had a girlfriend either."

"Oh." I swallow. Look at her. "So...girlfriends, then?"

She wraps her arms around me and squeezes me with such sudden strength that I have to gasp for breath, and then return the hug.

When we break, she holds me by the arms and looks at me. "I'd like that. Sol says I'll like the other girls, but... they haven't hoicked their asses all over fuckin' South America with me. We're blood sisters, Tat." My nickname, Tati, is pronounced *Tah-tee*, but she shortens it further to Tat, like the first half of the English word tattoo. "We've been through firefights and slogged through jungles together. Can't get any fuckin' closer than that."

"Tat." I grin. "I like that."

She passes a hand through her loose, chin-length black hair. "Used to be I'd tell you to call me Scar. You know..." she taps her scar. "Plus it's short for Scarlett. But I think you oughta call me Maria. I'll try it out on you before I let Sol call me it."

"Maria."

Sol glances over at us, leaning back from the conversation among the men. "What're you two into over there?"

Scarlett—Maria—grins at him. "Oh, nothin' much, baby. Just bonding over firefights, nicknames, and sore vaginas."

As if on cue, the whole lobby seems to go suddenly silent right as she says this, and I feel a host of eyes on us. I hold it in for a moment, but then laughter bubbles up and spews out of me, and Scarlett…it'll take time for me to adjust my thinking…Maria, I mean, laughs with me. The men look at us, curious, but we just laugh all the harder, and they shake their heads and go back to whatever manly things they were talking about. Guns and beer and weight-lifting, probably.

The ding of an elevator is a faint sound, swallowed by the ambient din of the bustling lobby. It announces, however, the arrival of Inez. We all see her approach at the same time, and no one seems to know how to react, how to greet her.

She's wearing a new pair of dark blue jeans, a plain black V-neck T-shirt, a pair of calf-height combat boots, and a black ball cap with the logo of a prominent sports clothing company, her hair pulled into a ponytail through the back of the hat. Her black eyes are in the shadow of the cap's pulled-low brim, making them somewhat less notice-able. She also seems to have applied some basic makeup to lessen the severity of their appearance. She walks with a slight limp and a shuffle, favoring her left leg, one arm braced across her middle to protect and support her in-jured ribs. Her face is carefully blank, as if she's working overtime behind the scenes to chide the pain she's in.

When no one greets her, she snorts sarcastically and rolls her eyes. "You all need to get your shit together. I was tortured, not raped, and I'm not dead. Quit tiptoeing around me. I fucking hate it."

Scarlett stands up and goes to her, reaches for her hands, hesitates, and then takes them. "None of us were sure if you had been, and we weren't sure how to ask. We all care about you, and we just want to support you."

Chance moves to stand behind her, resting his giant paws on her shoulders; she hunches and stiffens at his touch, but doesn't flinch away or otherwise resist. "And I say this with affection and respect, Boss, but you don't make it easy."

One by one, the men surround Inez and put a hand on her shoulders or back.

"We're here for you, Boss," Saxon says. "You saved all of us. We all owe you our lives."

Inez clears her throat. "This is all very touching, but—"

Rev speaks over her. "Receive it, Boss. Quit fighting it. The Ice Queen is no more, and we still respect you."

"Might be we respect you more," Kane puts in, "now that you've shown us that you're human."

I'm unsure whether I should be part of the group or not, so I hover just behind Nico, watching. Inez's eyes find mine, and she swallows hard, and then scans the eyes of her team. Grabs my hand and pulls me into the circle surrounding her.

She blinks hard, swallows again, ducking her head. "You guys came for me," she whispers, her voice thick with emotion.

"Of course we did," Silas says. "Like we'd leave you with that fuckin' monster a second longer than necessary?"

"You ain't just the boss, Boss," Kane says. "You're one of us. You're the original."

She nods, blowing out a shaky breath. "More so than you know." She meets every pair of eyes again. "You came for me. I'll never forget it, no matter what happens. Thank you, everyone." She looks at me. "You don't even know me, but you still fought for me, Tatiana. I am in your debt."

I shake my head, emotion riding high in my throat. "You are important to Nico. Where he goes, I go. What he fights for, I will fight for." I take her hand and squeeze. "There is no debt."

Inez hisses. "Goddammit," she whispers, blinking hard as tears drip despite her efforts to hold them back, to hide them. "Fuck you guys for making me cry. I hate it."

Chance laughs, wrapping his long, powerful arms around the whole group and pulling us all in closer, so we're crushing Inez in a group full-body hug. "Ya'll, Inez is crying. Someone take a picture for posterity."

Solomon's phone is out before anyone else can react, and he snaps a photo of Inez.

She reaches for his phone, but he dances out of reach. "Delete that shit, Solomon Cabot, or so fucking help me, I'll murder you in your sleep, oathbound or not."

Solomon just laughs "Oh, hell no. This one is getting printed, framed, and hung on the wall in the common room."

She glares at him. "I'll poison your protein shakes."

Solomon just laughs again. "Boss, the curtain has been pulled back. You're one of us now. Means it's open season for getting teased."

Rev chuckles. "I don't know, man. Might not be the best idea to tease the viper."

Solomon's phone buzzes in his hand and he glances at it. "Ride's here. Let's go."

An hour later, we're airborne—a short flight to Manaus, where we transfer to a larger cargo flight bound for an airbase somewhere in the States. That flight is, obviously, much longer—and cold and noisy and uncomfortable, but away from potentially deadly prying eyes.

When the flight lifts off, I let out a breath—we're finally leaving South America.

And I'm heading for my future in the States with Nico.

CHAPTER 21

FOUND FAMILY

LASH

INEZ SPENDS THE WHOLE FINAL HOUR OF THE FLIGHT into Las Vegas on her phone, talking to someone—the Big Boss, most likely. The flight from Manaus took us to a US military AMC terminal in Little Rock, Arkansas, where we transferred again to a private charter that took us to Vegas.

Now, as we land in Vegas, Inez is looking furious, nearly vibrating with rage. Once the flight stops and we deplane, I move up beside her as we make for the line of Mercedes-Benz G-Wagens that belong to the club.

"Something happened," I say. "What?"

She shakes her head. "Nothing."

"Inez." I grab her wrist, but she breaks my hold and yanks her arm away. "What is going on?"

She grits her teeth. "None of your concern."

"Inez, come on. You're not alone anymore. Tell me."

She looks at me, one foot in the footwell as she prepares to slide behind the wheel of one of the sleek black SUVs. "Rafael. He made a move on the safe house Ren is using. He handled it, but he has to move them."

"So what's our next move, then?" I ask.

"Your move is to take Tatiana home and introduce her to the other ladies and help her set up her business here," she says; she and Tatiana spent several hours on the way here talking together privately, and now I know about what. "The situation with Lorenzo and Rafael is mine to handle. You have all been through enough."

"Inez, Rafael is not *your* problem, he is *our* problem."

She puts her foot on the ground and turns to face me. "Lash—Nicolae. Listen to me." She grabs my arm and squeezes, shakes gently. "I *have* to handle this myself. You had to choose how to handle Pugli yourself. I have to handle Rafael myself."

I shake my head. "Not the same."

She frowns. "No, it's not. Rafael is technically still my husband. The marriage was legally binding, even though I didn't consent to it. The legal document will hold up in any court. He hasn't given up trying to make Reninho his heir, either." She shakes her head, sighing. "No. It's my problem and mine alone. I do not need or *want* help."

"You can barely walk, Inez," I argue.

She waves this off dismissively. "I'm fine. I have been through much worse."

"I can't convince you to bring even one of us with you?" I ask.

She shakes her head. "No. I'll see you all home and settled, and then I'll gather some supplies and head out."

"You were talking to the Big Boss?"

She nods. "I was."

"About? Anything that concerns us?"

"To a degree. We'll cover that later though, as a team."

I shake my head, sighing in frustration. "Just make me one promise, please."

She tilts her head to one side and lifts that shoulder toward her ear. "If it is a promise I can keep, I'll make it."

"If things go sideways, you bring us in."

She nods. "I can promise that."

I hold out my hand. "Repeat it and shake on it."

"My word isn't enough?"

"I want to hear you say it, and I want to shake on it. That way I'll know you have really given me your word." I keep my hand extended.

She stares at my hand for a moment, and then grasps it, squeezing firmly. "I swear on the brand and the oath that if I need help, I'll call you in."

I grin. "I'm tempted to question what you consider needing help, but I recognize I may be pushing my luck."

"It's good to see you happy, Nicolae."

I let out a breath. "Honestly, it is good to let myself *be* happy."

"That's part of why I have to do this, Nicolae. You all have had to deal with your pasts. Now it is my turn. Rafael has been haunting my life for far too long. If I want any chance at happiness with Lorenzo like you all have, then this is the only way forward."

I nod, clasping my other hand around our joined hands. "I understand. Just know that we're here for you. No matter what."

She nods. "I know. You've all more than proven that."

I say nothing to the others as we load up, but I see them all giving her looks, and I know they're all curious— and probably correctly guessing at what's going on with her.

We arrive at Club Sin in the late afternoon, with the hot desert sun blazing huge and bright low on the horizon. I sigh as we reach the door leading from the private employees-only parking lot down to our quarters—it feels like a lifetime has passed since I was last here. I see Solomon looking around and probably feeling similar.

I clap him on the shoulder as we drop what few belongings we have in the common area. "Sort of strange to be back," I say. "Everything about me is totally different since I was last here."

He nods, slinging an arm around my shoulders. "For fucking real, man. Last time I was in this building, I'd just found out my mother had murdered my father and killed herself. I was single, assumed Scarlett was probably dead or at the very least hated me, and figured I'd spend the rest of my life alone." He watches Scarlett enter the common room and look around, taking it all in. "Now look."

Tatiana is doing the same, and for a moment I see the common room with new eyes.

A long, narrow, high-ceilinged hallway runs from the exit to the parking lot on one side of the common room, with five doors evenly spaced on each side—our bedrooms. Pale gray epoxy floors sprinkled with blue flecks carry through the entire space—hallways, bedrooms, common room, everywhere. Stairs at the end of the hall lead up to the parking lot. Opposite the exit, the hall opens to the common room.

As you stand with your back to the hall, facing the common room, the kitchen is on your left—it's industrial, and huge. Two long cafeteria-style tables with built-in benches frame the space, running end to end parallel with the hall. Beyond that is a mammoth island with white cutting boards and roll-top chilled containers. Along the far wall is an eight-burner range, two matching glass-front, industrial-sized refrigerators, one for food and the other for beverages. There's a floor-to-ceiling rack stuffed with pots and pans and baking trays and cooking utensils and everything else you could possibly need, with a magnetic knife holder on one side cluttered with high-end culinary knives.

On the right side is the den. A U-shaped black leather sectional big enough for fifteen people to sit on without crowding each other frames the space, the open part of the U facing the wall and the professional cinema-grade projector and screen, with floor-to-ceiling speakers facing the couch, a subwoofer on the floor behind the couch, and more speakers in the ceiling hanging behind the couch facing the wall. A glass-fronted cabinet next to the TV screen contains all the requisite electronics, and a smoky, black glass coffee table fills the opening of the sectional.

The hallway continues past the common area, this one short and dead ending—closed doors on the left and right lead to, respectively, the Club Sin floor and the offices for the administrative portion of the Club; a third open doorless entryway in the center leads to a professional-grade gym filled with squat racks, machines, racks of free weight, racks of kettlebells ranging from dinky five-pounders to a cluster of monsters on the floor weighing upward of 200 pounds, and a cardio section with treadmills, assault bikes, rowing machines, and battle ropes, while another area features several heavy bags, a sparring ring, and speed bags.

Before Rev started this whole process, the common room was usually pretty messy. We're good about keeping our personal areas tidy, but the common room was often a bit of a mess. Now that there are women living here, all that has changed.

It's not just clean and tidy—it has personality. There

are brightly colored throw pillows on the couch, wicker baskets piled high with fuzzy black fleece blankets sit on either end of the sectional, and framed movie posters fill the empty spaces of the wall near the TV—*Apocalypse Now, Platoon, Jarhead, Saving Private Ryan,* and other military-themed movies, as well as lighter fare posters like *When Harry Met Sally, Sleepless in Seattle,* and *The Princess Bride,* with a few comedy posters thrown in for fun—*The Three Amigos, Blues Brothers,* and *Stepbrothers.*

There are vases of fresh flowers on the tables in the kitchen, bowls of fresh fruit on the island, and a giant three-wick candle burns on the coffee table, giving off a scent redolent of fresh cookies.

"Damn," I hear Rev say. "Girls've been busy."

"Gotta say, I fuckin' love it," Saxon says. "Feels homier."

Scarlett nods. "I was expecting barracks or a man cave, but this is nice."

One of the bedroom doors opens, emitting a sudden shriek of laughter and thudding music. Anjalee pokes her head out, sees us, and sprints toward Kane, holding her hands out strangely—she has fresh paint on her nails, I think. She slams into him full force, leaping up to wrap her legs around his waist. She holds her hands out to the sides, trusting him to support her as she bends down to kiss him so hard some of the guys wolf-whistle teasingly.

"Girls!" I hear Myka shout. "They're back!"

Naomi, Terra, and Annika file out behind Myka, and the women all hurry to greet their men—Naomi runs to Silas, Terra to Saxon, and Annika to Chance. The greetings are all unique to the couple. Naomi is reserved, gliding to her man and nestling in his arms, resting her cheek on his chest—I see her lips moving as she whispers something meant only for him. Terra is bold and enthusiastic, much like Anjalee, leaping into Saxon's arms and devouring his mouth with hers, her hands on his jaw. Annika, with her bad leg, limps and leans heavily on her cane—her limp is better now after months of rehabbing it in the gym, and she can even walk without it for short periods, but she'll always have a limp. When she reaches Chance, she slings her arms around his neck, cane clutched behind her neck in one hand, and kisses him—soft and gentle but passionate.

For a long moment, the room is silent but for the wet sounds of kisses.

Scarlett breaks the silence with a laugh. "All right, ya'll. Do Sol and I need to start making out? Jesus. Can I get some introductions?"

They all break apart then, and the men bring their women over to where Scarlett and Tatiana stand together between Sol and me.

Chance takes the lead on the introduction. "Scarlett Gutierrez, this is Myka, Anjalee, Terra, Naomi, and Annika." He points to each person as he names them. "Tatiana Juric, well…same."

Rev laughs. "Smooth, buddy."

Chance shuffles his feet. "Shut the fuck up."

Anjalee approaches Tatiana and Scarlett with a warm, welcoming smile. "Once the men have shown you to your rooms, please come to join us. We are doing the pedicures." Her lilting accent makes her voice musical.

Scarlett snorts. "Ain't had a pedicure in…well, fuck. Ever?"

Annika—once a professional athlete, laughs. "Girl, I

get it. But it's fun. Around here, you're gonna have to learn to have an open mind."

Scarlett scans the group of women, then looks at Tatiana. "Bet you've had plenty of pedicures."

Tatiana just laughs. "Yes, I have. I used to get manicures and pedicures every week. I must admit, I should like to have a pedicure. My poor feet have been through hell."

"Just your feet, huh?" Scarlett asks with a laugh.

Tatiana shrugs. "Not just my feet, no."

Terra strides forward and grabs both Scarlett's and Tatiana's arms and drags them toward the room from which music still noisily thumps. "Forget the tour—you can see it all from here and the rooms are all the same. C'mon. It's time to get to know our new sisters."

Scarlett blows a kiss at Solomon as Terra drags her away, and Tatiana looks back at me, somewhere between concerned and excited.

I wink at her. "Have fun, Lovely One. They are wonderful people."

And just like that, it's just us men again.

Kane looks around. "What happened to Inez?"

"She…" I sigh. "Rafael made a play for Lorenzo. She's gathering her stuff and going after him."

"Alone?" Chance asks, sounding pissed.

"The fuck?" Saxon growls. "After all that, she's just cutting us out?"

"No, it is not like that," I start, but I'm saved from having to explain by Inez's voice.

"I'm not cutting you out, I'm dealing with my issue myself. I made a promise on our brand that I would call you if I need you. But this is something I need to do myself, for a lot of reasons. And I'm sure you all understand."

Solomon nods, sighing. "Yeah, we get it."

Chance frowns. "Brand? You have the brand?"

Inez nods, tugging down the neck of her T-shirt to reveal the same brand we all wear on our arms, only hers is on the upper slope of her left breast. "I was the first to receive it."

Silas grunts something unintelligible and then shakes his head. "Inez, Boss, I don't like it."

She shrugs. "You don't have to like it, Silas. I'm not asking your permission. I'm still your direct superior. You answer to me, and I answer to J—to the Big Boss." That's the first time she's ever slipped, ever revealed even the idea that our nameless, faceless patron, employer, and savior has a name. She winces, annoyed at herself. "I appreciate the concern, and I understand you want to help take him down. But I must do this myself."

"You're in no shape to go anywhere," Rev says.

Inez glares at him, her stare full of the vicious, venomous ice we all know so well. "That is for me to decide, Rev."

He growls. "Fuck. Fine, then. Suit yourself."

She softens, just a little bit. "I appreciate the concern. I…." she tilts her head back. "When I return, things are going to be different. Change is on the horizon. That's all I'll say for now. Just be ready."

"We'll all sleep with go bags packed, Boss," Saxon says.

We all chime in our agreement, and then Inez claps her hands for silence. "I appreciate all of you. I appreciate more than I can ever say what you all did for me—that you came for me. We're all bonded by more than just the brand, now—we're bonded by this experience. I ask you to trust me. If I need help, I will ask for it—I have sworn this to Nicolae, and I will swear it again to each of you right now."

Chance rumbles. "Good enough for me."

Inez has a hard-sided, carry-on size rolling suitcase beside her, and she lifts the handle, looking around at each of us. Nods once. "Time to hunt down Rafael Sousa."

We all call goodbyes as she strides confidently down the hallway toward the exit, barely allowing any hint of the injuries she bears to show in her gait or posture. She pauses at the doorway where the women are cackling and shrieking and chatting, pokes her head in, says her good-byes, and then makes her exit.

"Think she'll call?" Kane asks.

Solomon stares after her. "Yeah, I do. I got a feeling our part in this ain't over, boys."

No one replies to that, because there's nothing to say.

With nothing to unpack and the women occupied, we all grab a drink and a snack and Rev turns on an old *Sons Of Anarchy* series DVD, and we kick back, relax, and listen to the joyful sounds of female laughter.

It may not be over, but this is pretty damned nice.

Especially when Tatiana floats out an hour or so later, her toes bright pink and her fingernails neatly trimmed and shaped and painted a vibrant purple. She curls up on my lap on the couch, steals a sip of my whisky on the rocks, and half-watches, half-dozes.

One by one, the women all filter out of the room and find their men, and at some point, someone turns on a rom-com from the early 2000s, and popcorn is popped, and drinks are mixed.

Tatiana puts her lips to my ear. "Is it always like this?"

I nod. "It wasn't always, but now, yes. We work on the floor at night and hang out during the day. But we do tend to spend a lot of time together."

She sighs happily. "Good. I am glad. I was nervous that I would not fit in, but they are all so kind and warm and friendly. I feel like I have known them all forever."

"You seem close with Scarlett," I note.

She nods. "I am. We bonded through that whole... adventure, I suppose you could call it."

I look down at her. "You are going to be happy here?"

She nods again. "I will be. I have a lot of work to do ahead of me to set up my business here, but it is work I look forward to. I have you. I have friends." She smiles up at me. "How could I not be happy?"

"I agree. I am glad. I don't want you to feel like you're leaving anything important behind, That you're missing something or stuck here."

She shakes her head. "I have never been to America, so it will be a change, and I will get homesick for Zagreb, but you will distract me."

I laugh. "I certainly will. At every possible opportunity."

She huffs a laugh, her breath hot on my ear. "Perhaps you can show me our room."

"It's not much," I warn.

She shrugs. "I will adjust. As long as you are here, I don't care. Truly."

I stand up and scoop her into my arms. "We are going to turn in."

"Great to meet you, Tat!" Terra calls, and the sentiment is echoed by everyone else.

I glance at her as I carry her to my—our—room. "Tat?" I question.

She grins. "Scarlett's name for me. I guess I am Tati to you and Tat to the women."

The room is small and I have almost no personal possessions—everything was burned in the fire, and I didn't bother accumulating things after that.

"I would welcome it if you put your touch on this room," I tell her. "I know nothing of such things."

She grins, looking around. "I can tell. Trust me, my love, I'll have it fixed up in no time." She shoves me backward onto the bed. "But that's not my concern at the moment."

"Oh no?" I ask, shimmying backward on the bed.

"Oh no."

She shows me what her concern is—several times. We fall asleep together, her head on my chest, sated and exhausted and travel-weary.

Before I fall asleep, I find myself almost wanting to thank Rafael for having my flight hijacked.

It led me to Tatiana, and Tatiana set me free, helped me lay to rest the ghosts that have haunted me for so long.

Yes, I am grateful.

Tatiana snuffles softly in her sleep, rolls to snuggle more fully on top of me, and her quiet breaths lull me to a deep, restful sleep.

EPILOGUE

THE ENERGY OF HATE

INEZ

EVERYTHING HURTS, BUT I WELCOME THE PAIN. It centers me, focuses me, motivates me. Fuels my fury and energizes my hate.

I have the windows down, letting the wind buffet me as I haul ass toward Texas. No music, no podcast or audiobook to pass the time, just me and my thoughts, stewing in my rage.

Rafael Sousa.

Flashes of what I endured at his hands sear through my mind. Beatings. Being shocked by car batteries attached to jumper cables, the alligator jaws clamped on sensitive skin. Sleep deprivation. Starvation. Sound assault—a hideously obnoxious old-timey commercial jingle for a long-defunct baking soda played on repeat at a deafening volume for hours upon hours.

I told the men the truth—Rafael never raped me, nor did his men. But they did…other things.

I can't go there. My fury is already boiling over, and if I dwell on that, I'm liable to go into a blind, murderous rage. Innocent people will get hurt—I know myself well enough to know that I am in a very, very dangerous mood.

My phone rings, so I roll up the windows and answer the call—the infotainment system of the G-Wagen automatically routes the call to the car's audio system and microphones.

"Inez." The voice is deep, smooth, cultured and refined, authoritative.

"Still fine," I snap. "I don't need you checking in on me every hour...sir."

"And yet, here we are."

I sigh. "Indeed, sir. Here we are."

"You should not be alone right now, Inez." The voice is almost affectionate.

"I am past any danger from a concussion. I had one, but it wasn't too bad. I'm well enough now, sir."

"Do you know where Lorenzo took them?"

"No. On purpose. I have to assume my calls are being monitored. Or his."

"The encryption app should take care of that."

"He's using a cheap flip phone burner. It won't support it. I use it but I'm still not trusting any details to a phone call, no matter how well encrypted."

"So, where are you going?"

"Texas. He'll have left me some kind of note or clue. I know where he was. I'll find him."

"And Rafael?"

I let out a snarling sigh. "Working on that. First order of business is hooking up with Lorenzo."

"I'd have thought you'd done that part already, Inez." The voice goes light, teasing.

"Not going there with you, sir."

"No sense of humor."

I suppress a snarky reply. "Not at the moment, no."

"How are the men?"

"Settling in. Happy to be home and not happy to be left out."

"You should have brought one or two of them with you."

"I can't. I have to deal with this myself."

"No, Inez, you don't."

"Yes, sir, I do."

"Did you discuss the next phase of Club Sin and the Broken Arrows with the men?"

"No. I told them changes were coming. I have to finish this, sir. That's the only thing that matters to me right now."

A heavy sigh. "I understand that."

"I suppose you would, sir."

"Just...come home alive and in one piece. That's an order, Sophia de Silva." He has never used my full, real name.

It's a little disconcerting.

"What will *you* do, sir? After this."

A moment of silence. "I'm not certain. Perhaps...well, best I keep my conjectures to myself for now, I think. We'll discuss the future of Club Sin and the Broken Arrows when you return. The only thing I know for certain is that whatever happens, you will be at the fore. You are important to me, Sophia."

"And you to me...sir." The one hard and fast rule is to never, ever speak his name over any phone line, even encrypted.

The dead aren't supposed to make phone calls, after all.

"Very well. I am satisfied that you are lucid and

coherent. But you must be smart. If you push your body beyond its limits, you'll be no good to anyone."

"I understand, sir. I'll be careful."

"See that you are. You are irreplaceable, you know."

"He could come after you, sir. It's not outside the realm of possibility. I think he knows of you, but not exactly who you are, or were. My point is you need to be on guard as well."

His laugh is predatory. Vicious. "I almost hope he tries."

I snort. "Honestly, sir, me too."

"We will speak again later, Inez."

"Yes sir. Goodbye."

He doesn't respond, as is his way—just hangs up.

I roll the windows back down and hang my hand out the window. I rip the hat off my head and pull the elastic band out of my hair, letting the wind flutter it every which way. I'll regret it later when I have to comb the snarls out, but for now, I need the tactile sensation of the wind in my hair.

Anything to keep me in the present.

Anything to keep the past from rising up in me like vomit.

Anything to center me, so I don't fall back into that pit, where Father's men took their turns on me while I was chained to a cot.

I shake my head as those memories threaten to surge up and overtake me.

No.

That's over. Those men are all dead. Ironically, it was Rafael who killed them, and some days I'm grateful while other days I resent it, wishing I had the closure of killing them myself.

I turn my thoughts to Lorenzo. My heart leaps at the mere thought of him—desperation to be near him rifles through me.

I *need* him.

I hate it, but I do.

He is the one human being on this planet who truly knows me. Even my employer only knows certain parts of me. Lorenzo? He knows it all. He knows me inside and out. All my secrets.

He knows the shape of the nightmares that haunt my dreams, keeping me from restful slumber.

My hope is that by finally erasing Rafael from this earth I will finally know a measure of peace. I'll be able to sleep at night.

Perhaps even find happiness.

With Lorenzo. If there is happiness for me on this earth, it will be with him. I just…I can't have that while Rafael lives.

I long to call Lorenzo. To hear his voice, just for a moment.

I wonder if he realizes how much he means to me, if he knows how totally he's woven into my being. I wonder if he knows I dream of him every night. That I have wept myself to sleep in the dark and solitude of my room, missing him. Craving him.

I press the accelerator, and the powerful SUV jumps forward. It's a twenty-some-hour drive from Las Vegas to Houston where Lorenzo last was, and I am lonely and in pain and angry and desperate. I should turn on the radio to distract myself, but I don't. I'm a masochistic like that—the pain and anger crystalize as I drive, become a single hard diamond at the center of me. Hour after hour, I fight my memories, my nightmares. And yet, with every hour and mile that passes, I feel myself drawing nearer and nearer to Lorenzo.

He's out there, alive, protecting my boy and the woman I chose to be his mother. I wish I could call him, hear his voice, get his advice, hear him tell me he loves me.

I dare not.

Instead, I drive faster, recklessly, illegally fast. Swerving around slower-moving cars, dodging oncoming traffic, and ignoring horns and middle fingers. At one point, I hear sirens behind me and see flashing lights—I pull off the freeway and lose them in a subdivision.

Back on the freeway, I floor the accelerator.

———— ◆ ————

Four in the morning. Houston is quiet, only a few early risers on their way to work filling the roads. I follow the car's GPS to the address of the safe house—it's in a rambling, run-down, lower-middle-class suburb on the outskirts of the metropolitan area, a neighborhood of narrow, tree-lined roads, tiny ranch homes with yellowing postage stamp yards and 20-year-old cars in the driveways.

The safe house is a carbon copy of every other house on the street—a pale yellow ranch with faded shingles and a buckling walkway to the front door, green shutters on either side of the picture window, and wobbly wrought-iron railings on either side of the microscopic concrete steps.

No car in the driveway, and the detached garage is open and empty. I park in the driveway, and leave the car running with the fob in my pocket. The front door is slightly ajar, and I instantly recognize the scent of death.

I know he's not here—he got a message to me that they'd been attacked and were fine but relocating. But still, the scent of death sends panic whirling inside me. I draw my pistol, slip the suppressor from my right hip pocket and screw it on as I nudge open the door with my hip. The door opens into the living room—white walls, old, stained, wear-flattened beige carpet, sagging faux-leather couch and mismatched loveseat, and an easy chair. Aging flatscreen TV.

Blood spatters the walls next to the door, and a pair of bullet holes pock the wall—rounds that went through a skull and into the wall. More blood on the floor between the living room and kitchen—a giant pool of it half on the carpet in the living room and half on the warped laminate floor of the kitchen.

The wall separating the kitchen from the living room is dented on the kitchen side as if a big, heavy body had slammed into it. The sliding glass door to the back deck is shattered, the remaining shards stained with blood, which is pooled on the gray, weather-faded deck. An old, rusty, Weber kettle grill sits forgotten in one corner of the deck, the lid slightly askew—that niggles in my brain, but I leave it for later.

I finish my examination of the house—more blood in the hallway. Empty bedrooms, drawers open as if the contents were thrown into a bag in a hurry. The bathroom door is closed. I open it, and the stench of death nearly bowls me over. The A/C is off and it's fucking hot. Bodies have been piled in the tub like cords of firewood—Rafael's mercenaries, eliminated by Lorenzo.

After my initial look-through is done, I go through more slowly, looking for clues as to where he may have gone.

Cabinets are empty. Nothing under the mattresses. Nothing in the fridge or freezer. Eventually, I go back to that grill out on the deck. It could have been bumped by someone, by a raccoon or the wind. But I doubt it. I go out and lift off the lid, sighing in relief. A glossy coupon flyer sits on the grate, advertising pizza specials for some mom-and-pop place in...I scan the flyer...

Austin.

I'm not sure how he managed to get a flyer from Austin to Houston, but I know without a doubt that it's the message from Lorenzo.

I pick it up from the grate and examine it more closely. He has circled numbers and letters in various places on the flyer—a coded message telling me the address of the next safe house.

I just have to crack it.

I fold the flyer and put it in my back pocket, walk around the side of the house to my SUV, and drive back toward the freeway. But instead of getting on, I recognize my own exhaustion and make the smart decision to call it a day—I drove straight through from Vegas, stopping only for gas and drive-through, and that was six hours ago.

I pick up a pizza from a nearby place and take it with me as I check into a Red Roof Inn near the freeway ramp. I devour the pizza while working on Lorenzo's code.

When I finally crack it, I burn the flyer in the sink, memorize the Austin address, and then burn the note-pad paper I'd written the address on while cracking it. A

Google search tells me the new address is similar to this one—a nondescript little house in the suburbs of Austin.

The question is whether I'll reach them before Rafael's mercenaries do.

As much as I want to leave now, I know I need sleep, so I lay on the bed fully clothed, and draw on years of practice to fall asleep quickly.

I wake after a few hours of fitful sleep and get on the road, stopping for coffee and a breakfast burrito.

———— ◆ ————

Three hours later, I arrive in Austin. The neighborhood is far from downtown, a quiet neighborhood, a bit more well-kept than Houston.

Scanning house numbers, I crawl slowly down the street, listening, watching.

I pass a shiny new Suburban parked outside one of the more run-down houses in the area—red flag number one.

The fit blonde woman pushing a stroller is red flag number two—I don't know why exactly, but my instincts don't like her, and I trust my instincts.

A flash of movement from a backyard is red flag number three—men in black tac gear carrying assault rifles.

"Fuck." I hit the single speed dial entry in my phone. It rings once, and he doesn't speak. "Contact," I say in Spanish. "Multiple targets. Front and rear."

"I understand," he answers in Spanish. "We are ready."

I hang up, shove the phone in my back pocket, and park the SUV beneath a big spreading oak tree. Reach into the second row and grab my vest, shrug into it, hissing as my bruised and cracked ribs protest painfully. I clip my

HK MP5K to my vest, shove spare mags in various places, secure my sidearm, suppressor off.

This will not be quiet or discreet.

This is going to be a firefight.

The woman with the stroller passes me, talking on the phone or pretending to. Pauses in front of a house a few doors down from where I'm parked. Bends over as if cooing at a baby I'm sure doesn't exist.

Movement between houses.

A pickup truck squeals around a corner half a mile away, engine roaring as it speeds in this direction.

Looks like three or four in the back of the house, the woman, and the occupants of this truck—four or five more, max—eight or ten people.

Easy.

The truck screeches to a halt at an angle across the driveway on the sidewalk, inches from the woman and the stroller.

The woman reaches into the stroller, comes up with a tactical shotgun, and jogs for the front door.

Four men in black tac gear pile out of the truck, moving in pairs after the woman.

Go time.

By the time I reach the front door, the thunder and rattle-crackle of gunfire have shattered the early morning quiet.

I kick open the door and step into a bloody hellscape.

Who's The Boss?
Can't figure out who the mystery Employer is?
Read Madame X and see if you can figure it out!

ABOUT THE AUTHOR

Jasinda Wilder is a *New York Times, Wall Street Journal,* and *USA Today* bestselling author of more than 100 titles including the #1 Amazon bestseller Falling Into You, the Audie Award-winning (best audiobook) Alpha, and the beloved, 17-book Badd Brothers series.

She and her husband Jack Wilder have sold more than 7 million copies and have been translated into more than 20 languages worldwide. You can find them at their fairy tale cottage by a lake somewhere in Michigan with their 6 kids, 5 dogs, 2 cats, 2 bunnies, and way too many ducks and chickens.

ALSO BY
JASINDA WILDER

Visit me at my website: **www.jasindawilder.com**
Email me: **jasindawilder@gmail.com**

If you enjoyed this book, you can help others enjoy it as well by recommending it to friends and family, or by mentioning it in reading and discussion groups and online forums. You can also review it on the site from which you purchased it. But, whether you recommend it to anyone else or not, thank you *so much* for taking the time to read my book! Your support means the world to me!

My other titles:

Forbidden Fruit

Wild Ride: Biker Billionaire

Delilah's Diary

Big Girls Do It:

Big Girls Do It
Married
On Christmas
Pregnant
Rock Stars Do It
Big Love Abroad

The Falling Series:
Falling Into You
Falling Into Us
Falling Under
Falling Away
Falling for Colton

The Ever Trilogy:
Forever & Always
After Forever
Saving Forever

From the world of *Wounded*:
Wounded
Captured

From the world of *Stripped*:
Stripped
Trashed

From the world of *Alpha*:
Alpha
Beta
Omega
Harris
Thresh
Duke
Puck
Lear
Anselm
Sigma
Gamma

The Houri Legends:
Jack and Djinn
Djinn and Tonic

The Madame X Series:
Madame X
Exposed
Exiled

The Black Room (With Jade London)

The One Series
The Long Way Home
Where the Heart Is
There's No Place Like Home

Badd Brothers:
Badd Motherf*cker
Badd Ass
Badd to the Bone
Good Girl Gone Badd
Badd Luck
Badd Mojo
Big Badd Wolf
Badd Boy
Badd Kitty
Badd Business
Badd Medicine
Badd Daddy
For a Goode Time Call...
Not So Goode
Goode To Be Bad

A Real Goode Time
Goode Vibrations
A Very Badd Christmas
Badd Apple

Dad Bod Contracting:
Hammered
Drilled
Nailed
Screwed

Fifty States of Love:
Pregnant in Pennsylvania
Cowboy in Colorado
Married in Michigan
Christmas in Connecticut

Billionaire Baby Club:
Lizzy Goes Brains Over Braun
Autumn Rolls a Seven
Laurel's Bright Idea

Club Sin:
Rev
Kane
Chance
Silas
Saxon
Solomon
Lash

Blood Heir
Blood Heir
Blood Rising
Blood Bonds
Blood Reign

The Cabin:
The Cabin
Christmas at the Cabin

Standalone titles:
Yours
The Parent Trap
Wish Upon A Star
Big Hose

Non-Fiction titles:
You Can Do It
You Can Do It: Strength
You Can Do It: Fasting

Jack Wilder Titles:
The Missionary

JJ Wilder Titles:
Ark

To be informed of new releases, special offers, and other Jasinda news, sign up for Jasinda's email newsletter.

www.ingramcontent.com/pod-product-compliance
Lightning Source LLC
Chambersburg PA
CBHW051549250626
47157CB00001B/242